In Both Worlds

by

William H. Holcombe

Double 9
BOOKS

In both worlds
by William H. Holcombe

ISBN: 978-93-65783-49-0

Published by

DOUBLE 9 BOOKS

2/13-B, Ansari Road
Daryaganj, New Delhi – 110002
info@double9books.com
www.double9books.com
Tel. 011-40042856

ABOUT THE AUTHOR

William H. Holcombe was renowned for his innovative contributions to modern literature. With a background in both philosophy and creative writing, his works often blended deep philosophical inquiry with compelling storytelling. He was particularly noted for his exploration of existential themes, human psychology, and the nature of reality, which were reflected in his complex characters and intricate plots. His most acclaimed works include a series of novels and essays that challenge conventional narrative structures and delve into the human experience with remarkable insight and originality. Through his writing, he explored themes such as identity, isolation, and the search for meaning, capturing the nuances of the human condition with both empathy and intellectual rigor. In addition to his literary achievements, his influence extended to academic circles, where his ideas contributed to critical discussions on literature and philosophy. His legacy is marked by a profound impact on modern literary theory and an enduring appeal that continues to engage readers and scholars alike. His innovative approach to narrative and thematic exploration remains a significant milestone in the evolution of contemporary literature.

CONTENTS

A STRANGE DISCOVERY IN LIEU OF A PREFACE

Many years ago I was enjoying in the harbor of New York the charming hospitalities of the officers belonging to one of the finest vessels in the British Navy. The company was gay, cultivated and brilliant. Student and recluse as I then was, I was perhaps more delighted than any one present with the conversation of those practical and polished men of the world.

After supper I was attracted to a small group of earnest talkers, of whom the surgeon of the ship seemed to be the centre and oracle. He was speaking of exhumations a long time after death, of mummies and petrifactions and other curious transformations of the human body. He stated that he had examined some of the skeletons which had been dug out of the ruins of Herculaneum. The bones were almost perfect after the lapse of eighteen hundred years. The complete exclusion of air and water seemed to be the only thing necessary to an indefinite preservation.

The chaplain of the vessel endeavored to give the conversation an æsthetic and semi-religious turn by analyzing the feelings of mingled awe, melancholy and curiosity with which most men survey the remains of a human form—feelings always heightened by the antiquity of the relic, and by the dignity of the person who lived and loved and labored in it.

"The fundamental idea," said he, "is a profound respect for the human body itself as the casket which has contained the spiritual jewel, the soul."

"Yes," remarked the surgeon; "nothing but the lapse of a people into cannibalism can obliterate that sentiment. When the Egyptian embalmers were ready for their work, a certain person came forward and made the necessary incisions for taking out the entrails. He immediately fled away, pursued by volleys of stones and curses from all the others. Hence also the dissections of the dead by medical students are conducted with the utmost secrecy and caution."

"Schiller," said I, "makes one of his heroes remark that the first time he plunged his sword into a living man, he felt a shudder creep over him as if he had desecrated the temple of God."

"Besides the feeling of reverence," continued the clergyman, "we have the awe which death naturally inspires, the melancholy excited by the vain and transitory nature of earthly things; and lastly, a tender and curious interest for the brother-soul which has tasted the sweetness of life and the bitterness of death, and passed onward to those hidden but grander experiences which await us all."

"Those shocking Egyptian mummies," said one of the officers, "are so disgusting that a strange horror is mingled with the gentler emotions you describe."

"I experienced that feeling," said another, "on reading an account of the exhumation of the remains, or rather the opening of the coffin, of King Charles I., two hundred years after he had been beheaded. It was increased, doubtless, by the idea of the separated head and body, and the strange and lifelike stare of the king's eyes, which collapsed like soap-bubbles when they were exposed to the air."

"There was something of the picturesque in that finding of a dead body by some little children who were playing in a grotto in France. It was seated on a stone bench and perfectly petrified, retaining, however, a sweet and placid expression of countenance. The man was an old hermit, who frequently retired into the deepest chamber of the grotto for religious contemplation."

"Imagine yourself," said I, "in the silence and shadows of Westminster Abbey, peering through some crevice in an old vault and getting a sight of the shrunken dust of Shakespeare."

"Passing from imagination to fact," said solemnly the old surgeon, "I have seen the body of a man lying upon the ground where it had lain undisturbed for eighteen hundred years."

"Eighteen hundred years!" exclaimed several voices at once.

"Yes, eighteen hundred years; and I was the first person who set eyes upon him from the day of his death until I got into the cavern where he perished."

"A romance! a romance!" cried the minister. "Come, doctor, be communicative and tell us all about it."

"It is not a romance," said the doctor, "but the facts were certainly very curious.

"When I was a young assistant surgeon, attached to the sloop-of-war Agamemnon, we were skirting leisurely the eastern shores of the Mediterranean, and anchored one morning in sight of the ruins of the ancient city of Sidon and opposite the westernmost spurs of Lebanon, the Mont Blanc of Palestine.

"There is only one picture grander than a view of Mount Lebanon from the sea, and that is a view of the sea from Mount Lebanon. I enjoyed the former so keenly that I determined to obtain the latter also. We got up a party of genial and stout fellows to ascend one of the highest peaks, armed with pick-axes, to obtain geological specimens on our way.

"We had advanced but a short distance up one of the cliffs, when we started from the scanty undergrowth some little animal—a wolf or jackal or wild dog, all of which abound on Mount Lebanon. We all joined noisily in the chase, and soon ran the frightened creature into one of the deep crevices or fissures made in the earth by the tempestuous rains of that region. Our picks were immediately brought into play, and in a short time, to our very great astonishment, instead of digging the fugitive out of a little hole in the ground, we opened our way into what was evidently the rear or back part of a cave of considerable dimensions.

"Our party crawled in one after another, myself leading the way. The contents of the place arrested our attention so strongly that we forgot the object of our chase, which had buried itself in some holes or burrows at the side of the cavern. The floor was of a yellowish-white limestone, and all eyes were immediately directed, in the rather dim light, to the figure of a man outstretched upon it.

"Yes, it was a man whose entire body, clothing and all, had dissolved into one blended mass, and so long ago that it looked rather like a great bas-relief of the human form projecting from the lighter-colored floor.

"The shape of the head and of the long hair and beard was complete. One outstretched arm lay along the floor, and the fingers could be traced by little ridges separate from each other. The protuberances of all the bony parts showed that the skeleton still resisted the disintegrating process of decay.

"What an awful death he must have experienced! For there was not a single other object in the small space which remained of the cavern; not a stone which might have served for a seat or a table; not an earthen vessel which might have contained a draught of water.

"The fate of this unhappy being was evident. Whether he had lived in the cavern or whether he had taken refuge in it from some great storm, he had clearly rushed to the back part of it to escape some enormous landslide and caving in at the front, which had opened toward the sea. He had been buried alive! Having exhausted the little air that remained to him, stricken down by terror, despair and suffocation, he had rendered up his soul to the great Giver in silence, darkness and solitude.

"These facts were so obvious that we all lifted our hats before speaking a word; thus paying the tribute of human sympathy to a fellow-creature eighteen hundred years after he had ceased to need it."

"How did you fix upon the date of his death?" asked the chaplain.

"You will see. A large cylindrical case of bronze was lying upon the breast of the dead man. He must have valued it highly, for he had clasped it to his bosom in the agonies of death. It was hermetically sealed with such ingenuity that we found considerable difficulty in breaking it open. It contained a parchment of great length, and rolled tightly around a little brass rod. The parchment was closely written in beautiful Greek characters. It was perfectly preserved. Two small gold coins fell out of the white dry sand with which the case had been filled. One of them bore the inscription of Tiberius Cæsar, and the other was stamped in the ninth year of the reign of the emperor Nero. Thus in the accidental grave of its author had his book been safely preserved amid all the mutations of the world."

The old doctor stroked his gray beard in silence, and I exclaimed:

"Who do you suppose this unfortunate man to have been?"

"That was revealed in the manuscript, but unfortunately not one of our party could read Greek. I sent the case with its contents to an old uncle of my mother, who had a little curacy near Binghamton. He was a great Greek scholar, and devoted to his classical studies the little time he could spare from the game of whist. I had a good deal of curiosity on the subject, and wrote several times to my uncle from different parts of the world before he condescended to reply. His answer was in substance this: that the manuscript purported to be the autobiography of Eleazor or Lazarus, whom Christ raised from the dead; that it was probably the work of some heretic monk or crazy philosopher of the second or third century; that, interwoven with romantic incidents in this world and the other, it gave expression to many absurd and false doctrines; in fine, that it was not worth my reading, and that I had better devote myself dutifully to killing his Majesty's enemies on the high seas, than to searching old caverns for apocryphal documents which impugned the sacred verities of the Apostolic Church.

"And so," concluded the old surgeon, "I have never thought any more about it."

"Your uncle was no doubt right in his conjectures and wise in his advice," said the young chaplain. "The number and extent of the apocryphal impositions upon the early Christian Church are almost incredible."

"Were you satisfied," said I, "with your good uncle's opinion?"

"I have always believed," replied the doctor, evasively and with a roguish twinkle of his eye, "that if the manuscript had contained the Thirty-nine Articles by anticipation, my uncle would have pronounced it divinely inspired."

"What became of it?" I inquired.

"Oh, it was sealed up again and sent to the nursery as a plaything for the children. It is probably still in the possession of one of my cousins."

The strange story of the old surgeon made a profound impression upon me; for in spite of the incredulity of all the other listeners, I believed from the first that the dust of that cavern was the dust of Lazarus, the brother of Martha and Mary, and that the manuscript contained something of genuine value to the Church and the world.

The opinion of the old curate and the echo of the young chaplain did not weigh a feather in my estimation. Young as I was, I had acquired that rare faculty of thinking for myself. Besides, I had had learned enough of human nature to know that legal reforms are rarely suggested by lawyers; that doctors always make war on a system of medicine better than their own; and that priests instinctively repudiate anything which demands a re-examination of the fundamental doctrines of their theological systems.

I had an inextinguishable desire to possess that manuscript, and set myself earnestly about it. I cultivated the acquaintance of the genial old surgeon, and contrived to render myself useful to him on more than one occasion. When he sailed for England I extorted from him a promise that he would send me the manuscript of Lazarus which his orthodox uncle has so flippantly condemned.

A good many years passed away, and I heard nothing from him. At length came a package, and a letter from England couched in very handsome terms, a part of which ran thus:

"My beloved father on his deathbed made up the parcel which I now send you, and requested me to transmit it to you with the following message, which he made me write down as the words fell from his lips:

" 'Forgive your old acquaintance for neglecting until death the matters of the dead. Read what Lazarus says, while I go in person to verify or invalidate his story. I have lived passably well, and I die comparatively happy. Good-bye!' "

I drew a deep sigh to the memory of the old surgeon, and set immediately to work studying and translating the manuscript. I found that a difficult task. It was not written in very classical Greek, and besides, was full of Hebraisms, which sometimes obscured the sense. There were not only many obscure things, but many things irrelevant, and many which would be regarded as absurd and even childish in the present age.

It soon became clear that a literal translation of the manuscript would not be of any great interest to the general reader. I determined to take the astounding facts narrated, as a skeleton or framework around which to build up a story of my own. This book is therefore a modern romance founded upon ancient facts. The original might be called a prose poem. Indeed, much of it is in the poetical form; the description of Helena, for instance, in the eleventh chapter.

The key to the whole book is, that here are the views and experiences of a man who, by what we may call a supernatural accident, was led into states of thought two thousand years in advance of his contemporaries.

I present it to the public in a dress of the nineteenth century, hoping it will reverse the decision of the old curate, who understood Greek and whist better than he did the inappeasable hunger of the soul after the unknown, and perhaps, alas! the unknowable.

I
CAST OUT

A serene and happy old age may delight in recalling the glory and the dream of youth, of which it is the crown and the fulfillment; but the wretched and desolate, nearing the grave, revert seldom to the past things of a life they are eager to exchange for a better.

A solemn sense of duty to mankind impels me to be my own biographer.

My story is the most wonderful in the world: so wonderful that the men of the present age cannot comprehend or believe me. I am spiritually alone.

None before me have penetrated consciously into the invisible world: examined its structure and its people: and returned to his fellow-men, enriched and burdened with its awful secrets.

This have I done.

I am Lazarus of Bethany, whom Christ raised from the dead.

I have lived and died, and live again; and I await a second time the bitterness of death.

"Lazarus," said they, "is asleep or dead. That is all."

Ah! how little did they know!

When I returned from the spiritual world, I had more wisdom than all the ancients, than all the magi, than all the prophets. I could have enriched the Church of God with spiritual treasures. I could have given light to every mind and joy to every heart. I could have satisfied the hidden hunger and thirst of the human soul. I was not permitted to do it. They would have rejected my gold and my frankincense and my myrrh. They would have turned from my offerings of spiritual truth as a wild beast turns from a man when he offers it bread.

I have lived many ages too soon. I will write what I have seen and heard. The world of mind will grow with the coming centuries into the capacity of comprehending what I alone now comprehend. These premature utterances will then be understood.

I was born in the little village of Bethany, which sits upon the eastern slope of Mount Olivet, embowered all summer in leaves and fruit. There were four children in the family; and our mother died in giving birth to Mary, the youngest and most beautiful. Our father was a man of great wealth and high social position, and we were reared in the lap of luxury.

My earliest recollection is that of playing in a large, terraced garden with my brother and two little sisters. The garden was full of olive, pomegranate, orange and date trees, and adorned with a great many shrubs and flowers. It was cool, fragrant and shady, and we sported about the tomb of our mother, which was cut in the solid rock, as merry and innocent as the birds and butterflies which shared with us the peace and beauty of the summer day.

I was ten years of age when Samuel, my younger brother, was taken from us. It was the first real grief of my life. Although five years old when my mother died, I was too young to remember the incidents. The angels are so near us in our infancy, that the troubles of the world, which are afterward engraved in marble, are then only written in water.

Little Samuel died calling my name. Oh that I could have obeyed his call, and followed him into that bright and peaceful sphere in which I saw him long afterward, and in which I shall soon see him again!

Early on the day of his burial our father went into the chamber where lay his little white body covered all over with whiter flowers. He knelt beside it and wept bitterly. He seemed unconscious that his three little ones had followed him, and stood pale and trembling at the door. When we heard the voice of his weeping we crept forward to the feet of our little brother and wept also. Our father kissed us all tenderly, and controlling his emotions and steadying his voice, he repeated from memory the beautiful verses of Scripture which describe the grief and resignation of King David at the loss of his child.

The body of our little brother was deposited in a niche in the rock close to the dust of his mother. The garden was avoided as a playground for a long while. I was busy with my books, Martha with her dolls—both rendered thoughtful beyond our years. One day little Mary ventured into the garden alone, but presently came running back and buried her golden head in her sister's lap in a shower of tears which needed no explanation.

Who can read the little child's heart? Perhaps some playmate bird had called to her: "Rosebud! rosebud! where is your brother?"

Then came the years of school and opening thought and expanding faculties, and the first appearance of affections and passions, no longer the dewdrops of the spring morning, but the beginnings of deep and swift currents in the course of life.

My sisters were remarkable women, differing in style and character; yet each a perfect picture of female loveliness!

Martha grew tall and firm and straight, with long black hair and black eyes, a brunette complexion and a finely-cut oval face. She was the impersonation of a pure and intelligent womanhood. She was active, observant and critical. She regulated her life by lofty principle as well as by noble impulse, and there was something about her that always impressed you with the idea that she was brave and strong as well as gentle and pure.

Mary was fragile in form, willowy and graceful in motion, soft and winning in manners. Her eyes were blue and sparkling with the tender dew of sentiment. The lily and the rose contended for supremacy on her face, and sunbeams nestled always in her hair. She was the impersonation of a loving and love-awakening womanhood. Her voice, her smile, her tear, expressed in the most extraordinary manner the sensitive emotions of her soul.

Mary was my lily; Martha my rose. Martha was my ruby; Mary my pearl. Martha was reason; Mary was sentiment. Martha was wisdom; Mary was love. Martha was faith looking fixedly at the stars; Mary was charity looking trustfully beyond them to God.

My father took a deep interest in the education and general training of his children. He provided us with the best teachers in every branch, but let nothing escape his own watchful supervision. It was greatly due to his intelligent care and the inspiring stimulus of his affection, that we attained a degree of mental and social development rarely witnessed in children of our age.

A dark cloud hung over this good and wise father and his happy little household.

His health had been gradually failing for a long time. He grew languid, lost appetite, and became slow in his gait and stiff in his motions. He abandoned his business in the city, and rarely went out of the house. He declined receiving visitors, until our home, which had been so gay and brilliant, became quite deserted and lonely. But his mental condition underwent a change altogether incommensurate with his physical symptoms. He became silent and melancholy, and so unlike his former patient and sweet self! He repulsed every attempt on our part to inquire into the nature or cause of his troubles. His mental faculties were also greatly weakened.

We could not comprehend the meaning of all this. We became very unhappy. We knew he was wealthy, honored and beloved—in possession of all that men covet for good or evil ends. The country was in a state of profound repose. It was incredible that the mere approach of sickness and death, could so change the character of a good and brave man.

My father was now frequently closeted with Caiaphas, a young priest of stately appearance and ingratiating manners. I became very anxious to learn the subject of these prolonged interviews. I once questioned Caiaphas at the gate about my father's condition; but he evaded me adroitly. At last my curiosity, prompted by filial love, triumphed over my sense of propriety, and I crept to my father's door one night, when he and Caiaphas were together, and applied my ear to the keyhole. For a long time the tones were too low for me to catch any meaning; but my father suddenly raised his voice in an excited manner—

"I assure you he is a thief and a robber, and addicted to magic. O Caiaphas! save my children and their property from this monster!"

I was terrified at these words, and slipped away in the darkness. There was the secret of my father's grief. He expected to die very soon, and was anxious for the fate of his children when he was taken from them. I wept on my bed nearly all night at the idea of losing my good parent. But who was this monster he so much dreaded? That set me to thinking.

When a man died, his minor children and property passed under the guardianship of his next of kin. My father had no brothers in Judea, for his only brother had wandered off more than thirty years before. He was an eccentric character who forsook his religion and changed his name. Beyond that we knew nothing of him. Nor did my father even know where to find him.

His only sister was married to Magistus, a citizen of Bethany. She was a confirmed invalid and never seen. In the event of my father's death we would fall to their care. Magistus then was this terrible monster, a thief and a magician. I was confirmed in this conclusion by the fact, that my father and Magistus had long been on bad terms; and my father was not the man to withdraw his friendship from a worthy person.

Magistus was a thin, sallow, ugly old man, with an immense hooked nose like the beak of a bird of prey. His black eyes were small, fierce and sly. He had a long dingy beard which he had twisted like a screw. Notwithstanding this sinister appearance, he had the reputation of being a good and wise man. People speak well of a rich man who seems always to retire modestly from the public eye. Magistus moreover was a great friend of the priesthood and a favorite with the priests.

I could not reveal to my sisters the approaching death of our father and the fears he had expressed about our legal guardian. I was astonished and somewhat relieved when he passed the warmest eulogy upon Caiaphas the next morning, and told us to look to him for comfort and to rely on him for help in the greatest emergencies. What astonished me still more was, that this reliable friend never visited my father again.

We were greatly distressed that no medical aid was called in. The suggestion was always repudiated with a strange earnestness. Whatever the disease was with which our father was afflicted, he was plainly growing worse and worse. At last he refused to quit his chamber, or to admit any one into it. He commanded a little food and water to be placed upon a table on the gallery underneath his window; and what was singular, he only took it in during the night when no one saw him. These things threw us into the saddest consternation. We began to fear that he was losing his reason. We were frantic with excitement. We determined to see him and nurse him. We knocked at his door and window and entreated him to show himself to his children.

At last he called out in a voice which showed he had been weeping:

"Calm yourselves, my children! and pray to God. A great evil has come upon us, which can be concealed but a little longer. My soul is overwhelmed with misery, but my heart beats for my children with the tenderest love. Ask me nothing at present; it is more than I can bear. If you love me and would obey me, keep away entirely from my chamber. Let no one come into the house—and least of all, your uncle Magistus."

We were reassured of his love and his rationality by these words; but they filled us with a vague terror and overwhelmed us with sorrow. We had no one to appeal to, no one to consult. We were commanded to keep everybody away. Thus several weeks of fearful suspense rolled by. The neighbors began to inquire about my father. His seclusion became the wonder and talk of the village. The interrogations, always disagreeable, became absolutely impertinent. The mystery had excited suspicion.

Worse than all, Magistus became a regular visitor to the gate. He questioned the porter in the subtlest manner. He obtained from him the facts that my father had never received any medical attention, that he had concealed himself in his chamber, and had not been seen for weeks, even by his children. He evinced the liveliest satisfaction. "The apple will soon drop," said he aloud to himself. All this was faithfully reported to us. Three little sparrows in a nest among the green leaves, could not have been in greater trepidation with an ugly bird of prey gazing at them from a neighboring branch.

The dénouement approached. We were whispering our sorrows together one day, seated by the little fountain in the inner courtyard of the house, upon which the door of our father's chamber opened. Suddenly voices and footsteps were heard approaching. A moment after Magistus appeared, followed by a venerable-looking old priest and stately Roman centurion. My sisters clung to me in terror.

Without noticing us, the party rapped loudly on my father's door, and commanded him to come forth. "In the name of the Mosaic law," said the priest; "and by order of the Roman governor," added the centurion. The words were repeated in a louder voice: the door slowly opened and my father stepped out, exclaiming, "Unclean! unclean!"

All fell back several paces.

"The scourge of God!" said the priest with deep solemnity.

"Damnable Eastern plague!" muttered the Roman soldier.

"Incurable! incurable!" exclaimed Magistus.

It was the leprosy!

That ghoul of diseases, which slowly devours a living victim, had made fearful ravages upon my poor father's frame. His eyebrows and eyelashes were gone; his chin and ears were much swollen, and a pearl-white scaly ulcer deformed his forehead; his hands had a sickly and withered appearance.

We now understood the meaning of his strange conduct. The disease began first about the joints and the covered parts of his body. As soon as it broke out on the skin, the poor man had shut himself up to conceal his affliction and to avoid contaminating his family. Knowing himself stricken with a disgusting and incurable malady, which would exclude him from society and drive him away from his children, he bore the burden of his awful secret alone. Magistus had discovered his condition, and anxious to revenge himself upon virtues he could not imitate, and to get possession of the property, he laid the case before the authorities, and insisted that the law of separation should be executed upon his brother-in-law.

As the unhappy man stood in the doorway, he turned his eyes upon the pale faces of his terrified children, and, silently wringing his hands, looked upward to heaven. He was turning away, when all three of us sprang forward at once, and with cries which would have moved the coldest heart, fell at his feet and clung about his knees.

"Touch me not! my sweet children!" he exclaimed, in a hoarse and feeble voice. "Touch me not. It is all over! Caiaphas will befriend my orphans."

He had not finished the words before several strange domestics, who had rushed in at a signal from Magistus, proceeded to drag us from the spot.

"Away with them!" said the hideous old man, fiercely. "Confine them in the farthest room. We want no young lepers—no more scourges of God."

"If it were a scourge of God," cried I, struggling to escape, "it would have been sent upon you and not upon my noble father."

We were carried weeping out of the courtyard. Looking back to the door, we saw the unhappy man waving his last adieu to us with his poor, sickly, withered hands.

The Mosaic law against the unfortunate leper was cruelly severe; but the Roman power which occupied the country and feared the ravages of leprosy among the soldiery, added greatly to its force and to the stringency of its execution.

The leper was sentenced to a social and civil death far more terrible to a man of sensibility than the mere separation of soul and body. He was driven from the face of his fellow-men, and dwelt in caves and hollow trees and deserted ruins. No one was permitted to touch him, to approach him, or even to speak to him. He was compelled to cry out, Unclean! unclean! so as to warn every one of his dangerous proximity. He became literally the wild man of the woods and the mountains and the desert—the companion and sometimes the prey of wild beasts.

Those who had friends and money had little huts erected for them in remote but safe places, and were amply provided with food and even luxuries by servants who deposited the articles upon the ground at a considerable distance from their habitations.

Such was the fate of our good and generous father—the idol of our hearts and the model of all social and heroic virtues.

We spent the night in tears, and the next day in an agony of grief. I do not know who witnessed the dreadful ceremonies of the law. He was examined by the proper inspectors, and pronounced unclean and incurable. He was led into the great highway. The people stood afar off. The priest in a loud voice pronounced the curse of God upon him—the service of the dead over the living body. He cut him off from the congregation of Israel. The guards then drove him before them into some uninhabited place, and he disappeared from the sight of men.

He was always visible, however, to the hearts of his three little orphans. We followed his steps with filial vigilance. We saw him toiling along in the sand of the desert, and we shared his burden of heat and hunger and thirst. We saw him seated under a palm tree, or in the shadow of some great rock, and we felt the sorrows of his thoughts as if they were our own. We saw him kneeling by the brook, and we mingled our prayers with his. We saw him sleeping in his lonely hut, lighted only by the moon, and we were comforted by his dream of angels and heaven.

II
CLOUDS GATHERING

We were now orphans, and of that kind most to be pitied, who have fallen into the hands of a cold and selfish step-uncle. He had a father's power over us, without a father's affection to regulate and sanctify it. There was no one to supervise his conduct toward us; no appeal from his baseness or cruelty, unless his acts were so flagrant and unconcealed as to call down the vengeance of the laws.

This uncle whom we so much dreaded and had so much reason to dread, wore at first a smooth and pleasing mask. He came every day to see us, and endeavored by as much civility and kindness as he could counterfeit, to soften our feelings and satisfy us with our condition. He professed the deepest sympathy for our poor father's calamity. He regretted the severity of the Jewish and Roman laws on the subject of leprosy, but excused them as a necessary protection to society. He assured us that our father had a comfortable lodge on the border of the wilderness, and that servants were despatched every other day with fresh supplies of food and wine and water. This assurance brought tears to our eyes and comfort to our hearts.

When the storm of our grief had abated a little, we requested to see our aunt; for we yearned for the presence and sympathy of woman. Magistus conducted us over to his residence which adjoined our own, but fronted upon another street. A high brick wall separated his garden from ours. He had a door cut in this wall so as to facilitate the passage from one house to another. His mansion was completely concealed from the public eye by a thick grove of trees which surrounded it. In the most retired chamber of this quiet and really beautiful place, we found Ulema, my father's invalid sister.

She was a middle-aged woman of extreme thinness and pallor. Her face was waxen-colored and ghastly. There was a wild terrified expression about her black eyes, which was absolutely painful. She had evidently been a great sufferer in mind and body. She received us with a faint, sickly smile, and then her features assumed an expression of profound pity. We supposed this was on account of the loss of our father. We did not know the reasons which the poor woman had for pitying any one who came within the shadow of Magistus.

After the interchange of a few commonplaces, our uncle cut short the visit on the plea of Ulema's feeble and nervous condition. This visit was repeated every Sabbath after the morning sacrifice. Magistus always accompanied us, and drew us away as quickly as possible. My aunt had always the same expressions of terror and pity. Thus our repeated interviews added nothing to our knowledge of her character. In vain we petitioned Magistus to let us live with our aunt, or to let us visit her oftener, or to let us stay longer.

Our own home was sadly changed. The furniture, the pictures, the statues, the fountain, the flowers, were all the same, but there was an air of silence and melancholy about the whole place, as if the inanimate objects had felt and shared the misfortunes of the orphan children. There was a different sphere around us, a different light upon us. The organizing and unitizing spirit was gone;—the good and wise father, who made all happy and cheerful about him, and held his little household together in the sweet bonds of perfect order and peace.

It was a cruel act of Magistus to substitute servants and creatures of his own for those who had been with us from our infancy. We were soon surrounded by strange faces, so that our father's house began to appear to us, what it really was, a prison. The domestics of an establishment acquire in time a coloring from the kind of life within it, as insects are colored by the leaves and bark of the trees they inhabit. Ours were respectful, obedient and cheerful; these were cunning, insolent and dishonest.

The chief butler or head servant was, however, a good character, who plays a remarkable part in my story. He was an African about thirty years of age, very black and homely. He was a eunuch, and dumb. These disadvantages, which at first excited a feeling of repulsion, were atoned for by a singular kindness, deference and sympathy, which were displayed in his features and manners The other servants held him in great awe; for he had been brought from Egypt about three years before by a magician, and was supposed to be gifted with supernatural power.

It was this advantage in command, as well as a certain kind of talent, industry and reliability, which induced Magistus to give him the supreme charge of both households. He had been with us but a few days, before he had quite won our hearts by his friendly attentions and evident sympathy for our distress. I, who had been made suspicious by my father's opinion of our guardian, detected in the face of Ethopus (for that was his name) the same expression of pity which shone in the features of our sick aunt.

All this, however, he concealed from Magistus with the greatest care; for he was always cold and impassive toward us in the presence of his master. Unfortunately Ethopus was dumb. His communications at this time might have been of incalculable service to us. I endeavored to learn something of the habits and character of my uncle from the other servants, but on that subject they were as dumb as Ethopus; for whenever I approached it, they manifested signs of fear, and invariably put the finger on the lip.

I became dissatisfied with this secresy. I resolved to teach Ethopus to read and write, so that he might tell me his own story, and initiate me into the mysteries and dangers of my position. He comprehended my idea at once, and came to me secretly at hours when he knew Magistus was absent. He had made some little progress,—though the difficulties of the first steps were very great,—when one evening Magistus walked slyly in and surprised us at our studies. We had been betrayed by one of the servants, who all acted as spies on each other.

Magistus was in a towering passion. He beat Ethopus severely, notwithstanding my protestations that I alone was to blame—and drove him from the room.

Turning fiercely upon me, he exclaimed:

"Do you not know the crime, the danger of teaching that man to write?"

"Oh, uncle!" said I, "what harm is there in bestowing the light of knowledge upon a poor dumb slave?"

"He was made dumb to keep him from betraying secrets."

"Horrible!" said I.

"Not my secrets," he added, cautiously, "but his former master's. If Simon Magus thought he could write, he would come all the way from Egypt to cut his heart out of his body."

After that event, the sphere of Ethopus' duty was changed, so that we rarely saw him.

Several weeks passed away, and we wondered why Caiaphas, from whom our father expected so much, did not come to see us. He was to aid and befriend us, and, as I hoped, to deliver us from the control of Magistus. He had evidently promised all that to our dear father. The priestly authorities, if properly applied to, surely would not permit the children of a good and devout man to continue under the influence of a thief and magician.

Caiaphas at last came. His visit was short: his manner constrained but polite. He sympathized briefly with our affliction; explained and defended the Mosaic laws against leprosy; eulogized our father in eloquent terms; and congratulated us on having such a worthy uncle, who would train us so carefully in the faith, and who would make our home so happy.

And this was the result of the secret interviews with my father, and of his solemn warnings against Magistus as a thief and a magician! I was puzzled and disappointed. I could not help saying:

"Did you know, O Caiaphas! that my father entertained a very different opinion of this good uncle?"

"Remember, my son," said he, somewhat abashed, "that your father was very sick, and his mind greatly impaired. There was no foundation whatever for his unhappy suspicions. Obey your uncle like good children, and you will find him all I have represented him to be." He then retired.

I was too young and ignorant of the ways and wiles of the world, to suspect that this priest had been all along in collusion with Magistus, and was to share with him in the plunder of the orphans of his friend.

The words of my father rang in my ear and continually haunted my mind: "He is a thief and robber, and addicted to magic."

I asked my uncle one day, in a very quiet manner, his opinion of magic.

He looked at me severely and answered:

"What are the words of Moses on the subject? Listen: 'A man or a woman that hath a familiar spirit, or that is a wizard, shall surely be put to death. They shall stone them with stones.' "

This did not convince me that my father was in error.

Months passed; and a gradual and saddening change was creeping over our life and its surroundings. I had detected no robbery, no magical practices; but I had no faith in my uncle. Cautious and reticent as he was, he could not conceal some of the ugly points of his character. He was violent and cruel in his dealings with his slaves. He was addicted to falsehood, and in both opinion and practice was destitute of charity. His strict observance of the ceremonial law and his intense ritualism, could not conceal from me the fact that his heart was wholly untouched by the spiritualizing influences of true religion.

He ceased after a while to take us to see our aunt. Our teachers in various branches were not re-engaged, or were dismissed. Education came to a stand-still. Company was excluded from our house. His own was opened at night to suspicious characters. By bribing one of his servants one dark night, I obtained admission to his courtyard, and discovered, by muffled sounds of music and dancing, that a bacchanalian revelry was going on underground. He sometimes betrayed the next day, in his face and manner, the effect of these midnight orgies.

In the mean time my beautiful sisters pined, neglected and sorrowful. Magistus rarely visited them; and when he did, he was guilty of coarse familiarities which shocked and repelled them. I summoned courage, boy as I was, on one of these occasions to reproach him bitterly for these things; for neglecting our education, our dress, our manners, our comforts; and for falling himself into habits which would certainly lead to the ruin of us all. He stared at me insolently, and said that I had better get my father's friend Caiaphas to revise his guardianship.

Like a man who sits helpless in a boat without oars, gliding down a swift current, and hears the far-off but inevitable cataract, I contemplated the dark future that awaited us. I grieved for my sisters more than for myself. We had just been mourning together one day over our sad fate, when Magistus came into the room. He had held a long private interview that morning with a strange man of gigantic size and very coarse manners, whose appearance, as he entered the guest-chamber, excited my gravest suspicions.

"You complain so bitterly," said he, looking reproachfully at me, "of the general decay and ruin into which everything about here, animate and inanimate, is falling, that it is surprising you have not yet intimated your doubts about your father getting his proper supply of provisions."

"Oh no, uncle!" said Mary, tenderly, "you could not forget so sacred a duty as that. Surely no one ever hinted such a thing. The thought of it would drive me mad."

"I wish you to satisfy yourselves perfectly upon that point," he continued, in the tone of a man who thought himself aggrieved. "A trusty servant is to convey to him a basket of things the day after to-morrow. Let Lazarus accompany him. Let his daughters send some little presents. His son can see him and even speak with him at a distance. He can see his lodging and satisfy himself that he is comfortably situated."

"Without confessing, uncle," said I, "that this visit is necessary for my faith in your attention to my father, I concede that it will give me very great pleasure."

"How long will he be gone?" said Martha.

"Is there no danger?" said Mary.

"He will run no risk and will return the same night," said Magistus, answering both questions in a breath.

This visit occupied our thoughts continually, and we delighted to imagine what joy it would give our poor father. I was out of bed before daylight that morning, impatient to start. I partook heartily of an extempore breakfast which Ethopus provided me. That personage to my surprise seemed sad and abstracted. I could say nothing to him, however, for Magistus was present. I kissed my sisters good-bye at the door of their room, for they too could not sleep for excitement. Magistus waved his adieu at the front door. I walked through the courtyard with Ethopus, who carried a covered basket on his arm.

We were near the gate, when Ethopus coming close to me slipped something into my hand. It was a long, thin, bright dagger. I concealed it immediately in my bosom.

"Ethopus thinks there will be danger," said I, to myself.

I would perhaps have said something, but I observed the porter admitting a person through the gate, whose entrance at that hour in the morning caused me the greatest surprise.

It was a woman; and at the age of sixteen a woman occupies a great deal of the field of vision before the masculine eye. This woman was very young—not more than fifteen, although perfectly mature. She was very beautiful—so beautiful that everybody must have turned to look after her. Her eyes were large, soft and hazel; her hair brown and wavy; her cheeks blended roses and pearls: her mouth small and curved like a bow; her voice and smile perfectly bewitching—all that I took in at a glance: nor did it need the splendid ear-rings and brilliant necklace and scarlet robe she wore, to impress it very deeply on my mind.

She bade me good-morning with the sweetest smile imaginable, and with the affable, self-possessed manner of a woman much older than herself. Startled and abashed, I could do nothing but bow profoundly and hurry into the street where Ethopus had given the basket to the person who was to be my guide.

I made signs to Ethopus, by a kind of pantomime we had acquired, to keep a watchful eye on my sisters. He replied by an affirmative motion of the head and a deep sigh, which was evidently on my own account.

This woman was destined, under the leadings of Providence, to make a greater and more lasting impression on my soul than all others. And this was our first meeting: I a bashful boy; she a strange woman, too gaudily dressed, entering my father's house at a strange hour. So two ships might pass each other on the Great Sea, merely exchanging signals of good-morning—ships destined long afterward to convoy each other beyond the Pillar of Hercules into the infinite unknown!

This woman was Mary Magdalen.

III
NIGHT BY THE DEAD SEA

With my thoughts fluctuating between the extreme beauty of Mary Magdalen and the danger which Ethopus seemed to apprehend, I walked some distance without regarding my new companion.

When I did so, I was surprised and puzzled at his appearance. He was a young man of singularly handsome features, the only drawback being a nose which was a little too aquiline. His black hair curled in short ringlets close to his head, and his face was thoroughly bronzed by sun and tempest. His dress was rather that of some foreigner attached to an Assyrian or Egyptian caravan, than the coarse and simple clothing of a Hebrew servant. And then there was something bold and free in his bearing, which precluded the idea that he was a menial either in character or condition.

"Are you engaged in my uncle's service?" said I.

He shifted the heavy basket from one arm to the other, and made no reply.

I repeated my question in a louder tone; but he did not seem to hear me, looking straight ahead at the road before him.

"This handsome fellow is both deaf and dumb," said I to myself. "My uncle has a curious passion for silent people."

Debarred the pleasure of conversation, I relapsed into reverie. I determined to make a use of this visit which my uncle little anticipated. I resolved to approach my father boldly, contagion or no contagion, and have an interview with him. I wanted to tell him of the neglected and unhappy condition of his children, of our increasing repugnance to Magistus, and of the indifference or treachery of Caiaphas. I wanted his advice. He could surely direct me to friends in the city, whose assistance might arrest our impending ruin.

Made happier by that resolution, as if it had already accomplished something, I let my mind revert back to the woman I saw at the gate, and a new cause of uneasiness arose as I reflected upon that accidental meeting. Boyish and inexperienced as I was, I discovered something in the dress and manner of the early visitor, which whispered to me that she was not a suitable companion for my sisters. She certainly was not a domestic. Who could she be? What could she want at our house just after daybreak? Perhaps she came to see Magistus on business. It was not the hour or the place for that. Perhaps she was one of the midnight revelers whom I heard singing and dancing in the basement story of my uncle's secluded residence. That idea startled me more than all. I determined to get back home by rapid walking before nightfall, and explore this disquieting mystery.

We had passed over hill and dale through a highly-cultivated country, full of vineyards and gardens and orchards, full of sweet little villages and beautiful rural villas. This did not last long, and we turned in a southeasterly direction. The villages disappeared; the houses became more sparse and humble; the trees became more stunted and bare; the rocks larger and the road more difficult. At the point where the highway leads down the steep hills toward Jericho and the plain of the Jordan, my guide turned suddenly due south into a rough, barren and wild country, where there was no road at all.

The sounds of life faded behind us. Vegetation almost wholly disappeared. No animals were to be seen but a few goats far away browsing among the rocks. The birds seemed to refuse to accompany us further. The silence of the desert fell gradually upon us. This was the wilderness of Judea.

We were winding downward to the Salt Sea, that great watery waste, in whose silent deeps Sodom and Gomorrah lie buried; on whose shores stand bleak and desolate mountains full of sulphur springs; the gloom without the glory of nature; the home of wild beasts and lepers and robbers and demons; mountains fearful in their nakedness and solitude; evil genii guarding in stern silence the eternal sleep of the lost cities of the plain.

I grew uneasy and melancholy as we approached these famous and dangerous places. The taciturnity of my guide, together with an increasing shadow on his expressive face, magnified my apprehensions almost into fears. I felt my boyish weakness and inexperience by the side of this strong, rough, silent man of the wilderness, who now seemed to my excited imagination to have got into his native element, and to be a part of the lonely and supernatural region into which we had entered.

Our attention was suddenly drawn to a neighboring eminence by sounds of so strange a character, that it was impossible to say whether they were animal or human. Four lepers appeared in sight, almost naked, holding up their long, withered arms, and screeching out from their hoarse throats and swollen lips their hideous cry,

"Unclean! unclean!"

I trembled at this sad spectacle and gazed intently, expecting and afraid to recognize my poor father in the group. My guide suddenly laid his hand upon my shoulder, and we both stood still. He then set the basket upon the ground, made signals to the lepers to approach, and drew me away from the spot. A horrible chorus of guttural thanks came up from the leprous creatures, who awaited our departure before pouncing upon the acceptable present.

"Oh, sir!" said I, resisting my guide, and forgetting that he was deaf and dumb, "you have given my father's food to those unhappy wretches! Where is my father? Oh, take me to him!"

He stopped and looked me full in the face.

"Oh yes!" I continued, in a supplicating tone; "that basket has food and wine for my poor father, the leper, and a bouquet and a letter from Martha, and a pair of sandals from little Mary—"

Overcome with emotion I burst into tears.

The guide drew a deep sigh; and when I looked up into his face it was radiant with a sweet and benevolent expression. He had either heard me or he comprehended intuitively the nature of my distress. He shook his head and made a deprecating gesture with his hand. He then drew me off strongly, but so gently that I was partially reassured, and walked meekly at his side, overwhelmed with surprise and sorrow.

After passing over several rough ridges we turned into a deep ravine. The guide made me go in front. The pathway down this narrow gorge, this cleft between two mountains, was rough and dangerous. There were deep holes or pits upon one side, and frightfully overhanging rocks upon the other. It was so dark and precipitous in some places that I could scarcely believe we were not descending into the bowels of the earth. We suddenly emerged from this monstrous fissure on a little mound made by the soil washed down from above, and found ourselves on the shore of the Dead Sea.

I had never seen such an expanse of water before, and was charmed with the sight. Away to the left was the plain of the Jordan and the sacred river of that name, invisible at a distance among its reeds and rushes. Opposite arose the reddish-brown mountain chain which borders the sea on the west. Far down to the right stretched a range of high hills of a bluish gray color. In front, and widening away to the south, lay the mighty surface of the sea, shining like a burnished mirror in the noon-day sun. A fine breeze was blowing; but there was only a faint ripple on the water, for its heavy salt waves can scarcely be stirred by the wind—like the soul of a wicked man, which cannot be moved by the Spirit of God.

I was recalled from that delicious reverie into which every one is transported by a view of the sea; for my guide pointed to a clump of stunted trees or rather large bushes near the beach. Half hidden by them was a tent of alternate white and red canvas, in front of which a large boat was drawn up on the sand. Two rough-looking fellows lay in the boat asleep. There was no human habitation anywhere about this lonely spot. These people belonged on the other side of the sea. They were ready for flight in a moment. They were wild, roving, secretive, fugitive. They were engaged in some unlawful business. I had fallen into the hands of robbers.

These disquieting thoughts passed through my mind as we approached the tent. Hearing our footsteps on the sand, the chief came out of it. He was tall and sinewy, a man of unusual weight and size. He was clad in a richly-embroidered crimson robe, with a splendid scimitar, jewel-hilted, at his side. A long beard, stained of a golden yellow by some vegetable dye, gave him a grotesque and never-to-be-forgotten appearance. All this barbaric ornament did not prevent me from recognizing the strange, coarse man who held the long interview with Magistus two days before. Then he was disguised; now his character was apparent.

We stood before him. My guide made a low obeisance and said in a clear voice:

"Barabbas! I have obeyed your orders!"

My astonishment on discovering that my robber-guide was neither deaf nor dumb, was turned into another channel when Barabbas exclaimed:

"Well done! Bind him tightly with the old Persian. If Beltrezzor's ransom does not arrive by sunrise, we will make way with them both together."

My uncle had betrayed me into the hands of the Ishmaelite to be murdered. There could be no doubt that the atrocious assassin had taken every precaution to prevent escape or failure. Resistance was impossible. There were four men in sight, either one of whom could have overpowered me in a moment. My heart sank in despair when my guide led me behind the tent, and bound me securely to a little tree, without evincing the least remorse or care at his own part in this shameful and cowardly transaction.

I now surveyed my fellow-prisoner, who was tied to another tree close to me. His gray hair and beard showed that he had passed considerably beyond the meridian of life. He had a serene and rather handsome face, full of thought and benevolence. Young and inexperienced as I was, I perceived by a kind of intuition that my companion in distress was a cultivated and superior man. He wore a rich Eastern robe and a bright-colored turban. He was smoking a long pipe curiously carved and twisted. He surveyed me quietly and nodded kindly to me, evidently pitying my childish terror and despair.

"We shall be murdered to-morrow!" I gasped.

"I learned a proverb in India," said the old man. "Brahma writes the destiny of every one on his skull. No man can read it"—and watching his smoke fade into air, he slowly continued, "and even the gods cannot avert it."

I was astonished at his coolness; but his fatalism did not console me.

"To die—to die!—to leave my poor sisters unprotected and to see them no more—Oh, it is horrible!"

"Not to be," said the Persian, in a voice of singular depth and sweetness, "not to be is better than to be; and not to have been is better than all."

In spite of myself and my fears, the calm and almost spiritual halo which seemed to surround this strange old man, began to quiet my agitation and to divert my thoughts from my impending fate.

"Are you a philosopher?" said I.

"I think," he replied; and drawing a long whiff from his pipe, he illustrated his remark by lapsing into a profound reverie.

I contemplated this serene philosopher a long time in silence, and made up my mind that he must have a good many beautiful things to think about as he sat there, bound and under sentence of death, smoking so placidly upon the arid shore of that dreadful sea.

When he indicated, by knocking the ashes from his pipe, that he had ascended from the ocean of dreams into which he had dived, I asked him how he had fallen into the power of these miscreants.

"Speak evil of no one, my son! Leave wicked names to the wicked. These gentlemen live upon the road and in the wilderness. They pay special attention to travelers, to caravans, and to small and remote villages. They cure some people of that chronic disease we call life, and they permit others to ransom themselves by large quantities of that evil thing we call money. They have set me down in the latter class, and I am awaiting a remittance from a friend in Jerusalem."

"Suppose your friend is dead, or absent from the city, or cannot raise the sum required, or refuses to do it?"

He pointed to the sea, shrugging his shoulders, and exclaimed:

"What is written, is written."

When it was quite dark my guide of the morning brought us a little food. The old Persian ate heartily, but I could barely taste it. The guide whispered in my ear, "Be silent and wakeful," and departed.

"Now sleep, my son," said my philosophic companion; "trust in God and sleep. Our angels and good genii befriend us most powerfully when asleep. When awake we scare them away by our villainous thoughts. Sleep."

The whispered words of the guide had inspired me with a vague hope, and I preferred trusting to his advice rather than to the invisible guardians of our sleep. I was therefore silent and wakeful. The moon went down long before midnight.

The hours passed away slowly, slowly, marked only by the coming up of the white stars from behind the eastern hills; while the long minutes were told by the dead plash of the water against the beach.

There were feasting and drinking and singing in the tent of Barabbas. This was kept up until long after midnight. Then there was silence, and the loud snoring as of some one in a drunken sleep.

It became very dark. The voices of man and nature were hushed. The hours passed, and all things seemed to sleep except the stars which continued to climb the heavenly dome, and the sad, gray sea which pushed feebly against the desert beach, and myself cruelly orphaned and betrayed, thinking alternately of home and death.

"Death at sunrise!" I exclaimed, thinking aloud to myself.

"The sun has not risen," whispered the Persian.

And Hope, the undying consoler within us, took courage at the words of the old man and at the slow-footed pace of the night; and thought it was long, long till the morning, and that the angel of Life might still come, and relieve from his awful watch the angel of Death.

An hour more of silence that could be felt, and of unutterable suspense — and a hand was laid softly upon my shoulder. The rope that bound me was disengaged, and my deliverer drew me stealthily along the beach, and away from the tent where Barabbas lay dreaming of plundered caravans and cruel uncles who enriched him for the murder of their nephews.

The guide did not speak until we stood on the mound at the mouth of the great ravine, where the Dead Sea first broke upon my sight.

"You are free," he said. "You are a child, abused and betrayed. You shall not be murdered. Robber as I am, there is something in my heart which is touched by your sorrows. Go back to life, if not to happiness. God perhaps will deliver you from Magistus, as He has through me delivered you from Barabbas."

"Come with me," said I; "leave this wretched and dangerous life in the wilderness. Share our fate and fortune in Bethany."

"Do not speak of it," he answered; "it is impossible. Hasten on your journey, or all may be lost."

"But," said I, clinging to him, "Barabbas will kill you when he finds I have escaped."

"No! I have contrived against that. I am cunning and I shall succeed."

"The poor old Persian will be murdered!"

"No! He will be ransomed to-morrow. Away!" he continued excitedly; "a moment's delay may be fatal. Away!"

"Stay!" said I, eagerly; "tell me the name of my benefactor, that I may repeat it in my prayers."

"I have no name, no home. I am the Son of the Desert."

He hurried softly away toward the tent, and I crept up the ravine in the darkness.

IV
IN THE WILDERNESS

Afraid of the dark and fearful gorge, full of rocks and pitfalls and unseen dangers; afraid of the unpeopled desert which awaited me above; afraid of wild beasts, serpents, lepers and evil spirits; afraid of the silence and solitude of night by the Salt Sea; afraid of all things behind me and all before; I ascended cautiously and painfully the narrow path, if path it might be called, praying to the God of Abraham, Isaac and Jacob, for protection.

I, who had never been out of my father's house at that hour of the night in my life, thus found myself amid a complication of circumstances which might have appalled the stoutest heart.

I had ascended two-thirds of the way, when my keen ear caught upon the night-wind the subdued but rough voices of several persons who were descending the ravine. My heart stood still and I almost fainted with affright. Fortunately, I remembered that I had just passed, a little lower down, a large side-fissure or chink in the great rock wall of the ravine. I went back with the utmost speed and caution, and got safely concealed in the black crevice before the objects of my terror came along.

They were no doubt some of the party of Barabbas, who were returning with or without the ransom of the old Persian. They were talking of ransom with oaths and laughter as they passed. I held my breath in suspense; nor did my heart recover its natural beat until they had descended a good distance, and their voices floated faintly upward like the mutterings of lost souls in some horrible abyss.

I was now afraid to start again lest I should meet another detachment of the robbers. I waited a long time, listening intently. It suddenly occurred to me that when the robbers reached the tent of Barabbas, my escape would be discovered, and the swiftest runners despatched to overtake me. This thought brought the cold drops to my forehead; and I hurried breathless all the way up the ravine, actually thinking that I heard the footsteps of men behind me, and voices calling my name.

Escaped from the robbers, I fell into the arms of the desert. I could have extricated myself from the new danger if the sun had been shining. But the day rose dark and cloudy, and I could not tell whether I was going east or west, north or south. I failed to recognize any of the spots we had passed the day before. I walked rapidly up and down the bare hills, over the rough gullies and through the sandy hollows. After some hours of this exhausting travel, both mind and body being on the stretch, I was shocked on discovering that I had been moving in a circle, and was near the mouth of the ravine again.

I would have stretched myself upon some rock in despair; but my dangerous proximity to Barabbas and his men, revived my fears and gave supernatural strength to my body. I fled away as fast as I could over new hills and gullies and sandy bottoms. It must have been two or three hours after noon, when I reached a hill overlooking a deep, narrow valley, the dry bed of some nameless brook, which, in the rainy season, poured along over the sands its little tribute to the sea. Thoroughly exhausted with hunger, thirst, fatigue, loss of sleep, fear and despair, I lay down upon the hillside. Lost in the wilderness, thinking of the still worse conditions of my father and sisters, my misery was too deep for tears. A strange torpor crept over my senses, and I fell into that profound slumber in which the weary are strengthened and the sorrowful comforted.

When I awoke, the setting sun, just freed from clouds, was shining in my face.

How life-giving, faith-giving, hope-giving is a sight of the sun, wrapping his mantle of softened glory about him, and descending trustfully to sleep in the kingdom of night, assured that Aurora will open duly her palace of pearl, and his golden chariot with its fiery steeds issue forth in the morning!

So does the Soul sink only to rise; sleep only to wake; die only to live: ever changing in state, ever the same in substance.

I was thus drawing new vigor from the rays of the sun, when a voice of heavenly sweetness broke upon my ear, a voice chanting this beautiful Scripture:

> "As the hart panteth after the water-brooks,
> So panteth my soul after thee, O God!
> My soul thirsteth for God, for the living God:
> When shall I come and appear before God?"

"Are there angels as well as demons in the desert?" said I, to myself.

A jutting brow of the hill concealed from me the source whence these sounds appeared to issue. I arose and advanced to explore the mystery. Rounding the intervening slope, I saw a young man seated upon a stone at the mouth of a large cavern. His quick eye detected me in a moment, and he advanced to meet me. He wore a single garment wrought of the finest camel's hair, which was secured about his waist by a leathern girdle. Simple toilet! But when you looked at his fine head with its long black hair curling about his bare neck, and his beautiful oval face soft as a girl's, full of all saintly thoughts and heavenly emotions, you knew that you were in the presence of one who was clad interiorly in fine linen and purple.

"Good sir," said I, "behold an unhappy youth, who has just escaped death by robbers, and is lost in this terrible wilderness!"

"One must have lived long in the desert to find his way out of it such a dark day as this. It will be clear to-morrow, and I will pilot you into the great highway. Meantime you are welcome to my poor hospitalities—a cave for roof, a bed of skins, water to drink, wild honey and locusts to eat; that is all."

"I gladly accept your offer; and were your proffered gifts still more humble, they would be sanctified by the light of brotherly love you throw upon them."

I seated myself on the stone while he went into the cave and brought forth his simple food and drink, of which I partook heartily.

"To whom am I indebted for this kind reception?" I inquired, as I finished my meal.

"I am John," he answered, "the son of Zacharias; and I dwell in the desert until the time of my showing unto Israel."

A deep human groan from the interior of the cavern now startled me, and I sprang from my seat.

"What is that?" I exclaimed.

"My poor old patient has awakened. I must go and examine him."

"He takes in the sick as well as the wandering," said I to myself. "Surely the angels must protect him in some peculiar manner."

John came forward again with an anxious countenance. "Alas!" said he, "the old man has rapidly changed. He fell into a soft slumber an hour ago, but he is now plainly dying. I knew he was very ill, for he has raved all day about his children and some magicians who wish to destroy them."

At these words a fearful tremor seized me. I could not speak. I sprang past the young man, and in a moment was kneeling at the side of my father! I seized his withered hand and covered it with kisses.

"My father! my father! Do you not know your son, your only son?"

The young hermit looked on in tears.

The old man slowly opened his eyes and cast a bewildered look, first at me, and then at John.

"Yes—you are angels," he said, "who have come to welcome my spirit into paradise."

He breathed heavily. I sank down weeping. John came forward with a little basin of water. "There is no time to be lost," said he in a low tone.

"Do you believe in God, and in Moses his lawgiver, and in the prophets his servants?"

"I do! I do!" said the old man, eagerly.

"Do you repent of your sins, and pray for the Holy Spirit to guide you?"

"I do! and God be merciful to a miserable sinner!"

"Then I baptize you with water, the emblem of purification,—and in the name of the Lord, the only God, into his spiritual Church and into the hope of immortal life."

Thus saying, he sprinkled some water on the old man's forehead. His own face shone with a meek and holy radiance. My father closed his eyes and seemed to sleep.

Suddenly he started, frowning, as if some great pain had changed the current of his thought.

"Tell my son to beware of his uncle. He is a magician."

"Here is your son!" I exclaimed, eagerly; "here is your son! Oh, speak to me, my father!"

He did not notice my grief; but, pointing slowly to John the Baptist, he said, solemnly:

"Behold the prophet of God!"

He then looked fixedly upward; and as I followed his glance to the roof of the cave, his spirit passed away beyond the blue dome, beyond the stars and the sun, beyond the entire realm of nature, into the paradise of Moses and the prophets.

I spent the night in prayer and tears by my father's dead body. Occasionally the young prophet broke in upon the stillness of the air with his silvery voice, chanting the sweet verses of Scripture. I was sorely tempted to rebel against the providence of God, which permitted such a good man as my father to be so cruelly dealt with. The presence, however, of the young prophet, was in itself a sermon, a blessing, a help to resignation. One could not be skeptical or even critical in his luminous atmosphere of peace and love. I reflected that there were many great mysteries which my youthful and inexperienced mind could not at present comprehend, and returning faith assuaged the grief it could not remove.

The next day about noon the young prophet offered a prayer over the corpse, and we consigned it to a humble grave dug by our own hands in a large cavern near by. I observed that there were four other graves in the same spot.

"Yes," said John, meekly, "this is my little cemetery. Here I bury my dead in ground consecrated to the Lord. This was a robber who was wounded in a fray and left by his comrades. He dragged his bleeding limbs into the desert. I found him and bore him to my home. I preached to him the new gospel of repentance and faith, and he died in my arms weeping like a child over the sins of his youth. He who occupies that grave was a madman, who broke his chains, and drove every one from him with knives and stones until he met me in the wilderness. He followed me to my cave, and would sit contented at my feet hearing me sing or read or pray. Under that mound is a poor slave who fled, mutilated and frenzied, from a cruel master. I kissed the wounds I could not heal; and he died clasping my hands smilingly to his lips. And that last one is the grave of another poor leper like your father, forsaken even by his wretched companions—but not forsaken by the Lord, whose Word I obeyed when I tended him in his long illness.

"I call it consecrated ground," he continued; "for these poor people are the children of God. The leper is cured of his leprosy; the slave is free; the madman is sane; the robber is forgiven."

"What induces you," said I, "to lead this strange, lonely life, so full of self-sacrifice, so full of terrors and dangers?"

"The Spirit of God!" he said, solemnly.

"Are you not afraid of the silence, the solitude, the darkness of the desert?"

He replied in the words of Scripture:

"The Lord is my light and my salvation; whom shall I fear? The Lord is the strength of my life: of whom shall I be afraid?"

I felt awed in the presence of this young man, who was not more than ten years older than myself. I was better satisfied to leave my father's ashes in his keeping, than if I had built above them the most splendid monument of Pentelican marble or Corinthian brass.

After a frugal meal we started for the public road. It was ten long miles to the nearest highway, and it was ten more from that to Bethany. We discoursed, as we walked along, about spiritual things; and although I did not understand half he said, he spoke with such eloquence and sincerity that he convinced me he had some great mission in the world. We parted a little before sunset with mutual embraces and blessings. I dropped some grateful and admiring tears as I gazed after the heavenly-minded hermit, picking his way with his long staff through the rough places, until he disappeared from sight over the brown, bare hill.

It was not until the comforting and sustaining power of his presence was withdrawn, that I recognized how exhausted and helpless and lonely I was. Fatigue, fear, excitement, sorrow, loss of sleep and inadequate nourishment, had considerably shattered my nerves; and now to appear suddenly in the presence of an uncle who thought he had murdered me, was a difficult and perhaps a dangerous task. I would gladly have turned in any other direction; but my sisters were in the power of the monster who had plotted my assassination. Nothing but a vague fear that those lovely women were in some trouble or distress, gave strength to my tired limbs and courage to my aching heart.

Night came on, and I had to advance more slowly. The full moon was shining halfway down the western sky, but a dark cloud had risen from the ashes of the sunset, and was advancing upward. It was important that I should make all the haste I could, before the light of the moon was obscured by that ascending blackness. To get out of the road might be to lose the whole night.

I moved so rapidly that I became exceedingly tired. If I sat down to rest, a mysterious fear impelled me to rise and press forward to Bethany. I have faith in those secret attractions, those silent monitors, those inexplicable warnings. A minute's repose of muscle, a minute's recuperation of breath, and I started again with renewed energy.

A wind came up behind the cloud and drove it furiously onward. It covered the moon and all was dark. I groped my way. I stumbled over obstacles. I advanced slowly. It was late, late in the night, when I entered the village of Bethany. No lights were visible; no sounds were heard. I traversed the streets alone. I passed my uncle's residence, brimful of maledictions against its wicked proprietor. Soon my father's house loomed up before me. I saw the long white wall in front of it, and the parapet of the house-top darkening above.

Suddenly a strong blast of wind stirred all the trees of the village. It sighed along the deserted streets and up into the sky. It lifted the lower edge of the cloud from the moon which shone out, low down, just above my father's house, as it were with a sudden brilliancy.

It revealed to me two astonishing things.

One was a large, strange, gilded vehicle drawn by two powerful horses standing before the gate.

The other was the figure of a woman on the house-top, between me and the moon—a woman with flowing robes and disheveled hair, raising her arms wildly to heaven, while a man was approaching her in the attitude of striking.

It was my sister Martha!

With a cry of horror I sprang against the gate, which gave way before me.

V
THE BANQUET

I am too deeply impressed with the vanity of our worldly affairs in comparison with the verities of the spiritual life, to employ my own time or engage a reader's attention with a biography, however pleasing or romantic, unless there was a subtle connecting link, which I expect to reveal, between the facts narrated and those eternal truths which overshadow all others in importance.

I, alone of all mankind, have lived consciously in both worlds long enough to discover their relations to each other. What my fellow-men have seen only on the surface, I have examined interiorly. I have seen the secret springs of human pride, ambition, passion and folly. I have seen the souls of men as they appear in the sight of angels. And my instructions in that world were all based upon my experiences in this.

It is now necessary to drop for a while my personal narrative, and to go back and relate, from the evidence of others, what happened in Bethany during my absence.

My sisters had been left with our atrocious uncle, like two lambs under the guardianship of a wolf. One capable of assassinating his nephew, a mere youth, would not hesitate at any wickedness against his beautiful nieces. This man's character was so cruel and wicked, that some explanation is needed of the singular maturity of diabolism to which he had attained.

Magistus had neither religion nor honor. Honor binds us in duty to our neighbor, as religion binds us both to God and the neighbor. It is a moon which shines brilliantly in the absence of the sun. The light of honor is also but the reflected light of religion. When both shine together, honor is absorbed and swallowed up in the more effulgent blaze of religion. The soul without religion or honor, is like the earth without sun or moon—cold, dark, desolate, hideous.

Such was the soul of Magistus.

Irreligion, like drunkenness, is sometimes inherited. The father of Magistus was a scoffer and sensualist. Fatal incubus of moral deformity descending from father to son! In this he was typical of the age. The hereditary pressure toward hell was so great, that a few more centuries of transmission would have brought the world into perfect sympathy with the lower regions. The advent of the Lord arrested that for a while.

Without religion or honor man is very close to hell. The veriest barbarian has some faint idea of natural religion, and some feeble impulse of natural honor, which distinguish him from the beasts and unite him to his kind. These are barriers against the influx of infernal life. He is ignorant of the devils within him, and the devils within him are ignorant of him. Wise and blessed provision! Were he brought into conscious rapport with his own attendant evil spirits, he would soon be one with them. Their life in hell and his life on earth would be animated by the same breath.

This had happened to Magistus.

Not that he was a barbarian. He was an educated, cultivated man, accustomed to the luxuries and full of the suavities of civilized life. Civilization and religion are not synonymous. Hell itself has a stupendous civilization. Magistus was a Pharisee by profession: a ritualist, and a strict observer of feast-days and ordinances and ceremonies. That, however, was not the man, but only his outer garment—his cloak. Supposed by the world to be virtuous and honest, this wealthy and reputable Pharisee was spiritually a whited sepulchre, full of dead men's bones and all uncleanness.

He was a spiritualist, a sorcerer, a necromancer, a magician. He at first sought and became familiar with these people, with their studies and arts, from natural curiosity. It was very pleasant to call up his dead father and various dead friends, and converse with them. It was agreeable to know that they were all happy, and advancing in various degrees toward the infinite divine perfection. They showed him wonderful things. They performed miracles in his sight greater than those which the magicians of Egypt performed before Pharaoh.

Then they told him that the Jewish Scriptures were not divinely inspired, but a medley of fables, passable poetry and childish philosophy. He had already suspected this; and he congratulated the spirits on possessing a critical genius so similar to his own. He finally acquired, from these supernatural instructors, a grand system of philosophy, revealing the divinity of nature and the laws of progress.

Having become convinced that there are great and subtle powers emanating from the spiritual world, unknown to most men, he determined to avail himself of those powers for his own private ends. He became a secret pupil and disciple of magicians and wizards. He communicated with spirits and permitted them to take possession of him, soul and body, so that they spoke through his mouth and wrote through his hand and came at his call.

He learned all the tricks and spells of legerdemain, the arts and formulas and incantations of magic, and the rites and ceremonies of the black art in its broadest sense. He obtained means of seeing objects at any distance, of producing hallucinations or optical illusions, of personating the dead, of finding hidden treasures, of reading men's thoughts, of sowing enmity between friends, of discovering secrets, and a thousand other astounding and almost incredible things.

The soul is not destroyed in a moment: it is the work of years. The evil spirits and demons with whom he was thus brought into contact, slowly poisoned the fountain-head of character; extinguished his reverence, his modesty, his respect for marriage; undermined his conscience; swept away all religious and even social and civil scruples; and fired and sustained all his evil propensities; so that, externally a faithful disciple of Moses, he was interiorly a devil, governed only by the love of self and the world.

This formidable hypocrite, the most of whose wealth had been obtained by secret frauds, and was not unstained with blood, had his dwelling in the centre of an immense area surrounded by lofty walls and concealed by a dense grove of trees. He received no visitors but those who came to him at night, and for no good purpose. He had the character of a recluse, devoted to sacrifice and prayer. He thus indulged his secret vices and carried on his diabolical incantations unsuspected. The dark shadows of his princely mansion enveloped a degree of Assyrian luxury scarcely exceeded by the Caprean court of the emperor Tiberius.

Caiaphas, the priest, was his best friend, who shared his private pleasures and maintained by constant applause his public reputation for sanctity and honor.

The influence of evil spirits who possess us is at first gentle and subtle, coinciding with our own inclination. Thinking to lead, we are led. When a man is chained so that he can no longer resist, they urge him headlong to a crisis. They fire his evil passions; they blind his perverted intellect; they inflate his pride and self-conceit; they make him scornful and regardless of others, impatient of all barriers to his self-gratification, and assure him of boundless immunity and protection. In this state of horrible fantasy and inflamed passion, he is ready to trample upon all laws human and divine.

To this fearful point in his spiritual life had Magistus arrived.

When my father was driven into the wilderness, Caiaphas and my uncle plotted together how to get speedy and sole possession of his great wealth. To get rid of or destroy his children was the first, and, indeed, the only thing necessary. But they resolved to allow some months to elapse—to let our misfortunes die out from the public memory, and even ourselves be quite forgotten. Hence the seclusion, the solitude, the systematic neglect to which we were subjected.

The plan was finally matured. The boy was to be decoyed into the wilderness and murdered by Barabbas. It was to be given out that he was a wild, incorrigible lad, who had run away from home and joined a band of robbers. After a few months a letter was to be received from Barabbas, whose fame as an outlaw was widespread, giving the particulars of his death in an attack of the party upon some caravan. This was to settle the matter for ever in the public mind.

It was more difficult to dispose of my sisters than of myself. A hundred schemes were suggested by the inventive villains, but all rejected or suspended. It was finally agreed to draw them out and test their characters, to make experiments upon them, to see what could be done with them. It was a delicate task; but Magistus had boldness and cruelty for anything, and Caiaphas was to back him incessantly with his private counsel and his public support. He had already begun his insidious work, by lamenting to sundry influential persons, with sanctimonious regrets, that the daughters of his old and dear friend exhibited so early a singular perverseness of character and disregard of their social and religious obligations. The result, he added, of that laxity of discipline and passion for individual liberty, which characterized the unhappy leper.

The first and best instrument of evil is always a woman. Mary Magdalen, left an orphan without relatives at a very early age, had fallen into the hands of a strolling showman, who taught her to sing and dance, accompanying herself on the timbrel. Her extraordinary beauty attracted attention in the streets of Jerusalem, and she soon passed into the possession of one of those connoisseurs who study the anatomy as well as the philosophy of art. She quickly disappeared from sight; and it was rumored that she had been sent to Ashkelon to serve in the gorgeous temple of Ashtoreth, the Venus of

Assyria. She had gone one dark night no further than Bethany, and had buried her talents and her shame in the princely mansion of Magistus.

On the morning of my departure this serpent was introduced into the dove-cote. Magistus represented her as a distant relative whom he had invited to spend several weeks with his nieces, hoping that her gayety of spirits would lighten the constant gloom of his little charges. The children, dazzled by her great beauty and won by her free and affectionate manner, were delighted with their new companion. She entertained them with curious stories of what she had seen and heard, refraining from any allusion which might reveal her true life and character.

But the plot of the two arch-demons did not work as they had calculated. Indeed, it worked in a way quite opposite to their expectations. They had counted on the corrupting influence of a bold, fascinating woman on the gentle and unsophisticated thoughts and feelings of innocent girls. They had not counted, cunning and sagacious as they were, on the possible influence of the girls upon Mary Magdalen.

That influence was astonishing. When she felt the pure and innocent sphere which surrounded the lovely sisters, a change came over the subtle emissary of Magistus. She forgot the instructions of her masters. The memories of her old life seemed to die out, and the unseen angels of her better nature to wake into strange activity. Young herself, more sinned against than sinning, her pity was awakened for these young creatures against whom such wicked ones were conspiring.

She made them tell her all about their poor father, and wept with them at the story. She took them into the garden and played over the green knolls, and ran in the graveled walks, and gathered flowers, and sang little childish songs, as if she were a child again. She asked a thousand questions about our mother and little Samuel, and about the babyish sayings and doings of my little sisters and myself. She frequently exclaimed "Oh, I am so happy! This is the happiest day of my life! Oh that I could live for ever so!"

Pausing before the tomb of my mother, and looking at a little vase of fresh flowers which stood before it, she suddenly fell upon her knees, exclaiming wildly:

"O God! if I could have offered flowers, also, at the tomb of a mother, it might have been different!"

She burst into a flood of tears; and the sisters endeavored to console her—not knowing the true nature of her wound—by kissing her cheeks and mingling their tears with hers.

They were interrupted in these sweet offices of mutual sympathy, by the voice of a servant asking Mary Magdalen if she had forgotten that she had to prepare herself and her companions for the grand supper at the house of Magistus.

She arose from the ground, and slowly recovering her composure, led the astonished children through the gate in the garden wall toward the house of our uncle. On the way she told them that Magistus had prepared a handsome entertainment for herself and them, and as a charming surprise to their brother, who was expected to return with good news from the father just about the hour of the feast. They need not be frightened, for Caiaphas alone was to be present.

We had never entered any portion of our uncle's great mansion except the small wing which contained the reception-room and the long passage which led to the private chamber of our invalid aunt. The three women now passed up a flight of marble steps into a portico leading into a vast hall, ornamented with statues and with vases filled with flowers. Hurrying through this hall, Mary lead them up another flight of stairs which had a gilded balustrade, into two exquisite bed-chambers which opened into each other.

The bedsteads were of carved ivory, exceedingly beautiful; the canopies, of blue silk fringed with gold; the coverlets, of fine linen and purple, curiously embroidered. The divans, the couches, the chairs, the tables, were all gems of graceful art. The floor was of polished cedar, with gilded moulding around the wall. The ceiling was a splendid stucco-work on which scenes were painted in brilliant colors; in one room, Actæon peeping from behind the trees at Diana and her nymphs in their crystal bath; and in the other, Venus beating her breast and tearing her hair at sight of the blood-stained thigh of Adonis.

The whole atmosphere was freighted with the most delicious and exhilarating perfumes. There were chests of drawers full of the richest female clothing, the fruit of the rarest material and the finest needlework. There were caskets lying open and revealing ear-rings and necklaces and bracelets of the most dazzling beauty. The sisters were overwhelmed with wonder and delight. They had never seen such things before; for our father, rich as he was, was plain, frugal and unostentatious in his tastes and habits.

"These are all ours," said Mary Magdalen, "the gifts of our good uncle who delights to make us happy. Come, let us dress for the supper."

Domestics came at her call, and the ladies were attired in robes of the greatest magnificence. Their hair was dressed in the most graceful manner, sparkling with alternate flowers and gems. "All this is for Lazarus," said the sisters to each other, as they followed Mary Magdalen, blushing at themselves, down into the supper-room in a deep basement almost under ground.

The supper-room was as gorgeously furnished as the bed-chambers. The table was placed on a raised platform at one end of the room, leaving a great space for which our bewildered visitors could not imagine the use. The ceiling had a splendid painting of Aurora driving the chariot of the sun, attended by the Muses and the flying Hours. The walls were adorned with solid upright mirrors of polished brass. In every niche and corner was some exquisite marble, some nude figure from the Grecian mythology; the most beautiful of which was Leda caressing the swan, concealing within its white form the passionate soul of Jove.

Caiaphas and Magistus reclined upon silken couches at a table which was loaded with savory viands and vessels of gold and silver containing delicious wines, and ornamented with brilliant vases of fruits and flowers. The scene was lighted by hundreds of wax candles of as many colors as the rainbow.

As soon as the women were handed to their places at the table, Martha exclaimed:

"And why could not poor aunt Ulema be brought down to enjoy this charming feast?"

And Mary added:

"And Lazarus, where is he?"

Ulema and Lazarus were the last persons in the world whom the host would have invited to his banquet. He paid no attention to Martha's question. To Mary's he replied by drawing a parchment from his bosom.

"Listen!" said he; "a letter from Lazarus!"

The faces of the young girls grew anxious.

"Dear Uncle:

"Excuse me for spending the night with my father. He is better, happy and well provided. But I have many things to say to him, and my visit has given him so much pleasure. I know I must submit on my return to the law of purification, which will separate me many days from my sweet sisters. Take them to your own house and make them happy. I will return to-morrow.

"Your loving nephew,

"Lazarus."

Magistus looked up: the sisters were weeping.

"I was half angry at first," he said, "at this strange disobedience. On reflection, I am satisfied. It confers immense happiness on both father and son; and their consultations may be of great service to you all. And, besides, it gives me such a good opportunity to become better acquainted with my charming nieces."

He passed the manuscript to my sisters, who inspected it closely. It was my handwriting without doubt. The reader need not be told that it was a base forgery; for at that very moment my poor father was ill in the cave of John the Baptist, and I was bound in expectation of death on the shore of the Salt Sea.

My sisters appeared to resume their composure and the feast proceeded, although they partook very lightly of its delicacies. Musicians came in, and the harp, the timbrel, the flute, the cymbals, the drum, and the silver bugle enlivened the entertainment. Caiaphas and Magistus grew warm and witty and convivial over their wine, which they pressed in vain upon the timid girls. Even Mary Magdalen merely sipped it in deference to both parties.

What a delicate thermometer is the heart of a young girl! Without thinking, how innocent! Without reasoning, how wise! A thoughtful shadow crept over Martha's face. Mary sank into a deep reverie, from which the playful sallies of the rest could not arouse her. These young girls were thinking, and their thoughts ran in the same channel.

The sudden change of Magistus from indifference to suavity; this gorgeous and secluded feast; Lazarus and his father away off in the wilderness; their poor aunt shut up in her sick chamber; this strange woman who wept so bitterly in the garden: these pagan pictures and statues so revolting to their chaste religious instincts: the lights; the music; the noisy laughter of these usually sedate men; all these things overwhelmed them with sudden apprehensions and vague terror. Each divined the feelings of the other by some secret sympathy; and bursting into tears at the same moment, they both rose from their seats.

"Stay!" exclaimed Magistus, nourishing his wine-cup and maddened by its contents—"Stay! you lose the cream and essence of the feast. I will show you now how the dancing-girls of Babylon intoxicate the king of Assyria."

At these words they fled from the room.

"Follow them," said Caiaphas to Mary Magdalen, "and quiet their apprehensions."

"Put your babies to bed," roared Magistus, "and come back yourself."

I will not describe the new parties who were introduced to the feast, nor how it degenerated into a revel, and the revel into an orgy. Mary Magdalen did not return to the supper-room; and long after midnight the drunken master of the house was borne off to a sleep from which he ought never to have awakened, and to dreams of conquests which he never achieved.

The shadow of other spheres more powerful than his own, was already approaching to thwart his plans and change his destiny!

An hour after all was quiet, a strange sound was made at the back gate in the wall nearest the lodging-rooms of the domestics of the establishment. It was a double sound; the first part of it being a loud and peculiar whistle, the last part a powerful and startling hiss or rattle. The first sound seemed to summon some one to appear; the second, to threaten him if he did not obey. The first was a call; the second a menace.

There was one person on the premises, and only one, who knew the full meaning of that strange summons. He trembled on his couch when he heard it. Great drops of sweat came out on his forehead as he listened. He strove to rise as if to obey it, but fell back as if paralyzed with fear. The call was twice repeated with a weird ferocity in its tone; and the black eunuch, Ethopus, staggered from his chamber and groped his way into the open air and to the gate. He opened it softly with a private key, and stepped into the street. Do not men, like moths, fly sometimes stupidly into the candle of danger?

A remarkable vehicle, drawn by two great black horses and driven by a hideous black servant, stood in the street. It was showily gilded, and had several little doors and windows in it. It resembled the chariots on which mountebanks and jugglers perambulated the country, but was of larger size and more tastefully constructed.

Ethopus paid no attention to this equipage. Right before him stood an object capable of inspiring him with the deepest horror. It was a tall figure with a huge yellow serpent coiled about his neck and body, and a leopard standing quietly at his side. The leopard growled and the serpent hissed as the black man approached their master.

"Be quiet, Moloch!" he said to the leopard. "Hush, Beelzebub," he whispered to the snake. "This is a friend and fellow-servant."

The poor black prostrated himself in the dust before this mysterious night-visitor and his bestial attendants. He signified his total submission by raising the man's foot and placing it on his head as he groveled on the ground. When he released it, he kissed it with the most abject servility. His abasement was extreme.

"That is right, Ethopus!" said his master, "that is right. I rejoice to find you in such a becoming frame of mind. Conduct me promptly to the secret chamber of magic. Then return to my servant and give him suitable accommodations. Inform Magistus of my arrival early in the morning. I have come on a grand errand to this village of Bethany."

Ethopus obeyed these orders without noise. All was at length silent. Perhaps all slept: the drunken proprietor, the wicked priest, the remorseful Magdalen, the frightened eunuch, the strange guest, and Mary and Martha locked in each other's arms, their beautiful faces bathed in tears, and their sweet souls dreaming that their angel-mother was watching them from heaven.

VI
THE CHAMBER OF MAGIC

There are few sights more touching than that of a man struck speechless in the course of disease, yet retaining his mental faculties. Death perhaps approaches; weighty business presses on his mind; solemn secrets demand revelation; confessions of soul struggle for utterance. He makes inarticulate sounds, incomprehensible gestures. He writhes; he moans with the burden of thoughts he cannot express. His eyes speak and plead with a mute eloquence. His ideas play upon his countenance like lambent lightning, but die away, voiceless, indefinite, unrevealed.

Such was the state of Ethopus, the dumb eunuch, the day after the treacherous banquet. There was a great solitude about the house; for Magistus, Caiaphas, and Simon Magus the magician, made an early and prolonged visit to Jerusalem. Mary Magdalen took the sisters over the beautiful and extensive grounds, and paid another visit to the tomb of our mother, carrying some exquisite flowers in her own hand as a little offering to the maternal shade. Ethopus flitted about here and there in a state of unaccountable excitement. He followed the sisters all day at a respectful distance; and when his duties called him off imperatively, he went precipitately about everything until he could assure himself again that they were free and out of danger.

"Ethopus has something extraordinary on his mind," said Martha, to herself; but she did not communicate her observation to her timorous and sensitive sister.

The case was evidently this: Ethopus had discovered the plot of Magistus against us all, and he felt certain that the arrival of the magician boded no good. He was struggling between his disinterested affection for us and his intense fear of his wicked masters. He felt his own weakness, increased by his inability to speak; and he was laboring to devise some plan by which the sisters could be brought to share his knowledge, and to concert measures of escape from some impending catastrophe.

He seemed to divine that Martha was more thoughtful, courageous and trustworthy than her sister. It was late in the afternoon when he made her a signal, seen by herself alone, to follow him. She understood his meaning, and contrived to withdraw without exciting the suspicion of her companions. Ethopus conducted her to the chamber of Ulema. Scarcely giving her time to exchange kisses with her aunt, he pushed her into a little recess in the wall which was concealed by a hanging curtain. Between the folds of this, Martha could peep cautiously into the room. In a few moments Magistus entered.

He seemed hurried and flustered, and had a dark frown upon his brow.

"No message from Barabbas to-day. Something has gone wrong. Put this woman to sleep immediately."

Ethopus adjusted a large mirror of polished metal on a table. Ulema arose from her couch without speaking a word, and seated herself in a chair about four feet in front of the mirror and gazed steadfastly into it. Magistus stood a little one side, and made rapid passes with his hands and arms from her head to her feet, nearly touching her body. His black eyes were fixed fiercely upon her face, and his heavy breathing could be heard by Martha at every pass he made.

There was silence for several minutes, during which Ulema gazed steadfastly into the mirror. Martha could not help doing the same; and she gazed at the mirror until a strange, tingling, bewildered sensation began to creep over her frame, and she averted her eyes to escape its magical fascination.

The victim of this singular experiment now became rigid, and made a convulsive sound as if in a severe spasm. Martha was terribly frightened; but her aunt suddenly became relaxed with a profound sigh. Magistus took a long needle and passed it through the skin of her hand. She did not flinch. He then put something which seemed to be a lock of hair into her palm, and closed the fingers tightly upon it.

"Follow this person," said he, "wherever he is, and tell me what you see."

The woman began, after a long pause:

"I am in a great wilderness of bare hills full of rocks and sand. The sense of solitude is terrible. It is cloudy but windy—and the sun will soon shine in the west."

"But the youth?—the youth?" cried Magistus, impatiently.

"Wait a moment. The youth? I must find him. Bless me! how he has wandered! how many circles! Ah! there he is! I see him stretched at full length upon the ground."

"That is good!" said Magistus eagerly; "that is good. He lies dead upon the ground. Go on."

"He is not dead," said the oracle slowly; "his heart still beats: he sleeps."

"Not dead?" screeched the old man, "what say you, not dead? Is he not wounded? Is he not stabbed? Is he not bleeding?" he continued in the highest excitement.

"No!" said the woman calmly; "he is not dead, he sleeps."

"Do you see no gashes upon his body?"

"No, I see only a bright new dagger."

"Furies!" exclaimed Magistus; "he has escaped me. I have been deceived."

Turning suddenly upon the woman, he seized her by the throat:

"Do you tell me the truth?"

"I tell you what I see. I fabricate nothing. I am now attracted around the hill. Ah! I see a young man with the face of an angel coming forth from a cave. He sings. Oh how sweetly he sings!"

"Angels and devils!" roared Magistus; "you have seen or reported falsely."

With that he seemed overwhelmed by a paroxysm of rage, and began beating the poor woman violently about the head and arms with a black rod he took from the table. She made no resistance, and did not seem to feel the blows. Ethopus raised his hands deprecatingly, and Martha was about to cry out from her place of concealment, when a low, fierce growl, from underneath the floor apparently, startled all of them but Ulema, who heard it not.

Simon Magus was feeding his leopard.

"The Master has returned," said my uncle, "I will consult him immediately. He may deliver me from this difficulty."

He left the room. Ethopus made rapid passes from her knees upward, and Ulema awoke. She rubbed her hands and eyes, looked wonderingly around her and exclaimed:

"I have had a long, painful sleep, and I must have seen sad things. Did I give him satisfaction?"

Ethopus shook his head sadly.

"Alas!" said she, with a distressed and puzzled air, "when will this cruel imprisonment cease, and this strange life of visions which I never remember?"

Martha now came forward and threw herself weeping upon the neck of her aunt. For a long time these sorrowful women exchanged those kisses and tears which are consolations. They then unburdened their hearts to each other. By questioning Ethopus and interpreting his pantomimic answers as well as they could, they learned that some secret dangers surrounded them, and that Ethopus wished Martha to spend the night in the chamber of her aunt. Martha thought it best to rejoin Mary immediately, and explain to her that Ulema was quite indisposed, and get her to sleep with Mary Magdalen, and permit the older sister to comfort and nurse the invalid. All of which was easily accomplished.

Ulema had been confined for years in that little room by her husband as the subject and victim of his magical art. She was a clairvoyant of extraordinary power; and when put asleep by the shining mirror and the waving hands, she would follow any clue given her, and the greatest physical obstacles seemed only penetrable shadows in the path of her mysterious vision.

She was thus employed by her husband to advance the schemes of his unscrupulous spirit. She was made to read the thoughts of others, so that Magistus became possessed of any man's or any woman's secret life whenever he chose. He obtained information in this manner which enabled him to make lucrative transactions in business, to plot in the dark against whomsoever he pleased, to destroy the peace of families, and to acquire a reputation for superior and almost miraculous wisdom.

She had long ceased to be anything but a mere tool in her husband's hands. She was locked up and taken care of as any other valuable instrument would have been. She was visited and inspected only when her services were required. Love, sympathy, interchange of sentiments, all this had ceased. She received nothing from him but contempt and threats. She lived within hearing of his midnight revels. She bore the ravages of these things in her pale and tearful face, with its sad and terrified expression.

Ethopus came softly into the room about midnight, and after many gestures expressive of the supreme necessity of caution and silence, he conducted the two women on tip-toe through a narrow passage. Near the end of this he paused, and pressing on a secret spring, he discovered a sliding panel in the wall. This opened and admitted them into a large, empty room. This room was only for the ventilation of a more interior and secluded apartment. A series of movable slats effected the communication between the two chambers. The light streaming through the shutters showed that the inner room was occupied. Looking down through the apertures, with very little danger of being discovered, the women beheld, six or eight feet before them, the floor of the secret chamber of magic.

Ethopus left them as stealthily as a cat, after placing them in the best position to see and hear what was going on in the den of sorcery. He pressed Martha's hand to his heart before he departed. Perhaps he wished to show how deeply he felt for them; perhaps also to intimate how deeply he suffered. Perhaps he asked for help as well as sympathy. The poor, dumb African would not only save them, if possible, from their subtle enemies, but would enlist the knowledge and power of a superior race, to effect his own deliverance from the crushing thraldom they had imposed upon him.

A thousand or two thousand years hence, magic as a science and an art will have ceased to exist. Generations unborn will enjoy the leafage and fruit of that sacred tree of Christianity, whose little seed we have seen planted in the dark ground. The hells now opened will be closed; the superstitions now triumphant will be a myth; the languages now living will be dead; the arts now flourishing will have perished; the civilization now dominant will be a historic shadow. Those who find this manuscript and give it to the world, will not be able to comprehend the meaning, or to believe the truth, of the strange things I am going to relate—and yet they are true.

Magic, which pervades to a greater or less extent all nations, and in some shape influences all individuals, had its origin in the corruption and perversion of the sacred truths of religion. It is the life of all false systems, the voice of their oracles, the inspiration of their prophets, the power of their mighty men. It was the medium by which evil spirits took possession of their victims. It is the falsity which antagonizes truth; the darkness opposite to light; the hell arrayed against heaven. To be under magical influence, is to be assaulted, betrayed, possessed, governed, by demons.

Simon Magus, who believed himself attended by Moloch and Beelzebub, two princes of hell, under the respective forms of a leopard and a serpent, was the most remarkable sorcerer in the time of Christ. He was a Samaritan by birth, but had spent his youth in Egypt, where he became addicted to the black art, and thoroughly conversant with all its mysteries. He was supposed by most men to be an Egyptian, and he took no pains to correct the mistake.

He was a man of unquestionable genius and boundless ambition. He was of majestic presence, bending weaker spirits easily to his will. He was brave to desperation, and eloquent as if he had been fed in his youth by the bees of Attica. He was the secret chief and leader of thousands of persons addicted to magic in different countries. His word was regarded as law; his power as irresistible; his wisdom as inscrutable.

Magicians generally resorted to remote caves and deserted ruins for their rites and incantations. Many of the most splendid temples, however, of the pagan religions, had private chambers devoted to their use. So also did the palaces of many kings, and the princely mansions of wealthy and powerful men. The magicians of Jerusalem and its neighborhood had a secret council-room in the quiet house of Magistus, in which they held their infernal conclave at every visit of the Master.

The two women peeped cautiously into this chamber of mystery. The floor and the ceiling were both covered with black cloth, the latter having a great many stars flaming upon it in imitation of night. Through them a vast comet trailed its fiery form. The walls were painted with figures of the most disgusting objects which creep on the earth, or fly in the air, or swim in the sea. Some of these figures had the heads of men and women: others had the heads of monsters attached to naked bodies in the human shape.

On a raised platform of black marble, and in a great arm-chair covered with crimson silk, sat Simon Magus, wearing a white robe of dazzling lustre, a leopard skin loosely thrown over his shoulders, and a gilt crown surmounted by an eagle with outspread wings. He wore also a massive gold chain around his neck, from which was suspended a little sapphire image, which was supposed to guide the Egyptian priest to the truth, as the breast-plate of precious stones did the Jew.

The short black hair of Simon Magus curled close to his head, and he had no beard after the fashion of his adopted country. His forehead was white as pearl and both wide and lofty. His eyes were large and brilliant. His whole face was illumined by the grand fires of intellect and passion. His expression was too proud to be pleasing, too fierce to be beautiful. He was a man to strengthen the heart of his friends, and to make his enemies tremble.

A large black table was before him, brilliantly painted with the signs of the zodiac. In the centre of it stood an image or idol made of black stone or ebony, having the head of a man, the breast and fore-feet of a lion, and the hind quarters of a goat. The serpent was coiled on the platform at his right hand; the leopard crouched at his left. A splendid globe of crystal hung from the ceiling constituting a lamp, burning perfumed oil and shedding a rose-colored light over the scene.

In this mystic and formidable presence stood twelve or fifteen men with bowed heads, down-hanging hands, and attitudes of the deepest humility. The women recognized only the faces of Magistus and Caiaphas. The former stood nearest to the table. Simon was addressing them in terms of reproachful eloquence:

"You have made no progress in our sublime mysteries during the past year. You have acquired no new powers over the spiritual world. You have not even given me information of the least importance. Alas! you are devoid of genuine ambition, without which whoever deals with spirits becomes a slave and not a master."

His voice became more sonorous and his eye more scornful as he warmed with his subject:

"Your tastes, your character, your life, are low and vulgar and sensual. You employ the powers of magic for paltry and contemptible ends. To obtain reputation for cunning and foresight; to get good bargains out of your neighbors; to cheat some widow out of her property; to find stolen or buried treasure and appropriate it to yourselves; to pry into the secrets of men's bed-rooms and store-rooms and kitchens; to seduce silly maidens; to create trouble between husbands and wives; to inflict all kinds of petty and scurvy revenges upon your enemies,—that is all you do with our venerable and awful art. The grander destiny which awaits us all by the development and centralization of our powers, your vulgar passions do not permit you to see or to appreciate.

"My example has been almost in vain. My spirit of self-sacrifice in achieving my lofty ends, is a mystery to your sluggish and ignoble souls. I have endured hunger and thirst and wakefulness and nakedness and heat and cold and solitude and plagues and wounds for mastery in the great path I have chosen. I have traversed the world from the frozen seas to the chasms of torrid heat. I have contended with wild beasts and with their guardians, the great spirits, by land and water. I have conquered the serpent and the leopard. The vulture lights on my shoulder like a sparrow; the lion crouches at my feet like a dog. Arch-demons come at my bidding, and hundreds of lesser spirits swarm at the signal of my curse."

He became violently excited; his eyeballs glared around in frenzy, and he continued in a fierce whisper:

"It would freeze your cowardly souls only to hear the spells, the incantations, the blasphemies I employed; the watchings, the tortures, the combats, I endured, before I brought Moloch and Beelzebub into subjection to my will. See there, how I have burned their names into my flesh with pencils of iron heated to whiteness!"

He turned back the sleeves of his robe from his white arms, and held them out. Upon one arm in great red letters was the word Moloch, on the other the word Beelzebub.

"It was dreadful! dreadful!—but henceforth they are mine."

The serpent writhed and protruded his tongue. The leopard showed his white teeth, but dropped his yellow head between his paws.

"I have told you," he continued, scornfully, "what constitutes your ambition. Now I will tell you mine. To me belongs the glory of having organized magic and associated magicians. I found them a horde of wandering hunters; I shall make them an invisible phalanx of soldiers. I have more than two thousand magicians, in seven different countries, who obey me as one man. By concerted action we have obtained the secret history, the hidden life of all the governors, consuls, warriors, kings and great men throughout that vast region. I am maturing my plans to get them all under my sovereign control. Other conquerors operate from without, by sword and spear and catapult. I conquer from within, by hope and fear and lust and passion and terror. Unseen, unsuspected, unknown, with legions of invisible soldiers, I shall get possession of all their treasures, all their palaces, all their thrones!

"Do you not see it?" he exclaimed, wildly, starting to his feet. "The lever which truly moves the world lies always on the spiritual side of our life. I advance from the right quarter to my designs. I shall subdue the souls and bodies of men. I shall possess myself of all they possess. I shall become emperor of Rome—yea, monarch of the world. Further still:—I shall advance from realm to realm, from sphere to sphere in the spiritual universe, marshaling around me my hosts of conquering spirits. I shall pronounce the Unspeakable Name. My own name shall become Unspeakable!"

While the magician's imagination soared away in this flight of boundless ambition, his form dilated; a fierce red flush came over his face; his eye, fired with a baleful brilliancy; and the maniac stood forth the very impersonation of that Self-Love which is the moving and controlling genius of hell.

His hearers trembled at his words and manner.

He sunk back into his chair and leaned his brow upon his hand. No one disturbed his reverie. All were spellbound by the speaker's enthusiasm. After several minutes he raised his head and continued in a subdued tone:

"But, alas! my friends! this glorious dream is far from accomplishment. If we had only to conquer the race of men, the difficulties would not be insuperable. But our fiercest fight is on the spiritual side. All are contending for the same prizes—power and glory. When we have beaten back the shining ones whom they call angels, our combat begins with each other; for each demands all for himself.

"Yet I despair not"—he added, after another pause and with a certain sadness in his manner—"I despair not of realizing my inexpressible dream. I have come into possession lately of an ancient and wonder-working formula, whereby I hope to take many steps forward. Listen!

"I discovered by secret means only to be acquired in Egypt, that in a certain wild spot of the Lybian desert one of the oldest and greatest cities of the world was buried in the sand; a city so old that it has no historical record; a people inconceivably wicked, in comparison with whom the people of Sodom and Gomorrah were children sporting in the golden dawn of innocence. This city and these people had been overwhelmed by the same Power which buried the cities of the plain in the Salt Sea.

"I found this spot. By the aid of spiritual powers I burrowed my way into their buried palaces and temples. I exhumed their remains. I made food and drink of their ashes. The spirits who accompanied me fled away, and I was left alone. I blended my being with that of the lost people. I became a skeleton among skeletons, a shade among shades. I conquered. I drew voices out of the silence, forms out of the darkness, life out of death. I summoned with difficulty and danger the ruling spirits of the perished race. I mastered their master. I made him my slave. I compelled him to disgorge the secrets of the wilderness and the grave. I have enriched myself with treasures of knowledge and power, of which no man even dreams."

Intense excitement pervaded his listeners—fear of the man and stupefaction at his words.

"I will show you," he continued—"by a strange art I have acquired, I will show you this new demon who is also one of the oldest. I have summoned this antediluvian monster to-night. He stands before me face to face, like man to man. You cannot hear his voice nor see his shape; but you shall feel his presence and mark his shadow on the wall."

He now let down a large white curtain against the wall, to the top of which it had been rolled like a great map. He resumed his seat and drew forth a curious cup from a drawer in the table. It had words and figures engraven upon it. He gazed intently into the cup, and pronounced some words in an unknown tongue.

A moment of awful silence ensued, every one gazing steadfastly at the curtain and hearing the beating of his own heart. Suddenly a strange, benumbing, paralyzing sensation invaded the nerves of all present. It was the approaching sphere of the antediluvian spirit.

"See!" said the magician hoarsely, "See! He comes!"

And sure enough! Like the shadow of a man which the moon makes when it is going down, there crept a shadow up over the curtain; dim, wavering, misshapen, which slowly settled into distincter form, and stood with bended head and sweeping beard, with tottering knee and outstretched arms, like a very old man of gigantic size begging alms.

All shuddered at the presence of this terrific spirit, more than Saul at the rising of Samuel in the cave of the witch of Endor.

"From this most ancient arch-demon of our art," continued Simon, pointing to the shadow, "I have extorted a method of incantation which promises more power and glory than all the combined rites and amulets in the world. He will confirm what I say."

The shadow slowly turned its old and hideous face toward the audience and made an affirmative motion with its head. It then passed away from the curtain like the shadow of a cloud creeping over a field of grain. All breathed more freely.

"This formula will procure me a liquid of such potent magnetic virtue, that a single drop of it put into a glass of wine will bind the woman who drinks it, entirely and for ever, soul and body, to the man who administers it. She will surrender friends, home, name, fame, everything to his wishes.

"Miserable sensualists that you are," he exclaimed, raising his voice and confronting his cowering audience, "the use for which you would chiefly value this inestimable secret has no attractions for me. My spirit looks upward, not downward. I scorn pleasure. I love glory and power. Through woman I shall conquer man. Woman herself shall be the agent of transferring all that husbands, lovers, brothers, sons, friends possess, to the great magician who shall be a god in her eyes."

"Glorious ambition!" exclaimed Caiaphas.

"When I have achieved the conquest of the world," said the earnest madman, "I will resign the women to you, as a conqueror throws the treasures of a sacked city to the soldiers who have won him a crown."

"And the liquid?" inquired Magistus—"how is it to be obtained?"

"That brought me hither from my subterranean palace in Egypt, where I was initiated into the sacred mysteries by Isis herself."

All ears paid him the strictest attention.

"I must obtain the body of a young girl and convey it to the buried city of the sands, where Ja-bol-he-moth, whom you saw just now, will assist me in the magical rites. We must take her alive. I have made every preparation. I have a vehicle specially constructed for concealment. That will convey us to Joppa whence I have just come. From there to Alexandria by a vessel which awaits me. Thence to the Lybian desert."

"And the young woman?" asked Caiaphas.

"She must be pure as the snow nearest heaven: innocent as the babe tended by angels: beautiful as Aurora when she treads the golden pavement with her feet of pearl: loving as the heart of Spring when she gives her life to the earth: holy as the spirit of prayer which breathed from the lyre of King David."

"And what would you do with this peerless maiden?" said some one in the group.

"Are you acquainted with the processes and powers of magic, and do you ask such a question? Do you know the virtues of the dust of a dove's heart? of the ashes of a viper's tongue? of the pulverized bones of a babe's head? of the blood of a living man? Can you not imagine what subtile forces we may extract from the essences of a virgin body?"

"Has your oracle directed you where to find this wonderful woman?" asked Magistus.

"My presence here is a warrant that it has. That woman is a Jewess, of the tribe of Benjamin, the youngest child, born at the death of her mother."

These were the last words heard by either Ulema or Martha. These affrighted women had been the silent witnesses and auditors of the extraordinary scene I have described. With increasing amazement and terror they found themselves unable to stand, and they sank softly upon the floor. When the object of Simon's visit to Bethany began to reveal itself, they trembled with intense fear. When the horrible idea took distinct shape in her mind, Martha had almost burst into a wild shriek of agony. The shriek was with great difficulty suppressed. The terror and agony were borne in upon the young soul, and she fell into a long and fearful swoon which seemed death itself.

After a long, long time, when all was still and dark, Ethopus approached as softly as he had departed. He aroused Ulema from her trance of grief, and the two bore the unreviving form of Martha back to the chamber. She was laid upon the bed; and as Ethopus passed out of the door, Ulema saw him by the dim light of the stars lifting his face and hands earnestly to heaven.

VII
SAVED

After Martha came out of her swoon, the night was spent in consultation between the two women as to the surest method of averting the catastrophe which impended. It was determined that the sisters should escape from the house early in the morning, and appeal for help to some worthy and influential residents of Bethany, friends of my father. They were so sure of obtaining succor and deliverance, that they became quite cheerful as the sunlight broke above the hills.

Magistus suddenly entered the room, and their hearts sank within them as they noticed the silent ferocity of his countenance. Without saying a word he clasped iron rings upon their ankles and wrists, and chained them securely to the bed-posts. Their tears, cries, inquiries, supplications, were all in vain. He took no notice of them whatever, and locked and bolted the door behind them, leaving them bound and in despair.

A different but equally painful scene occurred in the chamber of Mary Magdalen. Mary, my sister, had just awakened with a deep sigh, and began narrating an ominous dream which had disturbed her night's rest, when a loud knock was heard at the door, and a strange voice commanded them to dress and come forth immediately. They sprang up in great trepidation and obeyed the order. On opening the door they turned back into the room with a loud shriek.

Simon Magus stood before them with his serpent and leopard. He had these creatures about him almost constantly. It was to keep them in good training, for his personal protection, to excite wonder, to inspire awe, and to enforce his authority. They were admirable adjuvants to his pretensions and power. Every one quailed before them.

He assured the women that his pets should not hurt them, if they followed him in silence, turning neither to the right nor to the left. There was no alternative but to obey. He conducted them to our father's residence through the gardens and the gate in the garden wall. He had given every point a recent inspection. He passed into the inner courtyard, and led them down a flight of steps to a room in the cellar used by two of the domestics as a bed-chamber. Here he locked and bolted them in and retired.

Thus were the sisters secured without the possibility of communication or escape. The conspirators took every possible precaution. No one was permitted to leave the grounds, or to come in during the day. Magistus or Simon kept the black eunuch continually in sight. Whether his agitated and anxious manner betrayed him, or whether the magician really read his thoughts, his masters suspected that Ethopus meditated a revolt against the snares which had fascinated the leopard and the serpent. He was closely watched.

The situation of this poor fellow was very touching. His dark face was an index of a darkened soul, not by evil but by the absence of light. Under his homely exterior was a brave and generous heart. He was born and reared in a barbaric land, full of strange beasts and birds and stranger men, where Nature herself is wild and savage. He had been the victim of incredible oppression and cruelty. It is wonderful that the last spark of human feeling had not been trodden out from his spirit.

It spoke well for the native richness of the soil when good seed sprang up so luxuriantly as soon as planted. From the day he became acquainted with my sisters and myself, a new life had dawned upon him. Friendly voices, gentle words, kindly looks, sympathizing deeds, were food and drink to his amiable and child-like nature. His soul grew and expanded under them as flowers under dew and sunlight. Sincere attachment to us and hatred of our common enemies took possession of the whole man. He was ready for any labor, any danger, any sacrifice in our behalf.

Imagine the mental tortures of this humble and voiceless friend, when he saw the terrible fate which was impending over us, and found himself so helpless to avert it or to assist us!

Thus passed away the long, dreary, gloomy day - the day of my father's funeral. It was spent by my sisters in prayer and tears and unavailing struggles to escape or to make themselves heard. Mary Magdalen identified herself thoroughly with the gentle and innocent child with whom she was imprisoned. She taxed her ingenuity to the utmost to give her consolation and hope; and when invention failed, she resorted to tears.

"Do you ever pray to God?" said little Mary.

"To which God?" asked Mary Magdalen.

"Which God? There is but one God!"

"Magistus has the statues of a dozen gods and goddesses in his house; and he says that all of them answer prayer when they are presented with splendid gifts."

"Jehovah, the only God," said the child with sweet solemnity, "heareth the prayer of the humble and contrite heart. He heareth the poor and needy, and lifteth up all who are cast down."

"How beautiful!" exclaimed Mary Magdalen with a deep sigh; and she fell into a profound reverie with downcast eyes, while a solitary tear, the first pearl of genuine repentance, trickled down her cheek.

About nightfall Simon Magus unlocked the door and called Mary Magdalen out of the room. He closed the door behind her, so that Mary could not hear what he said. He put into her hands two cups of different patterns containing milk.

"This one," said he, "you will give to the child; this you will drink yourself. Be careful and not forget. Your life depends upon it. If you fail to obey me, I will feed your body piecemeal to my leopard."

Terror-stricken as well by his manner as his words, she took the cups mechanically from his hands and passed into the room. He carefully locked the door again.

Bewildered by this new blow, she took her seat in silence, a cup in each hand. She strove to collect her thoughts. Poison to Mary or death to herself! That was the alternative. Her nature was impulsive and passionate. She reached her conclusions quickly, and she acted upon them instantaneously.

"What is my wretched life worth in comparison with hers?" was the silent language of her heart, "What attraction has life for me, poor, guilty, forlorn, forsaken thing?" She drank from the cup intended for Mary.

"What is the matter," said my sister, who had noticed her singular abstraction and agitation. "What are you drinking?"

"Only some milk. I was so frightened by that terrible man that I forgot what I was doing. Excuse me for drinking first. Here is a cup for you."

The unsuspecting child drank it eagerly, having passed the whole day suffering from both hunger and thirst. Taken after fasting, poisons act quickly. It was not long before Mary Magdalen began to have strange swimmings in the head and benumbing sensations along the course of all her nerves. She felt sure that her death was approaching.

"Mary," said the brave girl, "when you are delivered from these dangers and your brother comes home and I go away, will you remember me sometimes?"

"You will not go away."

"Oh yes. I shall go away, far, far away."

"You shall live with us always," said Mary.

"I cannot! I cannot! When I am gone, and they tell you evil and cruel things of me, will you think of me kindly and love me still?"

"I will not believe them."

"But if you should believe them, would you love me still? I cannot live without your love."

"I will love you for ever," said Mary, throwing her arms around her neck. "Why do you speak so sadly? You frighten me. What is the matter?"

"I am sleepy, so sleepy," said Mary Magdalen, stretching herself on the couch.

Mary knelt at her side, chafing her hands, with some vague foreboding rising on her mind.

"Oh do not go to sleep so early. Do not leave me alone in the dark. Talk to me."

"Mary," said the stupefied woman slowly and with difficulty, "does Jehovah who accepts the offering of a contrite heart, ever receive into his heaven a very great sinner?"

"Certainly, certainly!" said the child.

"Then pray for me."

No words, no shaking, no supplications, no frantic screams could arouse her again; and Mary beat her bosom and tore her hair in the extremity of grief at the side of her inanimate friend.

About an hour before midnight four men stood in the inner courtyard of my father's house. Caiaphas and Simon Magus were engaged in earnest conversation. Magistus turned to the black mute whom he had compelled to accompany him everywhere, and said:

"I shall go half a day's journey with Simon. We will start now in ten minutes. Haste to the stables where his chariot and servant are in waiting. Drive quietly around to the front gate of this house. Here is the key to Ulema's chamber. After we have gone, not before, give those women some food."

Ethopus departed. He left the gate in the garden wall open. He hurried to Ulema's room. He released the astonished women. He drew them out upon the gallery. He pointed eagerly to the garden gate and over to my father's house. It was all he could do. He was wild with excitement, and the gestures of the dumb man were those of despair. He then ran toward the stables.

The women started on their dangerous journey, not knowing what was to be done. They hurried along the flowery walks in the greatest trepidation. On ascending our terraced garden, Ulema, weak, sick and overwhelmed with emotion, fainted and fell. Martha tried in vain to revive her. Time was flying. Faint screams now issued from the house. Mary was being abducted! She started up and without thinking,—for thought would have paralyzed her efforts,—rushed to the rescue alone.

The miscreants had descended into the cellar. Great was their astonishment to find Mary Magdalen in a profound stupor and the little Mary weeping at her side.

"This delays us," said Simon, with great vexation. "That traitorous woman has taken the opiate herself. It will be necessary to bind and gag the little one. No sounds must issue from the chariot, no suspicions be excited."

It was during this terrible process of binding and gagging that the screams were made which Martha heard in the garden. It was effected; and the three men were bearing the silent and muffled body through the courtyard, when Martha rushed toward them with a loud shriek of supplication.

"Silence!" thundered Simon, "would you betray us?" And uncoiling his great serpent from his neck (the leopard was locked up in the chariot), he threw it toward her. "Strike her!" he said, in a hissing tone. The serpent, as if acting intelligently, made an immense coil of its body and raised its head threateningly toward Martha. She fled in terror up the stairway leading to the flat top of the house.

"Pursue her!" said Simon to Caiaphas—"pursue her and keep her silent with your dagger until we have escaped."

Caiaphas bounded after her. She turned and faced him on the house-top. He threatened to plunge the dagger into her heart if she made a sound. She backed before him to the parapet. It was at that moment when the moon, suddenly emerging from the cloud, revealed to me, as I was approaching my father's house, the two figures; my sister raising her arms wildly to heaven, and the wicked priest threatening to strike.

At that moment I entered the courtyard and confronted Magistus and Simon, who were bearing my sister toward the gate. I drew the dagger Ethopus had given me, and plunged it into the side of Magistus who was nearest to me. He sank upon the ground with his burden, uttering a deep groan. Simon rushed upon me and in a moment we were engaged in a deadly struggle. He was a man of astonishing strength. He threw me at last upon the ground and had nearly wrested my dagger from me, when Ethopus who had been concealed behind the gate sprang to my assistance. He dragged the magician back by the shoulders, and at the same instant there was a loud scream from Martha on the parapet, and the sound of voices and footsteps at the gate. Two persons rushed in to our aid; and Simon suddenly springing from us all, escaped into the street, and in a second the wheels of his chariot rattled away with the utmost rapidity.

Caiaphas, seeing that his party was vanquished, fled away through the garden to the house of Magistus. Martha hurried down and rejoined her friends below. Ethopus brought lights as quickly as possible, although I had already recognized in the new-comers the good old Persian whom Barabbas held prisoner, and my late deliverer who had styled himself the Son of the Desert.

Mary was released from her wrappages and threw herself alternately into the arms of brother and sister. Ethopus enjoyed this scene with gestures of frantic delight. The happy party was suddenly startled by the groans of the wounded man, who had dragged himself away and was leaning against the wall of the house, bleeding profusely.

We laid him on the floor of the reception-room, and the Son of the Desert, who was an adept in such matters, stanched the blood and bandaged his hurt, pronouncing it severe but not mortal. When Magistus opened his eyes and saw the old Persian bending over him, he stared at him with amazement, and stammered forth:

"Surely this is my renegade brother-in-law, who has renounced the name and religion of his fathers and calls himself Beltrezzor."

He was right. Beltrezzor was our uncle, our father's only brother, our next of kin, our legal guardian!

This recognition gave us all the greatest delight. After mutual congratulations we hastened to recover poor Ulema from her trance, and to convey her and her wounded husband to their own home. Mary Magdalen was brought up into an airy, upper room, and every effort was made to rouse her from her comatose state; but in vain. A good nurse was placed at her bedside charged to render her every attention.

The Son of the Desert spent the night under our roof, and proceeded the next morning to Jerusalem with Beltrezzor. He refused to appear at the table with the women and declined all the rewards and presents which our gratitude induced us to offer.

It seems that Beltrezzor's friend had sent one-half of the ransom by the robbers who passed me going down the ravine, promising the other half in two days after, on the delivery of Beltrezzor himself at Jerusalem. Barabbas had entrusted the Son of the Desert with that mission. The old man had been slow in his movements, and night with its black cloud had overtaken them before reaching the highway. Reflecting that the trumpets of the Roman soldiery had sounded the evening tattoo, Beltrezzor had luckily suggested that they should turn aside into Bethany, where he had a brother whom he had not seen for thirty years. They came close behind my own weary footsteps, and I have told the result.

The second day after these surprising events, Mary Magdalen disappeared suddenly to our great regret, leaving no clue by which she could be traced. She awoke from her artificial sleep about daylight, and the nurse supplied her with food, and told her the wonderful things which had happened. She went away, notwithstanding the remonstrances of the nurse.

"Tell them," said she, "that I rejoice at their good fortune, and that I love them so much that I lift the shadow of my presence from the sunshine of their peace."

Poor Magdalen!

My new and real uncle, Beltrezzor, had a bargain to make with Magistus and his young friend, the hypocrite Caiaphas. It was easily affected. We were in possession of facts which would have exposed them both to public infamy, and have cut short the ambitious career of the talented priest.

Silence on our part was purchased at the following price:

Beltrezzor was a pagan, and objections might be raised in the Jewish Sanhedrim to his taking possession of a Jewish estate and the charge of Jewish orphans. Magistus and Caiaphas were to obviate these objections, and to secure him the legal guardianship.

Ethopus was to be declared a freedman.

Beltrezzor, my sisters and myself were to be permitted to visit Ulema every Sabbath so long as she lived.

In addition to his liberty, Beltrezzor presented Ethopus with a precious stone of considerable value, upon which was engraved a mystic name. This gem had great reputation in the magical fraternity for releasing its possessor from the spell of the most powerful enchantment. Whether some change really came over his spirit, or whether his imagination did the work, Ethopus acted as if some great burden had been lifted from his soul. He entered at once into our service, and his gratitude seemed only equaled by his humility.

Beltrezzor took possession of my father's estate, and to our great joy determined to reside at Bethany during our minority. Under his judicious and liberal management everything soon blossomed like the rose. He adorned our residence with all the chaste and beautiful treasures of architecture and art. He surrounded my charming sisters with every luxury that the most cultivated fancy could suggest. He devoted himself especially to our education, and our house became the favorite resort of all that was most learned and brilliant in Jewish society.

Thus several years passed happily away, overshadowed by no cloud. If a tear ever came into our eyes, it was consecrated to the memory of our dear father, and to the reflection that he had perished so sadly in the wilderness, without knowing the good fortune which was in store for his children.

VIII
BREAD ON THE WATERS

The impression made upon our minds by these extraordinary events was ineffaceable. After three days and nights of perilous adventure and suffering, from a youth I became a man. From little girls, my sisters became women. There was ever afterward about us a pensiveness, a gravity of manner, a too early maturity of thought, which excited the pity of those who had known us during our father's life, when a happy childhood broke forth into smiles and pleasures, like a genial spring blossoming out into perfumes and flowers.

Our six months of domestic life under the management of Magistus, with its gloom, its neglect, its suspicions, its want of love and liberty, stood in painful contrast with the merry sports, the delightful peace and the religious sunshine of our father's household. It was night compared with day. But the unmasking of the characters of Caiaphas and Magistus was a rude shock to our tender spirits. We had revealed to us at one view the utmost depths of human depravity. We had stood consciously amid the hideous and revolting spheres of hypocrisy, sensuality, robbery and murder. There was a leprosy of the soul as well as of the body; there were wild beasts of the spirit; there was a wilderness of the mind; there was a death masquerading in the garments of life; and we had seen them all. We had looked into hell.

This early and deep insight into the fearful connection between evil spirits and wicked men, and their combined influence over the world, was in one sense salutary. The recoil from the bottomless abyss into which we had peeped, produced a rapid and unusual development of the moral nature. In my sisters it took a religious, in myself a philosophical turn.

Those young girls, constitutionally pious and full of gratitude to God, sought renewed strength and comfort in the exercises of faith and religious duty. They devoted themselves to prayer and the study of the Scriptures. With the womanly nature of the vine, which must cling to something of firmer texture and stronger growth, they attached themselves trustingly to the priests and scribes and doctors of the law, with a natural and pardonable feeling. But they avoided Caiaphas.

I do not remember that I ever felt any decided respect or love for the religious institutions of my country. I was born, I suppose, with the element of veneration for the past left out of my mental organization. I never could understand why men look back to the infancy and childhood of the race for the oracles of wisdom. It is rather the business of each century to scrutinize rigidly the inheritance it has received from the preceding century, and to reject everything which is worthless, unphilosophical and immature.

I was largely indebted to my father for my progressive temperament. He despised pretension and ceremony. He conformed his life rather to the spirit than to the letter of the law. His understanding sturdily revolted against the mysterious and improbable. We were not trained after the strict manner of the Pharisees, but with that freedom of action which does not crush the individuality of the child. The reformer, the innovator, the man of new ideas and life, is seldom born of the narrow-minded literalist and bigot of an old system. The father is generally an intermediate link between the old and the new; adhering loosely to the old himself, and prophesying, inarticulately perhaps, the emancipation of his son from the thraldom of the past.

When we get rid of the conventionalisms of an old and perishing system, we become peculiarly open and sensitive to the grand intuitions of natural religion. The gorgeous ceremonies of the temple made little impression even on my boyish fancy: they were tiresome and disgusting to my riper years. But I melted into tender admiration at the thought of John the Baptist, praying and toiling in the wilderness, unseen of men, trusting in God, and receiving to his loving bosom and care, the leper, the robber and the lost ones of the world.

One of the teachers provided me by my excellent uncle Beltrezzor, was a Greek; and the study of that wonderful language and literature led me still farther away from the influence of Judaism, corrupted and failing as it was. I was not slow to assert that the poetry of Æschylus and Homer charmed me more than that of David and Isaiah; and that the philosophy of Plato exceeded in value all the learning of the Scribes.

My heretical opinions, candidly avowed on proper occasions, but never obtruded, had a gradual effect in breaking the spell of enthusiasm which bound my sisters to the priesthood and the ritual. But the examples and conversations of Beltrezzor had a still greater influence in lifting their minds out of that narrow and exclusive circle of thought, in which the typical Jew is born, lives and dies.

Beltrezzor was a man of most beautiful and lovely character. Simple in his own tastes and dress, frugal in his own habits, but generous and even lavish to others; cheerful and polite; active and industrious; truthful and unselfish; full of liberal opinions and tender sympathies; he charmed all who knew him by the purity and nobleness of his mind and the suavity of his manners. One of the most opulent and honored men in his adopted country, and an inveterate traveler by habit, he had quietly settled down in the little village of Bethany to consecrate several years of his life to our education and happiness.

Yet the model man, the like of whom we had never seen in Priest or Scribe, was in our eyes a renegade and a pagan. He had abandoned the doctrines and precepts of Moses for those of Zoroaster. His religion, which appeared so sweetly in his life, was a puzzle to us, for we expected to discover its quality in its outward observances. The following manifestations of the religious spirit were all we ever detected: He sometimes looked from his window at the rising sun, and muttered something like a prayer with bowed head. He always spoke of Fire with a strange reverence, and said it was synonymous with Power and Beauty. He kissed his hand to the first star he saw in the evening. On the last day of every year, he had fruits, flowers, wine and rice brought into his chamber, as offerings to the spirits of his departed friends, who, he believed, visited him on that occasion.

Behold the simple ceremonial upon which was based so much goodness of heart and so much wisdom of thought!

"Who was Zoroaster?" asked Martha one day of her uncle.

"Zoroaster, my child, was the friend and companion of Abraham. They lived together in Haran until the Great Being, Ormuzd, the King of Light, called Jehovah by the Jews, summoned them both to leave their country and fill a sacred mission. Zoroaster went to the east and Abraham to the west. Zoroaster like Moses received the book of God on the top of a burning mountain, and gave laws to the people."

"What kind of laws, uncle?"

"The essential moral teachings are as much like those of Moses as twin sisters are like each other."

"Then you do not worship idols?"

"No—we detest them."

"You do not worship any of the gods of the pagan nations?"

"No, my child! There is but one God, Ormuzd, King of Light. All religions come from him. Some are purer and more perfect than others. All true prophets and priests are his servants. False priests and magicians are in league with evil spirits. They are children of Ahrimanes."

"If there is such fundamental identity, why then, uncle, do you prefer the religion of Zoroaster to that of Moses?"

"Because its ritual is more simple, beautiful and sublime; because its doctrines are more rational and philosophical; because the people who believe it and live it, are more liberal and loving and enlightened than the Jews; because it brings the soul nearer to the Power and Beauty of the sun."

"Uncle," said Mary, affectionately kissing his hand, "are all the worshipers of Ormuzd as good and pure and sweet-tempered as you are?"

The old man blushed: "The teachings of Zoroaster tend to make men far purer and better than I."

The sisters sank into a deep reverie. They had a glimpse of that great world of moral light and beauty, which lay entirely outside of the limits of the Jewish faith. They gazed on it with wonder.

"But, uncle," said Martha, "in the great day of judgment will not the unbelievers be sentenced to eternal punishment?"

"In the last day, my child, all the metals in the world will melt with heat, and all human souls, living and dead, will pass in judgment through the fiery element. To the good it will feel like a fragrant bath of warm milk; to the evil it will be a torrent of burning lava. It will consume, however, nothing but the wicked lusts of the heart. Evil will thus be destroyed; and all men, freely forgiven by Ormuzd, will unite in a universal chorus of love and praise."

The sphere of our uncle's life and character taught us charity for even renegades and pagans; and the beauty and rationality of his singular doctrines made me suspect that truth had temples elsewhere than in Judea. I became fairly emancipated from the Jewish Church, and looked for the regeneration of mankind to the ennobling and purifying influence of knowledge, which, I believed, would finally illumine the world with its waves of rosy light. Beautiful and illusive dream!

My sisters, disgusted as they soon became, with the fanatics, hypocrites and impostors who thronged the temple, were not ready to cut loose from the faith of Moses or the ceremonies of the law. They deplored the corruptions and deadness of the Church. They shrank from the ritualists who had no religion, and from the devotees who had no love in their hearts. They sought consolation by looking eagerly for the Messiah, who was to restore the sceptre to Israel and rekindle the embers of faith and piety in the church.

Martha and Mary pondered upon all they had ever heard or read on this wonderful subject. Born of a virgin, "the Prince of Peace, the Mighty Counselor, the Everlasting Father," was coming in the flesh? They delighted to search the Scriptures for traces and predictions of his birth, his appearance and his mission. They loved to walk in the grove of olives which crowned the mount in rear of our house, whence they could see the marble colonnades of the temple and its vast roof all fretted with golden spikes, while they conversed arm in arm on their favorite theme.

Thus were we being secretly prepared by the experiences and circumstances of our life, for the reception of the new and strange religion of Christ. The thoughtful analysis of the past history of any human life, will reveal here and there the movings of the finger of God. We do not see the divine providence as an event approaches, but only after it has transpired. Jehovah showed his back, not his face to Moses.

Some may be surprised at the idea that certain minds were *prepared* for the reception of the Christian religion by processes directed by divine providence. They suppose that every one who saw the miracles and heard the words of Christ, could have believed in him and followed him if he had chosen. It is a mistake. There were many noble and pious Jews, to whose minds the words and miracles of Christ had no weight whatever; who rejected him unhesitatingly as a dreamer or an impostor. They were not prepared to receive him.

There have been several revelations or dispensations of Divine Truth; and there will unquestionably be more. The new revelation is seldom or never received by the adherents of the old. The force of the decaying system is first broken by schism. After schism comes a spirit of free inquiry, and skepticism is developed. The old foundations are broken up; new ideas, new influences, new life start forth. Then comes the possibility of a renewed development, a reconsideration of principles, the evolution of higher and more spiritual truth.

This fact was illustrated in the early days of Christianity. The first disciples were not the leading spirits and great lights of the old dispensation, who regarded themselves as the special guardians of religious truth. That class misunderstood Christ and rejected him. The men and women who forsook all and followed him had no special reverence for the Jewish law and its ceremonies. Singularly enough, they were not persons of strong religious convictions, however holy their life became after receiving the inspiration of the Holy Ghost. They had outlived or spiritually outgrown the Jewish dispensation. They cared little or nothing for the opinions of priest or scribe. They stood aloof from the Jewish ceremonial with skeptical indifference, waiting for Providence to give them something radically new. They knew Christ by intuition; their spirits had been organically prepared for his reception.

Christ rejected the Jewish Church long before it rejected him. He neglected its ceremonies; he violated its laws; he disregarded its superstitions; he ignored its magnates; he chose his associates from the publicans and sinners of civil life, and his disciples from the publicans and sinners of the moral world. If he ever comes again, the same phenomena will recur; for the Divine laws repeat themselves, like the return of comets and the revolutions of the sun.

I was acquainted with most of the persons who organized the infant Church of Christ. There were within my knowledge but two exceptions to the general law, that those who acknowledged the Messiah first and most cordially, were outside of the orthodox pale. Thomas Didymus was a rigid Pharisee and ritualist. He believed nothing which he could not see with his own eyes and touch with his own hands. He was the least spiritual of all the disciples.

Paul, the apostle to the Gentiles, was a man of ardent imagination, intense faith and great genius. His mind, however, was cast in the antiquated mould; and he was a stickler for orthodox observances. No logic or rhetoric, however eloquent and convincing, could ever have shaken him from his Pharisaic attachments. The miraculous interposition of heaven was necessary to turn him from the service of the Jewish Sanhedrim.

Not without influence also in preparing us for the new era, was the character of John the Hermit, afterward known as John the Baptist. For several years we paid two annual visits to the tomb of our father, and to the cave of the extraordinary young man who had befriended him in his last illness. One of these visits was made when the angel of spring had touched the snow-wreaths of winter with her silver wand and turned them into flowers. The other was made when the forests of autumn clothed themselves in their festal robes of crimson and gold, to celebrate the approach of death with its prophecy of resurrection.

We chose one beautiful and cloudless morning, and making an early start, mounted upon sure-footed mules, and well provided against those demons of the desert—hunger and thirst—we crept slowly along over the brown hills and through the desolate hollows. Ethopus and two or three more stout domestics always attended us as a bodyguard. We made a picturesque party, encamping in the mouth of the sacred cavern, startling the silence of the wilderness with happy voices, and breaking its wild solitudes with the enchanting presence of beauty and love.

John always received us with a graceful suavity, which seemed strange in one so unaccustomed to society. We first paid our visit to our father's grave, and offered our tribute of tears to the ashes and memory of the beloved. The prophet would improve the occasion to our spiritual advantage, by repeating with simple eloquence many appropriate verses of Scripture. We then returned to the cavern and conversed with the heavenly-minded recluse, startling the echoes of his lonely hermitage with incidents of life and travel and society, and with scraps of history, biography, poetry and philosophy, brought from the gay and busy circle in which we moved.

The prophet bore a quiet share in our animated talk, and partook sparingly of our ample repast. He was full of childlike earnestness and credulity, easily excited to smiles, easily moved to tears. The sphere of his thoughts and feelings was as different from that of the priests and scribes, as though he had been an angel descended from heaven,—full of love and wisdom, without creed, without doctrine, without forms, without ceremonies,—to mock with his sublime perfection the puny ritualist who imagined no religion possible without them all.

The young prophet seemed to enjoy these semi-annual disturbances of his thoughtful solitude. He always accompanied us on our return as far as the great highway. He was so fully convinced that he was driven into the wilderness by the Spirit of God, that we did not strive to allure him back to the haunts of men. I regarded him as a gentle and amiable fanatic. Martha pronounced him to be a young man of great promise, destined no doubt to be a prophet or leader in the Church. Mary's criticism was limited to noting the extraordinary sweetness of his voice and the softness of his hazel eyes. Once also a tear trickled down her cheeks, when we spoke of his lonely days and nights in his self-inflicted solitude.

It was in the third year after Beltrezzor's return, that, on approaching the cave of the hermit we saw a poor, emaciated creature, the skeleton, the shadow, of a man, seated on the stone at its mouth. It was long before we could recognize in this pitiable object, my generous deliverer, the Son of the Desert. On feeling the premonitory symptoms of a dangerous fever, he had left his band, which was then prowling about the Jordan, and had come to the cave of the young hermit.

"You nursed my wounded friend. Take care also of me. I am sick in soul and body. You are the only good man in the world. You alone make me believe in God."

These were the words with which he threw himself down upon the pallet of skins. Long weeks of illness had passed away—and he was restored, standing now on the border of life like a phantom flitting from the tomb. His great, sad, earnest eyes seemed to say that he neither cared to live nor was afraid to die.

We took a deep interest in this forlorn robber, who seemed to act, think and feel so little like a robber. This proud, handsome man, without name, without friends, was an enigma to us. He had sternly declined all reward for his eminent services to us, and we felt under painful obligations to him. When we bade him adieu with ardent wishes for his speedy restoration, Martha, with great dignity and self-possession, took a ring from her finger and deliberately placed it upon his.

"Do not forget us," said she. "Our fates may part us, but the invisible binds. On this ring is engraven the name of an angel. I give you my guardian-spirit as your own. May he lead you into peace."

He bowed his head low upon her hand; and when he raised it, there were tears in his eyes.

I noticed after a while that these visits to the desert had a singular effect upon Mary. For some time preceding them, there was an exhilaration of spirits, a flush of expectation, a vivacity of manner, which added a new lustre to her charms, a new glow to her beauty. During the visit, however, she was timid, reticent and abstracted: and afterward for weeks there was an unusual quietness of demeanor, as well as a tearfulness of the eye and a pallor of the cheek.

"Lazarus," said Martha to me one day, "had we not better bring our father's remains to Bethany and bury them with our mother's? It would spare us these long trips to the desert."

Keen-sighted, motherly sister! But I—who had not then met with Helena and knew nothing of love—I answered:

"Oh no! these visits to John are the most delightful events of the year."

On the fourth spring of these visits Mary took down a little flower-pot with a rose in it for John.

"I bring you a gem," said she, "of nature's light a lamp, a star, to illumine the darkness of the desert."

That evening when returning, Mary and John fell behind the rest of us, and when I turned to look after them, he was pointing out to her some rare beauty of the clouds about the setting sun; and her face, turned full upon him, was all aglow with a radiance not reflected from terrestrial skies.

The fall visit was looked forward to with unusual pleasure. It was a glorious day. Why was it that the desert seemed more solitary than usual? As we approached the cavern, the silence was appalling. There were no recent footprints on the sands. The spiders had spun their webs across the mouth of the cave. It was utterly deserted. John had gone. He had taken away his pallet of skins, his earthen vessels for food and drink, his sandals, his long staff. The flower-pot lay upon the ground with the little rose-bush in it, long withered and dead.

The sisters burst into tears; and Martha kissed the little one most tenderly on the cheek.

The Spirit of God, which impels men to the great missions of the world, drives them away from the bloom of nature and from the gardens of the soul,—away into the wilderness, where, tempted of devils and sustained by angels, they gather strength for the doom and glory which await them!

Our father's remains were brought to Bethany. Mary's cheek grew paler. The dew of tenderness trembled always in her eye. She searched the Scriptures all day long for the coming Messiah. At night she dreamed—

Ah! what?

Of the withered rose-leaves in the deserted cavern.

IX
SACRIFICE

My uncle summoned me one day into his presence, and told me that he wished me to enlarge my education by travel.

"You must visit Egypt, Greece and Italy," said he, "the typical centres of the world, and converse with the master-spirits in art, science and philosophy. I have made arrangements to keep you amply supplied with money at Alexandria, Athens and Rome, and with letters to agreeable and influential people.

"This will consume three years of your life; and if you are wise and prudent, they will be pleasantly and profitably spent. When you return I will surrender your father's estate into your hands, and make a handsome settlement upon your sisters from my own means. I am growing old and shall need but little for the rest of my pilgrimage."

"Then," he continued to my surprise and sorrow, "then I shall go back to the great East—nearer to the sun—to die."

"Go back to the East?" I exclaimed with trepidation. "Why so? Your old age requires the presence of loving friends and relatives. What can we— made your children by your kindness—what can we do without you?"

"Ah! my child, the grass soon grows in the footprints of man. We are easily forgotten. I shall be loved like one dead. I am weary of this Judean air; of this corrupt and discordant society; of these Roman trumpets and banners. I want peace and repose. I long to see once more the sacred fire burning upon the altars. After twenty years of life in Persia, one cannot be satisfied with the Mosaic sacrifices and the olive groves of Bethany."

Knowing my uncle's firmness of resolution, and how long he had restrained his natural restlessness for our benefit, I hung my head in mournful silence.

"Well, well!" said he in a cheerful voice, "we have time enough to talk about the whole matter. Get ready now for the scenes which fill the heart of a thinking man with supreme delight."

This plan of perfecting my education by travel, by coming in contact with idolatrous people and studying heathen philosophies, excited the fears of my good sisters, so contrary was it to the custom of the Jews. They regarded it, indeed, as almost a crime. My uncle, however, was grandly cosmopolitan in all his sentiments, and he had imbued my own mind with his enlightened charity.

Ethopus accompanied me as my body-servant. We had taught the dumb African to read and write after he was released from the bondage of Magistus and Simon. He acquired these accomplishments in a moderate degree with great celerity, so that our anticipations of rapid mental progress were sadly disappointed by the result. When he reached the intellectual development of a white child at twelve years, his onward march was arrested. No study, no assiduity could advance him a step farther. He was organically a child. His thoughts, his feelings, his opinions, his manners were all child-like; and so they remained.

Such is the general result of my observation and study of the African species. Susceptible as they are of a beautiful and indefinite moral culture, the development of their intellectual faculties is limited by the thick scull, the small brain, the black skin which they have inherited as a national curse. May it be different in the future! I have received nothing but kindness at their hands, and I feel nothing but kindness for them in my heart.

We learned from Ethopus, through the medium of writing, that he had been stolen by a party of marauding soldiers from his quiet and happy home in Abyssinia, where his father was a petty prince. He had been sold to some magicians in Egypt, who made him a slave, a football, a victim of cruel and unnatural experiments. He had been fed upon toads and serpents and creeping things. The blood of various animals had been injected into his veins. The operation of poisons was studied upon his body. Degradation and terror were imprinted upon his soul. He had been deprived of his manhood and his speech, to bring him into total subjection to his diabolical tyrants.

When I told him that I should go first into Egypt, he trembled; for the memory of Simon and his own early life troubled his mind. I could scarcely have induced him to accompany me at all, had it not been for the beautiful gem which my uncle Beltrezzor had given him. In its prophylactic powers against magic and magicians he enjoyed implicit faith. He had hitherto carried it always in his pocket. He now bound it over his heart, carefully secured in a leathern bag. He then declared himself ready for the journey. Less fortunate than he, I had nothing wherewith to fortify myself against evil spirits and the dangers of land and sea, but the consolations of Zoroaster's religion and scraps of the Platonic philosophy.

I had only one misgiving on leaving my sisters in the care of such an old man as our excellent uncle. The wicked Magistus was still living in the same house, separated from us only by a stone wall. He guarded my aunt in the same cruel seclusion, and no doubt kept himself informed by her clairvoyant powers of everything going on in our house as well as in others. He had never made any advances toward us, and there was no communication between us. I knew, however, that a fierce desire for revenge rankled in his heart; and his power was now greater than ever, since he had become a prominent member of the Sanhedrim, and his friend Caiaphas had been appointed high-priest of the temple.

I spent about a year in exploring the wonders of Egypt, and had reached Alexandria for a reluctant departure from that land of fascinations, when a letter was delivered at my door by some one who disappeared as soon as he gave it to the servant. This occasioned me some surprise, and I opened it immediately. On a little piece of parchment which fell out as I did so, I found these words:

"The original bearer of this letter was killed in a skirmish with our troop. I find it contains something which you will be interested to know. I therefore transmit it to you at some risk. Do not forget the unforgetting

"Son of the Desert."

The epistle was from my sister Martha. It ran as follows:

"A wonderful thing has occurred, my dear brother, since I last wrote. John, the young hermit of the desert, whom we have mourned as lost or dead, has appeared on the banks of the Jordan, baptizing the multitudes and preaching repentance and the remission of sins. He claims to be the forerunner of the Messiah, announcing the speedy approach of the King of kings. Crowds are flocking to him from all Judea and Galilee, and even from distant regions. His eloquence is so astonishing that many who go out of curiosity or sport, are stricken to the heart and receive his baptism.

"Mary and I have listened to the preaching of this inspired friend, and are convinced of its truth and power. We have been baptized also, confessing our sins, and vowing a life of repentance and good works. I assure you, my dear brother! when the prophet laid his hand on our heads, blessing us in the name of the Messiah, our minds were filled with a heavenly ecstasy, and we could scarcely refrain from shouting aloud for joy.

"When I came up out of the water, the first face I saw was that of our strange friend who calls himself the Son of the Desert. He was standing with many others on the bank near the prophet, and gazing earnestly at his seraphic countenance. When his eyes met mine, he looked down as softly as a young girl, and quickly withdrew from the crowd.

"My heart warms toward this poor, outcast stranger, who befriended you so nobly, and who leads, I fear, such an evil life. Is it not strange that the noble instincts, which he certainly possesses, do not cause him to revolt against his base surroundings? His name is continually in my prayers. Oh that he also would be baptized of John, forsake the troublous ways of the world, and receive the sweet delicious peace of the new life!

"Mary is so happy again! A new rose has come to her cheek, a new buoyancy to her step, a new beauty to her smile.

"Our good uncle accompanied us to the Jordan, although he despises crowds and excitements. His criticism on the preaching and baptism of John shows how thoroughly pagan are all his conceptions. He said he was a young man of splendid enthusiasm, who would have been a disciple of Zoroaster if he had studied the philosophy of fire instead of that of water.

"Perhaps the shining of this new star will guide you sooner home to our eyes and hearts. You linger in that old, frightful, sand-beleaguered magic-stricken Egypt, when this herald of the Messiah, Aurora prophesying the sun, is filling Judea with Divine light! Hasten with love, soon, very soon, to your loving sisters."

I was still meditating on this letter when Ethopus rushed into my chamber with a face full of alarm. I soon learned from his expressive pantomime that he had seen Simon Magus in one of the public squares, exhibiting some magical tricks to a great crowd.

"Did he recognize you?" said I, anxiously.

The African shook his head hopefully.

"Then we will take ship for Athens to-morrow. Get everything ready for the voyage."

Ethopus seemed delighted at these words, and proceeded with the greatest alacrity to execute my orders; not, however, until he had so disguised himself that I positively did not know him when he appeared before me. He was then so long absent on my errands that I became apprehensive for his safety. He suddenly entered the room with an expression of countenance which puzzled my practiced wit to decipher. It was the wildest joy strangely mingled with sadness. He found it impossible to convey his ideas by pantomime. The scene was ludicrous as well as pathetic. After several frantic and fruitless efforts, he seized a burnt coal from the hearth and scribbled on the white wall in great sprawling characters:

"I have found my brother!"

and making signs for me to follow him, he darted from the room.

We passed rapidly through the streets, Ethopus looking suspiciously about him all the while, until we reached a grand bazaar, where thousands of articles were exposed for sale. We forced our way through crowds of merchants, each crying his wares; through buyers and sellers and idlers of every description, chattering and chaffering in all the languages of the world. We came presently to some little rooms or stalls where a great many slaves on sale were exposed, almost naked. Ethopus pointed triumphantly to a tall young African of handsome and even noble features, and falling upon his neck, they wept together.

"They are brothers," said the trader. "Their meeting was both amusing and affecting. This dumb fellow recognized the other first, and fell upon his face, shoulders and hands with frantic kisses. The younger one, not comprehending such a useless outburst of affection, resented it as an intrusion, and would have belabored his brother soundly, had he not been so heavily ironed. The older one was in despair, but suddenly bethought himself of taking off a lot of false hair and beard, and baring his neck and bosom for inspection. The recognition was then soon effected, and they laughed and wept alternately in each other's arms."

"He is a slave?" said I.

"Yes—and a most unruly one. He was captured in the late war with the Abyssinians, and although very young, they say he was a superb soldier. I can well believe it. He has already passed through several hands, and was quickly got rid of by them all, on account of his fierce and dangerous character."

I studied the young man's physiognomy carefully, but could discover no trace of ferocity about the features. He seemed to be about twenty years of age, and had a manly and dignified bearing as he stood there manacled and exposed to the public gaze. I read his secret at once. He was a brave and high-spirited youth, accustomed to freedom, war, and perhaps to the exercise of power; and he did not submit to his chains as quietly as his owners desired.

The slave-dealer must have divined the admiration with which I regarded him, for he added with a quiet sneer:

"His braveries are at an end now, for he has been bought for Drusus Hortensius."

"And who is Hortensius?"

"Have you lived in the desert, that you never heard of Hortensius? Hortensius is the richest man in the world at present, and the greatest epicure in Rome. He imitates Lucullus, at least in pride and luxury. He makes suppers for his friends, of incalculable magnificence. His demand for nightingales' tongues has silenced half the bird-music in the world."

"Is Hortensius in the city?"

"In the city? No! He lives in Rome, which, he complains, is altogether too small for him. He has an agent in Alexandria, who has a standing order to send him about fifty refractory and incorrigible slaves every year."

"What does he want them for?"

"Want them for?" laughed the dealer. "Well, you must know that Hortensius has the greatest and rarest fish-ponds in the world. They are miracles of beauty. Hortensius is fond of fish as well as of nightingales' tongues. But common fish do not tempt his august appetite. Lucullus discovered, in the course of his epicurean studies, that fish fed upon human flesh have a remarkably fine flavor; and moreover that these aquatic cannibals have a special relish for the African species of the genus homo."

"Wretch!" I muttered.

"Therefore," continued the trader, without noticing my indignation, "Hortensius, imitating Lucullus, has a negro slave cut into small pieces and thrown into his fish-ponds every week. His children are taken out by their nurses to witness this choice method of refining the pleasures of the table."

Anthony, for so they had re-named the brother of Ethopus, had picked up a good deal of Latin, in which language the dealer was speaking. He had listened intently and had caught the horrible meaning of his words. The disdainful and defiant look of the young soldier, contemplating the fate which awaited him, was a study for an artist.

"How can I save him from this cruel bondage, from this hideous death?"

"He was purchased yesterday and will be called for to-day, as the ship sails this evening."

"Will you cancel that bargain and sell him to me?" said I eagerly.

"Yes—for a grand consideration."

I reflected that I had drawn my last funds from my uncle's Egyptian agent. Still, I might possibly borrow largely from him and wait a remittance. I named what I considered a liberal price. The trader coldly shook his head. I added a third more to it, determined to sacrifice a year's travel in order to save Anthony from the fish-ponds of the luxurious Roman. The trader declined without hesitation. I could make no greater offer without consultation with my uncle, and that was impossible. My countenance fell in despair.

The brothers had watched our conversation with intense interest; and although they did not comprehend its full meaning, they saw that I had made a great effort to redeem Anthony and had failed. The face of Ethopus was full of grief, that of Anthony of sad resignation. Ethopus suddenly sprang up smiling, as if some great idea had illumined his mind. He tore open his robe, and producing a little bag from his bosom, he took out the precious stone which my uncle Beltrezzor had given him. He extended the brilliant gem to the trader with one hand and pointed to Anthony with the other.

"Oh do not take that," I exclaimed. "This poor fellow values that stone more than life itself. Nothing but the most intense affection could prompt him to such a sacrifice. He believes that stone has delivered him from the bondage of a terrible magician, and wears it over his heart as a protecting genius. Accept my offer instead, which is of greater money value than his gem."

This speech had a singular effect. The slave-dealer had no generosity, but boundless superstition. He either had an intense fear of magic himself, or he was in collusion with magicians. He immediately acceded to Ethopus' offer, struck the chains from Anthony's arms and feet, and put the price of his slave smilingly into his pocket.

"I will replace him with that old fellow there, who would smoke his pipe as he is now doing if we were burying him alive. The agent of Hortensius counts heads and never looks into faces."

Anthony comprehended that an exorbitant price had been paid for his liberty, involving some great sacrifice on the part of Ethopus and he insisted on resuming his fetters, until I assured them both that the stone with such magical properties should be replaced by one similar, as soon as I could communicate with Beltrezzor.

Ethopus was now in a state of feverish anxiety to get aboard the Athenian vessel. The addition of Anthony to our company seemed to increase his fears and his sense of responsibility. I conveyed my baggage and my two servants to the ship, and put them in charge of the captain, while I returned into the city to finish my business and to make a few purchases.

When I reached the vessel again, Ethopus had disappeared! Anthony was in great distress, and the captain and sailors were highly excited. The story they told was a curious one. A tall, wild-looking man, fantastically dressed, came and sat down on the shore near the planks of the ship. Busily engaged in carrying on the small freight which crowds in just before a vessel leaves, the sailors paid no attention to him.

This man was heard to make some very curious sounds, a kind of double whistle, a signal which he repeated at intervals with increasing vehemence and impatience. Ethopus then came slowly out of the vessel, reeling and groping like one blind or drunk. He advanced slowly toward the stranger and knelt at his feet. The poor fellow suddenly started up with a great shriek and endeavored to escape. Several of the sailors rushed forward to rescue him from the man who had seized him and was dragging him off. The magician, for such he was, drew a huge yellow serpent from his robe, and flourished it like a whip at his assailants. Some of the sailors declared also that a jet of blue flame darted from his bosom. Certain it is that by some magical trick he so terrified them that they fell back in awe, and he escaped with his victim through the crowd which was gathering.

Poor Anthony, who had never seen a ship before, was walking about the vessel in childlike wonder while this terrible abduction was taking place. I was in the deepest distress. I took Anthony and the baggage back to my quarters. I remained a fortnight in Alexandria instituting the most thorough search after our lost friend. It was all in vain. I sailed at last for Athens with a heavy, heavy heart, and a new servant, leaving the poor dumb eunuch in the clutches of Simon Magus.

X
AT ATHENS

I lived at Athens a year, studying the philosophy and poetry of the Greeks. I longed to see my beautiful sisters and my good old uncle; but I cannot disguise the fact that I was greatly fascinated with Grecian life and manners. I frequently wished that I had been born a Greek and not a Jew, and that I could spend my days in sight of the marble-crowned Acropolis and the blue Ægean Sea.

I taught Anthony to read and write, hoping that he would prove to be of superior mental calibre to his brother. But the result was the same. He surprised me at first by his brightness and afterward by his stupidity. He was more impetuous than Ethopus, and braver; but then his spirit had not been broken and subdued by contact with the magicians of Egypt, those subterranean devils who defied the assaults of reason against their pretensions and the vigilance of government against their crimes. Ceasing to be a good soldier and incapable of becoming a philosopher, he proved an invaluable servant.

The letters from my sisters, who wrote alternately, were full of tenderness and piety. They continued to give glowing accounts of the power and progress of the teaching of John the Baptist. Martha quoted all the passages in the prophets alluding to the forerunner of the Messiah, and Mary dwelt upon the influence of his doctrines and baptism upon the hearts and lives of the people. Mary perceived intuitively that the only valuable thing in a religion is the life which it induces one to lead. One day I received a letter from this enthusiastic young girl, which indicated that some great spiritual ferment was working in the land of Judea:

"Dearest Lazarus:

"The hunger and thirst of our souls will soon be satisfied. I have seen him with my own eyes—him, the Son of God, the Messiah. Oh what grace! what wisdom! what goodness! what power!

"Do not think I am dreaming! Some time ago John baptized a young man, whom he pronounced by heavenly vision to be the Messiah, or as he styled him, the Lamb of God. This mysterious person disappeared from sight. It was rumored that he had retired into the wilderness, to undergo some terrible combat with the powers of hell, preparatory to his great mission upon earth. Our hearts have been watching eagerly for his reappearance.

"After a while we heard that a great prophet had arisen in Galilee, who had astonished all men by the wonderful spirituality of his preaching. He had also exhibited miraculous power by turning water into wine at a marriage-feast in Cana. Perhaps this Jesus of Nazareth was the promised deliverer! But how could the ignoble names of Nazareth and Galilee be connected with the Prince of the house of David?

"Not long afterward a strange incident occurred in the temple. The miracle-worker of Cana appeared, and assuming extraordinary authority, as if the temple were his own house, he drove out all the traders and money-changers and idlers who have so long desecrated the holy place by the connivance of the corrupt and wicked priests. They would no doubt have destroyed him in their anger; but the people, and indeed the better class of Pharisees also, applauded the courageous act of the man, who dared, single-handed, to vindicate the holiness of the Lord's house, and to scourge the profaners out of the sacred precincts.

"I was pondering over this incident, when our good and kind friend Nicodemus came in, and told us he had witnessed the scene himself, and that this Jesus of Nazareth was the same person whom he saw baptized by John in Jordan, at the time when John bare witness that he saw the Spirit of God descending upon him in the shape of a dove.

"Was not this cleansing of the temple prophetic of his spiritual cleansing of the Church, as well as of the purification of those little temples and churches, our own hearts?

"The good Nicodemus, who inquires into everything quickly, but into nothing thoroughly, paid Jesus a visit at night and drew him into conversation. He was astonished and puzzled at the new ideas of this spiritual teacher. Now, my dear brother, do not laugh at me when I assure you, that what seemed so unintelligible to a learned ruler in Israel, was a sun-burst of truth and beauty to the heart of your poor little sister Mary.

"How strange it is that I can see clearly what seems hidden from the eyes of those so much more capable than myself!

"Jesus said to Nicodemus:

" 'Except a man be born again, he cannot see the kingdom of God.'

"How stupid it was in the good old doctor to stumble at this sublime sentence, and to ask:

" 'How can a man be born again when he is old?'

"And the reply of Jesus, how beautiful! —

" 'Verily I say unto you, Except a man be born of water and of the Spirit, he cannot enter into the kingdom of God.

" 'That which is born of the flesh is flesh; and that which is born of the Spirit is spirit.'

"I understand it, Lazarus; I see, feel, know, comprehend the whole mystery. It may be the flower comprehends the sun better than the philosopher.

"We were born of water through the baptism of John. By the repentance and obedience taught by him, we are washed of the uncleanness and sensuality of our old life and enter upon the sweetness and purity of the new. Jesus will baptize us with the Spirit of divine love, as John did with the spirit of divine truth; and we shall be new creatures, born again as it were, into a spiritual kingdom of light and peace.

"The Sabbath after my interview with Nicodemus, I started with Martha to the temple, hoping to see Jesus with my own eyes. And I saw him, Lazarus, not only with my eyes, but with my heart and soul. We had reached the pool of Bethesda by the sheep-market, and were looking at the crowd of feeble and paralytic people, who were waiting for the periodical moving of the water, when a murmur arose: 'The prophet, the prophet of Nazareth!' I looked and saw Jesus standing in one of the porches on the first step that leads down into the water.

"The moment I saw his face I believed. My heart beat audibly within me. A divine ardor burned in my soul. A faith, strong as the mountains or the ocean, took possession of my whole being. My impulse was to rush forward, fall at his feet and proclaim him the Messiah to the assembled multitude. Martha held me back and said: 'Listen! he speaks!'

"Yes—he spoke; and I heard that voice I had so often heard in my dreams, dreaming of the restoration of Israel!

"He spoke to the oldest, the feeblest, the most forlorn-looking person in the crowd:

" 'Wilt thou be made whole?' he said, in a voice of infinite tenderness and beauty.

"Strangely enough, before the sick man answered, the same question entered into my own soul. I felt a deadly, paralytic sensation throughout my spiritual frame, and I knew that I needed to be made whole even more than the poor creature on the steps. The Divine question was put to the sick man, to me, to the Church, to the whole world. It was infinite. While I was ejaculating internally, 'Yes, Lord! yes! entirely whole,' the paralytic replied:

" 'I have no one, sir, when the water is troubled to put me into the pool, but while I am coming, another steppeth down before me.'

"Poor, old, helpless, friendless creature! Others had relatives or friends who assisted them to descend into the restorative waters; and day after day the selfish ones had pushed aside the weak, slow, pallid wretch. But the great Friend had come!

"Jesus, stretching forth his hand over the prostrate form, with a majesty indescribable, exclaimed:

" 'Rise, take up thy bed and walk.'

"And the paralytic arose amid the exclamations and plaudits of the crowd, which pressed about them until he and Jesus were concealed from our sight.

"I have seen the Messiah several times since that miracle. He was walking the streets with several fishermen of Galilee, whom they say he has chosen to be his apostles. The greatest takes up the least to connect all the intermediates with himself. The group is always followed at a distance by a woman clad in deep mourning, and wearing a thick black veil. She never approaches near enough to speak or be spoken to. No man knows where she lodges or how she lives; but the first dawn of light always reveals her dark figure opposite the house in which Jesus has slept.

"Who can she be? says every one to himself and to others. Whoever she is, her humility and devotion are very touching; and the Power which can work miracles no doubt reads her heart and is leading her to himself.

"Martha is profoundly impressed and greatly bewildered by the miracles and character of Jesus; but she cannot yet believe that he is the veritable Messiah predicted by the prophets. She thinks the Messiah must be a great Prince, who will restore the power of David and the glory of Solomon to the Jewish nation, and make our temple the temple of the whole world. Our hearts, I think, our purified hearts, are the temples in which he is to reign!

"Our dear, good, pagan uncle smiles quietly at my enthusiastic faith, and encourages Martha's doubts by telling us of great and good magi in Persia, who performed greater miracles than those of Moses.

"Ah, Lazarus! How can you linger away off in those beautiful and wicked cities of Greece, buried in spiritual darkness, and studying their foolish or insane philosophies, when the Source of all light has risen, and the Fountain of all truth has been opened in your own country! Oh hasten to your home in our hearts and see these great things for yourself. If you cannot share my faith, you will at least receive and reciprocate my love.

"Ever your   Mary."

If these strange things had occurred soon after my father's death, when the spirit of religious inquiry was strong, and when I loved to search the Scriptures with my sisters, I would have been deeply, intensely interested in them. But the hardest thing in the world is to make a devotee out of a man who thinks himself a philosopher.

My uncle had not converted me to the doctrines of Zoroaster, but he had convinced me that Zoroaster, Moses, and all the great leaders of religious thought derived their inspiration from the same source. I came tacitly to believe that no special Messiah was coming to the Jews, any more than to the Persians or Egyptians or Romans, all of whom needed deliverance from mountains of sin and wildernesses of error, quite as much as the Hebrew nation which constituted so small a fraction of the human race.

Moreover the influence of travel, and especially my free and happy life at Athens, had quite denationalized me. I was no longer a Jew.

I had breathed the mystic and magical air of Egypt, and had peeped into one of the very cradles of the human race; where I found everything so strange and so unlike what I had been taught by our childish Hebrew traditions.

I had trodden all the glorious and beautiful grounds hallowed in the immortal history and songs of Greece. I no longer wondered at the host of gods and goddesses which were conjured from the misty deeps of antiquity, to guard a nature so prolific and fair, and a people so perfect in form and so gifted in spirit.

The traditions of Greece, the poetry, the eloquence, the music, the philosophy, the art, and the divine architecture, which seemed a combination of them all, had so impressed and transformed my mind, that I looked back to my narrow circle of life and thought in Judea, as a man looks back upon the school-room and play-ground of his childhood.

After these things, it was impossible for me to believe that the Jews were the favored people of God, and that the descendants of the patriarchs were to govern the world. It was as easy to believe that the sun rose in Jericho and set in Joppa.

Therefore I smiled at my sister's pious enthusiasm, and said to myself:

This Jesus of Nazareth is some estimable Jew, full of philanthropy and zeal, possessed perhaps of extraordinary healing powers. With these he will so astonish the poor ignorant Hebrews, that they will call him a prophet of God, or even invest him with divine honors. In Athens he would be simply a philosopher or a physician, more or less profound and brilliant. His pretensions would be scrutinized by a thinking public, and he would receive applause in proportion to his merit and capacity.

There was, I must confess, another reason why I did not turn my face toward Judea; why the prophecies and their fulfillment had ceased to interest me; and why even my charming sisters were occasionally forgotten. While studying the theologies of the nations and poring over the ethereal pantheism of Greece, I met that wonderful divinity who flies ever with his golden shafts between the earth and the sun, and I became the devotee of a new religion.

I had seen the most beautiful, the most wonderful woman in the world, and—

And what?

I loved!

XI
HELENA

In the school of philosophy where the doctrines of Socrates and Plato were taught with an eloquence equal to their own, I met a young Greek resident of the city by the name of Demetrius. He was the son of Calisthenes, a very wealthy merchant, who, contrary to the usual custom, attempted to rival in his private residence the magnificent art which was bestowed only on the public works. He was ambitious that his only son should enjoy more than mercantile honors, and arrive at greater distinction than that which wealth alone could bestow.

As usual in such cases, his paternal aspirations were doomed to disappointment. Nine-tenths of the genius of the world comes from that great middle class which knows neither riches nor poverty. The possession of great wealth is generally a hinderance to intellectual or spiritual advancement. Demetrius was a handsome, amiable fellow, of mediocre talent, slothful by nature and indulgence, and more ambitious of social success than of a front place in the class of philosophy.

I know not how it happened, but he had attached himself more strongly to me than I to him. I attained the entrée of his father's house by a lucky accident. While we were rowing in the harbor one day, our little vessel was capsized, and it was only by my desperate exertions in his behalf that Demetrius was saved from drowning. Gratitude did more for the deliverer than friendship had done for the fellow-student: it opened the doors of the princely mansion, and showed me the household gods.

I was rejoiced at this, for I had heard one of my companions say:

"Helena, the sister of Demetrius, is the most wonderful creature in the world."

I verified the truth of his remark. It was indeed the echo of the popular lip. Helena was an institution of Athens, sought, seen and admired like its other wonders and beauties. No language can convey any adequate description of this cunning masterpiece of nature. There was no statue in all the rich collections of Grecian art, which excelled the matchless symmetry of her form or the perfect beauty of her features. She was the poet's dream of perfection, embodied in the delicate tissues of a splendid womanhood.

A neck and bust of immaculate beauty were surmounted by a head, every attitude of which was a study for artists and lovers. Her hair was a cloud of dark, brown waves faintly dashed with gold. Her broad imperial brow was pure as the silver surface of some cloudless dawn. Her soft, hazel eyes were radiant centres of inexpressible light and power. Her cheeks, nose, mouth and chin were miracles of shape, warmth and color. Her shell-tinted ears were hung with pearls less beautiful than themselves; and a necklace of golden beads made conspicuous a throat which it could not beautify. Her hands and fingers were so lucid, delicate and expressive, that they might be called features also, revealing in part the movements of her mind.

Poor artist that I am, I throw my pencil down in disgust. I cannot reproduce Helena to your eyes as she appeared to me.

To see this woman, for a young enthusiastic spirit, with his celestial dream pressing downward for realization, was to love her. The shaft of love flies from one eye to another; from the eye to the heart; from the heart to the brain; from the brain to the soul. I looked, I loved. I was smitten to the soul by that malady which has no cure but the cause which inflicts it.

Helena had not only an irresistible sweetness of voice and grace of manner, but she had a singular directness of attack, concentrating all her charms upon you at once; so that few men ever left her presence without feeling that she had absorbed and taken from them some portion of their life, which they could only recover by returning into the enchanted atmosphere which surrounded her beautiful person.

Thus bewildered by her beauty and bewitched by her fascinations, I lost my life when away from her, and found it again, enhanced and glorified, when I approached her footstool. I was attracted to her continually; and if I tore myself away, and climbed the mountain-top, or walked by the sea-shore, she became the inspiring genius of my solitary rambles; and the beauties of nature were only beautiful, because in some inexplicable manner they seemed akin to, or associated with her.

Thus, day after day, week after week passed by, and philosophy became as dry as dust, and my companions silly and unprofitable; and Egypt became a myth and Judea a dream; while the past was forgotten and the future uncared for, except in connection with her. Solitude became sweet, and reverie ecstatic, and the language of poetry the voice of common life. I created for myself an ideal world, romantic, ethereal, felicitous; for the greatest magician that ever lived is Love.

I was sometimes, however, sunk into the fathomless abyss of despair. I met in the splendid halls of Calisthenes so many distinguished and wealthy and powerful men; so many soldiers and statesmen; so many philosophers, artists and poets; all many degrees superior to myself, and all paying the same homage to the idol I worshiped, that my envy and jealousy were being continually excited; and I frequently shrank within myself, taciturn and melancholy, contemplating the awful distance which intervened between my feeble pretensions and the transcendent object of my admiration.

Then Helena, observing my silence and grief, would single me out from the crowd with a peculiar sweetness; would bestow a smile which seemed meant only for me; would drop a sentence of pearl which I felt that I alone comprehended; would solicit my early return in a manner so special and impressive, that I was fired with new hope and endowed with new life; spurned the dull earth beneath me, and was ready, like the daring boy of Apollo, to drive the chariot of the sun.

"Let no one ever despair," I would thus fondly say to myself, "of conquering a woman by love. Concentrate the passion of your soul upon her, like the rays of a burning glass, and sooner or later, you will melt her heart. The best philter to excite love is love itself. If you would ignite, you must burn."

With all this magnificent exterior, with the blended adornments of nature and art, this Helena was altogether unworthy of the pure and simple love I lavished upon her. She studied men as the angler studies the character, habits and locality of fish; solely to allure and capture them. She had the thoughtful brow and the words of wisdom for one class; the smile of the cupid and the laugh of the bacchante for another. She had an armory full of weapons; the tear of sympathy, the corruscations of wit, the meekness of modesty, the humility of religion, the splendor of dress, the ornament and even the exposure of person. Everything about her was the highest art in a garb of the sweetest nature.

She hesitated at nothing which would secure her a conquest. She was unhappy unless many were kneeling at her shrine. She lived upon the breath of adulation, the music of her own praises, the incense of delirious love. She wished to absorb everything; she gave nothing in return. She demanded for herself affection, thought, worship, life. She returned only smiles, hopes, dreams, shadows. She was a beautiful demon of selfishness. There were fascination, magic, spiritual death in her sphere; but the soul died listening to invisible music and dreaming of heaven.

This adoration of men and envy of women was more to be pitied than admired. She had a mother whose influence was a dark shadow cast upon her life. Neither beautiful nor gifted herself, she had determined that the gifts and beauty of her child should be turned to the utmost account. She had planted a wild ambition in her girlish spirit, as one plants a rose in a garden. She had nourished it and watered it carefully, until she brought it to baneful perfection. Her own evil nature was transfused into the child.

She taught her that power, wealth, fashion, glory, were the true objects of rational pursuit. She cultivated her vanity, her petulance, her imperiousness. She basked in the sunshine of her beauty and power. Fatal parasite! she drew from the virgin tree upon which she fastened, the sustenance she could not herself extract from the earth and air. The too pliant pupil accepted and improved all the lessons of the teacher; and behold the result!

Of the true character of Helena I knew nothing at the time. That discovery was the result of subsequent information and experience. Nothing occurred in those blissful days to break the spell of the enchantress. I did, indeed, once or twice notice the contrast between this Athenian goddess and my pure and sweet sisters. I did once or twice wonder that Sappho and Horace should be her favorite poets, and Aspasia her model of female character. But these shadowy doubts, like the faint threat of clouds which sometimes appear in the clearest heaven, soon passed away.

Helena, petted and spoiled, set all the regulations of fashion and propriety at defiance. She did as she pleased, and every one was pleased with what she did. Not every one; for she was the terror of rigid mothers and the scandal of prudish maidens. She walked unveiled in the streets. She made herself conspicuous at the theatre and the racing-grounds. She visited artists in their studios and poets in their chambers. She received very questionable visitors at very unseasonable hours. Her dressing-room even opened its doors to favorite lovers, or to those of whom she wished to make a convenience. All this was done so boldly, so gracefully, so naïvely, that no one dared to express a hint against her virtue.

She admitted me to her presence on a very familiar footing. One evening I called to see her, when she was dressing for a grand supper, and the servant ushered me into her boudoir. She was one bright blaze of jewels and beauty. The dressing-maid was giving the last caressing touches to her hair. She was scrutinizing the work in a metallic mirror with an ivory handle, which she held like a fan.

"Come! my Judean!" she said, casting upon me one of her most bewitching glances—"come and put this ring into my ear."

This captivating service I rendered with trembling hands and palpitating heart. The dressing-maid smiled at my awkwardness and trepidation. Helena never looked more resplendent. I felt helplessly bound to the chariot-wheels of her destiny.

The waiting-girl left the room, and falling at the feet of the unimpassioned beauty, I stammered forth my passion.

"Helena! do you know that I love you?"

She was contemplating her chin in the mirror, and replied without looking at me:

"Of course you do. Everybody does."

"But, Helena! I cannot live without loving you."

"That is charming. Love me then and live."

"Helena!" said I, sternly, "you mock me. You allure me as if I were a man; and then you treat me as if I were a boy. You invite me; you evade me; you tantalize me. Can you not love me?"

"Let me see," said she, looking up at the Judgment of Paris beautifully frescoed on the ceiling; "let me see: I love wisdom, riches, power and glory. When you are wise as Socrates, rich as Crœsus, eloquent as Cicero, and powerful as Cæsar, I will love you and give myself to you."

"Your combination is impossible," said I, proudly, biting my lip with failing heart and unconcealed vexation.

Her face suddenly became radiant with a yielding, tender and beautiful expression, and I added:—

"But if it existed, Helena, you would be worthy of it."

"To love such as yours," she said, sweetly, pressing my hands, "all things are possible. We have been dreaming in the boudoir; let us converse in the parlor."

She led the way and overwhelmed me with such civilities that I forgot the past which had wounded me, and had golden glimpses of that magical future which was to console and bless me. Such is the dream-land of love!

My sisters continued to write the most glowing letters, full of piety and tender affection. Their rehearsal of miracles and parables, and of voices from heaven, their enthusiasm, their faith, their zeal, all fell as dull and cold upon my ear as the monotonous songs of an old nurse.

XII
THE HALL OF APOLLO

I was awakened from my delicious dream by Demetrius, who importuned me to accompany him to Rome, whither he had been despatched by his father on business of extreme importance. This reminded me that a visit to Rome was an essential part of my uncle's educational programme. I had abandoned philosophy for love, and love cares nothing for thought, except as one mode of expressing the sentiments. My education, therefore, was at a stand-still. I hesitated and shuddered at the idea of leaving the charmed circle in which I stood entranced. I would, perhaps, have neither gratified my friend nor obeyed my uncle, had not Helena carelessly dropped the remark, that no student could truly regard his course of instruction completed until he had visited Rome. To acquire this title to perfection in the eyes of Helena, I endured the pangs of parting and the miseries of absence; became a compliant friend and an obedient nephew. I went to Rome.

Rome did not impress me so favorably as Athens. I was fond of art, but cared little for glory. The efforts of man to reproduce the beauties of Nature excited my admiration; his labors to immortalize himself and his deeds excited my contempt. The art of Rome was imported; her glory was self-acquired. I had soon seen all that I cared to see of the imperial city, which Augustus had found of brick and left of marble.

Demetrius had letters to some of the most powerful and influential men in Rome, so that we were soon introduced into the best society there. It was not long before we received an invitation to one of the splendid suppers of Hortensius, the richest man and the greatest epicure in the world. I remembered the conversation of the slave-dealer at Alexandria. I mentally resolved, as we drove through the magnificent arch of his palace gate, that, although I might taste of the nightingales of Hortensius, I certainly would take none of his fish.

"Beware of the fish-ponds," said I, laughingly, to Anthony, who accompanied us as footman.

This palace of Hortensius was an affair of Babylonian magnificence. Everything about it was of colossal proportions. It was said to have as many chambers as there were days in the year. Hortensius had twelve bed-rooms for himself, each named after one of the months, and gorgeously furnished in a manner to represent the month after which it was named. There were seven banqueting-halls named after gods and goddesses—the dreams rather than the creations of art. This grand structure was burned during the fire in the reign of Nero, and its splendors, no longer to be found anywhere on earth, are already regarded as fabulous.

We supped in the Hall of Apollo.

The company was altogether male, which I did not regret; for I did not wish to see or speak to a woman in the world but Helena or my sisters. It was composed of the magnates, the great stars of Roman society—soldiers, statesmen, senators, governors, etc.—the least of them immeasurably above the two young plebeian students, who, dumbfounded at all they saw, could not but experience a painful sense of their own insignificance.

On my right hand, however, at the table, was a noble and sedate Roman, Pontius Pilate, the governor of Judea. He had visited Rome to consult the emperor and the senate about the affairs of his province, and was on the eve of returning. He seemed pleased when he learned that my home was in the neighborhood of Jerusalem; and with great tact and urbanity drew me out of my abstracted mood, dissipated my bashfulness, and engaged me in an animated conversation.

The Hall of Apollo was a miracle of beauty. Its area was immense; its shape, circular. Supported by twenty-four golden columns, the ceiling rose to a vast height, as a blue dome painted to represent the visible heavens. The sun blazing up through masses of dense and crimson clouds; the intensely clear cerulean ether above; the horizon all around pierced by mountain peaks, overhung by rolling vapors of purple and gold, produced an illusion of astonishing power and magnificence.

Every object in the room, the pictures, the statuary, the bass-reliefs upon the columns, the carvings upon the couches and the gorgeous table, and even the engravings and embossings upon the splendid vases and vessels which adorned it, were all descriptive or symbolical of Apollo, his attributes and achievements. The wonder of the hall, however, was a golden chandelier of incredible size, containing a thousand rose-colored tapers, which lighted the scene with a brilliancy rivaling the day.

I will not attempt to describe the feast, having no particular fondness for epicurism. The bill of fare exceeded anything I had ever imagined. There was service after service, dessert after dessert, wine after wine, seemingly without end. The meat-courses, lasting about three hours, were presented by handsome boys of every nationality, clad in beautiful livery. The after-courses, of sweets and luxuries, were brought on by female servants, lovely in person and graceful in manner, revealing by their dress or otherwise every charm of the human body.

When the company was well filled and duly flushed by the delicious wines, the whole western wall of the apartment, by some hidden and admirable mechanism, suddenly opened or changed like a dissolving view, and revealed an interior apartment a little above the level of ours, which looked like a beautiful garden adorned and lighted in a style of Oriental magnificence.

The shrubbery and flowers of this garden were the concentrated beauties of the floral world in all regions, cultivated here by art, and offering an incense of perfume to these Roman rulers, who aspired to conquer not only man but nature. Ivory statues of gods and goddesses, of nymphs and fawns and satyrs, added greatly to the beauty of the scene. But when a dozen dancing-girls alighted as it were from heaven upon this miraculous stage, and whirled among these statues and flowers, less perfect and beautiful than themselves, the fascination, to those who regarded such enchantments, was complete.

"More music! more wine!" cried Hortensius from his purple couch a little elevated above the rest—"the feast of thought ends always in the feast of love."

The banquet progressed with continued variations of stimulus and entertainment. The guests were regaled by invisible music, repeatedly changed, and representing the airs and styles of every nation which had bowed its head to the Roman conqueror. The wine fell fast into golden goblets from vases composed of precious gems. The day dawned. The noise and excitement increased: the conversation degenerated into a babble, and the feast into a debauch; when a most extraordinary incident occurred, changing my uncle's programme and perhaps my whole fate in the twinkling of an eye.

A great clamor was heard outside of the door nearest Hortensius. Loud and angry voices, the rapid tread of many feet, curses, groans, shrieks, indicated the approach of some dreadful storm. It was a thunderbolt in a clear sky. All sprang to their feet and advanced toward the sounds, when the door was burst open with violence, and my servant Anthony rushed in, foaming at the mouth, bleeding profusely from several wounds and flourishing an immense knife over his head.

"I will kill him if I die for it!" he shouted, glaring fiercely on the brilliant crowd before him, and endeavoring to single out the object of his hate.

"What does all this mean, Anthony?" I exclaimed, leaping forward and seizing him by the throat.

"I have saved him from the fish-pond," he answered sternly, pointing to the naked form of a poor negro, whom the domestics had at last succeeded in hurling to the floor, and who had followed Anthony, defending him from his pursuers.

"And why did you not fly? madman!" I exclaimed, "why did you come here?"

"Oh! death was inevitable," he answered, in a tone of desperation, "and I determined first to kill the vile despot, the author of these cruelties."

"Slave! barbarian!" echoed from all parts of the hall.

"Slave I am: barbarian I may be!" shouted Anthony defiantly; "but in my country they do not feed fishes with men."

The crowd had stood back a little while we were speaking: but now there was a sudden rush upon us in front and rear. I was pushed forcibly aside, and Anthony was borne down, disarmed and bound with his fellow-prisoner, whose rescue had caused this great excitement.

"Throw the old one to the fishes immediately," cried Hortensius in a loud and cruel tone. "Bind this young villain by the pond and guard him till I come. I will cut him up, strip by strip, with my own hands."

A murmur of approbation ran through the assembly. Thrusting the bystanders away, I confronted Hortensius face to face.

"O most noble Roman," I exclaimed, "pardon something in this poor man to the spirit of liberty. He was born free, a prince in his little realm; and like you, he has been a brave soldier. Misfortune in war, not crime, has enslaved him. He is honest, faithful and noble. It was a fierce and glorious love of his own race which has fired him to this rash deed. His sublime self-sacrifice, his desperate courage surely deserve a better fate at the hands of a Roman and a soldier. Spare him and forgive him!"

It would be difficult to describe the fierce and haughty stare which Hortensius and his noble guests fixed upon me during this little speech. They wondered at my folly, my stupidity, my audacity. To plead for a black slave who had drawn his knife against a Roman senator! To accord the spirit of liberty to such vermin of the earth! To speak of them as brave, faithful, noble, glorious, sublime! They were stupefied at the novelty and heresy of such ideas. I was certainly either a fool or a madman.

Hortensius, lowering his voice and infusing into it a little suavity,—for he suddenly remembered that I was his guest,—exclaimed:

"The proper discipline of my palace, young man, demands the immediate death of this would-be assassin. I will replace your servant with a better."

"That is beyond your power," I replied impetuously; "your whole household would not replace him. I am indebted to his brother for my sister's life and honor. I am bound to this man's flesh and blood as if they were my own. I cannot, I will not desert him in his extremity."

There were loud exclamations of surprise, contempt and disapproval. Many, however, were silent, touched perhaps by a latent magnanimity.

"What will you do?" exclaimed a haughty old Roman in a most provoking tone.

"Do?" said I rashly, striking my hand upon the hilt of my dagger, "do?—I will defend him: I will die with him."

This caused a great uproar in the assembly. Loud cries of

"Away with him! out with him!"

"Insult a Roman senator!"

"Abettor of slaves and assassins!"

"Insurrectionist! Madman! Idiot!"

"Down with the base Judean!"

resounded through the splendid Hall of Apollo. My friend Demetrius, who had hitherto stood near me, now slipped into the crowd and disappeared. Having defied the supreme power of the place, I would probably have shared the fate of the wretched Ethiopian, had not assistance come to me from an unexpected quarter.

Pontius Pilate stepped between Hortensius and myself, and waving his hand with great dignity and grace, requested silence.

"Pardon, dear friends and most noble senators! pardon the wine which has made this rash youth forget both reason and duty. He is a subject of mine, being a native and resident of my province. I claim jurisdiction over him, and will punish him as he deserves. He is from this moment a prisoner in charge of my retinue. He shall be carried back to his native village, disarmed, bound and disgraced, so that all Judean youths may know what folly it is to insult a Roman senator."

There was a strong murmur of approbation throughout the assembly, and Hortensius nodded approval.

Pilate continued:

"I would not say a word to save this African from the death he so richly merits, were it not for one dark suspicion which crosses my mind and which will not permit me to be silent. I suspect this infuriate wretch to be a madman; and the insane, you know, are under the protection of the gods and, sacred from the fangs of the law. Permit me to convey this slave also in irons to Judea. I will have his case carefully studied by my own physician. If the gods have smitten him in their wisdom, let him go free as our laws direct. If he exhibits enough reason to be held responsible, I will have him driven into the dreadful desert beyond the Salt Sea, and sentence him to a perpetual exile in its awful solitudes. If he is ever discovered west of the river Jordan, his punishment shall be death, without question or delay."

Whether this proposition struck the hearers as remarkable, or what was more likely, the social and civil weight of Pontius Pilate bore down their opposition and silenced their scruples, Hortensius acceded to it and all seemed satisfied. After drinking again to the health of Hortensius, the company dispersed. I soon found myself a prisoner bound for Judea, deserted by Demetrius, exiled from Helena, full of sadness and dark forebodings, with the educational tour projected by my good uncle brought to a sudden and ignominious conclusion.

The only comfort I experienced during the long and melancholy voyage was the thought that I had saved the life of my high-spirited Anthony, whom I was not permitted to see, and whose daring conduct I more admired the more I thought of it.

I was struck also with the wonderful tact, courtesy and kindness of Pontius Pilate. I would gladly have thanked him for his services; but I was kept in strict confinement, and heard and saw nothing of the sedate governor. On our arrival at Jerusalem, I was unbound and taken privately before him.

"You are now free," he said. "I admire you too much to inflict any further punishment upon you for your incredible rashness. You cannot help being brave, but you can compel yourself to be prudent. Go, sir! When you get into trouble again, let me hear from you and I will befriend you, if possible."

"And my servant?" said I, hoping to intercede for Anthony.

"He has been driven into the desert."

An hour afterward I was trudging up the Mount of Olives, thinking of what a joyous surprise I was about to give to some dear little souls in Bethany.

XIII
MY FIRST DEATH

How beautiful was my old home, embowered in trees and perfumed with flowers! How charming were my lovely sisters, twin-stars of the social heaven, dropping sweet influence on all who received their tender light! How peaceful and pure was the self-sacrificing old age of Beltrezzor, over whose pagan heart, so full of simple love and wisdom, the most orthodox angels kept kindly watch!

A great sadness rested upon our little household, on account of the recent murder of John the Baptist by the cruel Herod, at the instigation of a still more cruel woman. That pure and good man had been cast into prison about the time that Christ began his ministry, and the morning star paled on the approach of the blazing Sun. He had ever been remembered with peculiar tenderness and gratitude; and heaven became dearer to us by receiving into its fold the gentle hermit of the wilderness.

My sisters had grown lovelier. On Martha's clear brow the sweet maturity of thought was imprinted. Mingled with the light of love on Mary's face was a touching sadness, of which none but Martha and I suspected the meaning. These women, so pure, so cultivated, so beautiful, were abstracted from the entire world. Sought by many lovers, they had discarded the very thought of love. They were wedded in heart to the heavenly bridegroom.

They had heard but once from our old friend, the Son of the Desert. A strange servant, no doubt a disguised robber, brought back the ring with a note from the wanderer, saying that he was unworthy to wear it; that it afflicted him with sorrowful dreams and burned into his soul like iron. Martha herself fortunately met him at the gate, and would not permit him to depart without an answer, as he was instructed to do. She sent back the ring with her love and Mary's to the savior of their brother, with the solemn assurance that the ring had a great blessing for him concealed within its curse.

I soon discovered that my sisters had but one idea, one study, one passion. Their individuality was lost in their perpetual concentration of soul upon one object. That object was Jesus Christ. They no longer spoke of him as the prophet of Nazareth. Martha had at last discovered with her eyes what Mary had seen with her heart. He was the Son of God: He was the Messiah. With subdued voices and reverent gestures they called him the Lord.

All this was very strange to me, fresh from beautiful and romantic Greece, where altars were erected to a thousand gods: fresh from the schools of philosophy, where the only deity taught was a spiritual essence, infinite, inconceivable, unfathomable. I listened, however, with interest to the recital of miracles which were certainly astounding; to parables which were replete with spiritual wisdom; and to discourses—for my sisters treasured all his words by heart and repeated them to me—which were radiant with a certain divine light and beauty.

I was ready to concede that this man must be the greatest philosopher of the age.

This was the opinion of our good uncle, who, however, took no trouble to see or hear the worker of such great miracles. He said there was nothing new under the sun; that all things repeated themselves over and over again; that all wisdom had been spoken and every miracle performed ages and ages ago. The Son of God was in his mind synonymous with a disciple of the Sun.

Beltrezzor was sorry that I did not remain a year at Rome, for he said the practical atmosphere of that city would have moderated and utilized the ideality I had drawn from Athens. He was greatly pleased, however, with my conduct at the supper of Hortensius.

"The man who sees any reason," he would say, "why Hortensius should be more wealthy, more powerful, more respected, more glorious than Anthony, has not incorporated into his soul the first ray of the divine principle of fire, and is altogether ignorant of the power and beauty of the sun."

A few weeks after my return, Beltrezzor transferred the whole of my father's estate, improved and augmented, into my hands. No reasonings, no entreaties could induce him to abandon or even to defer his long contemplated journey to the extreme East. A strange, sad home-sickness had apparently seized him; and he waited with a childish impatience for the arrival of the caravan from Egypt which was to escort him to Assyria.

It came at length; and our adieus were long and bitter. We were bound to him not only by a pious gratitude for his rich gifts and his unvarying kindness, but by a genuine love of his sweet, sincere and noble nature. We wept at the thought of the dear old man going away into that far-off, marvelous Orient, without a wife or child to comfort his declining years.

My sisters also seemed overwhelmed with grief, that one so good and so beloved had rejected to the last, with a quiet, polite incredulity, all the evidences of the divine mission of Jesus.

The old man's parting words to me, as he leaned from his camel, whispering in my ear, were these:

"Beware, my son, of the spirit of fanaticism which has fallen upon your good sisters. I bequeath you this verse from one of the sacred books in Persia. It is my last and best gift to you. Do not forget it:—

" 'It is more truly pious to sow the ground with diligence, than to say ten thousand prayers in idleness.'

"Adieu!"

A few days after my uncle's departure, we were invited to dine at the house of a worthy Pharisee, Simon by name, who was touched at heart with a secret admiration of Jesus. Preoccupied as I was with thoughts of Helena, and caring nothing about spiritual things, I would not have accompanied my sisters but at their earnest solicitation. They had been assured that Jesus would be present, and they were anxious for me to behold the object of their love and worship.

He came, and saluted us all with a charming grace and sweetness of manner. His face was handsome, thoughtful and benevolent, but did not strike you as majestic or sublime. There was a winning sociality in his conversation, which you did not expect from his serene and rather pensive countenance. He was quiet and modest in his demeanor; and instead of leading the thoughts of the company, he spoke less than any one present.

Reflecting, by the light of later and grander experiences, upon the first impressions made on me by this mysterious man, I am convinced that not only his face, his expressions, his words, but his whole life was comparatively a sealed book to the people who saw him in the flesh. They saw only the outside, the husk, the fleshly, not the heavenly part of him. They were ignorant of the sublimities, the infinities concealed within. Whoever sees only the physical and not at the same time the spiritual side of anything, sees little. The flowers, the gems, the clouds, all beautiful objects, on the spiritual side are full of sacred mysteries. Ignorant of these little things, how could the men of that day comprehend the Christ?

What a different banquet from that of Hortensius! A plain room, opening directly on the street; a plain table; a plain company. At Rome we had a wild ambition, aspiring to universal empire, and imitating even in its luxuries all the splendors of heaven and earth. Here were simple tastes, frugal habits, civic industry, neighborly love. There the presiding genius was the demon of pride; here it was the Divine Man.

The feast was nearly over, when a woman, closely concealing her face in a black veil, glided softly into the room and stood behind Jesus. This would not have attracted special attention, for people were coming in and going out all the time; but I remembered Mary's account of the mysterious woman who always followed Jesus and his disciples at a distance. I therefore watched the movements of this person with considerable interest.

She bent low over the feet of Jesus as he reclined on his couch, and I observed that she was weeping. She seemed deeply agitated. Suddenly she let down the great mass of dark brown hair from her head, and began wiping the feet of the Lord. Washing his feet with her tears and wiping them with the hair of her head! What touching humility! What contrition!

Then she anointed his feet with a precious ointment which she drew from her bosom.

My thoughts were concentrated on that kneeling figure. I entered so deeply into what I imagined to be her feelings and sorrows, I was so attracted by what must have been a secret spiritual affinity with her own soul, that I heard almost nothing of the conversation which ensued between Jesus and Simon, and which is recorded by the apostle Luke who was himself present.

When the divine voice pronounced the verdict, "Thy sins are forgiven;" a strange and bewildering sense of delight came over me, as if I myself had been the sinner who sought and found the pardon of sin. I was contemplating in amazement this reverberation, as it were, of the woman's sentiments in my own spirit, when Jesus said, "Thy faith hath saved thee: go in peace;" and the woman turned slowly around and walked sobbing out of the door.

Scarcely knowing what I did, I quietly withdrew from my place at the table and followed her. Suddenly, in some ecstasy of religious feeling, she threw her arms wildly toward the sky, the veil was lifted for a moment, and I recognized the beautiful, sorrowing and purified features of Mary Magdalen!

The spell which overpowered me was instantly withdrawn, and I returned to my seat. No psychology I had ever been taught, threw any light on this singular phenomenon; and it remained a mystery until solved by that special light of the spiritual world which I alone of all men have enjoyed.

After that the mysterious preacher and miracle-worker was a frequent visitor at our house in Bethany. I came no nearer to him than at first: I understood him no better. He was a good, wise, wonderful man; beyond that I could not penetrate. I became intimate with all his disciples; and I loved to dispute with them on theological subjects, and to puzzle their uncultivated brains with my philosophical doubts and quibbles. But in the presence of their master I had nothing to say. I stood abashed and silenced by some secret power which I could not explain. I never thought, however, of acknowledging him as the Messiah, or the Son of God.

The reason was, that my heart and mind were too closely riveted to nature and the things of sense, to rise to the conception and love of spiritual things.

While the faces of my sisters were growing more and more radiant and serene from the spiritual life which was deepening in their souls, mine became pale and haggard from the burden of concealed longings and the vigils of a burning but unfed hope. I had written and rewritten to Helena, but received no answer. I would have returned to Athens; but the fear of leaving my tender and helpless sisters so near to such a subtle enemy as Magistus, and Beltrezzor away off in Persia, detained me unwillingly at Bethany.

Absence extinguishes a feeble love; but intensifies a great one. I brooded in solitude. I took interest in nothing. Conversation was irksome. Religion and philosophy were alike neglected. I experienced that apathy which a great desolation of heart produces, and which men attribute to moroseness or stupidity. I was feeding with the intense hunger of love upon my treasured memories of Helena; devouring every word she had spoken, every look, every tone, every changing form, every shifting light of her miraculous beauty.

My love for Helena, for reasons which I did not then comprehend, was not of a soothing, ennobling, purifying type. It was a disquieting, paralyzing, corroding passion. The sphere of this woman, wholly incapable of the heavenly duties of wife and mother, did not lead me, encouraged and strengthened, into the sweet and useful activities of life. Like an evil spirit rather, it drove me into the wilderness; tempted me with stones which were not bread; and haunted me with wild dreams and insane ambitions.

Thus many weeks passed away, and the fever of my soul had so worn and wasted me that my sisters became seriously alarmed at my condition, not knowing the cause; for I had never divulged my pagan goddess to these pious little ones.

One day I was suddenly lifted out of the cavern of despair into the serenest sunlight of hope. I received a message from Helena that she was traveling with her father to the most noted places in Asia, and would spend a few days in Jerusalem; that she was the guest of Alastor, a wealthy Greek merchant of the city, and that her visit would be devoid of genuine pleasure unless she could see once more her esteemed friend, who had saved the life of her brother.

Now occurred a most curious mental phenomenon. The sudden reaction of joy in the feeble and excited state of my nervous system, overpowered my brain. I became the victim of an absurd, grotesque illusion. I leaped at once from the abyss of self-abasement to the maddest height of presumption. I transferred my entire experiences of heart and mind to Helena. She, I imagined, was pining with unconquerable passion for me. She was wasted and worn by unrevealed, unrequited love. She had suffered and faded in silence until longer concealment was death. Her father had brought her under cover of travel really to meet me again, to draw me once more to her feet, to obtain my confessions, and to receive new hope and life from my words. I was filled with an unspeakable tenderness, with a generous compassion. I would fly to her; I would console her; I would make her life and happiness secure by giving her my own.

Busied with these mad fancies, and muttering them to myself as I went along, I hurried to the house of Alastor. Ushered into the presence of Helena, I was surprised and abashed by the serene and smiling expression of her countenance, and her splendid physique, upon which neither time nor love had yet written the faintest trace of ravage. She received me without the least embarrassment in the gay and sparkling manner of a cold and polished queen of society. I saw in a moment that I was not loved, that she had never thought of me, that my hopes were dreams, my passion a madness. I read my doom in the charming suavity of my reception.

Disappointed, chilled, bewildered, heartsick, miserable, I maintained a broken conversation for a little while, until Helena, perceiving with her woman's wit, something, and perhaps all of my secret, broke off the interview.

"You are sick," said she tenderly, "you are feverish, you are in pain. You should not have come until to-morrow."

"Go home now," she continued, taking my hand kindly in hers, "go home and be cared for. When you get better you must come again, and we will talk of Athens and art, of poetry and love; and of all the beautiful things that ravish the hearts of men and women."

I do not remember what I said, or how I parted from her. On the portico I met a man going in, whose presence sent a strange shudder through my frame. My diseased nerves were very sensitive. He was a person of handsome face, imposing appearance and gracious address. He began speaking to me, but suddenly stopped and fixed his great, black, lustrous eyes fiercely on me. My first impulse was to resent this conduct as an insult; but I quickly perceived that my mind was becoming confused, bewildered, fascinated by his gaze, and I averted my face with a great effort and hurried down the steps.

I did not dare to look back. At the foot of the stairs I ran heedlessly against our old relative and enemy, Magistus, whom I had not seen since my return from Rome. Seizing him by the shoulders I gasped,

"Who is this man on the portico?"

"Simon Magus," said he, with a coarse laugh,—"Simon Magus, the prince of Egyptian magic, and he has evidently cast the evil eye upon you. Woe to you!"

I fled precipitately through the streets. When I reached home I was in a burning fever. At night I was in a raging delirium. It was a brain fever of malignant type. My mad and grotesque illusion about Helena was really the beginning of my illness. Days and nights of alternate excitement and stupor passed away; days and nights of physical torture and mental suffering. My sweet sisters watched and wept and prayed by my side.

Horrible fantasies besieged my fevered imagination. I thought that Mary was under the magician's knife, and that he would accept no substitute for her bleeding heart but that of Helena. I opened my eyes and started with horror; for Mary was seated by my side, with the heart, as I supposed, torn out of her bosom. Then again, Hortensius was cutting up the beautiful body of Helena for his fish-ponds, while the Egyptian held me fascinated by his terrible eye, so that I could not stir for her help.

I grew worse and the end approached. I had not realized my condition: I had neither fear nor hope: I had no thought of death or of Jesus. At last, however, when I was dying, I heard my sisters calling frantically on his name. The name must have touched some silver chord of memory. The sweet, benevolent face appeared before me, Mary Magdalen in her dark robe kneeling behind. The tender words, "Thy sins are forgiven," echoed in my ears. Mary and Martha seemed to me like two shining angels floating up into heaven. A sudden halo blazed around the head of Jesus. I reached out my arms to him with wonder and delight, fell back and expired with a smile upon my lips.

Yes! I was dead: and, wonder of wonders! I live again, to describe my sensations, and to inform my fellow-men what I saw and heard behind the veil which separates the two worlds—that veil which is so thin and yet seems so impenetrable.

XIV
MY SPIRITUAL BODY

Our sleep is an awakening: our death is a birth; our burial a resurrection.

The slumber of a babe upon its mother's breast, drawing from her bodily warmth the secret magnetism of life, is a picture of the true state of every human soul, leaning unconsciously upon the bosom of God at the moment when bereaved friends are exclaiming,

"He is dead! he is dead!"

They called me dead. My sisters and their companions rent their garments and covered their heads with ashes. Unconscious of their grief, I passed beyond the shadows of this world, beyond these voices and sorrows, into the pure light of a spiritual realm.

Dead, indeed! I lived most when I seemed to live least. Death is nothing but a name for a change of condition.

The first thing I remember on returning to consciousness, was a soft strain of distant and ravishing music. I could not open my eyes, nor did I care to do so. It was perfect bliss to lie there in sweet repose, and listen to those heavenly sounds which came nearer and nearer. I have been asked if there was music in heaven. Why, the least motion of the air there is musical. Music is to the ear what light is to the eye; and the sounds of heaven are as sweet as its colors are beautiful.

I next became aware of presences about me. How can I describe the new sense which informed me of their nearness! I did not see or feel or hear them. I perceived them, intuitively as it were, by a holy atmosphere of love and purity and beauty which came with them. So the flowers, without senses like our own, when the dark and chilly night is over, must feel the tremulous waves of light gladdening around them.

These invisible, inaudible attendants were engaged in some office of love about me. What it was I did not understand; but I felt as if my body was being drawn out of something, as a hand is withdrawn from a glove,— although no one seemed to touch me. I entered into a state of exalted and blissful sensations, totally new to me, and quite incomprehensible to men still lingering in the flesh. My affections seemed to be concentrated or detained upon pure, tender, lovely and holy things, so that nothing painful or doubtful or sorrowful should stain the shining mirror of the soul.

I do not know how long this exquisite state of happiness lasted. It must have been rounded off with a delicious sleep; for it seemed itself like a sweet and mysterious dream, when I discovered that I was wider awake than before, and surrounded by a different though still delightful and purifying sphere of impressions.

From the presences about me I seemed to absorb the power of thinking and remembering distinctly. I could not open my eyes, but I seemed to be contemplating a luminous atmosphere, an infinite variety of splendid and dazzling colors, a whole universe of light. The ecstasy of Joy with which, bewildered and fascinated, I studied this inexpressible chaos of light, is beyond my power of description. In the midst of it I felt that two persons were near me, one at my head and one at my feet. One of them seemed to bend over me, and to be reading my face as one reads a book. He then said to the other in a gentle voice:

"It is good. His last thoughts were about the Lord."

I pondered these words and asked myself whether I was dead or dreaming or in a trance.

My invisible friend then passed his hands several times gently over my face. He next drew a fine film from my eyelids and breathed upon my forehead. I instantly recovered my sight and looked around me. There were two men before me with beautiful and noble faces, and clad in robes of shining linen. I could not remove my eyes from them, there was something so inexpressibly tender and brotherly in their looks and motions.

"You are in the world of spirits, my brother," said one of them with ineffable sweetness. "Be not afraid, but rejoice! The world of spirits is the vast realm betwixt earth and heaven into which all men come when they are first raised from the dead."

"Raised from the dead?" said I, in extreme bewilderment.

"Yes—you have been raised from the dead. You have left the earth upon which you were born; you have left your natural body, which your friends will bury in the ground; you are now in a spiritual body and a spiritual state of existence."

I looked at myself and looked around me.

"I cannot understand it," said I, sorely puzzled. "You are certainly strangers to me, and you look so unlike any of the men I have ever seen, that I can readily believe you are angels. Nor do I see my beloved sisters,

Martha and Mary, who, I know, would not leave my bedside for a moment. But this body is the same body I have always had; this is the room in which I have been sick so long; and looking out of that window, I see the Mount of Olives and the familiar sky of Judea. Explain how this can be."

They looked at each other smiling, and one of them replied:

"The last impressions made upon the mind linger a while after death; so that the transition from natural to spiritual life may not be too sudden, and the sensation of personal identity may be fully preserved. This will change to you presently. We do not see the room that you see, nor the Mount of Olives, nor the Judean sky. These will all vanish from your sight after a little, and you will find yourself differently clad and moving about among novel and beautiful scenes."

"But,"—said I, incredulously,—"but this body of flesh and blood, in which I live, move and think, how came it here?"

"That body of flesh and blood you have left behind you. The soul is a spiritual substance organized in the shape of its natural body. The natural body resembles the spiritual as a glove resembles the hand contained within it. You have dropped the glove. You see the naked hand."

"Our mission," he continued, "is now ended, and another takes our place. We assist in the resurrection."

They made a motion of departure, but I seized one of them by the hand.

"Oh stay!" said I, "do not go. Your words interest me beyond measure. I would learn more of the heavenly life. Pardon my incredulity, pity my ignorance."

"One approaches," said he, "who is much nearer and dearer to you than we. Relatives delight to render to relatives these charming offices of comfort and instruction. He comes!"

"Who?" I exclaimed, eagerly.

"Your father!"

I looked in the direction indicated by the angel's face. Out of the darkness—which appeared to me and not to the angels, for it proceeded from my own mind and not from theirs—out of the darkness slowly loomed up a human figure. It brightened as it advanced. Then there stood before me a young man of radiant beauty, clad in a tissue of shining purple. His face was full of eager expectation, sparkling with love and joy.

While I was gazing at this form, which seemed to me a beautiful apparition, the other angels disappeared.

"My son! my son!" exclaimed the shining visitor in a voice of touching sweetness, and which seemed in some way remotely familiar. "Do you not know me?"

I was silent and troubled, for there was not the faintest resemblance between the splendid being who stood before me and the poor father I had buried in the wilderness.

"I am permitted for your sake," said he, "to return back into the mental states of my earth-life and to resume its forms. This is one of the wonders of the spiritual world, but one which you will frequently see and soon understand. Look steadfastly at the changes I shall undergo, and you will believe."

The light about him began to fade. The purple tissue darkened; his face grew pale; the lustre passed from his hair. His features gradually changed, becoming less and less beautiful, less and less youthful. Wrinkles appeared; his cheeks became haggard; his eyes sunken and sad; his head bowed and bare; his beard gray. Unsightly scars came upon his forehead; and when he held up his withered hands, from which two or three fingers had dropped, I knew the poor old leper whom the cruel law had driven into the wilderness.

"My father! my father!" I exclaimed, weeping at the sight which recalled so vividly the sorrows long buried in the soul, "I am satisfied. Return again into the beauty and glory of your heavenly youth. Let us forget the past. Let me see you as you are!"

His figure then underwent exactly the reverse series of changes; and when his angelic form was restored, I fell upon his neck and wept tears of joy.

I inquired into the philosophy of the astounding metamorphoses I had witnessed. I was taught that spiritual things—states of our affections and thoughts—are not so perishable as natural things; that they are stored away and preserved; and that they can be recalled and reproduced with a fac-simile of all the surrounding concomitants and phenomena. A spirit can be made to return into any state of his past life, when he will repeat his conduct to the least word and motion and incident. Thus nothing can be concealed; the entire past can be re-enacted; truth discovered and judgment given.

It was in accordance with this great spiritual law of changing forms corresponding with the changing states of the soul, that the disciples beheld Jesus from such different stand-points. If Thomas Didymus could have entered into the spiritual state of the three disciples on the mount, he would not have seen the Christ showing the wound in his side and the print of the nails, but he would have beheld him radiant—in his transfigured glory. It was the varying stand-points or mental states of the disciples, which give us such different manifestations of the Unchangeable.

I was not, however, thinking of these things at that moment. I was contemplating the youth and beauty of my father's spiritual body.

"I was told," said I, "that the spiritual body was a fac-simile of the natural body. How comes it that yours is so totally different?"

"When I first rose from the dead," he replied, "I seemed to myself to be in the same leprous body that I had in the wilderness; and like all men I found some difficulty in realizing the fact that I was living in a different world. The spiritual body or external form of the soul, changes rapidly according to the changes of its internal form, which is composed of affections and thoughts. In proportion as these are purified from the evil and false things imbibed during the natural life, the body is freed from its imperfections, its feebleness and its want of symmetry."

"And why do you look so young?" I inquired.

"Time," said he, "does not belong to the spiritual world. We have no computations here by months and years; no revolution of suns and planets, which produce day and night and the changing seasons of the world. Our external surroundings, what you would call our visible nature, are the immediate outgrowth of our own spiritual states. The exterior changes continually with the interior. All in heaven are therefore young and beautiful, because their soul-life is good and pure, and is fitly represented by youth and beauty."

My father then questioned me about the dear ones I had left behind. He manifested the deepest and tenderest sympathy in all that had happened to us since his departure from the world. He had heard of us frequently from new-comers into the world of spirits. We do not cease to love our earthly friends after death. But in the heavenly life there is such a thorough, soul-satisfying trust in the wise and merciful guidance of Divine Providence, that fears, doubts and anxieties about our absent loved ones, are utterly impossible.

"And my mother?" I inquired in turn,—"my mother and my little brother Samuel, where are they?"

"In heaven," said he, "where you shall see them, but not now. You will undergo sundry preparations of state, inexplicable to you at present, by which you will be fitted for the ascent into their resplendent abodes."

The angel who assisted in my resurrection was right. The objects which surrounded me at my death, and which lingered a while on my mental vision, had faded away. I found myself in a strange but beautiful world, the forms of which were similar to ours, but the laws which governed their appearance and disappearance very different.

I must confess that I was supremely astonished to find myself living, feeling, thinking, precisely as I did before my death. My mind indeed seemed more active, more penetrating than ever. My body had a buoyancy, a strength, a healthfulness pervading it, which were accompanied by a sense of intense pleasure. But it still seemed the same body in which I had previously lived; and I could scarcely comprehend my father when he told me that my sisters and friends were making preparations to bury my earthly form.

"Oh that I could look down upon them," said I, "could speak to them, could show them my true self, and lift their souls out of the fearful shadow of the tomb! Why is it not granted us to cheer the hearts and illumine the minds of those who are sorrowing so vainly over our cold dust?"

"They would not believe you, my son, if it were permitted. They would call your manifestation to them a vision, a hallucination, a dream. They are in such bondage to sensuous appearances, and to reasonings based upon them, that nothing but death will break their chains. It will take generations, ages, centuries, cycles of natural time to render higher thought on that subject possible. New civilizations, new churches, new revelations must arise before mankind can be delivered from this terrible darkness."

"And that natural body," said I, "laid in the grave, and food for worms, is not to rise again?"

"Why should it?" said my father. "Who wants it? What use could it subserve? Are we not in spiritual bodies clothed with all beauty and perfection? Are we not in a spiritual world vastly more beautiful and happy than the natural? Why should we return into nature? into a natural body? into an envelope of flesh and blood, however purified and etherealized?"

These ideas struck me as extremely rational and beautiful. Having passed the lowest round of the ladder of being, why should we reverse the laws of development and descend back to it again? Impossible! The natural body was only a vehicle of natural life with its thoughts and emotions. Spiritual thoughts and emotions demand a spiritual body, a spiritual world. Let those who choose, wed themselves to the grave and the worm and the dust and the darkness, and speak of their friends as sleeping in the cold ground, and satisfy their hungry souls with the hope of a material resurrection. But their ideas are far, very far from the truth; and the minds of men will some day be emancipated from such gross naturalism.

"Imagine," said my father, "the consternation of the good spirits, who are happy in heaven, at the thought that they must leave it, divest themselves of their beautiful spiritual bodies, and return to the natural world with all its painful limitations of time and space, resuming their old cast-off material bodies, which had been long since resolved into dust and forgotten!"

The thought is monstrous! monstrous! And yet the poor blinded people in the natural world dwell upon it as if there were some special consolation, some glorious promise in it. Incomprehensible freaks of the human spirit! He who preaches a material resurrection, has made but one feeble step beyond the infidel who preaches none at all.

"Men still in the flesh," said my father, "do not know that our spiritual world inhabited by spiritual bodies fulfills all the imperative demands of the soul for a perfect and final resting-place. We have here life and form, organization and objects, weight and substance, sounds and colors all more beautiful and wonderful than those in the natural world. All these things, invisible, intangible, inaudible to men, are as real and solid to our senses as the earth was to you when you were a man upon it.

"Yet this external world surrounding us is not material and fixed like yours. It is what we call substantial or spiritual. It is plastic to spiritual forces. It changes, not according to your natural laws, but according to the changes in our own spirits. This is the key to the great difference which exists between the world you have left and this glorious one in which you are to live for ever.

"Our light here changes. It is day or night with us according to our own spiritual relations to the great Fountain of life. In one state of mind we are in the city, in another in the country. Certain emotions carry us to the mountain-tops; others place us among the sands and shells of the sea-shore. In one state of thought we are walking in flower-gardens of ethereal beauty; in another we are sitting by rivulets which echo the music of our own hearts. Thus mountains, fields, rivers, cities, houses, animate and inanimate objects come and go, appear and disappear, according as they represent or symbolize the interior changes of our spirits."

"All this," said I, "is so beautiful that it seems impossible. Liberated now from the thraldom of time and space, I understand you; but I doubt whether the most gifted philosopher in Athens can conceive of a world without time or space; of a world so phantasmagoric in appearance, yet said to be so genuine and eternal in reality."

"Our spaces are determined," said my father, "by spiritual affinities. Similarity of thought and feeling determines presence; dissimilarity makes distance or absence. When you here direct your thought to any person on the same plane of life, as we call it, with yourself, having at the same time a desire to see him, that person becomes aware of the fact, and, responding to your desire, is face to face with you at once.

"Let us both," he continued, "fix our thoughts intently upon our noble and lovely friend, John, called the Baptist, who was beheaded in prison, and is performing here a similar office to that which he so well executed on the banks of the Jordan."

We did so; and in a moment there was a beautiful flash of azure light, like a great sheet of water reflecting the sun and sky.

"That," said my father, "is the sphere or symbolic appearance which always precedes and announces the coming of the gentle herald of the Lord."

Then stood before us the young prophet of the wilderness, beautified, etherealized, glorified beyond conception.

He saluted me with brotherly warmth, and we entered into a long conversation which I shall not repeat; but from which I learned a thousand interesting and wonderful things about the spiritual world—things incredible to men in the flesh, most of whom, like birds of night, are satisfied with the darkness of nature.

XV
THE WORLD OF SPIRITS

I was greatly astonished at the nature and importance of that intermediate state of life which I have called the world of spirits. Although the doctrine of a place of departed spirits, called Sheol or Hades, is distinctly taught in Scripture and by tradition, it seems to have made a very feeble impression on the minds even of the most devout. Most men think they will go immediately to heaven or to hell when they die. They are mistaken.

The world of spirits receives into its vast bosom the mighty congregation of the dead from all nations and climes. It is the first grand receptacle of the whole human race after death. It is the place of judgment, special and general. It may be compared to the stomach, into which all articles of food and drink are collected; where they are all comminuted, concussed, expressed, decomposed and digested; and what is found good and nutritive is taken up into the blood and makes a part of the living man; while the hard, unwholesome and innutritious portions, which cannot be dissolved or appropriated, are cast out of the system as useless or injurious.

Let not the reader smile at this anatomical metaphor. When he gets an interior view of the human body such as I have enjoyed, he will see that it is an epitome of the universe; that the mysteries of nature, the wonders of philosophy and the secrets of heaven are all written upon its organs and tissues.

In the present state we are strangely compounded of good and evil, both hereditary and acquired. He who thinks that all good people on earth are ready, at death, to pass at once into heaven without further preparation and instruction, has formed a mistaken idea of heaven. Our life in the world of spirits is a judgment upon ourselves, an unfolding or unrolling of our true characters, a revelation of our evils under the best possible circumstances; where by the assistance and instruction of angelic friends, our imperfections, if our ruling love be good, can be finally removed, and our souls fitted for that perfect social organization based upon supreme love to God and the neighbor, which men in the flesh cannot understand or even imagine.

"But," says some one, "all that is done for us instantaneously at death by the miraculous power of God."

God works always by organic and eternal laws. The spirit, like the body, grows, develops, progresses by definite means. Seeds do not expand instantaneously into trees. A diseased tree is not changed in a moment into a healthy one. The soul which attains heaven does so by regular and progressive steps, many of which (if there has been a commencement on earth) are taken in the world of spirits. The idea that miraculous power changes a bad man into a good one, an impure soul into a pure one, in a moment of time, in answer to prayer and faith, is a childish fallacy disastrous to the life of true religion.

The population of this world of spirits is immense. Not only the dead from our world are there, but angelic spirits from heaven and evil spirits from hell all meet on this grand arena of spiritual combat and instruction. In the time of Christ many generations and centuries of human life were accumulated there; for evil had become so predominant, and the spiritual element in man so nearly extinguished, that few or none could be prepared for heaven. Unless, indeed, God had descended in the human form and executed a great judgment in that world, casting the evil into hell and revealing a higher dispensation of truth, mankind would have perished and heaven itself have been threatened with chaos.

But all this is myth and mystery to those who have busied themselves only with the historical movements of the natural world, not even knowing that the world of spirits above and around them had far grander historical movements,—the key and cause of all others.

Every human being living in the natural world, is attended by two good and two evil spirits who are living in the intermediate state. I saw the spirits who had accompanied me during my life; and, what is singular, although I had never seen them before, they appeared like old acquaintances and friends whom I had known from my youth. Let no man suppose that he will rise from the dead into the world of spirits, and find himself a stranger there, friendless and alone.

It seemed very wonderful to me that this mighty realm of spirits should be so near to men, secretly connected with them by affections and thoughts, flowing down into them, giving them life and power, and instigating them to good or evil, and still that the human race should remain ignorant of the stupendous fact—benighted by all kinds of false philosophies and false religions.

"Why," said I to my father, "are not our earthly friends permitted to see us in this better and brighter sphere, to converse with us, and establish social relations with us?"

"They are in natural bodies," said he, "and they cannot see our spiritual forms with their natural eyes. Their own spiritual eyes would have to be opened before they could see us. The opening of their spiritual senses would bring them into conscious communication with the world of spirits."

"Well," said I, "so much the better. They would then see all these wonderful things for themselves, and their doubts would be wholly dissipated."

"Ah! you know little as yet of the world of spirits. It is full of evil and wicked ones, who share the bad passions and prompt the sinful deeds of men on earth. If men came, by the opening of their spiritual senses, into visible and audible communication with their own attendant evil spirits, the power of hell on the earth would be immeasurably increased. The power of a wicked companion in the flesh is great; but the power of an evil spirit enthroned in your bosom, possessed of your entire memory, and governing from his more interior stand-point every movement of your brain, would be fearful indeed!"

"No," he continued; "it is the mercy of the Lord which in the present evil state of the world keeps these two realms of being from a conscious intermingling. The offices and uses of the two worlds are different; one begins where the other ends. To throw them together would be to produce inextricable confusion, to destroy free-agency, to confound good and evil, to thwart regeneration, to arrest the judgment, to close heaven and to open hell.

"All this can only be made clear to you by a thorough system of religious philosophy, embracing a true psychology and the organic relations of God to the universe, and of the different parts of it to each other. All these will be the subjects of your delightful study, and may possibly be revealed to mankind in some far-off futurity, when men become capable of receiving and utilizing such sublime mysteries.

"To seek to penetrate the veil which separates the spiritual from the natural realm, to invite an open intercourse with spirits, to consult them about earthly affairs, is one of the terrible crimes denounced and forbidden in Scripture. It is the secret source of the power and mysteries of magic. To seek such intercourse is perilous to the soul's best welfare. Therefore it is that consulting with 'familiar spirits' is forbidden in the Word. It is forbidden for man's own good."

"These are new ideas to me," I said, "and I cannot fully comprehend them. How should I, filled as I am with fallacies which need exposure and removal! But I am appalled, my dear father, at the thought that the world of spirits is so full of evil, and that we enter on a state of fearful explorations, combats, temptations and judgments on leaving the natural world."

"Yes, my son. In heaven only there is rest. There only are perfect peace and order and love. The road to heaven lies through the world of spirits, through its instructions, its purifications, its judgments. The pathway is pleasant and beautiful to the good man; for at every step he lets fall some hateful thing that clung to him in the past, and he rises into new light, new glory, new joy."

"You spoke," said I, "of general judgments occurring in the world of spirits, as well as the particular judgment of each individual. What do you mean by that?"

"At the end of every church, every dispensation, every old order of things, and at the beginning of a new church, a new revelation, a new era, there is a great judgment executed in the world of spirits. This judgment is effected by the light of divine truth streaming down through the open heavens, searching people to the core, revealing their true characters, separating the evil from the good, casting the former into hell, elevating the latter into heaven. It is a destruction and reconstruction of the world of spirits. This stupendous event is described in Scripture as the great and notable day of the Lord, the day of wrath, the judgment day, the end of the world.

"You have come into the world of spirits at a period when you can witness the mighty events foretold by Isaiah and Ezekiel. There is a judgment now going on upon the last remains of the Jewish Church, and on all the pagan nations in the world of spirits; and preparations are being made for the institution of a new and more spiritual church on earth. The Messiah has come and judgment follows."

"You astonish me," I exclaimed. "The people on earth know nothing of these things. They are expecting a fulfillment of the prophecies in the material world. They expect the Messiah to come in splendor and power, to invest the Jewish people with supreme dominion, and to wreak his vengeance on all the disobedient and idolatrous."

"Poor blind ones, led by the blind! They interpret literally what was written in the language of symbols and given to them for spiritual uses."

"Why the necessity of this judgment?" I asked.

"Because the church is corrupt and dead; the priests are drunk with the wine of false doctrine; the people blind and without a shepherd. Therefore iniquity abounds. The flood-gates of hell are opened. The world of spirits is crowded with evil ones, who prevent the good from ascending to heaven, and infuse the most direful evils and falsities into men on earth. The prophets are dumb. The magician and the sorcerer are in the ascendant.

"Let me tell you something," he added in a solemn and subdued tone, "which, if you comprehend its full meaning, would make you tremble with fear. The order of the universe has been so far broken that demons have issued from hell; and there is a general insurrection of the evil spheres against heaven itself. Unless these hells are subdued and these evil ones cast out from the world of spirits, the people on earth will be obsessed, soul and body, by wicked spirits, human society will be destroyed, and universal chaos reign."

"You appall me by your prediction. But my wonder is, how such dangers can be impending, and the human race know nothing about it."

"Because they know nothing of spiritual things—nothing of this world of spirits in which are the cause and origin of all things. Because they look downward, and not upward. Because they have eyes and see not; ears and hear not. Because they have perverted and nullified the Word of God by a sensuous interpretation of its meaning."

"Alas! then," said I, "how can the lost order be restored and the world saved?"

"By one arm alone; that of the Creator, the Supreme Being, the Lord."

"Oh," said I, "this Being of supreme power created man in his supreme wisdom, gave him angelic attendants, a written Law, an established Church—and behold the result! What new influences can He bring to bear upon his fallen and doomed creatures?"

"Listen. He has clothed Himself with clouds and come down to us—to men on the earth. As the sun clothes his consuming rays with an atmosphere of vapor, which moderates them and accommodates them to the states of man and beast, so has God clothed himself in a finite human form and thus come down to his creatures. He is now engaged in spiritual combats with all these evil spheres. He is casting these lions of wickedness into their dens and shutting their mouths. He will purge and purify the world of spirits, deliver heaven from the assaults of the wicked, lift the great shadow of chaos from the world, restore man to his free agency and make him hereafter capable of a higher and more spiritual life. God is, henceforth, in the eyes of his children, not an invisible Spirit, but a Divine Man."

"These are mysteries and dreams to my understanding. I cannot comprehend how the Supreme Being, infinite, omnipotent, omnipresent, can assume a human body and live like one of us."

"It shall be made clearer to you. You shall see Him. Indeed you have seen Him, but you did not know Him. You shall see Him again—and know Him."

"I shall see the living God?" said I, in a state of solemn trepidation.

"Yes"—said John the Baptist, who accompanied us—"you shall see Him. I have surrounded you, by divine permission, with an atmosphere which will enable you without pain to endure his coming."

I cannot convey to mortals an adequate idea of the sense of awe which crept over me at these words. My knees smote together; my hands dropped; my heart trembled; my brain reeled at the thought of standing face to face with the living God!

XVI
THE CHRIST ABOVE NATURE

I now approach a subject so sublime and awe-inspiring, that it is necessary for us, like Moses before the burning bush, to take off our shoes from our feet; for the place is holy ground.

Let not the scoffer or unbeliever suppose that a stronger mind, a firmer reason, a clearer light, are the cause of his incredulity. He will disbelieve and repudiate what I am about to narrate, only because, in the progress of development, his own spirit has not yet reached that stage when he can comprehend and receive the most beautiful and holy truths.

We had been walking in an easterly direction during the latter part of our conversation. Suddenly there appeared before us a vast golden-colored sheet or blaze of light in the east. It was exceedingly brilliant, but at the same time inexpressibly soft and beautiful. In the centre of this great luminous field there was a snowy dove with outspread wings, bearing an olive branch in her mouth.

"The sphere of the Lord in the world of spirits!" exclaimed my companions in a breath; and they knelt with bowed heads and reverent faces at the approach of the resplendent symbol.

"This was the sphere which I saw," said John, "at the baptism of Jesus. My spiritual senses were partly opened, and this golden light which surrounds the Lord, appeared to encompass his natural body; and the dove, which represents the Holy Spirit of love and peace, rested upon Him; while a revelation was made to me, that this man whom I had baptized, was truly the Son of God."

I scarcely heard these words, nor did I understand them; for my mind was in a state of great agitation. I had never been pious: I was scarcely even religious in an external sense. I knew little or nothing of conviction of sin, penitence or repentance. I was, therefore, amazed at the new sensations I experienced. There was a painful sense of my own unregenerate condition; a terrible self-reproach, self-loathing, self-abasement; and with tears of contrition and humility I prostrated myself on my face. It was the sphere of the Lord, the light of heaven, the Spirit of God penetrating my soul and revealing me to myself.

My father now raised me from the ground, and fell upon my neck weeping.

"Be not astonished," he said. "These are tears of joy! You have been tested by the divine light. There are remains of goodness and truth in your soul. You will be saved. Heaven is yours."

This was more incomprehensible to me than anything yet, but I said nothing; for a sweet calm overspread my senses, and I became aware of the proximity of holy and august presences. I looked around me. I saw a great multitude of good spirits before us. All faces were directed to a group of figures which occupied a little knoll in their midst. In the centre of that group, I recognized Jesus of Nazareth!

His face shone as the sun, and his raiment was white as the light. Dazzling as his form appeared, his features were perfectly familiar, but etherealized and glorified, Moses and Elijah stood by him, one on his right hand and the other on his left. I recognized them at once; for every Jew has seen the statues and pictures of those national worthies.

Notwithstanding all that John the Baptist and my father had said, my obtuse understanding had not yet grasped the idea, that Jesus Christ was the Messiah—the Supreme Being.

"Has Jesus of Nazareth died also," I inquired, "and been raised like myself from the natural into the spiritual world?"

"Oh no!" said John, smiling sweetly at my bewilderment. "He exists in both worlds, in all worlds, at the same time."

"You speak enigmas," said I; "interpret them."

"Whom do you suppose this Jesus to be?" inquired John, earnestly.

"Some great prophet of God sent to perform miracles in Judea, and to preach a new gospel of peace and love."

"Jesus, the anointed One, is God himself," said John, with deep solemnity.

I answered nothing, for my mind was blank with astonishment. I gazed at the shining form with solemn awe. I now observed that Jesus was speaking or preaching to the multitude around him. I did not, however, hear a word he said.

"These are good spirits," said John, in explanation, "whom the Lord has liberated from the bondage of the evil spirits who infest this intermediate state. He is teaching them the spiritual truths adapted to their new condition, which correspond to the truths he is simultaneously teaching his disciples on earth.

"You are not permitted to hear what he says, because the fallacies of your natural life have not been sufficiently removed; and your mind would pervert his divine truths, or change them into the opposite falsities. You will be instructed in due season, and all things necessary to your life and happiness will be given you.

"In the mean time," he continued, "let us be seated under this beautiful tree, whose boughs make mysterious music, while I endeavor to bring it clearly to your mind that Jesus is God; for without an acknowledgment of his supreme divinity, no genuine spiritual truth can be received. The idea of God is a fundamental idea; and every one's state depends upon it or is determined by it. If that be false all is false; the mind is a dark chamber full of motes and cobwebs.

"Did not the Jews stone Jesus for affirming his equality and identity with God? Did not Jesus declare his pre-existence in saying that before Abraham lived, he lived? Did he not teach his omnipotence, his infinity, when he claimed to be one with the Father, and told his disciples that whoever had seen him, had seen the Father? Is not his name Immanuel—'God with us?' "

"Yes."

"Did not the prophets affirm that the Messiah who was to be born of a virgin, and to redeem Israel in the form of a man, was really the mighty Counselor, the Prince of Peace, the everlasting Father, Jehovah? Did they not repeatedly mention the Holy One of Israel, the Messiah that was to come, under such titles as 'the Lord of hosts,' 'the God of the whole earth,' and other names applicable only to the Supreme Being?"

"True."

"Why then should you be astonished that God is present in both worlds at the same time? Is He not omnipresent? ubiquitous? Unlimited by time or space, does He not manifest Himself to his creatures in all times and in all places? Can He not, if He will, appear simultaneously to all created intelligences in all the natural and spiritual spheres He has created?

"This Jesus, the Messiah, is everywhere. If you ascend into the heaven next above us, on fitting occasions you would see Him there in a more glorified form. If you mount still higher, you will only be coming nearer to Him, and behold Him in still more transcendent glory. Sometimes He appears to the angels as a Divine Man standing in the sun of the spiritual world. It was this truth, transmitted by tradition to the ancient people of

Asia, which gave rise (as they fell into naturalism) to the worship of the natural sun and the adoration of fire."

At these words I seemed to see my good and generous uncle Beltrezzor bowing his head reverently to the great luminary, from which the celestial face of Jesus looked down, smiling benediction upon the childlike old man.

"What you tell me," said I, "of Christ, is so strange that at first sight it appears incomprehensible. I perceive, indeed, that if Jesus be the supreme God of the universe, He may be seen simultaneously from every standpoint in the spiritual world, in every sphere, in every society, and by every individual soul, and everywhere take on a form accommodated to the spiritual states of those who behold Him. The difficulty in my mind lies in identifying the man Jesus whom I knew in Bethany, with this sublime resemblance of Him that I see in the world of spirits; and in comprehending that they are one person leading a simultaneous life in two spheres; and, finally, that this one person is the Supreme God.

"My difficulty is increased when I remember that Jesus in his earth-life is accustomed to call himself the Son of God. Although he said plainly that he and the Father were one, yet he sometimes speaks of the Father as greater than himself: of praying to the Father for his disciples; and of ascending to the Father on the consummation of his work."

"He has certainly left the impression upon his hearers that there are two persons in the Godhead; one higher, superior, interior; the other, a man among men; and that between these two there is some mystical union incomprehensible to the human mind."

"Most of his disciples accept this idea blindly, as a holy mystery. Persons of philosophic culture, who have studied Jesus as a phenomenon, regard him as a Son of God, or rather an emanation from God, in the same sense that Brahma, Osiris, Zoroaster, Moses, and Plato, are sons of God, or manifestations of divine truth. The mystical union between Father and Son is supposed to be an incorporation of the soul of man, by a life of obedience and goodness, with the essential Divine nature from which as a parent it was derived.

"In estimating the difference," said John, "between Jesus and other teachers of divine truth, the fact of deepest significance is, that he was born of a virgin. The soul of man is derived from his father. Jesus Christ had no earthly father; therefore, as to his inmost he was different from all other men. He was not some angelic form returning into the flesh, or let down from heaven into it; for that is impossible. And if it were so, his claims to omnipotence, infinity, eternity, the Godhead, would be preposterous. No: the soul of Jesus Christ was not introduced into his earthly body through the agency or intermediation of any created intelligence. His soul is the Divine Life, the Supreme Spirit.

"Seen from this earthly side, Jesus has no father. Seen from the spiritual side, he is the Father. Spirits and angels know Him only as the Father. They have never heard the term Son, in the earthly sense, applied to Him. There is no Father beyond him or above him. Here he never prays to the Father. Here he is himself recognized as the Father, Jehovah, the I AM.

"The term Son of God is used in accommodation to the sensuous states of the natural mind. It is peculiar to the earth-life, and cannot rise above the plane which separates the spiritual from the natural. It is only the human natural mind, divorcing the spiritual from the natural, that sees God in a double form, calling Him when invisible, the Father, and when visible, the Son."

"These things are wonderful," said I; "but how to explain them to men, who cannot think spiritually, however much they may think about spiritual things?"

"There is another and profounder reason," continued my instructor, "why Jesus speaks of himself on earth as the Son of God, and so frequently prays to an invisible Father. By subjecting himself in a finite form to the limitations of time and space, he subjects his own spiritual consciousness, so far as it is united, to obscuration. In his human body he thinks and feels as a finite being, the Son; while at the same moment in his spiritual form here He thinks and feels as the Divine Wisdom itself.

"The grand purpose of the incarnation was, to assume a human form in which he could be tempted as we are, in which he could be assaulted by evil spirits and devils; in which he could conquer death, hell and the grave, and become the Mediator, the Way, the Life and the Resurrection. The infestations of evil ones obscure his mental vision and take away from him at times his perception of identity with the Father. Thus he has two earthly states of life, one of glorification or spiritual insight, when he feels conscious of his Fatherhood; and one of humiliation, when he is sorely tempted and tried, and when he lifts his heart in prayer to that Fountain of love and light which is the centre of his own infinite bosom."

"These things amaze me," said I, "beyond expression. Nor do I believe that any human being has any true conception of the character of Jesus, of the mission he is filling, or of his plan of redemption. Certainly none of the thoughts you have communicated to me have ever dawned on the minds of his disciples."

"Nor is it probable," said John, "that mankind will be prepared, for many centuries, to understand what can only be comprehended from a spiritual stand-point. The least portion of the work of Jesus is apparent to men in the world. The sublime and far more difficult portion is wholly invisible to them, as it occurs here in the world of spirits which is not open to their perception."

My angelic friend was about giving me further light on this lofty theme, when Jesus and the happy multitude that surrounded him seemed to approach nearer to us.

My reader—if this manuscript ever finds a reader—may wonder why I did not approach the Divine Man and speak to him, after I had discovered that my earthly friend was the Supreme Being manifested in the human form. Ah! they know nothing of the sphere of the Lord! I could not even lift up my eyes to his feet. I was overwhelmed with wonder and awe. Had not so many other spirits been present to engage my attention, to divert my thoughts and to impart courage and life to me, I should have swooned and fallen.

Oppressed by the heavenly sphere, whose nearer approach I was not prepared for, I seized my father by the hand and he led me away. The scene faded behind us; and we went down into a little green valley filled with small white flowers and watered by a little brook. There I was freed from the terrible sense of oppression, and recovered my composure. We sat down in this valley of humiliation, where the small white flowers were the innocent thoughts of the new life, and the musical voice of the brook was a hymn of contrition.

"O my father!" said I, "is it always thus in the spiritual world, that the divine sphere of Jesus agitates the mind and pains the heart, so as to almost suffocate the life within us?"

"When the sphere of heaven approaches those who are in evil and falsity," answered my father, "it occasions intense pain in their interiors, and they cry out; 'Why art thou come hither, O Christ! to torment us?' Such is the judgment: and the wicked call upon the mountains and the rocks to hide them from the wrath of God."

The wrath of God! monstrous conception!

It is the gentle breath of the Divine Love which is converted into a burning fire when it enters the perverted and corrupt forms of their own souls!

"The same sphere of divine light approaching those who have some remnants of good and truth, and who can be saved, produces a profound self-abasement, a trembling contrition, a suffocation of the old life with all its wicked desires, and an inexpressible longing for a new life of purity, peace and love."

I now understood it all. I felt the self-abasement, the contrition, the inexpressible longing. The sun had already disappeared. The sun of the spiritual world does not rise and set like ours; but it brightens or pales in appearance with the changing states of the spirit. Then shone out innumerable stars in a blue dome, like the friendly faces of cherubim and seraphim smiling on us.

At length the wearied new-comer into the spiritual world passed into that mysterious realm of profoundest sleep, which is common to all worlds, and in which the unconscious soul is alone with God.

XVII
JUDGMENT OF THE JEWS

When I awoke, the sun was shining through a golden mist: the dew glittered like a rainbow fallen upon the grass and flowers: the air was full of sweet odors and the voices of birds: a strange warmth and vigor pervaded my body, and a delightful activity reigned in my soul.

"Come," said my father, "the first awakening thought should be always a prayer."

He then repeated those beautiful words by which Jesus taught his disciples to pray. I will not describe the spiritual phenomena which attended this prayer. The multitude of ideas and influxes and perceptions which were crowded into every sentence, would be incomprehensible to men. It seemed to be an epitome of the universe, and to bring the soul into loving contact with all the spheres of the divine creation.

"Has Jesus taught that prayer in the world of spirits also?" I inquired.

"Yes. This prayer is the universal prayer which binds the heavens and all the angels together. It is the holiest thing of religion. It descends from God to angels and men; and blessed is he who receives it into his heart!

"We are now ready," continued my father, "by the divine permission and under the divine protection, to explore some of the evil spheres which have congregated in the world of spirits, and which infuse their deadly poisons into men in the world. You will then understand a part of the great work which Christ is performing in this intermediate state."

Thereupon he examined my face, head and hands with the utmost minuteness. A man's whole life is written upon these; and angels, having a perfect knowledge of correspondences, the key of symbolism, can read from them your whole history as from a book.

"I perceived," said he, "that in your earth-life you have been brought into contact with the corrupt sphere of the Jewish Church, with the sensuousness of Grecian art and philosophy, with the splendors of Roman ambition, and with the ancient and subtle power of Egyptian magic. You have seen these things on the natural or earthly side. I will show them to you on the spiritual and interior side, so that you may comprehend the dreadful condition of the human race, and see the necessity of the Divine incarnation."

The geography, if we may use the expression, of the world of spirits is ever changing. The Church of the Lord, meaning those who come from the world and possess a divine revelation, always occupies the centre; other nations with different religions are arranged in successive zones around it; the farthest off in the circumference being those pagans who have received the least portion of the divine light and life.

"Behold the mutations of the world," said my father. "Those remotest people, away off in the darkness and cold of the circumference, were once the chosen people of God, his church, occupying the centre, immediately under the down-falling rays of the Divine Sun. They proved faithless to their trust. They became so evil that a terrible spiritual catastrophe overwhelmed them, described as a flood, — for they were engulfed in a flood of falsities. They were the antediluvians, of celestial genius, the most richly endowed, the most beautiful of all; and now their descendants, the most hideous and debased, are the black and bronzed barbarians and savages of the world."

"We are accustomed to think," said I, "that those lower types of mankind are the last created, and therefore the least perfect."

"No! they are the descendants of the first created and most perfect. They are not imperfect but degraded types. Imperfect types would progress upward and onward by natural law. These barbarians of Africa will never make the least advance until new causes which do not now exist, are put in operation. This great mystery of the Divine Providence will not be solved for many, many ages to come.

"After the destruction of that antediluvian church, another succeeded, possessing a written Word, a splendid ceremonial and boundless treasures of spiritual wisdom. They also forfeited their birth-right and betrayed their trust. Their judgment occurred in this world of spirits when Sodom and Gomorrah were destroyed by fire. Abraham and his family were the remnant saved from that church for the beginning of a new, as Noah and his family had been the remnant saved from the preceding.

"The descendants of this lost church compose chiefly the nationalities of Asia. They have remained for ages and will remain for ages to come in a stationary, semi-petrified condition, possessing no genuine truth, no vital religion, no element of progress; but living upon fables and myths which are the fragments of spiritual truth, whose interior light has long been lost to their understandings.

"For many centuries now of natural time, the Jewish Church has held the centre of the world of spirits. It also has become thoroughly corrupt, and is about to be removed to the circumference. Its great judgment is impending; its destruction approaches; but of this, that church itself is profoundly ignorant."

During this conversation we had ascended by insensible degrees to the summit of a high mountain. I was astonished at the splendid panorama spread out beneath us. It was the whole land of Canaan, from the Jordan on the east to the borders of Philistia on the west; from Damascus and Antioch gleaming away to the north, down to the great desert that frowned along the southern boundary.

Immediately beneath us was a city of Jerusalem, ten times as large as our earthly capital; and a holy temple of corresponding proportions, all transcending in glory and grandeur anything ever seen on earth.

"Behold," said my father, "the creation of spiritual fantasy, the imaginary heaven of the Jews, which will pass away like a scroll at the breath of the Lord when He comes in judgment upon them.

"You seem astonished," he continued, "that spirits should reproduce around themselves these spiritual semblances of the cities and countries they have left behind. Nothing is more simple and rational. These people are gross and sensual in their nature, with little or nothing of the celestial or spiritual about them. They loved material things exclusively; their thoughts never rose above outward, civil, and political affairs. Here their interior life is reproduced in exteriors. Therefore they create around themselves their old homes, cities, and countries; and re-enact, as far as possible, their earthly life, because all their affections and thoughts are earthly."

"This mountain," said I, "upon which we are standing puzzles me; for there is no similar elevation in the neighborhood of Jerusalem."

"This mountain," answered my father, "is symbolical of the lofty state of spiritual pride and presumption in which the Jewish Church now is—a state of self-glorification which precedes its judgment and final destruction. It is only from this height, corresponding to their own spiritual state, that you can see the holy city and temple as they appear to them.

"Is it strange that a people, so gross, so unspiritual, so near their extinction as a church, should be so inflated with spiritual and theological conceit? They appear in their own eyes to have the most glorious city, the most holy church, and the most august ceremonials that ever existed; accounting all others unfit for heaven and unworthy of the Divine favor.

"It was on the pinnacle of that colossal temple which you now see, that the evil spirit placed Jesus, and attempted to infuse into his heart the arrogant self-glorification of the corrupt priesthood, which imagines itself the special care of all the angels of heaven."

"We had always supposed that that temptation occurred on the temple in Jerusalem."

"Oh, no!" said my father, "the temptations of the Lord always occur in the world of spirits. Evil spirits do not move around upon the temples and mountain-tops of the natural world. The Lord's spiritual senses were opened into this world, which is the scene of his trials, his temptations, his combats with hell; and will be the scene of his final glorification and ascension."

"These ideas are all new to me," I said, "but very rational."

"You will now see," my father continued, "how this imaginary heaven of the Jews, with its proud and worldly magnates, appears in the genuine light of heaven. An invisible angel accompanies us, who is commissioned to let in the heavenly light upon these scenes, to show you the internal and real character of this church."

Thereupon a ray of white light seemed to shoot down from the zenith. A black cloud immediately arose from the Salt Sea, and spread itself like a canopy over the whole land. Fearful thunderings and red lightnings issued from the bosom of this terrible cloud. The whole country around became a desolation—a dreary waste full of stone-heaps and pitfalls. The holy city sank into the earth; and in its place there rose a great lake, black as a mountain tarn unruffled by the wind. Floating in the midst of it was the gorgeous temple converted into a huge wooden house or Noah's ark, from the innumerable windows of which looked out the hideous faces of wild beasts and the heads of enormous serpents.

I was at first terrified at these sights; but my father observed:

"This is a representation, a pictorial prophecy of a reality yet to come, before Christ has finished his conquering work in the world of spirits. These people do not see the things we see. This heavenly light has come into our minds that we may discover what their interior life really is,—devoid of all spiritual vitality; desolate, dark, lurid; full of evil beasts and unclean birds and creeping things."

This sphere of ecclesiastical pride and presumption is not peculiar to the Jewish Church or nation. It is predominant in all religions, churches and individuals, when the religious instincts are satisfied and delighted with grandeur, power, numbers, fashion, wealth and glory.

"What will be the effect," I inquired, "of this disastrous judgment in the world of spirits, upon the Jewish nation in the natural world?"

"There will be fearful dissensions and conflicts; wars within and without; the city and the temple will be destroyed; the country made desolate; the people scattered as exiles and vagabonds among all nations. Their descendants, coming into the world of spirits, will recede toward the circumference among the pagans. A new church springing up among other nations, will take the central place, and give rise upon earth, after great struggles, to a purer religion and a nobler civilization.

"You will now see, in symbolic representation, the three great classes into which the Church will be dissolved at its judgment."

Then there appeared before us a great many domestic animals; oxen, horses, asses, camels, sheep, fowls, etc.; all mingled together in confusion, and all looking poor, jaded, filthy and wretched.

"These are the beasts of burden," said my father; "the ignorant and innocent masses, presided over by a corrupt and cruel theocracy, which desecrates the name of God by imposing upon his children a spiritual despotism.

"Advance nearer to these creatures, and you will behold a wonderful sight, such as can never appear in the natural world, but is common enough in the world of spirits."

We came nearer, and lo! all the animals were found to be men and women. Some of their forms and faces seemed taken from my memory; for I thought I recognized the crowds which followed Jesus in the world.

"From these people," said my father, "the remnant will be taken—the remnant about which the prophets speak so often. This remnant of Israel, starting with the apostles chosen by Christ, will be the seed and starting-point of a new Church.

"Such are the forms of those who are interiorly good. Observe now the forms of those who are interiorly wicked."

The former scene passed away and three wild beasts appeared standing at the mouth of an immense black cavern, in front of which many human bones were scattered. The animals were a wild boar, a wolf and a tiger, all of gigantic size and terrible ferocity.

We advanced nearer to these also, and they changed into men; the wild boar into Caiaphas, the high priest; the wolf into the cunning and cruel Magistus; and the tiger into the robber Barabbas. The meaning of this tableaux I perceived intuitively without explanation.

"Between these two extremes," continued my father, "is a great class who are in mixed states of good and evil. Their sufferings will be severe before they can put off either kind of life so as to live entirely in the other; for a separation of good and evil must be effected,—if not upon earth, at least in the world of spirits."

A sandy wilderness then arose to view, in which I saw but two figures; a zebra, wild, beautiful, intractable, snuffing proudly the air of the desert; and a white dove which was struggling frantically to escape from the jaws of a monstrous serpent.

These I approached more eagerly; for I was impelled by an earnest desire to caress the beautiful zebra, and to rescue the dove from the fangs of the serpent. They changed also in the twinkling of an eye. The zebra was our friend the Son of the Desert, and the dove was Mary Magdalen. As the latter stepped forward, a shining and beautiful woman, the serpent shriveled and fell behind her like a black garment cast upon the ground.

As the last picture faded away, my father resumed his instructions.

"The scenes you have witnessed are phantasmagoric, but symbolical and full of spiritual truth. They illustrate the law of appearances which governs in the spiritual world. The phenomenal world around us, animal, vegetable and mineral, is all representative of the life within us; not by accident or with confusion, but according to fixed and eternal laws.

"The sphere of life radiates from a spirit like heat from the sun, or like perfume from a flower. It flows forth and falls into successive zones or belts of spiritual substance, in each of which it produces some spiritual form representative of itself. Outside of his human sphere, the life of a spirit takes form in the first zone as an animal, in the second as a planet or flower, in the third as a mineral, a stone, a drop of water, a cloud, a star.

"The life which animates a wicked spirit becomes a corresponding wild beast in the first zone; a loathsome fungus in the second; a poisonous mineral in the third. The sweet spiritual life of a good heart becomes the innocent lamb in one zone; the beautiful rose in the next; the brilliant gem in the last.

"Observe, however, that each spirit always appears to himself in the human form; and always so to others when they are near him. He only takes on these typical or correspondential forms in the eyes of others, when he recedes to or approaches from a distance."

"What a deep philosophy you are unfolding!" I exclaimed. "I see already in what you have told me the germs of a thousand brilliant ideas.

Oh that I could teach these beautiful things in the porticoes of Athens! How they would ravish the Grecian heart!"

"You are mistaken," said my father. "Some simple soul from whom you least expected it, would accept your doctrines, weeping for joy. The great, the rich, the learned, the powerful, would scornfully reject them as fables or dreams."

"That is strange and sad."

"Yes—but it is true. The mind which is wedded to falsities in religion or philosophy, is proud, self-reliant, self-satisfied, bigoted and intolerant. The genuine truth which makes the soul free, makes it also liberal and loving."

"Will the Jews on earth reject the Messiah, proving his mission as he does by stupendous miracles?"

"Yes: miracles avail nothing with the unbelieving. Truth is not seen merely because it is truth. No truth is received or seen but that which corresponds to some love in the heart. The hatred which these Jewish spirits feel for holy things, will descend by influx into the priests and scribes at Jerusalem: and the tender seed of the New Dispensation will be sown in darkness and watered with tears and blood.

"Do not suppose," added my father, "that spirits and angels have any special power to foresee the future. Oh no! We only live nearer to the Fountain of causes, and reason more acutely from cause to effect."

I treasured these strange things in my mind, having only a faint perception of either their truth or value. I was especially surprised at the fact, that a church could actually come to an end, a dispensation be spiritually closed and a new one inaugurated, while the adherents of the old were in the full flush of power and numbers, and regarded themselves as the favored repositories and faithful interpreters of divine truth!

XVIII
IMAGINARY HEAVENS

After these things we were taken up another high mountain, whence we had a view of all the kingdoms in the world of spirits at once. Hither it was that Jesus was carried by the evil spirit who offered him all this power and glory, if he would fall down and worship him. There is no mountain in the natural world from which such an outlook were possible.

"This great height," said my father, "represents the infernal sphere of self-aggrandizement, which aspires to universal dominion. It is that ambition which corrodes the heart with envious passion so long as anything remains unconquered. This spirit is common to nations and individuals, to the greatest and the least. This mountain rears its awful summit in every human breast. This is the spiritual mountain which is to be cast into the sea by faith."

Looking down, I now beheld a city of Rome as before I had seen a city of Jerusalem. Beautiful, shadowy pictures of cities, homes of spirits, vastly magnified and made glorious with ethereal colors! Man cannot imagine the splendid creations which spirits can instantaneously produce from the plastic substance of the spiritual world. These cities and countries, however, are peculiar to the intermediate state. They do not exist in heaven.

The Romans risen from the dead had reconstructed their imperial city of precious stones, so that it always shone from afar as if some grand illumination were going on, whose splendors were again reflected from the clouds which floated above it.

We looked into this marvelous city, its capital and palaces, its temples and amphitheatres. The great avenues were crowded with a vast and gorgeous procession. Many kings and queens and nobles were walking in chains, brought as prisoners from so many conquered countries. The treasures of these plundered captives were borne by thousands of slaves of all colors and nationalities, in massive and curiously-carved vessels of gold and silver. Specimens of wild animals from all regions of the Roman world, drawn in gilded cages, and of the more wonderful plants and flowers carried upon the shoulders of men, and screened from the sun by flaming canopies of silk, added to the picturesqueness and grandeur of the scene.

The Roman senators, generals and magnates were seen heading the different divisions of this vast multitude, riding in blazing chariots drawn by superb horses richly caparisoned. On both sides of the captives marched the victorious armies of Rome; so that the very air above them was golden with the flash of helmets, spears and shields, and the gleam of Roman eagles.

These were the spirits of that vain-glorious and indomitable race who had changed the geography of the natural world, and were now celebrating their victories with transcendent magnificence in the intermediate state. The sphere of their interior character was wafted to my spiritual perceptions, and I felt as I did in the Hall of Apollo when Hortensius and his guests fixed their haughty and contemptuous gaze upon Anthony and myself.

"How unutterably base, cruel and sensual," exclaimed my father, "is the spirit of man when he loves himself supremely, and overreaches and overrides his fellow-creatures. Behold the spiritual side to this magnificent exterior!"

Thereupon the light from a higher sphere streamed down, and the pomp, the glory, the beauty of the whole scene disappeared. We beheld a vast crowd of beggars in filthy rags, and a confused heap of low buildings made of mud and straw. The proud and fierce Romans were all slaves themselves, wearing long chains and driven by infernal spirits in the shape of grinning apes. Where the Capitol had stood, appeared a pool of blood-colored water, in which a dragon of hideous dimensions lay, spouting from his mouth a stream of fire. A lurid twilight hung over all, prognosticating a wild and tempestuous night.

"Such," said my father, "will be the fate of ambition when the Lord comes in judgment. Let us now descend to a lower region, and see a people greater than these, but who have sunk into darker depths; a people now destitute of spiritual pride or civil ambition; a degenerate, effeminate, corrupt race, dead to all genuine and ennobling aspirations, and immersed like beasts in the life of the senses."

We seemed to go down to the sea-coast—for the blue ocean girdles also the world of spirits. Soon we came into the sphere of the Grecian souls who had risen from the dead, and who had reconstructed about them, according to spiritual laws, their own charming and ethereal country. The scene was not far from Athens, whose marble-crowned Acropolis gleamed in the distance, with clouds more beautiful than itself floating above it.

The poetic faculty, full of the inspiration of Grecian art, can alone appreciate what I next witnessed. The Hall of Apollo in the palace of Hortensius was a beggarly chamber in comparison with this great hall of nature in which Pan presided, and in which earth, sky and ocean had each its part. The guests also of the luxurious Roman were mere schoolboys in comparison with the august assembly before us, which was gathered to a feast in the imaginary heaven of the Greeks.

We seemed to be standing on a hill that sloped and fell by beautiful green terraces down to the silver beach of a placid sea. The summit of that hill was long, broad and level, and crowned with a grove of extraordinary beauty. The trees were far apart, and rose like emerald columns to a great height before they branched. Their foliage was pruned and led by threads of invisible wire to intertwine overhead, forming a delicate arch for a roof. The ground was carpeted with an inwrought tissue of living flowers, which yielded elastically to the tread, sending up continually a delicious perfume.

In this immense grove were spread a thousand tables seemingly of solid precious stones, and crowned with great vases of wine and cups of crystal, and adorned with ethereal fruits and flowers. At these tables were seated or reclining thousands and thousands of the ancient heroes and heroines of Greece, served by thousands of beautiful nymphs, Dryads and Naiads, who had left the woods and the waters to bestow their charms on these happy souls.

The gods and goddesses were also in attendance; for heaven and earth were thrown together in such admirable confusion that each partook the qualities of the other. The sky and the air were literally full of divinities. On a rose-and-purple cloud condensed into a throne, and lowered half-way between the ceiling and the floor, sat Venus, crowned with myrtles and presiding at the feast. The Graces were kneeling at her feet, while her swans and doves were grouped about her. Near by stood Cupid twanging his bow, and laughing at the sight of his empty quiver; for every heart in the crowd had been pierced by one of his golden arrows.

Looking out to the sea, we saw Neptune, of colossal proportions, riding in his chariot constructed of shells, and drawn by horses with brazen hoofs and gilded manes. Myriads of sea-nymphs and sea-monsters sported and gamboled about him, sometimes in the air, sometimes on the shining surface of the deep.

In mid-sky Apollo in person drove the chariot of the sun, attended by the Muses and the flying Hours. In the west, Iris the messenger of Juno, planted her rainbow on a passing cloud, and smiled in colors to the world. Afar off, in the east, the Seasons had opened the massive Gates of Cloud, and we had a glimpse of the old Olympian gods in conclave august, feasting upon ambrosial food.

Thousands of these beautiful figures were nude; and I saw the spiritual models which had inspired and immortalized Grecian art. Thousands also were draped, and with such infinite variety and beauty, that it seemed no work of human ingenuity, but as if Nature herself had invested them with her forms and colors.

"Oh, my father!" said I excitedly, "surely this is real; this is heaven. These things will not vanish also, or change into something hideous and terrible."

A shade of sadness came over my father's face; for he saw that the subtile and powerful sphere of this Grecian nature-worship had awakened the activities of my own sensuous life.

"Yes, my son; these are phantasms. These are wicked Grecian spirits who are personating their gods and goddesses, their heroes and heroines. You see before you what wonders spirits can achieve by magic and fantasy. This is the sphere which flows into and governs the present population of Greece. These spirits would, if they could, obsess and control the human race. The interior state of these souls is terrible."

"O, do not show it to me yet," I exclaimed. "Let me contemplate a little longer this marvelous scene."

"When all these spirits are judged," continued my father, "and cast out of the world of spirits, the Greece and Rome of the natural world will become feeble and death-stricken. Their oracles will become silent; their arts will fail; their glory perish; their civilization decay. Their very languages will die. Their exact modes of thought will no more be possible to men. Ages of bondage and darkness will ensue, after the light they have perverted and the liberty they have profaned."

I scarcely heard these last words; for the vast assembly of gods and men, which had been in comparative repose, became suddenly animated by a wild excitement. There issued from the cool and leafy forests on all sides a crowd of beautiful nymphs headed by Diana, resplendent as a statue of pearl, clad in an apron of green leaves and flowers, and with a constellation of fire-flies in her hair.

Her merry troop of nymphs, arrayed like herself, were flying in affected fear from the jolly god Bacchus, who appeared in pursuit, crowned with vine leaves and berries and drawn by his Indian tigers striped with ebony and gold. He was followed by a rabble rout of Fauns and Satyrs and bacchanalian revelers, male and female. This beautiful chaos threw itself pell-mell, reeling and whirling and dancing, shouting and singing, into the midst of the brilliant assembly.

A scene of the wildest carnival followed. The heroes and heroines caught the contagious frenzy, and soon all were entangled in the embraces of the maddest dance that ever was witnessed. Neptune and his water-nymphs sprang high into the air to view the scene; and all the deities in Olympus crowded down to the Gates of Cloud, which they illumined afar off by the sun-like radiance of their presence.

I was gazing on this scene with the utmost astonishment, when my eyes fell suddenly upon Helena, the beautiful daughter of Calisthenes.

"My father," said I, with profound emotion, "do you not see that superb figure of a woman more beautiful than all these goddesses, leaning against yonder tree and clapping her hands with delight at the drunken Bacchus making love to Venus? That is Helena of Athens! the dream of my life, the idol of my soul."

"Not so," said my father, "it is a phantasm—a spirit resembling your earthly Helena; perhaps some cunning Syren who has assumed her form to allure you to herself."

"Oh no!" said I, "impossible!" feasting my eyes and heart on the lovely apparition.

"Every one," continued my monitor, "fresh from the natural world, who enters this magical and fantastic sphere, sees, or thinks he sees, some wondrous woman, whom he declares to be the idol and dream of his soul. Beware, my son, of these seductive emotions. The light of heaven will dispel for us all these illusions."

"Oh no!" said I, wildly, "it cannot; it must not. This, this, is heaven, and all else is illusion."

My heart beat with passionate fervor, and I sprang forward to meet my beloved. My father suddenly disappeared from my sight! In the spiritual world, when two persons enter into totally different states of thought and feeling, they mutually vanish from each other's sight. Heaven and hell are thus separated, and the existence of each is even unknown to the other. I noticed the fact that my father had vanished; but I cared nothing about it, for my infatuated soul thought only of Helena.

I advanced toward her. She turned upon me a look of beautiful recognition; and stretching out her ivory arms, exclaimed with a sun-burst of her old bewitching smiles:

"My boy-lover of Bethany! welcome! I thought I had killed you with love!"

"Then love me back into life!" I exclaimed.

When an appalling change came suddenly over all things. The light of heaven streamed down upon me, and those other lights were turned into shadows, the beauty into ugliness, the joy into horror, life into death. The deities became phantom skeletons grinning as they fled away into the darkness. The men assumed the forms of filthy swine or goats, and the women those of writhing vipers. The charming creature into whose delicate arms I was about throwing myself, became a scaly serpent of frightful size. I fell swooning to the ground, with the terrible sensations of one who is falling headlong from a precipice into the sea.

I returned slowly and painfully to consciousness, like one who has had a long sleep and harassing dreams, and finds it difficult to pick up the fallen thread of his yesterday's life. I found myself pillowed on a soft green bank in a delicious atmosphere of repose. Without opening my eyes I reverted to all that had happened, and a feeling of desolation came over me, and a sense of deep shame and contrition. What a revelation of the sensual affinities of my own interior nature! What blindness! What madness! Alas! how low had I fallen! I was afraid to meet my father and the good John. I was wretched.

My meditations were interrupted by the voice of some one near me, singing in low sweet tones, pervaded by a certain divine sadness, the beautiful words of Scripture:

> "Rejoice not against me, O mine enemy:
> When I fall I shall arise:
> When I sit in darkness
> The Lord shall be a light unto me."

Then another voice overhead, clearer, more thoughtful, more musical than the first, sang sweetly:

> "Jehovah upholdeth all that fall,
> And raiseth up all who are bowed down."

Thereupon the first voice near me proceeded in the same low sweet tones full of sadness:

> "But as for me, my feet were almost gone,
> My steps had well nigh slipped."

The higher, nobler voice continued the heavenly consolations of Scripture:

> "Nevertheless I am ever with thee!"

The voices, the music, the refrain, the holy words of the Psalmist, stirred in the tenderest manner the very depths of my soul. I wept. A new faith, a new hope, a new divine resolution were born within me.

Like a singer who has been overcome with emotion, but dries her tears and resumes her singing,—the sadness overshadowed by a modest courage,—the first voice was heard again:

"Thou hast held me by my right hand,
Thou shalt guide me by thy counsel,
And afterward shalt receive me into glory."

Then there was a burst of divine music as from a hidden choir of angels, in which the two voices joined; and this was the hymn:

"The Lord is my Shepherd;
I shall not want:
He maketh me to lie down in green pastures;
He leadeth me beside the still waters;
He restoreth my soul!"

The strains died softly away, lingering long on my charmed ear and leaving my heart in a sacred calm.

I prayed with intense earnestness:

"From self-love and the love of the world; from self-righteousness, presumption and hypocrisy; from pride, ambition and sensuality; all of which I have seen so fearfully unmasked:

"Good Lord! deliver me."

I opened my eyes, and my father and the seraph-faced forerunner of Jesus stood before me.

The latter took my hand tenderly in his own, and said:

"All the experiences of life, both in the world of men and in the world of spirits, are given to teach us the difference between good and evil, between the true and the false; to show us the deformity of sin and the beauty of holiness; to deliver our souls from the bondage of hell, and lift them into the peace of heaven."

XIX
THE MAGICIANS IN HELL

We had then a long conversation about the mysteries of regeneration or the new birth, scarcely any of which are known to mankind, or would be believed if they were revealed. This knowledge is so peculiarly spiritual and angelic that it seems useless for me to say anything about it. If a church on earth ever comprehends these divine arcana, it will only be when the Lord sees fit to open his heavens anew, and to unfold the spiritual meaning of his Word.

"You have now seen," said my father, "the three great spheres which represent the three degrees of the human mind. That Jesus Christ met and resisted the powers of hell in all these spheres, is shown in his temptations in the wilderness. By conquering these evil spheres in his human form and through his divine power, He is enabled henceforth to deliver all men from similar infestations. This was the great purpose of his incarnation. His temptation will appear to men as an historical event enacted at a certain time and space. To angels it seems a condensed statement of his whole spiritual life, of his entire redemptive work, from the assumption of humanity to his final and perfect glorification."

"Who is the devil," said I, "that was capable of tempting the Holy One so severely?"

"The devil is no single individual, but the whole combined evil world, speaking and acting through one medium. You seem surprised; but nothing is more common in the spiritual world than for a whole society of spirits, even millions in number, to think, feel, and express themselves simultaneously through one of their number.

"Do you not remember that when Jesus asked a certain maniac his name, the devil within him replied:

" 'My name is Legion: for we are many.' "

This led to the strange subject of demoniac possession. I told my father that the Greek philosophers and physicians, who were considered the profoundest thinkers in the world, scouted the idea of evil spirits taking possession of men. They attributed all such cases to the effect of physical disease.

"They know nothing whatever," said my guide, "of the relation between spirit and matter. Their philosophy of man, history, and nature is superficial and false. Their boasted light is darkness to our spiritual perceptions, and their scientific verbiage the merest babble.

"It is true, my son, that devils are continually aspiring to break through from hell into the world of spirits; and by means of evil spirits in this world, especially those fresh from the earth, to possess and govern men in the natural world. If the divine hand were not put forth to arrest this influx of hell into the world of nature, three centuries would not elapse before all mankind would be imbecile or insane, and would destroy each other like wild beasts."

"Mankind," said I, "are totally ignorant of the fearful dangers which hang over them."

"Of course they are. These dangers come from the unseen spiritual side. They know nothing and believe nothing of the unseen."

"Can you tell me anything of the spiritual philosophy of magic?"

"A sphere inconceivably subtle and wicked! It obtained its first foothold in Egypt ages before the historic period, and has penetrated thence, under different forms and names, into all the countries of the world."

"We had some painful experiences with it soon after your departure from the natural world; but my philosophic studies at Athens led me to suppose that magic was an imposture based upon absurd superstitions."

"Magic, my son, is at present a fearful reality. It is the means by which the wicked can summon around them the worst spirits, and obtain control over man and nature. By its means they can overcome physical obstacles; can see and hear at incredible distances; can produce dreams and illusions; can make one thing appear another; effect transformations which seem miraculous; call up the spirits of the dead; take absolute possession of the fancy and the will, and control their victim in all his thoughts and actions. They can give wise answers and frequently foretell future events. They can imitate good and heavenly things with such marvelous accuracy, as to impose themselves as illumined teachers and prophets upon mankind."

"How could such a fearful thing have originated? Whence is its power?"

"From the perversion and profanation of holy things; from the abuse of the knowledge of correspondence, which is the secret bond between spirit and matter, and for that reason is now concealed from mankind. When the sons of Aaron put strange fire upon the altar of the Lord, they were consumed. When the sons of the prophet shred the wild vine into the pot, there was death in the pottage. That strange fire, that wild vine is magic. Magic is the perversion of truth—the science and the religion of hell."

"Can you foresee the future of this terrible power?"

"Yes—so far as we can infer that certain material effects must flow in time from certain spiritual causes. The great judgment which Christ is now executing in this world of spirits, will cast all these magical powers into hell and shut them up for ever. This is a part of the saving work of the Redeemer. He delivers men, not from the punishment but from the bondage of sin. Magic will then cease upon earth. The fragments and shadows of it may annoy mankind for ages; but its central power will have been bruised and broken, and it will become such barefaced superstition, trickery, and sleight-of-hand, that future generations will find it difficult to believe that it ever was anything else.

"Come!" he added; "I am permitted to show you one of the old Egyptians at his work."

We now descended into a dark cavern which appeared on our left, but which I had not noticed before. It sloped downward, with ragged black rocks protruding from its walls. The atmosphere was at first so stifling that I could hardly proceed. We emerged after a while into a level country under a sky of a dark gray color. A blood-red sun, never setting, stood low in the west, casting a lurid light over all things. Our path was along the bank of a large river, moving sluggishly and darkly between gigantic reeds and rushes. Huge crocodiles and monstrous beasts I had never seen before, lay here and there, half in the mud and half in the water. Away in the distance rose many colossal forms, pyramids, sphynxes, obelisks, palaces, temples— vast shadows as it were against the sky. Now and then we passed a statue of stone or bronze, higher than the tallest trees, and so sad, stern and lifelike, it was difficult not to believe that it was the lost soul of some old Egyptian king, doomed to perpetual misery in the outward form of eternal repose.

"You must know," said my father, "that to enable us to enter these awful gateways of hell, an invisible guard of thousands of angels is necessary."

I was relieved by this thought; for a sensation of fear had already begun to oppress me. I had learned enough of the spiritual world to know that all this wild and grotesque scenery was the outbirth of the life and memories of evil spirits, and could be dissipated in a moment, or changed into something horrible by the revealing light of heaven.

We now came to a great palace which seemed built of ebony, with foundations, doors, and cornices of bronze. The gates leading to its courtyard were of immense size, and constructed of dingy brass. A strange inscription ran across the arch, which I asked my father to interpret.

"That," said he, "is the Ten Commandments reversed, representing the laws which govern in this evil sphere. Much of it is too dim for one to read; but see!

"Thou shalt kill.

"Thou shalt steal.

"Thou shalt commit adultery."

"Hold!" said I, "what profanation! what blasphemy."

"Yes, my son! Hell is the opposite of heaven."

The courtyard was laid out in curious geometric figures, and adorned with many extraordinary plants and flowers, but mainly of yellow and purple hues.

"Flowers at the doorway of hell! I thought that flowers were the children of heaven, the fragments of divine wisdom showered upon men in the disguise of beautiful forms, fragrances and colors."

"So they are," said my father; "and the floral kingdom here is antipodal to the floral kingdom in heaven; the concentration of all that is malignant and baleful in the thoughts and feelings of the inhabitants of that doleful place."

I shuddered as I passed these infernal flowers; and we mounted the iron steps of the palace, walking between the statues of two great brazen bulls as we entered the hall.

A servant came forward to receive us, of such hideous form that I started back in terror. He was nearly naked, and thousands of hieroglyphic figures had been burned into his body in black and red colors. His face was the face of an embalmed person, long dead, shriveled and ghastly.

While we were speaking to this frightful personage, a hoarse, sepulchral voice issued from a half-open door:

"Bring them in. I have felt their coming."

We passed into a chamber of immense size,—for everything in the shadowy world seemed to me colossal. I instantly perceived that it was the counterpart of the chamber of magic in the house of Magistus, so minutely described to me by my sister Martha.

"Behold the source of inspiration to Simon Magus!" said I to myself.

I recognized all the objects mentioned by the eyewitnesses of that remarkable scene between Simon and the magicians; the marble platform; the black table with the zodiac upon it; the images on the wall. Even the leopard and serpent were there. The magician was an old man, stern-featured, cruel-eyed, worn and wasted, with some personal resemblance to Simon Magus.

"I have had violent pains about my heart and difficult breathing," said the evil spirit slowly, "ever since you entered my kingdom. I know who you are and who protects you. Your presence tortures me; so be brief with your mission. I will answer you truthfully, for the experience of ages has taught me that it is useless to resist that sphere. Be quick and release me."

"This," said my father, "is one of the magicians of Egypt, who imitated the miracles of Moses and Aaron. He is the most cunning and powerful of the species."

Addressing the magician, he continued:

"I am instructing this novitiate spirit who accompanies me, in the relation between the spiritual and the natural worlds. I have told him that all false and evil things are breathed into men by wicked spirits: that magic is the science of evil springing from the perversion of good, and a means by which you attempt to govern men."

"You speak truly," said the evil spirit, rubbing his hands with glee; "you speak truly. Our power is immense: our wisdom is incredible. We have vastly more influence over men than the angels. You have heard of the witch of Endor who brought Samuel from the dead. We can reverse that wonderful art. We can bring those living upon earth into our presence. I will show you one of my favorite slaves, a fellow of great capacity and boundless ambition; a genius worthy of the grand inspiration with which I animate his soul."

Thereupon his servant unrolled a great white curtain against the wall. The spirit went through sundry unintelligible incantations: and slowly the perfect portrait of Simon Magus appeared before our eyes.

"He seems to be in a paroxysm of rage," said I.

"Yes," answered the spirit. "He derived it from me a few moments ago. I was foaming with passion just before you entered my palace: and now the fury is expending itself on him."

"The evil passions of men," said my father, "have previously passed through the dark and filthy souls of evil spirits."

"Ha! ha! ha!" laughed the magician. "My victim thinks it is original with himself. Indeed, the deluded fellow believes he controls me and a vast number of other spirits. The merest tool in our hands, the dull, slow machine through which we work our fiery wills, our stupendous plans; he conceives himself to be possessed of miraculous power! Men who think they control spirits, are always controlled by them. Ha! ha! ha!"

"Beware," said my father; "are your own inspirations original? Have you ever heard of Ja-bol-he-moth?"

"Yes—and seen him," he answered trembling.

"Alas! alas!" he added slowly and painfully. "We govern men from our stand-point: but there are deeper and more direful hells that govern us. We are slaves also.

"Oh! if Ja-bol-he-moth," he suddenly exclaimed with a fierce earnestness, "if Ja-bol-he-moth and other great antediluvian giants could only escape from their imprisonment, we would soon transform the whole earth to our liking."

"Unhappy spirit!" said I, "do you find pleasure in the contemplation of such a thought?"

"The only pleasure that is left me," he replied; and passed into a frigid state with a deadly, stony stare, more like a statue than a man.

"Come," said my father, "our sphere has paralyzed him. I have one more strange thing to show you before we return to the world of spirits."

We left the ebony palace; and turning from the dark river with its colossal reeds and rushes, we passed into a wilderness of sand, over which hung a gloomier twilight than any we had before witnessed.

Presently there appeared before us a great black dome of iron, reaching across the horizon from east to west, and sloping upward from the sand even to the sky. The blackness, the immensity, the gloom of this strange object cast a fearful shadow on my soul.

"This," said my father with deep solemnity, "is the tomb of the antediluvian world, which none can open or shut but Christ. In the terrible abysses underneath are imprisoned the evil spirits whose judgment is described in the Scriptures as a flood. Unless the Messiah had come in the flesh, this antediluvian sphere would have broken forth and deluged the world of spirits and the world of men."

"What would be the consequence?" said I.

"The total suffocation of the spiritual life, as the natural life is suffocated by drowning; a complete torpor of the moral sense, a paralysis of the intellectual faculties. Mankind would relapse into barbarism. The physical system would degenerate. The skin would become black and fetid; the hair woolly, the nose flat, the forehead low and debased. One step more, and from barbarians men would become beasts.

"This process of degeneration had already made sad havoc with a large portion of the human race, when the closure of the antediluvian hells and the institution of a new order of things arrested its march. So the African now stands torpid, unprogressive, sensual, barbaric, bearing on his very body the typical shadows of hell."

"Is there no hope for him?" said I, sadly, —for my mind reverted to my trusty friends, Ethopus and Anthony.

"Oh yes," said my father, "Jehovah is good to all, and his tender mercies are over all his works.

"The Lord in the form of a Divine Man will close these ancient hells and beat back the waves of evil. Great organic changes will go in the spiritual and natural worlds. In the far-off ages there will be a last judgment in the world of spirits and a new church upon earth. New causes will be set in operation; and these Africans at last will be delivered from their hereditary curse, and restored to the form of beauty and wisdom which their ancestors enjoyed in the beginning of the world."

I rejoiced at this glorious prophecy. And while thinking of the tender and noble emotions which seemed to govern the only Africans I had ever known, we ascended into the world of spirits, whose beautiful and peace-giving light I hailed with unspeakable pleasure.

"How little the inhabitants of earth know," said I, to myself, "of the spiritual philosophy of history!"

XX
FRIENDS IN HEAVEN

Heaven is above the world of spirits, as the latter is above the earth. The way to heaven is through the world of spirits; but it is not reached by a process of death, but by a process of preparation. We are prepared for heaven by putting off the evils and falsities and imperfections that we carry with us from the natural world. We are then taught to feel, think and act in unison and love with thousands and millions of other beings. It takes a long time and a great deal of instruction in the world of spirits to bring some people to this degree of social development.

The harmony of souls in heaven is like that of an immense choir of music. Each has a distinct part, and each must be perfect in his part. Imagine thousands of good and pure spirits living in choirs of thought, choirs of feeling, choirs of acting; and you will begin to have a faint idea of the order, peace, beauty and felicity of the social life in heaven.

New-comers into the world of spirits are always anxious to be admitted into heaven. There is a process by which they can be elevated into heavenly societies, and shown the wonders and glories of the celestial life. This favor is extended to all, and their legitimate curiosity is gratified. They then return into the world of spirits for judgment and preparation, and to undergo those organic changes which are necessary to a permanent residence in the higher spheres.

I was delighted to hear my father say that I had been unconsciously prepared for this wonderful journey. Walking along with a glad heart, engaged in pleasant conversation about the difference between the world of spirits and heaven, I suddenly perceived a beautiful road ascending a mountain deeply shaded with overhanging trees and bordered with brilliant flowers.

"This is our way," said my father. "The roads which lead out of the world of spirits, either up into heaven or down into hell, are invisible to all but those who have been prepared to follow them. There is no danger of any one going astray. No mistakes are made here; no revelations but to the proper parties. All the art and cunning of Simon Magus or his master demons could not enable them to discover this little road leading up into the heaven where our loved ones reside."

How easy, how buoyant, how charming was that ascent! No fatigue, no hurry, no impatience, no terrestrial sensations. Our bodies seemed to grow lighter and stronger, and our minds clearer and happier as we ascended. The air grew fresher and sweeter; the trees and flowers more beautiful; the sky softer and more brilliant. As we neared the summit we saw the most exquisite green lawns and terraces, which seemed to have been dipped in a golden ether. Here and there was a flock of sheep. Now a swarm of pearl and crimson butterflies would sport around us; and then a flock of birds like little flying rainbows would illumine the air.

"These things," said my father, "are typical of the thoughts and affections of the blessed people whose homes we are approaching."

The vista from the summit exceeded in magnificence and beauty everything I had ever imagined. There were two interminable series of green knolls, one on the right hand and the other on the left, separated by a charming little valley with the softest, brightest verdure I had ever seen. On every knoll was a resplendent palace built of precious stones. The grand rainbow-like illumination produced by these mineral splendors flashing in the sun, is altogether indescribable. Away in the east where the palaces seemed to approach each other, the view was terminated by a great temple resembling the temple at Jerusalem, and shining like a gem in the distance.

The valley between these palaces was laid out in lawns, parks and gardens, adorned with flowers, statues, fountains, lakes, and picturesque walks and arbors. These things are common enough on earth; but here each of them exceeded the corresponding earthly form in all the elements of artistic beauty, as much as the most precious diamond in the world exceeds the commonest pebble on the sea-shore.

This was the heaven of a society of angels, all belonging to the tribe of Benjamin, and all interiorly united by similar thoughts and affections. Now for the first time I learned that all angels were once men upon our earth or some other; that the physical universe is the indestructible basis of the spiritual; and that all things first receive root and form and substance in the former, to rise and expand indefinitely, in the latter. The earth is the footstool of the Lord, and is established for ever.

I now noticed that I had on different garments from those I had worn in the world of spirits, and much more beautiful.

"These garments are given you," said my father, "to adapt you to the sphere which you have entered. We are clothed here imperceptibly to ourselves, as the trees and flowers in the natural world are clothed with forms and colors by a generous nature. All our external things arise spontaneously around us, without our thought or care or labor, being perfect correspondences and mirrors of the things within us."

"Here is the home of your brother," said he; and we stood before a palace of marvelous splendor. Twelve steps of lustrous pearl led up to a grand piazza covered with a dazzling arch and supported by twelve columns of gold. We entered the spacious hall, and before I had time to observe its beauties, a youthful spirit advanced, strongly resembling my father; and with a face full of light and love, and a voice overflowing with kindness, welcomed me to that little spot, as he called it, of the Lord's spiritual kingdom.

"You shall see me as I used to be," he said "and then you will know me better."

Thereupon he underwent the same series of spiritual changes by which my father revealed himself to me as the poor old leper of the wilderness. He returned into the states and forms of his boyhood, as a full-blown rose might shut, leaf after leaf, contracting itself slowly into a beautiful bud again. He was the same little Samuel who sported with my sisters and myself in our garden in Bethany, and whose withdrawal from us had left so dark a cloud on the sunny places of our childhood.

Reassuming his angelic form while I gazed at him with admiration and joy, he pointed to a chamber, the half-open door of which was one superb crystal. From it there issued a beautiful female form, clad in a silk robe of lustrous white. Her face was radiant with smiles and beauty, and a single rose was in her hair. The extreme gentleness and gracefulness of her movements, her manners, her tones, revealed the pure soul of this bright angel.

"Behold my wife!" said my brother.

Bewildered and delighted, I pressed timidly a brotherly kiss upon her cheek, and said:

"This is to me the greatest wonder of all in this realm of wonders. Married in heaven! Husbands and wives living together in wedded bliss! Enlighten my darkness; tell me something of this great and beautiful mystery."

"I perceive," said my brother, seriously, "by the glance of your eye and the tone of your voice, that you cannot yet be initiated into the sublime and heavenly secrets of the spiritual marriage. You have not been sufficiently divested of your earthly and sensuous state of thought to penetrate those truths which are only visible in the light of heaven. Be satisfied for the present to know that sex and marriage are universal and eternal; that love is inextinguishable, and becomes purer and holier the higher it rises; and that conjugal pairs live together in heaven in eternal youth and eternal bliss."

"A most delightful and ennobling thought," said I; "and I am willing to believe what you say, and to wait my own spiritual development before being able to comprehend its meaning."

I was then seized with an intense desire to see my mother. And lo! before I could give it utterance in words, she appeared before us, an angel as young and beautiful as my sister-in-law, but grown the female counterpart of my father by long and loving contemplation of his virtues.

"I was attracted hither," she exclaimed, in charming trepidation, "by strange gushes of maternal feeling. Who is it that calls me?"

Mother and child passed simultaneously into the old forms of the earth-life, and into the long dormant states of the natural memory. She was a Jewish matron in Bethany, and I a little boy of five years old. How frantically she kissed my face and hands! How madly she pressed me to her heart! How we wept together!

When we came back to our last form and state, she exclaimed, still weeping for joy:

"Oh that I could see you continually in that charming little shape! I shall make you resume it over and over again, until I satisfy my hungry heart with the graces of your boyish form. Ah! nothing is lost. All is given back to us."

We discoursed on a thousand topics, and floods of spiritual light were poured upon my benighted, undeveloped mind. Walking with these angelic friends on the grand piazza of the palace, and gazing at the architectural grandeur which surrounded us, I was filled with an exhilaration of spirits too great for earthly utterance, never to be comprehended by any one until he meets his friends, whom he calls dead, in the divine light of the heavenly world.

When I new recall these things, poor, old, desolate, heartbroken man that I am, bearing my earthly burdens again and doomed to another death, they all seem to me like a delightful dream! That I walked and talked with friends in heaven! surveyed their houses! discussed their laws, their government, their worship, their occupations, face to face as man with man! Impossible! Incredible!

What did I say?

It was no dream. It was no hallucination. It is possible. It is credible. It was a fact. My memory does not betray me. My imagination does not mislead me. It was all true; and I shall see them, hear them, live with them again, never to return to earth, so soon as I once more give up this mortal breath and render this feeble body back to the dust whence it came.

How long, O Lord! how long?

I learned from my brother that the societies in heaven, which are innumerable, are arranged according to the uses they perform, which depend upon the bent of the inclinations and the expansion of the intellectual faculties of those who compose them. Men on earth receive their vitalizing impulses, their attractions to all that is good and true, from these societies through the medium of good spirits in the intermediate world.

Some of these societies inspire the love of nature and art; some the genius and power for civil government; some the taste for science and practical life. Some animate especially the devotional nature; some the social; some the poetic; and others, again, act as intermediate powers, balancing and harmonizing the different activities of the soul.

The society to which my brother belonged was one which presided over and secretly vivified the architectural tastes and genius of man. Near by, upon mountains whose purple summits I saw in the distance, was a large society which presided over music. Great societies which were the secret life and soul of poetry, history, oratory, statuary, painting and other fine arts, were grouped around, more or less remote, all holding the most delightful communications and interchanges with each other.

I was astonished to learn that the peace and joy and highest happiness of the angels spring from the exercise of their faculties in the performance of useful service to each other. They are never idle, but continually engaged in doing something useful from the love of use. I learned that in this the angels find their chief delight; and that, although they occasionally meet for formal and social worship, and unite in prayer and songs of praise as people do on earth, they nevertheless regard the loving and faithful performance of the duties of their respective vocations as the highest kind of worship. This they call *real* worship; and the *formal* kind in which they sometimes engage, is merely to fit them for the higher and more real kind.

"Do you ever see your earthly friends," I asked, "struggling and toiling in the dark abyss of nature, before they cast off their earthly covering and rise into the light and beauty of these higher worlds?"

"Not directly!" replied my brother, "for there is no continuity between spirit and matter. To speak philosophically, there is continuity and correspondence; but spirit and matter are not degrees of the same substance, differing only in tenuity, as is commonly supposed. It is impossible for us to see or hear anything in the natural world, except through the medium of some living man whose interiors have also been opened.

"Wonderful as it may seem to you, the spirits of men still living in the flesh are really in the spiritual world, all the time connected secretly with spiritual societies. They are invisible to us, however, because their thoughts, affections and senses all open downward and outward into nature. They become dimly visible, but do not communicate, when they are in states of profound abstraction or great spiritual elevation.

"We see them occasionally also by correspondences, which would appear to you like visions or dreams. In every society these manifestations are different, depending on the nature and functions of the society. In ours, for instance, the mental states of our earthly friends are sometimes revealed to us architecturally. That is, we see them as in a dream building houses: and without knowing their names or earthly whereabouts, we judge of their characters by the materials, the progress, the execution, even to the minutest details of the work they seem to be doing."

"Wonderful and beautiful!" I exclaimed.

"I can show you this wonderful thing more easily than I can explain it. We have here the power, incomprehensible to you at present, of recalling these symbolic images and making them appear before us again, as if they were external and real things.

"Look," he said, and the horizon toward the north seemed overcast. A thin veil of mist arose before us, and through it we discovered a dim range of hills, upon each of which a house was in process of erection.

"Every man in the flesh," said my brother, "is always engaged, unconsciously to himself, in building his future house in the spiritual world; for the entire spiritual life of a man is represented symbolically by his residence here and its appointments. All the activities of your hands, heart and brain in the good and true things of the earthly state, are so many contributions to the materials, style, form, color and finish of your eternal home.

"Observe," he continued, "that some of those houses are nearly finished, others are barely begun. Some of them are in styles of great grandeur, others are very plain. The materials, too, and the execution differ immensely.

Observe also that a man alone is at work on some; a man and a woman on others."

"Why is that?"

"When a man and woman are truly married, they assist each other in building the same house; for they will live together as husband and wife for ever in heaven. Sometimes persons not married in the world, are seen working together here. Such persons have strong interior affinities, unknown it may be to each other on earth, and will be united in heaven."

"Strange and beautiful!" said I.

"And true!" he exclaimed, earnestly. "The true is always strange and beautiful.

"If you will look closely," he continued, "you will see many faint and shadowy forms that are earnestly assisting these men and women in carrying the heavy materials and putting everything into its proper place. These are attendant good spirits invisible to the workers themselves. When a house is finished, we know that the architect has been released from the bondage of the earth-life, and will soon occupy the same house vastly beautified and glorified in some heavenly society."

Thus are spiritual houses—houses not made with hands, eternal in the heavens—builded by our prayers, our faith, our hopes, our loving thoughts, our useful and unselfish deeds.

"I see some houses," I remarked, "upon which no one is working. They seem to be falling to decay."

"The builders have been led away into temptation by evil spirits. The work of regeneration appears to be arrested or retroceding. The Lord will lead them by ways they know not, and they will renew their labors."

While gazing at this strange scene and scrutinizing these shadowy architects of future homes, I suddenly recognized my own figure toiling along under a great beam which was to constitute one of the door-posts on the ground-floor. My house was scarcely begun.

"See, brother," said I, "I have passed into the spiritual world and my house is not finished."

"I never saw it so before," he said. "I would say confidently from this, that your earthly mission is not ended."

While he was speaking, my attention was arrested by a woman in a black robe on the side of the hill opposite to where my own figure was. This woman was bent almost to the earth under a great block of stone, which she was bearing to put into the walls. Several shadowy forms were busy around her assisting in the difficult task.

"And that woman?" said I.

"Is probably your future wife."

An insatiable desire immediately seized me to behold her face. Forgetting my painful experience in the imaginary heaven of the Greeks, I thought only of Helena.

"It is she," said I, to myself. "She is a pagan. She is surrounded by evil spheres. She is unregenerate. Her regeneration will be painful and difficult. The good angels are assisting her. The foundations of our house are laid; the structure will rise; the joint work of our secretly united souls. I always knew it and felt it. It cannot be otherwise!"

In this ecstasy of thought I watched the bowed figure in the black robe.

"Oh that Helena could see and know that I am with her and she with me, laying the invisible foundations of our eternal home! What felicity that would be! Let me speak to her! Let me see her face!"

The intense desire of a strong will is at once granted in the spiritual world. The woman in the black robe slowly raised her eyes to heaven and turned her face toward me.

It was the pale, sorrowing face of Mary Magdalen!

Mary Magdalen!

The blood all seemed to rush back upon my heart, and I stood with a chilling, suffocating sense of disappointment hard to describe. But the loss of Helena, grievous as it was, was not the only ingredient in my cup. There was vexation as well as disappointment. A deep sense of mortification overpowered me at the substitution of Mary Magdalen, a woman without character or friends, recently possessed of seven devils—a creature miserable, outcast, forlorn.

Secret feelings of social superiority, self-righteousness, and offended dignity, embodied themselves in my exclamation of contempt:

"Mary Magdalen!"

I brought upon myself immediately the operation of one of those spiritual laws which excite so much astonishment in the new-comer. My angelic friends were total strangers to earthly passions, to the frenzy of love, the rage of disappointment, the sentiment of superiority, the feeling of contempt. Loving all alike with infinite tenderness and pity, the angels of God do not see any difference between the self-righteous saint and the audacious sinner.

My outburst of unregenerate passion separated me at once from my heavenly companions. It appeared to them that the ground opened and swallowed me up. They no doubt exclaimed to each other:

"Poor fellow! He is not yet prepared to enter upon the heavenly life. We will wait on the Lord, who bringeth all things to pass."

My sensations were different. The architectural heavens of the tribe of Benjamin vanished from my sight; all was dark for a moment; and, remitted into my former state, I found myself in the world of spirits just where I had been raised from the dead.

My faithful friend John the Baptist was near me, and extended his generous hand.

"Have I visited heaven," said I, "or have I been dreaming?"

XXI
THE SPIRITUALLY DEAD

"You now understand," said my father, who had rejoined us, "the spiritual law which separates heaven from hell. Similarity of mental states produces presence; dissimilarity separates. Societies are held together by the cohesive power of spiritual affinity. In heaven they are all in perfect light and perfect peace, because they all obey the spiritual attractions of the Sun of heaven, which is the Lord."

"Heaven, then," said I, "is open to all, but none can live there save those who are as good and wise as its inhabitants?"

"Precisely so. Whenever a false or sensual idea arises in the mind of the new-comer, or some unrighteous feeling is aroused in his heart, he disappears from his heavenly associates and they from him."

"How then can one be prepared for heaven?" asked I, sadly; "for it seems that I am very, very far from that state of perfection."

"One is prepared for heaven by his life on earth. The life of a man is the aggregate of his loves. The state of the heart determines the hereafter. It is the intellect only which is anxious about many things—many dogmas, many creeds, many questions. To the heart there is but one thing needful, one care, one duty—to cast out the love of self, or duly subordinate it to the love of the Lord and the neighbor.

"Kindly feeling toward the neighbor, acts of civility and charity unconnected with the hope of reward, deeds of self-sacrifice, generous emotions, pure affections, the spirit of forgiveness, reverence for God, obedience to law, humility, patience; these are the angels of the heart and the powers which build up the heavenly character in the soul, and the future heavenly world in which it resides."

"My life upon earth is then a poor warrant of a life in heaven," I answered pensively. "I do not know that I have any faith at all. I have no purified motives, no fixed principles. I have no love for spiritual things. I have a certain taste for the true and beautiful, a certain admiration for the pure and good. I am kind and affectionate by hereditary organization; but I have never thought of devoting myself to the good of others. No aspirations beyond the sensuous life have been kindled in my soul."

"Do not despair, my son. You have, without doubt, the basis on which the heavenly superstructure can be reared. Your house in the heavens was not finished, but it was begun. You will pass through various stages of instruction, and even through trials and sufferings in the world of spirits."

"And in the world of nature also, where his period of probation will be extended for many years to come," added John the Baptist.

As we both looked to him anxiously for an explanation of these singular words, he continued:

"As the herald of the Lord, forerunning His work in the world of spirits as I did in the natural world, I have become acquainted with an extraordinary fact, which it is my business here to announce. You are to leave us and return into your natural body. You disappeared from your earthly friends and became visible to us; you will now disappear from us and become visible to them. Christ will recall you from the dead after your body has lain four days in the grave. You will be the subject of a great miracle of the Lord; and your story will animate the faith and hope and love of the Church in all ages of the world."

I was bewildered at these words.

"How can I return into nature?" said I. "How can I get back into the natural body? How can I die here when there is no death?"

"The difficulties which seem to you impossibilities," said John, "are easily met. The process is perfectly intelligible from the spiritual stand-point. Attend to my elucidation of it; for it involves the true nature of miracles and of the redemptive work of the Lord.

"You understand that Christ exists consciously and actively in both worlds at the same time; in his spiritual body here, in his natural body upon earth. You know this, for you have seem Him in both spheres.

"He is performing a series of divine works in both worlds at once; and a wonderful parallelism exists between his works here and his works there. What he does in this sphere is repeated in that in a different but corresponding form.

"This is the world of causes, that is the world of effects. There is no effect without a cause. It seems to men in the flesh that the miracles of Jesus are performed by his word alone—by the breath of his mouth. That is a mistake. They are the natural effects of spiritual causes. Jesus is engaged in this world of spirits in instituting a series of causes which are to produce certain natural effects; among them, his benevolent works called miracles.

"Miracles are not violations of natural law. They are only proofs that spiritual or divine forces govern in all the transformations of matter. They teach men the true source and origin of causes, and the true relation between the spiritual and natural worlds. All things are miracles. They are only wonderful when the events are new, extraordinary, not understood, or misinterpreted.

"Christ could not restore natural sight to a blind man, unless he excited into activity those spiritual causes which produce both spiritual and natural sight. Imparting spiritual light or wisdom to the spiritually blind in this world, he originates a force which, passing through his own natural body, restores vision to the correspondingly blind man on the earth upon whom he lays his hands.

"He here infuses moral vigor into souls who had lost the power of performing their spiritual duties. This becomes a cause producing a corresponding effect upon earth; namely, that the touch even of the hem of his garment will restore muscular strength and will to the paralytic.

"When the Divine Man resists and subdues the evil spirits who would destroy him, the natural effect is, that He stills the tempest and treads upon the waves,—that even the winds and the seas obey him.

"When he preaches spiritual truth to those who have never risen above the perception of natural things, and their minds are lifted from the natural to the spiritual degree of thought, the natural effect is, that he turns water into wine.

"So of all his miracles, even that of raising the dead. When he imparts spiritual life here to those who are spiritually dead, he sets in operation a spiritual cause which imparts life again to those who are dead in the natural sense.

"Such is the spiritual philosophy of miracles, which men in their ignorance suppose to be contraventions of natural law, designed to prove the possession of divine power. God violates no law either spiritual or natural. He is Law itself. It would be a contravention of the eternal organic law if miracles did not ensue, after the institution of their specific causes in the world of spirits."

"You draw indeed," said I, "a wonderful and beautiful parallel between the spiritual and the natural works of Christ. It is clear that the biography of the Divine Man can only be written from the spiritual side. I understand also, in some measure, your philosophy of miracles; still I do not perceive how I am to get back into the natural world."

"I will make it plain to you presently. When you come within the power of an evil sphere, it endeavors to absorb your individuality, and to assimilate you entirely to itself. If you approach the sphere of spiritual pride and self-righteousness, unless you are under divine protection, you will become proud and self-righteous. Approach the sphere of ambition, and you become fired with the insatiable lust of dominion. Approach the sphere of sensuality, and your heart, blood, brain, are all set on fire with hell.

"Such is the contagion of evil. Contagion, whether moral or physical, is simply the influence of spheres—the imposition of one's state upon another—the transference of conditions.

"Now if under certain circumstances you enter the evil spheres of this world, you will be reduced to the state of the spiritually blind, deaf, dumb, paralytic or dead as the case may be. You will then be connected interiorly and by correspondence with the blind, deaf, dumb, paralytic or dead, in the natural world. Do you not see?"

"Go on," said I, following with deep interest the chain of his reasoning.

"Well, you will descend among these people whom we call the spiritually dead. You will enter into their spiritual state. Your spiritual body will be then reconnected by correspondence with your natural body now lying in the sepulchre; all without your co-operation, without your consciousness."

"Well—and then what?"

"When Christ in his judgment approaches the sphere of those who are spiritually dead, he will cast out the evil spirits who possess them. Spiritual life will begin to dawn on their souls. Both spiritual and natural life will spring up for you simultaneously."

"Why for me alone? Why will not *their* dead bodies also arise?"

"Because their connection with nature has been long and totally sundered. On the contrary, you have still a natural body not yet disorganized; indeed, preserved by special providence for your resumption at the proper moment—thus manifesting the power and glory of God.

"Your spiritual companions will be delivered from their bondage to hell, and will emerge into the activities of spiritual life. You will be correspondently delivered from the bondage of hell and the grave; and will be raised from the dead and restored to your friends in Judea."

I contemplated with awe the extraordinary fate that awaited me. I felt some reluctance at leaving a sphere so bright and beautiful, where I had been initiated by such charming friends into high and holy truths. I felt deeply convinced, however, that I was unprepared for heaven, and was grateful for a more extended probation on earth. An encouragement also to resignation was the thought that I was going back to comfort and protect my loving and lovely sisters, Martha and Mary.

"But these people who are spiritually dead," said I. "Are their corpses here, also, and sepulchres and monumental inscriptions?"

"Oh no!" said my father, who took up the conversation; "you are now thinking from your natural stand-point. The spiritually blind are those who are blind to spiritual things. The spiritually dead are those who are dead to spiritual things. They comprise an innumerable multitude of souls who have lived a merely sensual life, and who have no knowledge or love of anything higher or better or purer than the wretched existence they led in the life of nature."

During this conversation we had been advancing toward the north. We came now to the brow of a great hill, whence the country sloped suddenly downward and spread into a vast plain. It had a cheerless and wintry aspect; for the cities and villages and fields were all covered with snow. Afar off along the line of the horizon was a dim blue ocean, full of icebergs of enormous size. A gray twilight hung over this cold region, the darkness of which was occasionally illumined by electric flashes in the sky.

"There are spiritual as well as natural zones," said my father—"zones of thought and affection, in which the heat and light vary in intensity according to the interior states of the dwellers. Cold and darkness arise always in this world from the want of spiritual heat and light, which are love and wisdom.

"Here we take our adieu," he continued, in a tone which revealed a touch of sadness. "That great light just rising in the east and south indicates the approach of the Lord with all his hosts of ministering angels and spirits. His presence will disperse the demons of darkness, who have so long sat like ghouls upon the hearts of myriads of feeble and helpless beings.

"Ah! how the love and faith of the Church in heaven have watched over these dead souls! and have wept and prayed for them, like two lovely sisters weeping and praying over the body of a dead brother! How have they longed for this day of the Lord, and how have they wondered, sorrowing, that He has so long delayed his coming!

"He comes! He who is the resurrection and the life! and these dry bones shall live; these dead souls from all pagan lands shall come out of their graves; and the power of death and hell shall be overthrown!

"Descend, my son, into the grave that leads you back into life."

My spirit-friends now bade me a tender adieu, pronouncing benedictions upon me and speaking words of encouragement. Bewildered and amazed, wondering and fearing what would happen next, I went down the steep slope toward the cold and silent plain. As I moved along, a great change came over my spirit. There was a perceptible closure of some window from above, through which the vital currents descend into the soul. This was followed by a loss of memory, a vanishing of thought, a sense of fainting or death.

The last thing I remember was the music of a sweet hymn wafted softly from the brow of the hill. The words were these:

"Yea, though I walk through the valley of the shadow of death, I will fear no evil."

It was my father and John the Baptist comforting to the last the forlorn spirit that was sinking in the waters of Lethe.

Of what occurred after I reached the plain, I have not the slightest recollection, if indeed I ever knew. What kind of people I saw, what they were doing, what Christ and his angels did, what changes followed—all is a perfect blank to me. I cannot account for this fact. It will all be made plain to me when I ascend again into the spiritual world. Certain it is, that a sublime scene of judgment and deliverance took place, but that it did not come within the range of my consciousness.

The first thing I became aware of, was a sense of infinite pity. I did not know whether I was in the spiritual or in the natural world. I was flooded with a vast, deep, boundless spirit of compassion. I wept—I did not know why. This was the communication to my soul of the life flowing from the Divine Man.

"Jesus wept."

He was not only weeping for me, as the Jews supposed who witnessed the external side alone of this wonderful scene. The loving heart of the Divine Being was touched with infinite, celestial pity for the innumerable multitude of the spiritually dead. It was a drop of that infinite pity which stirred my soul from the sleep of death. It was a drop of that infinite pity which trickled down the face of Jesus, as he wept in the garden for the brother of Martha and Mary.

That communication of the divine grief to me must have come from the spiritual side of my perceptions. I passed again into a dreamy, almost unconscious state, from which I was aroused by a clear sweet voice, saying,

"Lazarus! come forth!"

I started to my feet. Blind, bound, bewildered, I staggered toward the voice. The fresh air struck sweetly on me, and I revived.

The voice continued:

"Loose him and let him go!"

Oh how many myriads of invisible but happy spirits heard at the same moment similar words of deliverance and comfort, from the omnipresent God speaking in the world of spirits as He had spoken on earth!

I was freed from the shackles of the grave and looked around me. I was in the sweet garden of Bethany, standing by the stone which had been rolled away from the sepulchre, beneath a bright and beautiful sky. A crowd of friends, with faces full of wonder and joy, were grouped around. My sisters had swooned at the feet of Jesus, who was smiling benignantly upon me.

I took in the whole situation at a glance. Remembering everything; remembering my former unbelief and indifference; remembering the wonderful scenes I had witnessed; remembering Jesus in his spiritual body, seen also by the three disciples on the mount; remembering his divine character, his warfare with hell, his judgments, his mercies; and now understanding in part the divine mystery of the incarnation; I knelt at his feet in the deepest humility and the most undoubting faith, exclaiming,

"My Lord and my God!"

XXII
BACK TO EARTH

I was borne to my bed-chamber by my friends; for I was not able to walk. The curious crowd followed us to the gate, but very few persons were admitted into the house. They judiciously forebore attempting to converse with me, and I fell immediately into a refreshing sleep.

When I awoke my sisters were ready with stimulants and nourishment. Looking up into their sweet, eager, happy faces, I found stimulus and nourishment of a higher kind.

"Back in the world again!" I exclaimed, as soon as I could breathe for the kisses they were showering upon me.

"Yes—raised from the dead!" said Martha; "Praise be to the Son of God!"

"Raised from the dead!" echoed Mary with deep solemnity, her voice faltering with emotion.

Trying to recall what had happened, I was struck with a curious impression which had been left on my mind. It was the impression that a very long time—months, years, many years, had elapsed since I died. I had passed through so many wonderful states, had seen so many astounding things, and been initiated into so many spiritual mysteries, that when I came to think of them from my earthly stand-point, it seemed impossible that so much experience could have been crowded into a few days.

"If this be really Lazarus," said I aloud, "he ought to be a gray-headed old man, and his sisters wrinkled old women; for surely many years have passed since he fell sick in Bethany."

The words disquieted my sisters, who were afraid of returning delirium. They enjoined upon me absolute silence on the plea of my great weakness. So I lay upon my couch, looking alternately out of the two windows of my room. One of them opened upon the inner courtyard with its little fountain of water, as beautiful to my eyes as if it had been a great column of crystal. From the other I saw the summit of the Mount of Olives, beyond which lay the Holy City, concealed as heaven is concealed from us by the intervening heights of our earthly passions.

Mary sat near me engaged on some fine needlework; Martha at a little table close by, poring over a beautiful golden-clasped parchment of the Psalms of David. They occasionally lifted their eyes with watchful interest to my face. It was a soothing pleasure to contemplate these lovely women. There was a soft, pure, heavenly atmosphere about them, which reminded me of the heaven I had left; and I understood the words of the Psalmist, that man was created only a little lower than the angels.

"Where is Jesus, our benefactor?" I inquired, breaking through their injunction to keep silence.

"Gone into Jerusalem," was the reply.

"If our good father was here," said I, "he would tell us what great change in the world of spirits was coming next; for every movement of Jesus on earth is significative of wonderful things going on in the sphere above us. But alas! from this earthly point of view, all is darkness!"

The startled expression of my sisters' faces showed that they thought my mind was wandering. They only replied by putting their fingers warningly upon their lips.

So I shut my eyes and addressed myself to sleep again; but pictures from that museum of Art which memory builds for us all, came floating before me. Mary standing silent and downcast at the mouth of the deserted cave; the Son of the Desert, the zebra of my vision, wearing in his wild life the ring which Martha had given him; Ethopus parting with his treasure to rescue his brother; the haughty stare of the guests of Hortensius in the Hall of Apollo; Helena, the beautiful, leaning against the emerald tree and clapping her hands at the drunken Bacchus; Mary Magdalen toiling up the hill under the terrible load, and comforted by invisible spirits; the great snow-fields and ice-mountains of the spiritually dead, whom I felt but did not see; all these things and many more passed and repassed before my mind's eye, until, lulled as if by the ceaseless patter of rain, I fell a second time into a deep slumber.

I was thoroughly restored when I awoke the next morning. I immediately repeated the Lord's Prayer after my father's example; and entered, upon the first page of the book of my new life, a firm resolution to prepare my soul by faith and obedience for an eternal home in the heaven I had visited, but for which I was yet unfit.

As my strength increased I gave audience to my friends—to very few at first; but recovering day by day, I soon had the house thrown open to all who wished to examine for themselves the facts in evidence of the great miracle.

The story had gone far and wide. The death, the burial, the four days in the grave, and the resurrection, were all susceptible of positive proof. There were scores of intelligent and truthful witnesses on every point. Crowds of people came to see the house, to inspect the grave, and to converse with me. I was examined and cross-examined by Scribes and Pharisees, by Jews and Greeks, by Romans and Egyptians, by infidels and disciples.

I soon discovered that, although everybody was intensely interested in the story of my sensations when dying and when coming to life again, very few appeared to be long entertained by my wonderful experiences in the world of spirits. They seemed instinctively to refer all my statements on that point to the class of dreams and visions.

At first I was astonished and even annoyed at this indifference and unbelief. But I soon learned that man at present is so immersed in the life of the senses, that faith in a spiritual world is more nominal than real; a faith so vague, shadowy and fanciful, that he will not accept as true any positive statements about the spiritual world.

Men yearn for the great veil to be lifted; to communicate with departed friends; to see the patriarchs and prophets; to learn the mysteries of the heavenly kingdom. Oh that some one, say they, could return from the unseen world and tell us all about these things! With what solemnity would we listen to his words! with what joy! with what faith!

They are the victims of delusion. If their dearest friends were raised from the dead after a year's burial, they would find themselves disappointed. They would regard them at first with wonder and awe. They would believe until they began speaking. But when they described the resurrection which happens to all as it did to me; when they taught the doctrine of a spiritual body; the reality and substantiality of the spiritual world; the civil, social and religious life of heaven; doubt after doubt would crowd upon their minds, until they would reject the whole story as a dream or a fabrication.

Christ himself declared that the appearance of one from the dead would convince no man. It is a strange declaration, but my own case is evidence of its truth.

The grounds upon which the incredulity of my visitors was based, were of the most contradictory and sometimes of the most irrational nature. One disbelieved because I had not seen Abraham, Isaac and Jacob; and because I declared that no earthly names exist in heaven, and that respect is there entertained, not for persons, but for character or quality. Another doubted my report because I said that David was not king of all the Jews in the spiritual world.

One man, a great patriot, was indignant because I affirmed that all the Romans did not go to hell. Another, equally zealous for Judea, was personally abusive because I declared that more people were saved from the pagan or gentile nations than from the Jewish Church. Another was shocked because I said the angels were not always engaged in singing and praising God. Another, an ideologist, scouted the idea that there was any form, shape or substance to the soul, or even in the spiritual world.

The most ignorant and conceited of the Scribes and Pharisees denounced me bitterly as teaching doctrines utterly at variance with Scripture and subversive of the interests of vital religion. On the other extreme, our worthy old Greek gardener laughed at my narrative as a tissue of hallucinations, because I had not been rowed over the river Styx by Charon the ferryman, but honestly declared that I had seen neither Charon nor the Stygian river.

The majority insisted that I had not been dead at all; that my condition was only a trance, which had often occurred before, and had been prolonged to even a greater period. To this the Pharisees added, that it was no doubt a trick of magic in which I was guilty of collusion, and which was designed to extend the fame and influence of Jesus of Nazareth.

Some believed in the fact of my resurrection; and the more enthusiastic went so far as to affirm that my body had been decomposed in the grave. These were actually angry with me when I declared that, although I was so far dead as to be living consciously in another world, yet my separation from nature was not organic and final, my natural body being preserved in a peculiar manner for a reunion with its spiritual form.

I soon became wearied and disgusted with unprofitable discussions, and with credulities and incredulities equally absurd. Failing to convince my hearers, or to elevate their minds into the heavenly light which I myself enjoyed, I became more and more reserved; and at last I would not speak on the subject to any one but Mary and Martha.

These dear women listened with unfailing delight to all I had to say. The divine intuitions of woman recognize always a new truth before the calculating reason of man endorses it. Martha indeed doubted occasionally and criticised sharply, but was always satisfied after consulting the Scriptures and comparing what I related with their sacred teachings. Mary, full of love and trust, believed unquestioningly every word I said.

When the crowd was greatest and the excitement highest, our old enemy Magistus, assuming the garb of friendship, came to see me. He had heard of my death with great pleasure, for he expected to regain possession of the property and of my sisters. He was at heart greatly incensed at my return to life, and vowed to wreak his vengeance on the Divine Man who raised me from the dead.

He entered with affected friendliness of manner, and congratulated me on my happy escape from the world of shadows. He hoped, with sanctimonious earnestness, that after this solemn warning, I would discard all my pagan ideas and proclivities, and consecrate my whole soul to the service of the only true and living God.

I told him that I was rather to be pitied than congratulated on returning to a world so vastly inferior in beauty, peace, and joy to the one I had visited. I told him also that I had been instructed in the true doctrine of God in the world of spirits, and that I had seen the terrible dangers which were impending over the Jewish people and church on account of the blindness and wickedness of their hearts.

"You will be delighted to hear," I continued, "that my guide and instructor was my beloved father, who passed from the wilderness into heaven, exchanging a poor leprous body for the radiant form of an angel."

Whether my looks and tones displeased him, or my statements aroused his anger; or whether the sphere of truth, like the revealing light of heaven, compelled him to show himself in his true colors; Magistus dropped the mask, scowled upon me with a face full of hateful passion, and retired, turning at the door to exclaim:

"Beware, young man! lest this pretended resurrection prove the cause of your real death."

I had hardly felt myself in full and healthful possession of my natural body again, when I made inquiries after that beautiful and fascinating woman, the love of whom, unrequited and consuming, had been the principal cause of my death. One might suppose that after my strange experience with Helena or her attendant demon—an experience seemingly designed to apprise me of her true character—she would have been the last person on earth I desired to see.

Alas! it was not so. The enchantments of the senses strike deep into the soul. The dream of love first engendered in the fervid brain of youth is not easily forgotten. Her beautiful face and bewitching figure were constantly before me. And it was with the deepest anguish that I heard she had fled from her father and friends, and had gone down into Egypt with Simon Magus.

I found it impossible to turn my thoughts from this Greek siren whose own evil passions had thus borne her out of my reach, and to concentrate them upon that other woman whom Providence had decreed to be my eternal partner, and who was silently, painfully, unconsciously, co-operating with me in building that palace in the architectural heaven of my tribe.

Mary Magdalen followed Jesus as usual, and came occasionally with the crowd into the front courtyard of our house. The love of Helena so preoccupied my thoughts and desires, that I could not make up my mind to speak to her forlorn rival, or to invite her into the guest-chamber with the other disciples. So the future wife of my soul stood without among the unwelcomed crowd, outcast, solitary, unfriended, patiently bearing the burden of life for both herself and me.

Jesus spent his evenings at our house, until the violent spirit of the chief Priests and Scribes, on account of my resurrection, became so apparent, that he withdrew for a season to Ephraim, where he had several devoted followers. He passed the time in pleasant conversation with his disciples, or in reading and expounding to us the Scriptures.

With what eyes and thoughts, different from the others, did I now regard this Divine Being, seated as a man among men—among the creatures of his own breath! My spiritual experiences with regard to Him had cast a spell of silence and awe upon my soul. I could not speak to Jesus as before. In his presence I could scarcely speak at all. Sometimes I found it impossible to lift my eyes to his face. While the others ate and chatted respectfully but familiarly with this Divine Man, knowing Him only as a man, I sat silent and reverential, my heart humbled in the dust before Him, thinking of the great golden light which preceded Him in the world of spirits, and of his divine face shining like a sun upon the angels of the celestial heaven.

XXIII
IMPRISONED

Jesus at length came up from Ephraim and prepared for that triumphal entry into Jerusalem which aroused the animosity of the Sanhedrim to the highest pitch, and gave color to the charge which they brought against him, that he meditated a political conspiracy and sought the temporal authority and kingdom of Judea.

Many, indeed, of his ignorant followers expected him to seize the reins of civil government, and to maintain his position by miraculous power. Then they supposed he would raise Jerusalem and the Jewish people to the pinnacle of earthly glory. These boasted openly of their expectations; and the chief priests and rulers no doubt congratulated themselves, in their subsequent proceedings, that they were extinguishing a false religion and a civil war by the same energetic blow.

On the eve before this entry into Jerusalem my sisters gave a supper to Jesus and his disciples. It was a brilliant and beautiful scene, crowned, however, with a certain solemnity and sadness; for the great events about to transpire cast shadows before them which fell upon every heart. It was there that my sister Mary drew forth, from a golden box which had been given her by our good uncle Beltrezzor, a costly Persian ointment and anointed the feet of Jesus. Judas Iscariot reproved her conduct as extravagant; and Jesus responded that she was anointing him for his burial. This prediction of death on the eve of apparent triumph and glory, bewildered the minds and saddened the hearts of his hearers.

If I had known at that moment, upon what a frightful precipice I was standing, and what lifelong tribulation awaited me, I would have been the saddest of them all. But the skeleton stands invisible at our feasts, and the serpent coils undiscovered among the flowers.

Jesus, with his favorite disciples, Peter, James and John, lodged at our dwelling; but most of the guests returned to Jerusalem at a late hour. I accompanied them through the grove which crowned the Mount of Olives, and down the western slope, over the spot where Jesus was afterward betrayed, and from which also he ascended to heaven. I parted with my friends at the long arched bridge which crosses the valley and lands you near the gate of the temple called Beautiful.

As the last footsteps died away on the bridge, I turned to go back, when I was startled by the dark figure of a man advancing from behind a tree. The moon had just gone down and the wind sighed mournfully through the olive leaves. This man was Judas Iscariot.

"I have something," he said in a low tone, "of the deepest importance to reveal to you. I know your attachment to our Master. I know your discretion and your courage. I have discovered a plot against the life of Jesus. Two hirelings in the pay of the Sanhedrim, conscience-stricken, or more probably afraid of the miraculous power of Jesus, have betrayed a part of the plan. They are now underneath one of the arches of that bridge, waiting for me. I wish you to accompany me into the valley, to question these men, to satisfy yourself of the nature and extent of the danger, and to aid me with your counsel and if necessary with your arm."

I was deeply agitated at these words. I knew the animosity of the chief priests to Jesus, and I believed they would not hesitate to employ the knife of the assassin, if they could not arrest his career by a public process. I had no cause to doubt the report of Judas; but for some inexplicable reason I had a great aversion to the man.

He must have read doubt or suspicion in my manner; for he immediately exclaimed in a tone of surprise:

"Why do you hesitate? Is my word not sufficient? I have chosen you to share in this mission of honor and danger, because you are indebted to Jesus for your own life, and because he is at this moment a guest in your house. Had I communicated this to the brave Peter or the resolute James—"

"Enough!" said I, interrupting him and taking his arm; and we groped our way along the narrow path that wound down the steep hill into the valley. Reaching the level ground, Judas gave a low whistle and four men started up from behind the pillars of the bridge. One of them led a mule by the bridle. We approached them.

"Here is your man," said Judas, suddenly stepping behind me and seizing me with great strength by the shoulders. The men rushed upon me, and notwithstanding my desperate struggle they bound me hand and foot in a few seconds.

"Vile traitor!" was the only exclamation that passed my lips before they were tightly closed by a strong leathern muzzle which was strapped securely over my head and behind my neck. I was then blindfolded and put upon the mule. We moved around to one of the city gates. The passwords were given, for the party were emissaries of the Sanhedrim. We traversed the streets a good distance, when we halted and I was conducted into a house. When released from my bonds I found myself in a large stone chamber with a small iron door and two lofty, iron-grated windows.

"In prison?" I exclaimed.

Judas, who stood in the doorway, rubbed his hands with insulting glee and said:

"Your uncle Magistus pays me handsomely for this."

"If Jesus is ever murdered," said I, with indignant scorn, "you will be the murderer."

He sneered and went out. I saw him no more. Alas! I never saw the natural form of Jesus again. He who betrayed the disciple, was already bargaining for the thirty pieces of silver at which he estimated the life of his Lord.

The cause of my imprisonment was not doubtful. I had become obnoxious to the Sanhedrim from the mere fact of my resurrection. The attention it attracted, the prestige it conferred on Jesus, the increasing crowd that followed him, all annoyed and vexed them. I was a living proof of the power and glory of the new religion, a standing protest and menace against the old. It was necessary that I should be put out of the way.

I was shut out from the world; a pallet of straw for my bed; a rough table and a stool my only furniture. A fierce, silent guard brought me a daily supply of water and coarse food. I saw and heard nothing of the great sea of human life which was surging outside of my stone walls.

Several days and nights passed in this manner. What had become of my sisters? What had become of Jesus? If I had been made the first victim, surely these others would fall shortly beneath the malice and cruelty of such unscrupulous enemies. These thoughts, attended with gloomy forebodings, pressed with painful reiteration upon my mind. I could not eat. I could not sleep. I was all eye, all ear.

I was startled one night by a strange uproar in the street. I was so watchful, so quick of hearing, that I detected it a great way off. It gradually came nearer and nearer. It was a riot or street-fight or battle creeping in the direction of my prison. There were at last plainly heard shouts, groans, curses, the hurrying of feet, the clash of arms, and all the exciting accompaniments of a bloody contest between two enraged factions. From the triumphant cries and the great flare of torches which came in at my window, I perceived that one party had driven the other before it, and now occupied the ground in front of the building in which I was imprisoned.

I put the table against the wall and the stool on the table. Mounting thus to one of the windows, I could see partially what was going on in the street.

What a crowd of ruffians of all nations and colors, fantastically dressed and variously armed!

While I was gazing on this hideous rabble, a man of huge proportions rode up on a horse finely caparisoned, which had evidently been the late property of some dashing Roman officer. This man had a horribly bruised and swollen face, and an immense, dingy, yellow beard. I recognized Barabbas the robber.

"Break open the doors and release the prisoners!" he cried in a terrible voice.

Beams used like battering-rams were soon brought to bear upon the iron-barred and bolted doors, until the whole building resounded with the tremendous strokes. How my heart leaped at the thought of a speedy deliverance! I determined in the confusion to elude both parties and escape to Bethany.

At this moment a great outcry arose: "The Romans! The Romans!" and the swift clatter of horses' feet and the renewal of all the sounds of a fierce fight, assured me that the rioters had been attacked by a squadron of Roman cavalry.

Suddenly I heard a loud, clear, sweet voice shouting with wild enthusiasm:

"Death to the Romans!"

"Freedom to Judea!"

I recognized the familiar tones before I discovered the tall figure of the Son of the Desert.

He was bare-headed, and his fine bronzed face, his scimitar and his crimson scarf gleamed in the torchlight as he rushed bravely forward. Anthony, my old servant, was at his side, watching his movements with admiration and echoing his words. The Son of the Desert was bringing up a large party of stalwart fellows, armed with pikes and scimitars, to meet the advancing column of horse.

I called to him loudly, waving my arms eagerly between the bars. At that moment a strong pressure backward from the front, held the party stationary for a second. My old friend looked up at my window surprised, and smiled his recognition. He kissed his hand to me and pointed to the ring on his finger which Martha had given him. Anthony also recognized me, and saluted me with frantic gestures and every demonstration of childish joy.

The party suddenly surged forward, and the Son of the Desert raised his battle-cry:

"Death to the Romans!"

"Freedom to Judea!"

Just then my guard, who had entered the room, commanded me to come down from the window, threatening to transfix me with his javelin if I did not obey. I descended and seated myself quietly on the stool, listening in silence to the progress of the fight. Knowing the irresistible power of the Roman arms, and wondering why the Son of the Desert had been led into such a hopeless enterprise, I was grieved, although not disappointed, when I distinguished by the varying sounds of the conflict, that the disciplined cavalry of Pilate's legion were masters of the field.

The torchlight faded away; the tumult ceased. Nothing was heard but a solitary horseman patrolling the deserted streets. The enterprise, whatever it was, had failed. I was not to be rescued. I was not to rejoin my sisters. I was to know nothing that was going on in the busy world around me. I sank upon my straw, dispirited, despairing. Toward daylight I slept; and I dreamed of that terrible night by the Dead Sea and of the words of my uncle Beltrezzor.

It seems that the riot made my jailers suspect that my prison was insecure. A few nights after this grand excitement, I was startled by several men in masks entering my room. I was bound, muzzled and blindfolded again. I was placed in some kind of a vehicle. We traversed the city; we passed the gate; we descended a slope. The fresh air of the country broke sweetly and soothingly upon me. We ascended a long hill, as I knew by the motion to which I was subjected. No one spoke.

At last the vehicle stopped. I was led between two men into a house. We walked through a very narrow passage where only two could pass at a time. Suddenly I was stopped, seized by the arms, and let down into a kind of vault. Previous to this I was stripped of my bandages; but it was so dark that I could distinguish nothing.

It was not deliverance. It was not death, that happiest deliverance of all! It was a change of prisons—from dark to darker. My heart sank within me. I trembled.

Strange sounds above me at the point of my entrance now attracted my attention! I listened with the utmost tension of ear, endeavoring to conjecture what my jailers were doing. At last I comprehended it! They were bringing brick and mortar, and all in the dark! They were walling up the space by which I had been lowered into the vault.

Horrible idea! My former prison was a dungeon; this was a grave! I was to be buried alive!

The thought overpowered me and I swooned.

XXIV
BURIED ALIVE

When I recovered my senses I examined as well as I could the strange place into which I had been plunged. It must have been broad daylight out of doors, for there was a kind of twilight about me that revealed plainly the contour of my dungeon. When evening came on I was shrouded in impenetrable darkness. Such was the only difference between my day and my night.

The chamber was about ten feet square, and its walls rose to a considerable height. It was evidently an old secret dungeon partly underground, damp and mouldy, the scene perhaps of many sufferings and many crimes. There was an opening into this vault, so that I was not literally buried alive. The workmen who had sealed up the space by which I had entered, had left a little square hole like a window about ten feet above the flooring. I could see a brick wall beyond it, so that there was evidently a narrow passage by which some rays of light came to me. When a door, opening into this passage, was left open, the light was considerable.

If I could have reached that window I could have escaped; for it was large enough to admit the head and shoulders of a man, as I soon had occasion to know. I made many frantic efforts to do so, but could barely touch the edge of it with the tips of my fingers. There was not an object in the room to assist me in reaching it. My chamber was perfectly bare—not a stool, not a pallet of straw.

While I was contemplating sadly the frightful fate which was in store for me, a little lid or trap-door in the ceiling about a foot square was opened, and a basket was lowered by a cord. This basket contained a loaf of bread and a bottle of water. I took out the bread and water; the basket rose again by the cord, and the lid was closed. This was the routine, day after day, without variation. Not even an arm or a hand could be detected when the lid was raised. Nothing could be seen or heard.

There was one thing that varied the monotony, and only one. Every day, about noon, the door in the passage was opened, the light admitted, and the ugly face and head of Magistus were protruded through the little window. There he stood gazing at me for some minutes, sometimes for half an hour, on several occasions for one or two hours. He did not speak. He glared at me with a stony malignity which is indescribable. When he had satiated his cruel appetite with a sight of my sufferings, he retired.

Thus passed away week after week, month after month. My sufferings were horrible. I wasted and weakened day by day both in mind and body. The air of the dungeon had become foul and sickening. The bread and water had become tasteless and repulsive. The silence, the solitude, the darkness, were fearful.

Magistus came every day to enjoy with secret satisfaction the cruel death he was inflicting on me. I regarded him with such repugnance and scorn, that I did not speak to him or even look at him. This no doubt inflamed his hatred. I walked about my narrow prison, whistling or talking to myself until he went away. My insulting indifference did not seem to disturb him in the least. He did nothing to attract my attention. He only looked.

And now a strange and almost incredible thing occurred. I do not believe any one can comprehend what I have to say, unless he has been shut up alone in the dark for weeks and months; with the mind preying morbidly on itself for want of external objects to give it healthful activity; wasted by low diet and a mephitic atmosphere, by silence whose terror is indescribable, and by solitude which of itself can drive to madness.

I did not look at the stony, cruel face of Magistus; but the idea that he was looking at me began to take a singular and painful possession of my mind. I could not get rid of it. I walked, whistled, talked, sang to myself, all in vain. The idea that a hideous face was in the window; that the black, fierce eyes were fixed upon me; that I could not prevent it; hung over my mind like the vultures gnawing at the heart of the chained Prometheus. It became a positive torture.

An irresistible desire to look him full in the face seized me. Whether it was a secret magnetic attraction compelling me to do so, or whether I thought it might mitigate my painful and absurd tension of thought on the subject, I yielded at last. From that moment his triumph was complete. It was veritably the fascination of the bird by the serpent. I could not help gazing at him. He seemed to absorb my whole nervous life, to suck out the very spirit of my blood, so that I was left breathless, dizzy, bewildered, helpless, after each of his terrible visitations.

Thus I lived a daily death for many weeks; ignorant of all things without; never hearing the sound of a human voice; buried alive; until hope died in my bosom, and despair became my bedfellow, and fear my familiar, and even memory ceased to weave her beautiful airy tissues, consoling me for the loss of a future by her glorification of the past.

At first I used to love to review all the incidents of my life, both on earth and in the world of spirits. I spent my long and lonesome leisure in organizing my knowledge, analyzing my experiences, and building up from them a grand philosophy of mind and matter.

I saw plainly that such a philosophy was needed to give intellectual strength and stability to the young church of Christ. I knew that no height of piety, no fervor of faith, no frenzy of love can secure a church from the cold and critical assaults of the human understanding. Devotion may be the soul of a church, but Truth is its body: and no religion without an impregnable basis of philosophy, can be anything but a transient fervor. It must inevitably perish by a gradual disintegration. For this mode of thinking I was indebted to the Athenian philosophers.

The disciples of Christ had no such foundation upon which to erect the great theological truths they were going to teach. I saw plainly that such a philosophy cannot be discovered by the human intellect: and moreover that it can only be revealed to mankind through some one who has lived consciously for a while in both worlds. By divine permission and protection I had so lived. I had been put into possession of truths of the utmost importance to the infant church and the world. Surely I could not thus perish in a dungeon! Surely the Lord who had raised me from the dead, would deliver me also from this great snare; so that I could delight and instruct mankind with what I had seen and heard in the spiritual world.

I therefore arranged all my ideas into philosophical form, and contemplated with intense pleasure the perfect system of spiritual and natural truth which I had eliminated from my accumulated materials. It is astonishing how one spiritual truth leads to another; how all things are connected together; so that the greatest things are repeated in the least, and the smallest fragment is an image of the whole.

With increasing debility and despair I ceased to think steadily of these grand and beautiful subjects. I spent much of the time in praying for deliverance, and much in brooding over the possible fate and sorrows of my poor sisters. After a while I discovered that my ideas were strangely confused, especially after those terrible visits of Magistus, which I began to regard with absolute horror. I could not distinguish between what had happened in one world and what in the other; between dreams and realities; between my hopes and my fears. The awful suspicion broke upon me that I was losing my reason, that I was on the verge of madness.

Then it was that my courage failed and my pride humbled itself; for when Magistus next appeared, I raised my hands supplicatingly to him and exclaimed:

"Oh, my uncle! why do you thus persecute an innocent and helpless creature? May God have mercy on your soul as you shall have mercy on me!"

He made no reply, but stared fixedly at me. Not a muscle of his face moved. No ray of emotion was visible on his features. He seemed to be as deaf and dumb as a statue. I might as well have appealed to a tiger or a crocodile for pity. I was about to repeat my supplication, but his look appalled me; and I sank, pale, rigid and stupefied under the old spell of fascination.

There was no hope.

Let no one suppose that this instance of cruelty is incredible. Its hereditary germ is concealed in our hearts. It begins developing in the child when he tortures the dumb creatures in his power. To delight in witnessing pain is the basest and most infernal of all our passions; but it is common enough. Every court, every camp, every government, and alas! almost every religion in the world, has its secret records which could unfold tales of horror worse even than this. Man invested with irresponsible power, is naturally a tyrant; and the difference between a tyrant and a devil consists only in their different degrees of development.

I learned, moreover, in the spiritual world the singular fact, that men or women addicted to sensual pleasures unregulated by religious ideas, however kind and gentle they may seem, have in their hearts a tendency to the most direful cruelties which rarely come to the surface in this world, but which rage in hell with unabating fury.

One morning a wonderful thing occurred. How small a thing may seem wonderful to those who are shut out from the sweet presences of man and nature!

On taking the bread and water out of the basket, I found a delicate little rose-bud at the bottom of it. Let those who see every day a thousand flowers in the golden palaces of the spring, pity and excuse the frantic pleasure which this tiny one gave to a poor prisoner, who had been shut up for months in darkness, surrounded by stone walls and demons.

I seized the sweet messenger of love, for such I construed it to be; strained my eyes in the twilight to discover the green and crimson of its livery; and imagined that its delicate perfume was a little voice whispering to me of pity and of succor. I wept over it. I kissed it. I invested it with life. I called it Mercury, Iris, Hebe, Cupid, Apollo—as a child endows her doll with vitality, speaks to it, caresses it, nurses it. Perhaps all nature would be alive to us if our hearts were only childlike.

This flower was a link that reconnected me with the great world above, so long lost to me. It was a delicate thread that led me up into the open air under the blue sky, and out into the green fields and into the gardens where the winds wrestled playfully with the trees, and all the flowers ducked their little heads at the great rough sport of the larger creatures. The beautiful forms and colors of a luxuriant nature rushed upon me with a ravishing sweetness. My memory and imagination were stimulated into rosy life. I wept for joy.

The secret of all this happiness was, that the rose-bud reconnected me with my fellow-men. Some one had got hold of the basket who knew my sad story, pitied my fate, and had sent me a message of comfort. I was confirmed in this idea when I broke open my loaf of bread; for I found a slice of meat concealed within it, juicy and delicious. This was the first variation from my diet of slow starvation. It was clearly the secret, cautious work of a friend. Help was coming; my heart danced with hope.

This little event shed still greater light and blessing upon me. My mind became clear; my memory acute; the fear of madness left me. My past sufferings seemed like a dream. With hope I received new life, new courage. When Magistus came, I found that I was freed from the spell of his fascination. I did not look at him. I sat down immediately underneath his window. I repeated comforting verses of Scripture to myself until he went away.

That day was spent in the most delicious castle-building. At night I slept, but was visited by a disagreeable dream. I thought Magistus had taken my rose-bud from me, and buried it in the ground; and I awoke with a great cry, for I suddenly remembered that what we had called the rose-bud was my sister Mary.

How eagerly I watched the next descent of the basket, for more comfort, more tokens of love, more hope! It came; but there was in it only bread and water. My heart sank within me. I would have called out loudly to my unseen friend, to know why I was deserted; but I feared my unseen enemy; for I felt certain that Magistus always watched the person who let down the basket.

Magistus came as usual; and I sat, not noticing him, underneath the window. He seemed annoyed at my indifference. He shifted his position often and stayed a great while. He missed the pleasure of contemplating his work in my ghastly and pallid face.

The same things occurred the next day and the next. No more flowers; no more meat; no messages; no hopes; only bread, water and Magistus. Was it all a hallucination? Again I began to sicken and despair.

One morning the basket came down with only bread in it. No water! I knew it was a sentence of death. Magistus was revenging my escape from the fascination of his evil eye. Before night I began to feel the horrors of thirst. Awful sensation! I dreamed of water; of the fountain in my father's courtyard; of the blue Ægean near Athens, so soft, so beautiful; of the Salt Sea and the tent of Barabbas; of the snow-fields and icebergs of the frozen zone in the world of spirits.

All, all depended on the next descent of the little basket. I watched its coming as a prisoner listens to the voice of the judge, for life or death. Alas! bread alone; no water. Torture, madness, death, were now inevitable.

I took out the loaf, which somehow or other seemed heavier than usual. To my amazement, the basket did not rise, but was jerked impatiently up and down by the person holding the cord.

"What can this mean?" said I to myself.

I broke the loaf. It was scooped out and contained, in the cavity thus formed, a piece of parchment and a very small ink-horn with a pen.

I hastily examined the parchment and found on one side of it in great sprawling letters, like a child's writing, these words:

"What shall I do?"

A light came into my mind as brilliant as the sun. I was calm and self-possessed; my good angel recalled to me the friendly words of Pilate at our parting:

"Send for me if you get into trouble."

I wrote as clearly and as rapidly as possible in the dim twilight:

"Tell all to Pontius Pilate. Be quick or I die!"

I put the parchment into the loaf and pressed its crust closely together again.

I now heard the stern voice of Magistus exclaim to some one:

"What are you dallying about?"

The basket ascended. I trembled. I almost fainted. My entire hope, my life, hung upon a thread—upon a hair!

How fortunate it was that I did not send up the parchment alone! My good angel guided me. Magistus looked into the basket, and seeing it ascend with the loaf in it, exclaimed,

"He is too weak to take out his bread. I will give him a little wine."

He seemed to walk away and my heart commenced beating again.

At that moment another little flower, another sunbeam, fell from the ceiling to my feet: and the lid was closed.

High hope in my soul obliterated for a time even the torture of thirst. I was calm. I was happy. My invisible friend had received my message. If he delivered it, I was safe: for Pilate would certainly release me. What if Pilate was absent or dead or displaced? Such thoughts were torture. Still, the new governor, whoever he was, would befriend me. I determined not to give way until night.

Magistus came earlier than usual, and threw me down a goat-skin bottle of wine and water. I thanked him with the utmost deliberation. He did not speak in reply. He only wished to fan the embers of life, to prolong my sufferings. Human nature revolts at the contemplation of such a demon. Such men are indeed rare, but such evil spirits are common. They are present to our souls; cunning, cruel, malignant; infusing their poison into our thoughts and affections; endeavoring to make us such as Magistus.

The worst evils here are moderated and repressed by the counteracting pressure of good spheres. To see evil in its true light, you must see it in the world of spirits and in hell—evil utterly divorced from good, projecting itself outwardly in its own brutal forms, and working out its frightful destiny.

I waited for my deliverance with a sublime hope, a calm and fixed faith. I knew it was coming. It came.

Magistus had at length reached, as all wicked men do either in this world or the next, the limit of his power, the fatal line; after which comes the rebound, the reaction, the punishment, the disgrace, the sure recoil upon one's self of all the evil he meditates against others.

Early in the afternoon I became aware that a great commotion was going on in the house. The door into the narrow passage was broken open by axes; for Magistus always carried the key, and he could not be found. A Roman centurion soon appeared at the window where Magistus had so often stood. Oh what a picture was his brave, handsome, indignant face! Soldiers came in. The brick and mortar were soon torn away. I was lifted out and carried into the open air. I was so overcome with joy that I fainted.

The men who beheld my ghastly features and emaciated form were loud in their curses of Magistus. I was laid on a bed in the house, and nurses were assigned me. The kindly centurion did not leave me until I was comfortably fixed and had recovered from my swoon.

"Pontius Pilate," said he, "desired me to present you his congratulations, and to say that he will visit you to-morrow when you have been refreshed and strengthened by food and a night's rest; and will then hear your story from your own lips."

I thanked him warmly.

"And my deliverer?" said I, "my unseen, faithful friend and deliverer! Where is he? Who is he?"

No one present knew anything about my deliverer.

XXV
WHAT HAD HAPPENED

Pontius Pilate fulfilled his promise; and I told him my whole story from the time of my resurrection until my happy release by his good centurion. When I was speaking about the invisible friend, the flower let down in the basket, and the parchment with its rude letters, his face grew sad. When I finished by asking him to inform me how and from whom he learned my condition, so that I could discover, reward and love my deliverer as he deserved, he drew a deep sigh and said:

"I fear I have done a very hasty and cruel thing!

"The man who informed me of your condition was the African who accompanied you to Rome, and who endeavored to rescue the slave from the fish-pond of Hortensius."

"My brave and good Anthony!" I exclaimed eagerly.

"He eluded my guards; and although wounded by one of them for his temerity, he rushed into my presence as I was finishing my morning meal. The words he spoke were substantially these:

" 'Lazarus, whom you brought from Rome, is confined in a dungeon underneath the house of Magistus, in Bethany. They have starved him nearly to death, and he has been without water for a day and a night. Send help to him speedily, or it will be too late.' "

"Noble, courageous Anthony!" I exclaimed. "He shall have half of my possessions!" but I was disquieted by the darkening brow of Pilate.

"I asked him," continued the Roman governor, "if he had been in your employ since our return from Rome.

" 'No!' he replied, 'I have seen him but once, and that was in prison.' "

"He spoke the truth," said I; "he always spoke the truth!"

"I thought he was a messenger sent by some friend of yours. I remembered him immediately, and I remembered also my promise to Hortensius. I saw in him only an audacious criminal, returning without leave from an exile which had been decreed perpetual."

"And you threw him into prison?"

"If I had known of his beautiful and heroic devotion to you, his fate would have been different."

The evident remorse of Pilate startled me.

"And his fate? What was his fate? He is not dead," said I, elevating my voice.

"He was beheaded immediately."

"O cruel, cruel, cruel fate!" I exclaimed; and regardless of ceremony, I mourned for my dead friend with bitter tears and bitter words in the presence of his august murderer.

"I feel," said Pilate, when he bade me a friendly adieu—"I feel that I have discharged a severe duty in this matter; but the generous conduct of this African,—for he certainly must have known that he endangered his own life by appearing before me,—would have entitled him to a full pardon, which I would have given with pleasure for his own merits as well as for your sake."

As soon as my Christian friends heard of my reappearance, they crowded to see me. From them I learned the sorrows and trials my sisters had undergone, as well as the strange events which preceded, accompanied and followed the crucifixion of Jesus.

Magistus and Caiaphas had set afloat the story that I was engaged in the raid upon the city of Jerusalem, made for the double purpose of robbery and murder, by Barabbas and his party; many of whom were deluded into the enterprise under the idea that it was a patriotic rebellion against the Roman yoke. They also suborned witnesses to prove that I was killed in the night attack, and was buried by them with a crowd of other rioters who fell by the Roman arms.

This led to the confiscation of our estates; and as Mary and Martha were helpless and beautiful young women without relatives to protect them, they were assigned to the special guardianship of Magistus. Caiaphas approved in strong terms this decree of the Sanhedrim, eulogized Magistus for his generous character and patriarchal virtues, and congratulated the sisters of a vile robber, themselves the disciples of a base impostor, on their extraordinary good fortune in being placed under the enviable protection of one of the shining lights of Israel.

The wickedness and duplicity of this high priest will be almost incredible to future times. But the age was evil; the church was corrupt; and public and private morality reduced to the lowest ebb. The priesthood was a matter of bargain and sale. The office of high priest, the holiest and highest in the

Jewish theocracy, was obtained by bribery and fraud and in more than one instance by murder. Caiaphas was one of the most consummate hypocrites that ever entered the holy of holies. He might have changed places with Barabbas, and justice and religion would not have fared the worse for it.

My sisters, terrified at the thought of falling into the power of Magistus, their remembrance of whom was anything but pleasant, fled from our house and concealed themselves with some of the disciples of Jesus. The two chief miscreants of the Sanhedrim seemed determined to get possession of these unhappy and forlorn women; and they instituted the most rigorous search through the houses of all persons who were suspected of harboring them. Their evil passions seemed only half gratified by my destruction and the seizure of our property. Fearful would have been the fate of these angelic friends of Jesus, had they fallen at that time into the hands of his fiercest enemies.

Spies and detectives fully authorized to search, arrest, bribe, intimidate and even kill, were set upon their track in every direction. The country became so unsafe for them, that they were conveyed by stealthy night marches to the hut of some friendly fishermen away down on the sea of Galilee. Even there they were pursued; and Peter the apostle rowed them across the sea on a dark and stormy night, and concealed them in the very tombs whence issued the maniac out of whom Jesus cast a legion of devils.

After many sufferings and hair-breadth escapes, they were conveyed out of the country, and at that moment were living concealed in the city of Antioch, at the house of a poor but worthy man—himself a Christian, for Christ had cured him and nine others of the leprosy; and he alone of the ten had turned back to give thanks.

I wept when I thought of the unhappiness of my poor sisters; and I felt an urgent desire to regain my shattered strength and rejoin them.

The story of the crucifixion of the Lord struck me with wonder and awe. I was not surprised that Judas Iscariot had betrayed him. But the pathetic incidents of his last supper, his betrayal, his trial, his crucifixion, his resurrection, his appearance to his disciples, and his ascension, affected me to tears, and filled me with a spirit of humility, love and prayer.

"Those are pictures," said I, to my friends, "which will be painted on the heart of the Christian Church in the colors of heaven, and which the powers of death and hell can never efface.

"If such," thought I to myself—"if such is the effect of this divine history as it appears in the literal form to man, what must be the power and glory of the spiritual signification of these great and holy things, when they are studied by angels in the light of heaven!"

Barabbas and his bravest lieutenants, including the Son of the Desert, had fallen into the hands of the rulers. Barabbas conveyed to Magistus a threat, that if he were not released he would expose to the Sanhedrim his attempt to murder his nephew. Whether Magistus and Caiaphas, who acted always in concert, feared an exposure of this kind, which is not probable, considering the source whence the charge would come, or whether they followed spontaneously the wicked instincts of their own souls, they procured the release of Barabbas and the crucifixion of Christ.

The mercy extended to Barabbas was not given to his followers; and two of them were selected to be crucified with Jesus, to increase the ignominy of his execution. And so Christ was crucified between two thieves—or men so reputed.

One of these was the Son of the Desert.

This brave, wild man, strangely compounded of good and evil, was heavily ironed and cast into the deepest dungeon. Magistus had a habit, consistent with his cruel disposition, of visiting prisoners condemned to death, and enjoying the terrors with which they contemplated their approaching fate.

The Son of the Desert did not gratify his passion for witnessing the sufferings of abject misery. He was singularly cheerful and buoyant. He declared himself not only willing but anxious to die. He had nothing to contemplate with pleasure when he looked back; and as to the future, if the soul were really immortal and a second life were given him, he was determined to start upon it with new principles and motives.

Magistus was astonished at the calm, philosophic spirit of this poor wretch, who had never heard of philosophy.

When Magistus was leaving, the Son of the Desert took a ring from his finger and said:

"You are not too proud to do one little favor for a condemned criminal. Give this ring to Martha, the sister of Lazarus. Tell her it has accomplished the mission upon which she sent it. She can touch it without shame. It has been an angel of light to me. Since I have worn it, I have seized no man's goods, I have taken no man's life except in lawful battle. If I have adhered to my band, it was to moderate their passions, to stay the hand of violence, to plead for mercy, to assist the captive, and where possible to make restitution. It found me a slave, it has made me a freeman. It found me a robber, it has made me a patriot."

He was about to say more, but suddenly checking some rising emotion, he clenched one hand upon his heart, and waving the other, exclaimed:

"Adieu! adieu!"

Neither the message nor the ring was delivered to Martha. The story was told to members of the Sanhedrim, in whom it awakened no generous sentiment, but only excited their amusement or mockery. The ring was taken to Ulema, my poor aunt, who still retained her wonderful clairvoyant power, which indeed seemed to increase as her general health declined. Magistus expected by the ring to obtain knowledge of all the movements and actions of the formidable band of Barabbas; for the clairvoyant can see the past as well as the present, and with the proper clue, can go far back, on the stream of time, to the very origin of things. Rumor says that the ring made strange and unexpected revelations, not only about the band of Barabbas, but about the early history of the Son of the Desert. Ulema found in the last possessor of the ring her own only and lost child, who had been stolen from the court-yard by one of a prowling party of Egyptians, when he was a very little boy. No discovery was ever made of his whereabouts, and her grief at the event was one cause of her after seclusion and ill health.

Magistus was astounded, and perhaps pained, on finding that his own child had been crucified with Jesus. It was too late to do aught but bury the whole matter with the other painful things in his memory. He said nothing to Ulema on the subject, who was of course unconscious of it all in her waking state.

A strange thing, however, now took place. The moment she passed into her trance state, she began to weep and wail over her lost child. Her clairvoyance put her in full possession of all the facts of his life and death. The mother's heart broke under the immense sorrow. She pined rapidly, and her white hands were soon folded in that sweet sleep which precedes the celestial waking.

We have a life within our life, like a wheel within a wheel!

With no knowledge of his parentage, no friend in whom to confide, no heart to receive and give a last adieu, the Son of the Desert bore his own cross up Calvary, and was nailed upon it by the Roman soldiers.

He had never seen Jesus before. He had heard of him only through enemies. He supposed him to be some fanatic or impostor, or perhaps some political maniac who aspired to the crown of Judea. At first he joined his fellow-sufferer on the other side of Christ in railing against the king and miracle-worker, whose sceptre and miraculous powers seemed so useless to himself and others in his last extremity.

But the conduct and words of Jesus smote him to the heart. Through that secret affiliation and sympathy by which one brave and good man recognizes another in the hour of sternest trial, the Son of the Desert, educated only in heart, perceived with the heart that the kingdom of Christ was a spiritual kingdom. Divining intuitively the mission of infinite love in which the Lord was engaged, he confesses his own sin, rebukes and silences his fellow-sinner, and pleads for remembrance in the hour of triumph which he sees is approaching for the King of kings.

Brave, repentant soul! Jesus is everywhere; in heaven; in earth; in hell. And shortly thou wast with Him and He with thee, in that paradise or garden of the soul, in which the new life, forgetful of the old, begins to bud and blossom!

The great tragedy was enacted. The disciples at first stood afar off. But as the death-scenes drew nearer, and the curiosity of the crowd increased, military discipline was somewhat relaxed, and the people were permitted to press closer, and those who had special claims were allowed to come up and stand very near the dying sufferers. It was thus that the Apostle John, and Mary the mother of the Lord, were in speaking distance in his last moments. It was then that He gave each of them so tenderly to the other.

Aside from this awful central scene, which will shine in all history as the pivotal event of the world, a pathetic side-scene was enacted, of which there is no historian but myself; and even I was not present, but relate it at second-hand. My authority, however, was a man of truth, John the Apostle, the exile of Patmos.

Far off in the crowd was a solitary being whose eyes were fixed continually on the Son of the Desert. He stood with his brawny arms folded spasmodically across his chest. Great tears ran slowly down his cheeks. That man was poor and ignorant and ragged and black, but he had a noble soul. It was Anthony, the Ethiopian, who, exiled by Pilate into the desert, had there met Barabbas and his band. He soon attached himself by a certain instinct to the only noble spirit in the party. He followed the fortunes of this man; and, true to his African genius, he imitated his character. The Son of the Desert was not ashamed of his humble disciple.

Anthony escaped death and capture on the terrible night of the riot. But his master was taken; and the faithful servant prowled about the suburbs and the prisons, risking detection and arrest in order to catch a glimpse, if possible, of him whom his soul loved. It was all in vain. He followed the vast crowd which went out to the crucifixion, pushed aside by the spears of the soldiers, and found himself on Calvary a witness of the last act in the great drama—an act which disclosed the mighty power of Love, and foreshadowed and meant the redemption of the world.

When the people were permitted to approach nearer to the crosses, Anthony came very close to that whereon his master, the Zebra of the Desert, hung in agony. No one noticed the ragged black man. He at last caught the eye of the poor sufferer, who smiled a sweet recognition. He was cheered. He felt happy to have one follower, one soul that loved and pitied him. Poor Anthony wept as if his heart would break.

He procured a large goat-skin bottle full of water, and stood at the cross bathing his master's wounded feet with the cooling stream. The guards wearied, sickened with the prolonged sufferings of the victims, did not prevent him. He listened to the conversation between Christ and the repentant sinner; and for the first time he seemed aware that there was another great tragedy going on besides the one in which he was especially interested.

He sat or squatted upon the ground in front of these dying men, looking first at one and then at the other; studying also the faces of the group of holy women, who with the good John stood near the central cross. A great idea was dawning on the benighted soul of the Ethiopian, a great light, a great glory.

Why is it that the beams of celestial light pass by the palace and illumine the hut?—pass by the cultivated and learned and gladden the hearts of the simple and child-like?

When the Divine Man, praying for his enemies, gave up the ghost; when the great shadows came over the sun; when the bereaved women raised their wail of sorrow; when the centurion exclaimed, "Truly this was the Son of God;" another convert—humbler, lowlier than they all—was kneeling at the foot of the cross, praying to Him who hung upon it: "Lord, remember me also when thou comest into thy kingdom." Anthony assisted the disciples in taking down the body of Jesus from the cross. That night, aided by John and two other disciples who had witnessed his tender devotion to the Son of the Desert, he took down the body of his master, wrapped it in a new winding-sheet, and buried it in a corner of the Potter's Field.

When washing the body for this lowly burial, they discovered some beautiful red letters pricked or burned into the skin immediately over the heart. They were these:

"Martha, sister of Lazarus."

Anthony followed John to his home and became his servant. He soon learned the anxieties and conjectures which prevailed about my sudden disappearance. Remembering my face at the prison window, he became convinced that I was still a prisoner. He determined, with John's approval, to devote himself to finding and delivering me. He had no adviser, for John was busy in saving my sisters from the cruel Magistus, and was at Ephesus when I was delivered from the dungeon.

How well he executed his trust, the reader already knows. But how he did it; how he discovered my whereabouts; how he got into Magistus' employ; how he obtained the post whence he could aid me; his difficulties, his hopes, his fears, his emotions—all were buried with him—alas!

He will tell the whole story to me when I meet him in heaven, as I most assuredly shall.

Poor Anthony! brave to impetuosity, extravagantly generous, meek to the deepest humility, faithful to the last degree! In his short, obscure life is concentrated a glory superior to all Greek or Roman fame.

One more piece of news occasioned me as much surprise as anything already narrated. This, however, unlike the rest, was joyful. About a week before my deliverance, my good uncle Beltrezzor had arrived in Jerusalem from Persia. He had heard, through his correspondent in the Holy City, of my supposed death, of the crucifixion of Jesus, and the mysterious disappearance of my sisters. He at once suspected some evil, and determined to hasten to their assistance. He found considerable difficulty in converting all his property into jewels and precious stones; and still more in bringing everything safely through countries which were at war and infested by prowling bands of deserters and thieves.

He had started for Antioch only the day before, having heard that John had conducted my sisters safely to that city.

Pilate was not slow in bringing Magistus to justice. Finding that an exposure of his infamously cruel character was already made, and that the Roman governor himself had taken part against him, hundreds of people whom he had injured in person or property came forward to assist in the prosecution. He was convicted of many crimes, his estates confiscated; he was exiled the country and forbidden to return under penalty of death.

It was ten days before I was able to travel. I chid the tardy hours that kept me from my beloved sisters and my dear old uncle, the disciple of Zoroaster.

At last the word came:

"To Antioch!"

XXVI
THE CITY OF COLONNADES

Strange things were going on at Antioch.

Antioch, the seat of the Roman government in Syria, was a centre in which met all the peculiarities and eccentricities of the civilized world. It was situated on the river Orontes, several miles above its confluence with the sea. By an extensive system of artificial works the river was made navigable for the largest vessels, so that Antioch was in rapport with the maritime world. It was the city of amalgamations; the point of contact between the East and the West; the receptacle of all races and nations.

Notwithstanding its wealth, beauty and splendor, the society of Antioch was inconceivably corrupt and degraded. All kinds of strange doctrines and unhealthy superstitions were rampant there. Magicians, sorcerers, miracle-workers, impostors, buffoons and courtesans were in high favor with all classes. Life and death were equally disregarded. Races, games, fêtes, debauches, combats, processions, seemed to occupy the whole time of the excitable and licentious populace.

Simon Magus, after spending three or four months in Egypt with Helena, came to Antioch and began an extraordinary course of public teachings. It was a rich field for his peculiar genius. He combined philosophy with sorcery, theology with magic. Of his cruel deeds, his infernal plots, his insane ambition the world was ignorant.

He was greatly changed. The inspiration of evil had taken demoniac possession of him. He had grown leaner and darker. His eye, always eloquent and powerful, was fierce and restless. He had a singular habit of grasping at his breast, with an expression of suffering on his face, as if a violent pain shot through his heart. He had lost much of that calm, self-possessed, imposing exterior which commanded respect by its apparent strength and dignity. He was louder in his speech, more rapid in his gestures, prouder and more defiant in his attitude. This gained him a larger but more vulgar audience.

The magician was on the eve of madness, if not actually mad.

It was the age of insanity. It was the age of imposture and false miracles, of convulsion and persecution, of moral and physical turpitude, of direful cruelty and bloodshed, of the wildest fanaticism, of the most revolting excesses, of actual possession by devils. Nothing like it was ever seen before or ever will be again, because all these things were the effects and collateral issues of the spiritual combat between good and evil, between Christ and hell; the throes of the great demons of past ages before their final expulsion from their thrones and the inauguration of a new spiritual power in the world.

Such was the state of society at Antioch when Simon Magus appeared in that city and claimed to be an incarnation of the Deity, exercising miraculous power. He seemed to be possessed of boundless wealth. The splendor of his palace, the rare and gorgeous beauty of his equipage, his singular and dazzling dress, the wild grandeur of his manner, the wonderful eloquence of his speech, and the astounding feats of magic which he certainly did perform, all created a bewildering impression on the excitable and unthinking people of the City of Colonnades, as Antioch was called on account of its architectural beauty.

On his first arrival he had directed his subtle energies to obtain the ear and the faith of the ruler of the province, the Roman governor, whose name was Lelius. The appliances which he brought to bear upon the heart, the brain, the senses of this weak and vain man, were finally successful. In a few weeks Lelius was not only the dupe, but the mere creature of Simon Magus. Helena shared with her pretended husband the glory and the shame of this royal conquest.

Such was the state of things when the apostle John arrived at Antioch with the two unhappy fugitives—my sisters. They were attended by Mary Magdalen in the humble capacity of servant. This zealous disciple of Christ had kept modestly aloof from them in their prosperity; but when thrown together by common sorrows and persecutions, she tendered her services and proved through life a most faithful and efficient friend.

John obtained lodgings for the party with Salothel, the restored leper. Hoping still further to shield them by drawing the pursuit after himself, he traveled on westward as far as Ephesus, where he had friends, and where he began preaching the new gospel of Christ. The sisters remained concealed for a long time, until their fears were quieted and they began to be intensely anxious to hear from Judea. They had always doubted the story of my death, and were continually hoping to get news of me.

Emboldened by their long repose, Mary and Martha closely veiled took a walk one afternoon with Salothel through the grand street of colonnades, and sat down to rest in one of the beautiful public squares. A triumphant procession in honor of the Roman arms was passing by; and it was precisely in a great crowd, passing and repassing, that our recluses thought there was least danger of being specially observed.

Suddenly two men stopped near them, and one gazed earnestly at the sisters. That man was Simon Magus, thoroughly-disguised. He had received letters from his old disciple Magistus, telling him how his nieces had eluded his vigilant pursuit, and requesting him to keep a lookout for them. Simon also had not forgotten the defeat of his great scheme at Bethany, and he desired above all things to get possession of Mary for his own private ends.

It is needless to say that when a man of Simon's genius and power gets upon the fresh trail of a poor helpless woman, it is but a short time before he secures his prey. Mary, innocent, unsuspecting, loving creature as she was, the very next day was decoyed from the house of Salothel by a very old gray-haired, heavenly-faced man, a devout Christian, who managed to see her alone, and who wished to conduct her without a moment's delay to her suffering brother Lazarus. Of course the devout old Christian was a disguised emissary of Simon; and Mary found herself immured in a secret chamber of his palace.

What to do with her? was now the question.

Simon Magus had such intense faith in the incantations of Ja-bol-he-moth, the old demon of the Lybian desert, that he was ready to abandon his great theological mission and convey Mary to the ruins of the ancient city which was buried in the sand. If he had permitted Helena to remain in possession of his palace under the protection of Lelius, that beautiful person would have approved his enterprise, and would have given him her blessing with her farewell. But Simon was obstinately resolved that she should accompany him, and share the dangers and the glory of the expedition.

Helena positively refused to return to Egypt; and as she was as fierce and implacable as she was beautiful, Simon was at last obliged to submit to a compromise. Mary was not to be conveyed into Africa; but she was to be murdered, her heart extracted, burned into a cinder and pulverized, to constitute a magical powder of extraordinary virtues. Thus Simon was to be gratified by an addition to his necromantic treasures, and Helena was to enjoy the dissipation of Antioch.

"And how it will delight our friend Magistus!" said Helena.

Simon felt too insecure in his new surroundings to venture upon the secret murder of the young girl. It might be difficult to dispose of the body after the heart was abstracted. The untried creatures and slaves around him might discover the deed and betray him. His new claim to divinity would be sadly compromised by his sudden exposure as an assassin.

Simon and Helena devised a cunning plan by which they could attain their ends without the least danger to themselves. Simon represented to Lelius that a strange and dangerous conspiracy against government and religion was taking root in Antioch. He described Jesus as a subtle impostor, who, under the cloak of extraordinary sanctity, meditated the grandest political revolutions. He painted the disciples in the blackest colors as the secret enemies of peace and order.

"The leader," said he, "of these turbulent spirits was crucified by Pontius Pilate, whose probity and leniency are known to the whole world. His followers, driven from Jerusalem, have spread as firebrands in different countries; and secretly associated together, they are now plotting against the stability of all existing civil and religious institutions."

He claimed to have discovered their plots by magical power; and he solemnly assured his credulous listener that he had not exaggerated their importance or danger. He predicted that in a few years a decree of extermination would be issued by all civilized powers against these people, and he begged Lelius to initiate those measures of destruction which would entitle him to the gratitude of mankind.

"I know," he continued, "that one of the most cunning of all these emissaries is now in the city: a woman, beautiful, accomplished, designing; concealing under the garb of modesty and humility, the spirit of universal anarchy. She anointed this Jesus as king in the presence of his chosen officers and lieutenants on the night before his grand entry into Jerusalem, when the mad populace shouted his claims to the throne of Judea. To satisfy your mind of the true nature of this formidable doctrine growing up around us, let me bring this woman before you and question her in your presence."

Lelius assented to this proposition, and Mary was led or rather dragged into the august presence of the Roman governor. Simon Magus proceeded to question her in the most adroit manner, drawing from her exactly such answers as were best calculated to shock and disgust the ignorant and arrogant pagan who held in his single hand the power of life and death.

Mary, terrified and unsuspecting, answered all his queries in a simple and truthful manner. She was thus made to say, that she had known and loved Jesus of Nazareth; that she had anointed him on the eve of his royal entry into Jerusalem; that she believed his teachings; that he had risen from the dead and ascended into heaven; that she prayed to him as God; that he was coming again to restore Israel and to judge the world.

This seemed like the wildest folly and fanaticism to the proud Roman; and he smiled at the thought that there were people with the semblance of rationality who could credit such absurdities. But Simon's work was only half done. Questioning and cross-questioning his artless victim, he drew from her facts of a far more serious and practical bearing.

Mary believed, and candidly acknowledged it, that all the religions sanctioned by the laws of the Roman empire, were false religions; that their gods were no gods at all, or demons; that their boasted oracles were evil spirits; that the tendency of these religions was only evil, and that their devotees were living in sin and doomed to hell. Moreover, that the religion of Christ was to supersede them all; that no compromise could be permitted; that it was a life-and-death struggle between the old religion and the new gospel.

In addition she was made to say—never dreaming to what conclusions her admissions were leading her pagan judge—that Jesus had set apart a great many persons, twelve at one time and seventy at another, to go forth into the world and preach this gospel; that he had given them miraculous power wherewith to achieve their ends; that angels delivered them from prisons; that they could strike their enemies blind or dumb or powerless; that they could raise the dead; that they had a secret organization with signs and symbols; that they had started or were going to start on their grand mission which was to overturn the powers of pagan darkness and prepare the minds of men for the universal reign of Christ at his second coming.

When Mary was removed by the guards, Simon had no difficulty in convincing Lelius that his own allegations had been well founded. Torturing the meaning of Mary's words and giving them a purely literal construction, he inflamed the indignation and zeal of Lelius to such a pitch, that he despatched private letters to the governors of the neighboring provinces, informing them of the existence, motives and plans of this new and desperate conspiracy against all that was stable, glorious and venerable in the civilizations of Greece and Rome.

The next thing was to determine what should be done to extinguish a heresy which meant revolution, in his own province. To this conference Helena was admitted; for Aspasia had less influence over Pericles than Helena over Lelius. The Roman governor was weak-minded, easily led, and without moral sensibility. He was passionately fond of new sensations, extraordinary excitements, and the bloody sports of the amphitheatre. He was soon induced to sanction a magnificent scheme concocted by that subtle brain which received its inspiration from the old magician of Pharaoh.

Our good uncle Beltrezzor arrived at Antioch the day after Mary's disappearance. He found the household of Salothel in the profoundest consternation and distress. He was welcomed with frantic joy, and joined them in the most painful and laborious search for his lost niece. Day after day these sad, anxious souls traversed the city, walking, looking, inquiring everywhere. Among half a million or more of people the lost are not easily found, especially if cunning and unscrupulous power gets them in its clutches and conceals them from view.

In the course of his inquiries, Beltrezzor discovered that Simon Magus lived in the city in great grandeur and authority. A fearful suspicion entered his mind; for he remembered the night-scene in Bethany, and the foiled abduction. He did not communicate his fears to Martha or the rest, but insisted upon their remaining in the utmost seclusion, while he conducted the search alone. He said he had discovered something important, but which demanded great caution and secresy; and he endeavored to inspire a hope which he did not feel.

The next day, passing a crowd in one of the squares, he observed the herald of Lelius reading a proclamation to the people, which excited the greatest enthusiasm. He came near and listened to its second reading.

It announced officially, with great pomp of words, that the government, determined to protect the safety and morals of the people, had taken measures to extirpate a certain secret association of conspirators, which had been founded in Judea by one Jesus Christ, whom Pontius Pilate had crucified as an impostor and revolutionist. That the first step in this righteous undertaking, would be the public execution of a young woman, who was an agent and emissary of these outlaws, and who had anointed the said Jesus king of the Jews, according to the old Jewish custom of installing into the royal office. That in order to strike terror into these evil-doers, and to warn them of the fate which awaited them if they attempted to teach the doctrines of Jesus, the young woman, Mary of Bethany, high-priestess of this new and dangerous religion, would be thrown to an immense Næmean lion just arrived from Africa, in the grand amphitheatre on the afternoon of a certain day which would be the second Sabbath following, according to the Jewish calendar. That, to illustrate the clemency of the government, a full pardon would be given to the said Mary if she publicly recanted her heresies and revealed the names of the other conspirators.

Beltrezzor stood aghast at this terrible document, full of false affirmations. The old man's heart was pierced with grief and terror in contemplating the frightful toils into which his innocent and beautiful niece had fallen. To conceal the awful fact from Martha was his first thought—and then he was prepared for any labor, for any sacrifice to rescue Mary.

The whole city was in a blaze of excitement over this new sensation. It was the great topic of conversation everywhere.

And her crime? Oh! said the people, it is terrible! A female atheist! denying all the gods, and worshiping a Jew who was crucified between two thieves!

All agreed that she deserved her fate; and that it would be the most entertaining sight of the season, and a death-blow to the conspiracy.

"And see!" said they, "the noble mercy of Lelius! If she recants at any time before the opening of the amphitheatre, she will be released."

Then they all agreed that it would be very cowardly and disgusting in her to recant. They admired an unbending and not a repentant sinner.

Beltrezzor was a plain, childlike man, having no ingenuity for indirect attacks, or for unraveling difficult questions. Thoroughly truthful and honest, he always went to work in an open, straightforward way. He felt that, in the great work before him, he had but one hope, one resource—his immense wealth.

If he had loved money more than he did, his hope would have been greater; for he would have believed that all men could be bought with a bribe. Unpurchasable himself, he doubted the power of money. Still he was compelled to test its efficacy, for it was plainly his only resource.

He studied the situation thoroughly, deliberately. He became convinced that the whole thing was the conjoint work of Simon Magus and the Roman governor. He was sure that Simon Magus, a fanatic almost to lunacy, could not be deterred or withheld from a favorite project by pecuniary considerations. The government could not withdraw its proclamation without a sacrifice of dignity; and if Lelius were approached on the subject, he would probably refer it to Simon, by whom all proposals would be rejected.

He thought it best to keep away from these high dignitaries altogether, and to sound the subordinates. He was afraid, moreover, that if Simon learned of a wealthy element working in Mary's behalf, he would increase his vigilance and double his guards, so that bribery and escape would be alike impossible. It was best to let him believe that Mary was alone, helpless and friendless.

He visited the amphitheatre and sought out the keeper of the prison connected with that immense establishment. The keeper had already been questioned out of his patience by crowds of people to whom he gave surly and unsatisfactory answers. He was a Gaul by birth, a Roman soldier by captivity and necessity, Euphorbus by name. He was taciturn and apparently ill-natured.

Beltrezzor went straight to the point. He asked him no questions. He said softly:

"A word to you in a private room may be valuable."

Euphorbus looked fixedly at him a moment, and led the way to a small office within. Beltrezzor produced a sparkling gem of considerable value.

"I wish to speak with the young woman who is confined in the amphitheatre."

"Impossible!" said the keeper, gruffly.

"I am her uncle."

"No admittance to anyone on pain of death," said the Gaul, casting a wistful eye on the jewel.

Beltrezzor drew forth a precious stone of remarkable size and immense value.

"These are yours, my friend, for a single brief interview with my niece."

"Hark you!" said Euphorbus, taking the jewels into his hand. "I am willing to gratify and befriend you; but there are four Roman soldiers at the door of her cell, who permit no one but myself to go in or out."

"Are they not under your command?"

"No. They belong to Simon Magus, and obey only his word."

"Lead me to them."

The old man made a touching appeal to these rough men for permission to see his niece. Some large gold coins that he offered them had more influence than his eloquence. The assurance of the keeper that he would shield them as far as possible, decided the matter; and Beltrezzor was admitted into Mary's dungeon.

The meeting between uncle and niece was affecting in the extreme. Mary had greatly changed since her imprisonment. A deadly pallor pervaded her beautiful countenance, and she had the air of one whose delicate nerves had almost given way under prolonged terrors. The old man clasped her in his arms, and the bitter tears fell from his face upon her golden hair.

"Oh uncle!" said she, "is it not horrible to contemplate? A young girl stripped and thrown to a lion before thousands of people! Are they not devils in human form who can witness such things?"

She trembled; her eyeballs started with horror; the cold drops stood on her forehead; she clung frantically to her uncle.

"Oh! I have thought of it," she said, "until I shall go mad! And then to hear the lion roaring at night! It is fearful. He is kept very, very near me. Is not that cruel, cruel? I hear every sound he makes. I hear him growling and crunching when they feed him. I hear him yawning and whining as he impatiently paces his cage. Then at night he roars as if he thought he was in the pathless forest. Oh it freezes me! I cannot eat. I cannot sleep. I shall die!"

The head of the young woman fell upon the old man's breast.

"Have you never thought, my child," he said, tremulously, "of saving your life by renouncing your religion?"

"No, uncle! never! never!"

"That's a brave girl!" said he, tenderly kissing her forehead; "and you shall be saved without it."

"I am not afraid of death, uncle, but of the lion. But I doubt not—oh! I doubt not that Jesus will support me even in that last extremity. I cannot, however, control my fears."

The old man cheered her with many tender words and promises of help and assurances of speedy rescue. Promising to visit her twice every day, he departed to mature some plan for her deliverance.

That evening he was plunged in a deep and painful reverie. Neither Martha nor Mary Magdalen could engage him in conversation. He sat with head between his hands. He retired early.

During the night Martha heard groans issuing from his chamber. She lit her lamp and entered softly. Beltrezzor, pale and haggard, lay upon his back with his face upturned to heaven. He had been weeping in his sleep. His lips were moving as if in prayer.

Faithful, loving old man!

XXVII
HELENA AGAIN

When my uncle came out to his morning meal, a strange transformation had taken place. He was buoyant and cheerful; his face was radiant with a pleasing vivacity. Indeed he was absolutely mirthful. Martha regarded him with profound astonishment, which gave way to fear that the dear old man had lost his reason, when he burst out into the following speech:

"Rejoice, my friends! rejoice, my children! I have got it fixed. I see our way clearly out of all our troubles. Get ready, as quickly but as quietly as you can, to leave this horrible place. Be silent as the grave. A ship will be ready for us on Sunday afternoon; and while these mad people are yelling in their vile amphitheatre, she will weigh anchor, slip her cable, and with Mary on board and angels smiling on the voyage, her prow will point steadily for the land of Gaul."

During this speech he was rubbing his hands with glee; and at the conclusion of it he waved them over his head in an excited manner. His listeners showed by their silence and the tears in their eyes what they thought of this singular conduct.

"Come, come!" said the old man, resuming his usual gravity, "I am in earnest. God has revealed what I must do, in a dream. I know exactly where Mary is. She is well and will soon be happy. You must obey me. Ask me no questions. Trust in me implicitly. All will be right."

Seeing Beltrezzor so thoroughly in earnest, the little group became hopeful and cheerful, and proceeded with alacrity to make preparations for the sudden and strange journey. Beltrezzor went out into the city, and was incessantly occupied in arranging and working for his remarkable enterprise. He barely came home to sleep at night, so much had he to do in so little time.

He continued as vivacious as ever. His spirits, his hope, his assurance, seemed to rise every hour. At last, the evening before the Sabbath, the little party with their baggage were quietly transferred after nightfall from the house of Salothel to a beautiful new ship anchored away up at the very end of the long pier which adorns the river front of Antioch.

When they were all safe on board the vessel, Beltrezzor took Martha into the cabin, and opening a closet, he showed her several boxes of rosewood bound with brass bands.

"This," he said, "is full of golden coins of various sizes and value. This contains jewels of incalculable splendor wrought by the greatest artificers in the East. This conceals precious stones of great beauty and high price. And this last contains some genuine diamonds, brought from the remotest India, and which would excite the envy of kings and queens.

"Here are the keys to them all. Take them."

"And all this immense wealth," said Martha in amazement.

"One half of it is for you and Mary."

"And the other half?"

"Is for the man who brings Mary to this vessel to-morrow and conducts it to Gaul."

"Oh, generous uncle; and for yourself?"

"Something far more valuable than all that."

My uncle returned to the house of Salothel to sleep, fearing lest its sudden evacuation should excite the suspicion of the neighbors. Several servants also, bribed to profound secrecy, were to remain until after the Sabbath. Beltrezzor was obliged to move with great caution. A single false step might ruin everything. If the parties who were plotting the destruction of Mary obtained the least clue to his movements, his whole scheme might be thwarted. Mary would be given to the lion, the rest seized and perhaps murdered, and his splendid estate confiscated. He could not sleep a moment under the weight of such tremendous responsibilities.

It was the next morning, the day of the Jewish Sabbath, when the grand exhibition was to take place at the amphitheatre, that I arrived at Antioch. Just as my uncle was leaving the house for ever, he met me at the door. I thought he would have started from me as from a ghost. But he was one of those quiet men whom nothing ever surprised. He gave me a sedate but cordial welcome, just as if he had been expecting me. He had difficulty in calming my excitement and fury when I learned what a shocking fate was impending over my youngest and most beautiful sister.

He would not tell me anything about the means he had adopted for Mary's deliverance. I was very restive under this burden of secrecy and mystery.

"Be quiet, my son," he said, "or you will mar all. You have come into the fight too late to understand the exact state of the parties and to take command. Be patient. Do the part I give you. Do it well, and trust to me for the rest. We must not be seen together, for you may be watched, and that might betray me. You must not go to the ship until the hour of starting, for you might be followed there, and that might ruin us both.

"Stay in the house until nearly four o'clock. At four o'clock precisely be at the north-east angle of the amphitheatre on the opposite side of the street. You will see a chariot standing there with the letter G in gilt upon its side. A servant will be holding a gray horse a few paces off. At four, precisely, two persons will come out of one of the rear doors of the amphitheatre. They will enter the chariot and drive away rapidly. Mount the horse and follow them. Ten minutes afterward you will be in the arms of your sisters!"

I was very much dissatisfied with this arrangement. I felt that the stake was too immense and sacred for the whole work to be left to the knowledge, the discretion and the energy of one man. But my uncle was resolute in keeping his plan for Mary's deliverance entirely to himself. He bade me adieu. There was a singular tenderness in his words:

"Good-bye, Lazarus. I need not conceal from you the fact that there is danger in this enterprise. You may never see me again. You will take care of your sisters in my place. Be honest, be faithful, be good. If my plan succeeds, this will be the greatest, happiest day of my life. Courage! Adieu."

The old sweet smile irradiated his face, and he went off as gayly as if he were going to a feast instead of entering upon a dangerous enterprise.

I went up stairs in the now deserted house of Salothel, and sat down at an open window, looking out on a beautiful public square. At any other time I would have been delighted with the scene. My heart would have been cheered by the tender green of the soft grass, by the rustling of the leaves in the wind, and the twittering of the birds among the branches. I would have admired the splendid domes and spires of Antioch rising all around above the tree-tops, and the brilliant tints of an eastern sky flecked with fantastic and fleecy clouds.

But the glories of nature and art were alike powerless on a spirit sunk into the deepest abyss of sorrow and fear. My heart was full of the direst forebodings. The morning hours passed gloomily away. My restlessness became insupportable. It must have been about noon, when, looking down into the public square, I saw a young man seated upon one of the iron benches, whose face immediately riveted my attention. It was my old friend and fellow-student, Demetrius, the brother of Helena.

A powerful temptation immediately assailed me. It was to do something for my poor sister independently of Beltrezzor's schemes, so that if one failed the other might succeed. One resource only seemed so little to depend upon. I was nearly frantic waiting thus in idleness for the fruition of an unknown plan which might fail at the very moment when its success was expected.

I said to myself:

"I will speak to Demetrius. He has a good heart and a clear brain. He may suggest something which may lead to good. He may enlist Helena in our behalf, if Helena is here. I cannot see what harm can come of it."

I went down into the square. Demetrius was overjoyed to see me. He did not, however, seem surprised to find me in Antioch. We sat down together and I told him all our troubles. I unbosomed my whole grief to him like a brother. I had the discretion to say nothing of Beltrezzor, resolving to let the old man work out his own plan alone. If harm came to any one, it could only be to myself.

Demetrius knew that the condemned woman was my sister, and professed the deepest interest and sympathy in her case. I pleaded the youth, and the innocent and sweet character of Mary, against the charge of foul and dangerous heresy.

He seemed to think the heresy was bad enough, for he indulged in the most contemptuous expressions against Jesus and his disciples. "But," said he, "it is all the work of Lelius. No one can aid you so efficiently as Simon Magus. Great magician and sorcerer as he has been and is still, he is a noble and generous man. I am confident he will assist you in delivering your sister from her fearful peril. He is now lecturing to a select audience on the great points of his new philosophy. Come with me to his palace and hear him. When he has finished, we will consult together as to what is to be done."

I followed him; and ascending the marble steps of a princely mansion, and passing through a great hall adorned with statues and immense vases of flowers, we were ushered into a room of moderate size, but superbly furnished. The audience nearly filled the place, for there were but two or three chairs near the door.

Simon Magus, on a raised platform, was in the very heat and height of an eloquent discourse. His subject was the nature of the soul and its transformations. His voice was winning, his gestures expressive, his eye a blaze of intellectual fire. His language was full of Orientalisms and Egyptian mysticisms. Taught in the severer school of Grecian philosophy, and blessed with the far greater analytic light of spiritual knowledge, I perceived at once that the influx of ideas into his mind came from cunning, subtle, evil spirits, and that the tendency of his words was to bewilder, dazzle and betray.

"You saw me," said he, "turn water into wine just now. You saw me turn silver into gold. You saw me resolve a rose into nothing; you saw me restore it as it was before. These things, I told you, were symbolic of spiritual transformations.

"When the spirit by prayer, by faith, by watching, by study, by abstinence, by suffering—is purified and etherealized, it undergoes similar transformations, and from water becomes wine; from silver becomes gold; from human becomes divine. Thus it is that I have become the power of God—the Son of God—the Word of God; and that I have still a holier name, incommunicable to you.

"In this state I have supreme control over matter. You saw me a little while ago take up a deadly serpent. It bit a dog before your eyes and the creature died in a minute. It fastened itself upon my hands and my cheeks; I was unhurt. You saw me swallow balls of fire. I am unharmed. So I can float in the air like a bird; I can live under water like a fish. I can point my finger at a tree, and it will wither. I can call to a cloud, and it comes to me. I can curse a city, and it will sink into the sea."

There was an excited and admiring murmur among his credulous hearers. The fanatical impostor continued:

"These powers are awful and incomprehensible to you who do not possess them. They are only given to the wise who use them wisely. But I have attained to a height of glory, in comparison with which these first labors and results are insignificant. Having become the emanation of God, I can create souls out of nothing. I can restore souls to life which had been given to annihilation. I will show you a soul I have created."

There was a great murmur of astonishment and applause. The curtains were now drawn and the room darkened. The wall behind Simon appeared to open, and the most beautiful sight was presented to view that I have ever witnessed. The chamber beyond was one resplendent glory of golden light. It did not seem to be lighted, but to be filled with light as a golden vapor. In the midst of the room, half-way between the floor and ceiling, both of which seemed to be mirrors of shining brass, hung or floated a rosy cloud, shaped like a throne, over which was a canopy of celestial azure. On that throne was seated Helena, my first and only love.

I turned to look Demetrius in the face at this splendid creation (?) of his gifted brother-in-law. Demetrius had left the room unobserved.

"Simon," said I to myself, "has lost his old sublime faith in his diabolical art, and has resorted to magical impostures."

I turned my attention to Helena. Now I solemnly avow that the woman, her chair and all, whatever they may have been, were ten feet in the air, entirely unsupported by anything visible to mortal eye. Whether this was some magical trick, really explicable by natural law, or effected by the assistance of evil spirits, I do not know. Of this, however, I am certain, from experience and knowledge acquired in the spiritual world, that evil spirits can, under certain conditions, lift the heaviest articles high in the air and keep them there for a considerable time.

"This," said Simon Magus, enjoying the ineffable amazement of his hearers—"this is the soul of Helen of Sparta, who caused the Trojan war. She was annihilated for her extreme wickedness. I have recalled her to life; and, wonderful to relate, I have purified and spiritualized her whole nature by the sanctifying influence of my presence."

I gazed upon this strange scene with intense interest, and was soon enchanted with the face of Helena. Never in this world have I seen features of such exquisite beauty; and neither in this world nor in the other have I seen a face expressive of such womanly love, tenderness, sweetness and purity. The white peace of heaven was enthroned upon her brow, and the softness of infinite pity beamed in her eyes. If she was a picture, it was a subject for boundless enthusiasm. If she was living, she was an object for profound adoration.

So thought every one who looked on. It is strange that I did not remember what I had been taught in the world of spirits, that syrens and wicked women there can counterfeit angelic forms so cunningly as to deceive the angels themselves for a while.

"There," said I, to myself, "is a gentleness, a holiness, a purity, a mercy which I know will save my sister from the lion."

The curtain or wall or whatever it was, was closed, and Simon went on with his lecture. I did not hear a word of it, so rapt was I in the contemplation of Helena's seraphic face.

"Oh, if I could speak to that vision of superlative beauty, I am sure she would befriend my poor sister."

Suddenly Demetrius touched me on the shoulder and whispered:

"My sister wishes to see you."

I followed him, asking no questions, bewildered, unthinking, but whispering to myself, "Helena wishes to see me!"

We passed through the superb hall, and opening a door near the end of it, Demetrius ushered me into the room without entering himself. Helena advanced to meet me. I was delighted with the extraordinary warmth of her reception. If we had been passionate lovers long separated, she could not have manifested more pleasure at seeing me!

Superbly beautiful as she was, that heavenly radiance and purity which I had seen upon her countenance a few moments before, had vanished. There was nothing spiritual in her expression. She was plainly no spirit and no soul just created, but a perfectly formed, glowing, enchanting woman of flesh and blood. I was about questioning her on the subject of her extraordinary deception, when she spoke:

"I knew you wanted to see me. I sent Demetrius out to look for you. You are in trouble, and I long to assist you. Sit down with me on these cushions and tell me all your story."

She touched a little bell, and a tall, stately servant appeared at the door.

"Wine and refreshments," said Helena.

We sat down together, and I told her all about poor Mary, still wisely omitting the part of Beltrezzor. The tears glistened in her brilliant eyes, and she exclaimed:

"As soon as Simon finishes his lecture, I will persuade him to grant your request. I have great power over him."

A pang shot through my heart as I thought of Simon—the husband of this resplendent object of my youthful adoration. Alas! what was Helena to me? Why did I not remember the fatal effect of her love upon me? Why did I not remember the lessons of the spiritual world? Are there not passions which we can never conquer, struggle as we may? Are there not Canaanites of the soul that can never be expelled?

The wine and refreshments were brought, and Helena whispered something to the servant. I heard only the last words, "Tell him to make haste." I thought it was a message to Simon, and that my dear benefactress was impatient to intercede for my sister.

"Come," she said, "pledge our future joys in this delicate wine, and then tell me all about that wonderful voyage they say you made into the world of spirits."

Fool that I was! excited by the powerful liquor, and still more intoxicated by the presence and smiles of that bewitching woman who repeatedly took my hand in hers, I profaned sacred things by lowering them to the level of her vulgar and sensual mind. She seemed vastly entertained by my story; and when I described the great feast of Grecian spirits, and her own splendid appearance in the scene, and her terrible metamorphosis, she laughed uproariously, and said it was one of the most charming stories she had ever heard in her life.

There was a sound of footsteps in the adjoining room.

"Come," she said, filling my glass, "drink to the morrow which shall be happier than to-day."

There was a rap or signal upon the wall.

"Simon's lecture is over," she said, rising. "This is his audience-chamber in which he receives a few pupils who question him on the deeper points of his subject. Their conversation would be very dull to us in our mood. Let us retire into my chamber, until they disperse, when we can speak to Simon alone."

I followed her to the door of the room from which the signal had come. I hesitated, abashed, at the thought of entering her chamber.

"Oh come along," she said, grasping my arm. "Do not be afraid of my chamber. It has carpets which render your feet inaudible. It has pictures and statues which ravish your senses."

With that she drew me into the room.

I was immediately seized from behind by several powerful men, and thrown to the floor. With a peal of devilish laughter, my betrayer fled back into the audience-chamber.

I looked up, and Magistus was regarding me with a diabolical smile. A man was standing by him who riveted my attention. He was black, but his face was full of hideous white spots. One eye was gone, lids and all, so as to leave a frightful deep hole in its place. He wore a red turban. This strange, repulsive creature stooped to fasten a kind of iron bracelet on my feet. I watched him in silence. He softly kissed the top of my foot unseen by the others.

I knew him. It was Ethopus. Poor Ethopus!

Helena peered in at the door with her beautiful, laughing face.

"How does my boy-lover like my bed-chamber?"

"How could you betray me in this atrocious manner?" said I, indignantly.

"Magistus offered me a beautiful diamond ring to get you into his power. You know we women could never resist the fascination of diamond rings!"

"And my poor sister!" I exclaimed, in despair.

"True, I had forgotten about her. It is time to dress for the amphitheatre. The gladiators interest me very little, but I would not miss seeing a woman eaten up by the lion, even for a diamond ring. Good-bye."

The demon departed. The vision of the woman-serpent in the world of spirits was a prophecy.

I had fallen again—this time how low! into what an abyss!

The amphitheatre was open! and great Heavens! I was bound hand and foot and cast into a dungeon.

XXVIII
TO THE LION

The day preceding these surprising events, Beltrezzor had taken the keeper of the prison aboard the new ship which lay at the pier. He had shown him the immense treasures in his rosewood boxes—the accumulation of a long life and successful trade in the far Eastern countries which abound in diamonds and precious stones.

Euphorbus opened his eyes in great astonishment. He had never seen so much wealth before. To his feeble arithmetic it was absolutely incalculable.

"Euphorbus," said my uncle, looking toward the blue line of the sea which was visible in the distance, "if this vessel sails from this point to-morrow evening at four o'clock, do you think she could get out of the river and to sea before night came on, to escape any vessel started in pursuit of her half an hour after she weighed anchor?"

"Yes, she could not be overtaken by any sail now in the river?"

"I make liberal calculations. I say half an hour, but she will have an hour or two hours the start."

"Then she is perfectly safe," said the other.

"Euphorbus!" continued my uncle, looking him in the face, "you are a Gaul. Away over there lies your beautiful country, with its glorious mountains, its swift rivers, its rich fields, its vineyards, its brave warriors. Do you not wish to see it again?"

"Yes," said the soldier with a sigh.

"Here you are a stranger, an exile, a prisoner yourself. What are these Romans to you, hereditary enemies, that you should obey them? robbers and murderers of your friends and countrymen, that you should love them?"

"I despise them," said Euphorbus, gruffly.

"In Gaul you could be happy. You could return to your old home perhaps."

"The Romans have burnt it."

"You could rebuild it. You could take care of your mother in her old age. You could have a wife at your side and children about your knees."

"Do not talk about these things!" said the Gaul. "They sadden me."

"Talk about them? You shall have them; they are yours. This vessel is yours; one-half of that immense treasure is yours."

"Mine? mine?"

"Yes, yours, on one condition."

"What condition?"

"That you bring my little Mary out of the amphitheatre to-morrow —" and the old man, overpowered by the strain upon his feelings, burst into tears.

Euphorbus was deeply moved.

"You ask an impossibility! Oh that I could —"

"Will you if you can?" exclaimed the old man, earnestly seizing him by the hand.

"Certainly I will —"

"It is all I ask!" said Beltrezzor. "Leave it to me. Let me into your private room at three o'clock and I will explain everything to you. If you are not satisfied you can then refuse."

"You speak mysteries," said the Gaul; "but you yourself are a mystery. Come, as you promise. My life is not much, and I am willing to risk it for you and your little Mary as you call her."

My uncle had been twice every day to visit his niece. The more he saw of her helplessness, her purity, her suffering and her terror, the more she entwined herself about his heart, and the more resolutely did he labor to achieve her deliverance. She clung to him so tenderly, and as the fatal hour approached her fear of the lion became so heartrending, that the old man could hardly tear himself from her embraces.

The Roman guard, accustomed to him, received his coins smilingly and scarcely noticed his coming out. For three days before the Sabbath he had worn a green shade over his eyes.

"I got dust in them," said he to the soldiers, "and an old man's eyes are weak."

Three o'clock, Sabbath, arrived. Beltrezzor was admitted into the private room of the keeper. The amphitheatre was crowded, and crowds were still pressing on the outside for admission. The games and combats were going on, to the great delight of the immense audience, for they occasionally shook the building with shouts of laughter and thunders of applause. The huge lion, irritated by these noises and raging with hunger, sent up roar after roar, which appalled the stoutest hearts among the spectators.

Euphorbus, stern and pale, came into his office.

"Now for your plan," said he to Beltrezzor. "It is now or never."

My uncle drew from the ample folds of his robe a package, which he laid on a table.

"Now," said he, "attention! Mary and I are to change places. She is to come out with you, disguised as her uncle. I am to remain in the dungeon, disguised as Mary."

Euphorbus staggered back with protruded eyes.

"And to be thrown to the lion yourself?"

"It is the only way," said the old man, slowly and meekly.

Euphorbus fell upon his neck and kissed his cheek:

"I have heard that heroes were sometimes elevated into gods; but you are the only man of whom I could believe it."

"You see," continued Beltrezzor, "here is a mask of the finest parchment, painted in imitation of Mary's face, with long beautiful golden hair attached to the headpiece."

"It is indeed an astonishing likeness. The face is perfect. And where is the mask in imitation of yours?"

He untied a string behind his neck, and drew off his hair and beard at once. He was a beardless bald old man. He wore his mask.

"Any one wearing this would be mistaken for me. There was one difficulty about the eyes. We got over that by wearing the green shade. There was another about the nose and mouth. She must hold her handkerchief to her face, as is natural in grief. The illusion will be complete.

"Here are two flat pieces of cork," he continued, "to be put into my sandals, which are peculiarly constructed so as to conceal them. That will add an inch to Mary's height. Then you see my turban is so arranged that a little traction here elevates it an inch more. That will make it right, for she is nearly as tall as I am. The robes you know we can simply exchange."

The old man dwelt upon these details until he convinced Euphorbus that the singular exchange was perfectly feasible.

The voice of Simon Magus was now heard in the courtyard. He had just looked into Mary's window to see that his victim had not escaped. He threw the guard some money. He then spoke to three men who stood before him with long poles in their hands, each pole having an iron hook at the end of it. He spoke so loud that Mary and every one heard him:

"You will stand inside the iron railing and watch the lion's attack. So long as he eats the neck and shoulders or the lower half of the body, let him alone. When he begins upon the chest, drag the body away from him with your hooks. Remember! I want the woman's heart uninjured. If you cannot do it, I will give the signal for the keepers to throw in the murderer Trebonius. That will save my prize and satisfy the people."

After this horrible speech he entered the amphitheatre by a private way and resumed his seat near the gorgeous chair of Lelius.

"The coast is clear," said Euphorbus. "Now is our time."

They entered the courtyard. Euphorbus gave the guards double money.

"Our poor old friend," said he, "is overwhelmed with grief to-day. He cannot speak. It is his last visit."

They passed into the dungeon. Mary was crouching in one corner, white as a corpse. She sprang to her uncle's arms. She could not speak; she could not weep. Terror had paralyzed the fountains of thought and sorrow.

"I have come to save you, my child," said the old man, "Courage! and you will be free in ten minutes. Lazarus is in the street waiting for you. Martha is on a beautiful ship waiting for you. In one hour you will be on the blue sea sailing away from this awful city."

Mary stared at him in wild surprise.

"Free? Lazarus waiting! and Martha?"

The transition from total despair to hope was too much for her weak nerves. She swooned.

The old man knelt by her side, kissing her hands and chafing her temples while the great tears rolled down his cheeks.

"Too bad! too bad!" said Euphorbus, "when time is so precious" — and he busied himself in forcing a stimulus into her mouth.

She revived presently and sat up.

"You say I may be saved, uncle. Now tell me how. I am calm and can comprehend you perfectly."

Beltrezzor proceeded to explain everything as he had done to Euphorbus. She heard him patiently, and then said in a quiet tone:

"And, poor good man! do you think I will permit you to be eaten by the lion in my place? Oh no, that is impossible. Think of some other plan."

"There is no other way. I shall not be eaten by the lion."

"Why not?"

"Because I am not a Christian. You are condemned for heresy. I am a Gentile."

"But they will kill you for contriving my escape, and this good keeper also."

"Oh no! That offence is not punishable with death. They will fine me heavily, but I am rich and can pay. The keeper will escape with you and protect you."

After much persuasion and argument on one side and many doubts and questionings on the other, Mary's scruples were at last overcome, and the transformation in both parties effected so adroitly that detection seemed impossible.

Mary suddenly turned her earnest eyes on Beltrezzor's face.

"Uncle, if you deceive me in this matter, it will kill me."

"Courage! my sweet girl," said the old man, smiling—"come what may. I shall rest better to-night than I did last night; and the sun will shine for me more beautifully to-morrow than it has to-day."

"Come, come," said Euphorbus, "we must be going."

Oh the anguish of that parting!

Mary put the green shade over her eyes and the handkerchief to her mouth and walked slowly but bravely out with the keeper. The guard let them pass. One fellow looked closely after them, and then stepped to the window and looked in. Mary with her golden tresses falling over her shoulders was kneeling in prayer!

Who can imagine the thoughts of that brave old man, as he knelt in the woman's dress, with the lion's growl in his ear! How eagerly he listened! How freely he breathed when he heard no interruption in the courtyard; no outcry; no alarm. They are safe! How he lifted his heart to heaven!

Did he spend that last hour in prayer? To what God did he pray? What faith did he offer up as his claim to salvation? What matters it? Had he not kept the commandments of God?

Was not his soul free from irreverence and profanity and theft and murder and adultery and perjury and uncharitableness? Did he not love his neighbor more than himself?

This disciple of Zoroaster, was he not a child of God?

The hour passed. There was a solemn hush in the grand amphitheatre. The dead gladiators were dragged from the arena. Sliding panels were withdrawn and the great Næmean lion was seen behind his iron bars furiously lashing his sides with his tail.

The herald of Lelius cried with a loud voice:

"Bring forth the woman!"

There was a great rustling and stir in the vast audience. Every one held his breath. A sudden outcry was raised from the prison:

"She has escaped!"

It was echoed by a thousand hoarse whispers in the crowd—"She has escaped!" There was a tremendous excitement. All stood upon their feet. How? where? when? by whom? echoed from all sides. Simon Magus, a picture of flaming wrath, leaped into the arena and ran through the walk enclosed by iron railings that led into the prison.

He returned in a moment dragging the poor, old, bald-headed and beardless man by the arms, and holding up the female mask in the air, he exclaimed:

"The woman and the keeper have fled; but here is the miscreant; here is the criminal! Clear the arena and give him to the lion."

"Give him to the lion!" echoed thousands of voices, followed by thunders of applause.

A tall, stern-looking man, in the front row of seats, sprang to his feet and looking over to Lelius, exclaimed:

"Justice! justice! This man is no Christian; this man is no heretic."

"To the lion—to the lion!" interrupted the multitude with fiercer yells than before.

Simon Magus motioned significantly to the governor.

"To the lion," said Lelius, waving his hand.

"I defy you," said the speaker, in a loud and stern voice—"I defy you to throw him to the lion.

"In the name of the Senate and people of Rome I warn you that this man, Beltrezzor of Persia, is a Roman citizen."

Silence was partly restored; all eyes glaring upon the speaker as he continued.

"Not by birth nor by purchase, but by special decree of the Senate for commercial services rendered the Roman empire by this man, one of the wealthiest and noblest men of the East. I am his agent and correspondent for Antioch. I have seen him before. I know him, and I can prove what I say."

"Release the Roman citizen," said Lelius in a proud and haughty tone, rising from his seat.

Whilst he was speaking Beltrezzor sank gently to the ground. He had been released by an authority higher than that of Rome.

"He is dead!" exclaimed a thousand voices at once.

"He died of fear," said Simon Magus.

"He died of joy," said the voice from the benches; "for that face is the face of an angel."

XXIX
CHRISTIAN CANDLES

Of all these things I was ignorant. I was bound and in prison, helpless, unfriended, unable to communicate with my friends. I bitterly repented having disobeyed my uncle's orders. I cursed Demetrius and Simon Magus and Helena and Magistus. I cursed myself. Mary perhaps was devoured by the lion! Or if saved, she and Martha and Beltrezzor were out on the blue sea, and I left to perish in my folly.

A day or two afterward I observed that our prison ward had received a considerable accession of captives. I was then told by the keeper that a female heretic condemned to the lion had escaped, and that Lelius had ordered the arrest of all the Christians in the city, hoping to ferret out the parties who had assisted her. How my heart leaped for joy! My sister was saved!

My own captivity became a little more endurable. I delighted to think of my friends sailing away over the white-crested waves for the happy land of Gaul. I seemed to feel the fresh sea wind in my own hair and to hear the cool water dashing against the sides of their vessel. Alas! my own fate, how different!

I expected every hour to see the ugly and cunning face of Magistus peering in at my door. Several days and nights passed, and he did not come. I knew he had not forgotten me. I knew he was only preparing himself for some extraordinary villainy and cruelty against me. I was right.

Late one evening my door suddenly opened, and Magistus entered the dungeon, followed by Ethopus. The latter bore an immense roll of some kind of cloth under his arm.

Magistus stood contemplating me for several minutes with folded arms and the old diabolical sneer on his face. Ethopus stepped behind him with downcast eyes.

"Now," he said, slowly, "for the greatest, sweetest revenge which any man in this world has ever enjoyed.

"You have been the bane, the curse, the evil genius of my life. I have always hated you; I know not why, but that it so pleased me. If you had perished in the desert as I designed, all would have been well. Simon would have procured the body of Mary, and we should have been gods in power and glory and pleasure. If you had not escaped my dungeon in Bethany, I would not be at this moment an exile and an outcast. You have eluded me twice. You are cunning. You have eluded the grave itself; but now, my amiable nephew, your time has really come.

"I respect my family too much, I respect your own distinguished merits too much, to doom you to any common ignoble death. Your friend Helena and I have put our brains together to devise something for your especial honor. We have achieved it. It is striking, original, charming. Listen.

"Our plan could not be carried out without absolute power. I have it. Do you see this diamond ring with this great seal upon it? That is the ring of the Roman governor. He who presents it to any officer, soldier, jailer, servant of the government, is to pass untouched, unquestioned. His word is law. When he speaks, it is obedience or death. This absolute power is given me for this whole evening by virtue of the ring.

"Helena obtained this favor from Lelius. Who but she could have done it? Who can say how she did it? Ah! she is deep; she is cunning; she is irresistible.

"Now see what we intend to do. This cloth is a stiff heavy woollen, thoroughly saturated with bituminous substances. We intend to bind your arms down to your side and roll your body tightly up in this cloth, merely leaving out your head. This, when ignited, will burn slowly but brightly, and make a beautiful candle of you.

"But you will fall over, you say. Oh no: a strong iron rod run deep into the ground will pass through the outer layer of the cloth and keep you steady by penetrating in a long, sharp, needle-like point under your chin and through your mouth. Could there be anything more ingenious than that?

"You will be taken out in a cart to the great public square opposite the palace of Simon. There are twelve of you. Christian candles I have named you. You will be stationed immediately opposite our grand portico. Helena and I, arm in arm, will witness your combustion from that point. It is pleasant in a great crowd to know where one's true love is standing.

"It is time for the fireworks to begin. The square is already crowded. We have rolled up the others snugly. They will call for you in a few minutes. All the orders have been given and they will be obeyed.

"Come," he continued, turning to Ethopus. "Come, my old jolly, spotted dog of Egypt! get to work. Simon says his last training made a perfect machine of you. Be quick and bind this old friend and master of yours."

My feelings of horror and of terror during this diabolical monologue, can be better imagined than described. I was dumbfounded. I said nothing. I regarded a speedy death as now inevitable. I looked anxiously at Ethopus, who stoically unrolled the cloth. He took out a strong leather band or girdle. He advanced toward me. He seemed impassive as a stone. I gave myself up in despair.

A moment of awful suspense — and all was changed.

Quick as thought Ethopus turned and dashed Magistus against the wall, throwing the band over his head at the same time. He pulled it down over his chest and buckled it tightly, securing his arms at his side. He drew the signet-ring of Lelius from his finger and threw it to me. Curses and struggles were in vain; for Ethopus seemed strong as a lion and animated with a terrible fury.

In another moment Ethopus hurled him upon his back, and seating himself upon his body, took a knife from his pocket and cut off half his tongue. He then deliberately passed a stout pin through the stump and tied a strong thread behind the pin. He thus stopped the blood which was pouring out of the wretch's mouth and gurgling in his throat. He was now dumb like Ethopus. He could not betray him. He could not escape him.

This was one of the most horrible scenes I ever witnessed. It had evidently been deliberately planned. I was chained against the wall and could not stir. I called out to Ethopus to stop, not to cut out his tongue, not to roll him up in the cloth, but to leave him bound and gagged until we escaped. He paid no more attention to my entreaties, to my excitement, than if I was not present. He seemed deaf, dumb, blind, insensible to everything except to the one master resolution of his soul.

He wound the body carefully up in the bituminous cloth and secured it with leather thongs. It was a shocking sight. He then removed my bolts and chains and set me free. He led me sternly and forcibly to the door, and we passed out, leaving Magistus to his terrible fate. He had fallen into the very pit that he had dug for me.

There was no one in the hall as we came out. Ethopus took the opposite way from that by which he and Magistus came. We soon met officers and guards. I showed the signet-ring; no questions were asked; and we shortly found ourselves in the street and free. What a release!

I did not know which way to go. Ethopus drew me toward the public square. It was crowded with people. Swinging lamps of all colors were suspended from the trees. There were bands of music and fireworks, and dancing-girls and flower-girls, and men with trained monkeys, and all the strange sights and sounds which make a great city in high carnival so brilliant and attractive. Heralds had announced in the afternoon that twelve favorite disciples of the Jewish impostor would be burned, in the shape of candles, that night. The interest was intense.

We came very near to Simon's palace. It was brilliantly illuminated. I recognized the figures of Helena and Lelius and Simon and Demetrius promenading with others on the grand portico. The carts or wagons came along with the unhappy victims. There was a great bustle in the crowd. The figures were set up on a green knoll which elevated them above the heads of the people.

One of the Christians sang, with a clear, sweet voice:

"Glory to God in the highest!
Peace on earth and good-will toward men!"

The mob hooted and yelled and applauded, each in an uproarious manner.

"Ready," cried an officer.

The torches were applied; and twelve bright pillars of flame rose in the air. There was wild cheering from the crowd; but I heard a wilder cry from the spectators on the portico of Simon. The cry was:

"Magistus! Magistus!"

His own friends recognized his face and witnessed his death-struggles!

Such was the origin of the Christian candles, a mode of fatal torture afterward adopted on a grand scale by the emperor Nero in his persecution of the disciples at Rome.

Poor children of Christ! They faced death in every shape. They were crucified; they were flayed alive; they were thrown to wild beasts; they were cast into pits full of serpents; they were stoned; they were starved; they were frozen; they were burned; but there was no form of death which excelled in atrocity this invention of Magistus and Helena.

Helena! Beautiful, enchanting, detestable woman! From this point our currents of life diverged never again to meet. When I look back, I can scarcely comprehend the causes of the wonderful control she exercised over my spirit. I was young, enthusiastic, and impressible; and the senses, educated first, prolonged their sway over the rational faculties. I have been so long delivered from the bondage of the sensuous life, that I am astonished that I ever found any beauty unallied to goodness, or any fascination in aught but a pure and virtuous love.

Women who are given to luxury and pleasure; who aspire to captivate men by the charms of the senses; who live upon the flattering incense of lovers and admirers; who are cunning, proud, vain, ambitious and contemptuous toward others, are Helenas at heart. Circumstances beyond their control may curb their wills and prevent the outward development of their characters. But the revealing light of the spiritual world will show them to be selfish, sensual and cruel to a dreadful degree; and they become the syrens of hell.

These characters are so fearfully wicked, that some may think them gross exaggerations. Exceptional they may be, even in these evil times; but they are the genuine offspring of our natural lusts unsubdued and uncontrolled by the sacred laws and life of heaven. They are the common, every-day characters of the spheres of the unhappy in the spiritual world, and they exist in potency, if not in act, in every human being whose heart is alienated from God, or whose ruling love is the love of self.

I had no time to philosophize in this manner, when I knew that the friends of Magistus had recognized his face before it was concealed by the fatal flames. A keen and rapid pursuit would immediately follow in every direction. To get out of the city was our first thought, our only safety. If we took the roads to the interior of the country, we could certainly be overtaken. If we struck out eastwardly for the sea-beach, we might pick up some fisherman's boat and escape to sea. We took the latter course.

We walked rapidly, and were many miles up the coast before midnight. I was fresh and under high excitement, and Ethopus seemed capable of all endurance. I occupied the time in telling him the whole history of his brother Anthony, and in thanking him over and over again for my extraordinary deliverance. The poor, dumb man could only manifest his delight by shaking my hand and patting me on the shoulder, which he repeatedly did.

Several hours more and I was thoroughly fatigued. Just before dawn we lay down under a great tree on the banks of a little stream which was perpetually tripping from the mountains toward the sea, bearing its crystal tokens from the spirit of liberty in the one to the kindred soul in the other.

When I awoke, the sun was high in the heavens. Ethopus was bathing his feet in the little river. He could not bear to disturb me, as I appeared so exhausted and so sound asleep. He pointed smilingly to a little boat, which we had not discovered in the darkness of the night. There was one ark of hope and safety. I felt reassured. We had nothing to eat but some apples, which we had plucked by the way. We made this frugal meal, and if we had put to sea immediately, the whole story of my life, from this point, might have been different.

The morning was bright and balmy. A little silver mist rose softly from the woods, the leaves of which were twinkling with dew. The sea's surf, which at times is so white and boisterous, rippled gently against the yellow beach. The singing of birds was heard here and there in the branches, and now and then a great shining fish flapped up out of the water. The air was sweet and serene, the sky soft and pure. "This heavenly peace and repose of nature," said I to myself, "is neither silence nor solitude!"

One of the most beautiful things in the world to me is a little stream of clear water, afar off in the country among the green hills, breaking into sounds and colors over the stones and pebbles in its path. I could sit by the hour on the banks of such a lovely rivulet, looking into its face and listening to its music. It is there, if ever, that the breathings of the spirit world upon the heart endeavor to break forth from the lips in poesy and song.

Touched that morning with this delightful and child-like love of nature, I could not rest satisfied until I had bathed my weary limbs and body in the cooling stream. I dallied a long time among the ripples and in the shadow of the overhanging trees, forgetful of the painful past and the uncertain future.

A sharp cry from Ethopus, who was getting the boat ready, suddenly aroused me from my dream. He pointed down the beach. Before I had put on my robe, I heard the tramp of horses, and in a few moments we were surrounded by a troop of cavalry and taken prisoners. Bound tightly and mounted behind two of the soldiers, we were hurried back to Antioch and cast into separate dungeons.

I lay there for several weeks neglected and alone. I had at least no fear of a visit from Magistus. A visitor, however, at last appeared. It was Demetrius.

"Lazarus," said he, "I reproach myself for the part I took in decoying you into the house of Simon and betraying you into the hands of Magistus. It was not well done toward a fellow-student of the Platonic philosophy. I have labored to make you amends. I have saved your life, but it was a hard struggle. Ethopus was thrown to the lion. Helena pouted and fumed because you did not share his fate. Lelius was for a long time inflexible. I have gained something for you, although not much. You are condemned for life to the chain-gang of criminals who are compelled to labor on the public works. It is a sad fate, but you are young. Time, the revolutionist, sometimes releases the bound."

"Life is sweet," said I, "and I thank you. I forgive your wrong to me. I forgive Helena and Simon. I will pray for them and you. And, oh, Demetrius, let a man, henceforth dead to the world you live in, beseech you to extricate yourself from this terrible network of evil that surrounds you. Aspire to be free, just, true and good, and you will be happy."

"Where did you get this religious philosophy?"

"From a greater than Plato—from Christ."

He turned away.

XXX
THE GREAT COMBAT

Behold me then at the age of twenty-five, innocent of crime, sentenced to the life and labors of a convict! My associates were the lowest ruffians imaginable. My fare was coarse and sometimes revolting. I was locked up alone at night in a dark cell. I slept on a pallet of straw. From sunrise to sunset I was compelled to labor on the public works, chained by the leg to another creature as miserable as myself.

Young as I was, I had already met with strange adventures and made hairbreadth escapes. I was long buoyant and hopeful, and was constantly expecting some lucky turn of the wheel of fortune. There was, indeed, very little rational ground of hope. My uncle Beltrezzor was dead. My sisters had escaped to the other end of the world, and were not likely to return. Not one of the few Christians of the city knew anything about my being there, for I had seen no one but Beltrezzor. Demetrius alone knew my whereabouts, and by command of Simon he had entered a false name for me on the books of the prison. So I was lost and buried from the social world in which I had moved.

I did not believe that my imprisonment would be of long duration. Young, educated, wealthy, I thought I was needed by the infant Church. The subject of the greatest miracle of Christ, my very presence was an argument in favor of Christianity. Then my experiences in the spiritual world had given me knowledge superior to that of all the disciples; knowledge necessary to the organization of the faith upon truly rational principles. To suspect even that one so valuable to the holy cause could be imprisoned for life, without a future, without a mission, was to doubt the wisdom of Providence and the verity of my death and resurrection.

It was thus that the secret pride of my selfhood buoyed me up in the direst adversity, and that my own self-righteousness became the fountain of hope!

Notwithstanding all this, I remained a captive at hard labor for forty years of my manhood! As long as the children of Israel were in the wilderness, so long was I in the convict prison of Antioch! Terrible thought!

When I emerged from my prison-grave into the world and the Church again, I was old and feeble and bronzed and broken, forgotten by all men, a cipher in the sphere of thought and life in which I had expected to occupy so commanding a position.

The wicked and detestable emperors, those monsters of nature, Tiberius, Caligula, Claudius and Nero, had successively governed and cursed the Roman state. The Christian religion had spread into all countries; into Syria and Parthia and Arabia, into Egypt and Abyssinia, into Spain and Gaul and Britain, by the zealous labors and fiery devotion of Paul and Peter and Barnabas and Philip and James and hundreds of lesser lights of the new faith.

All this and thousands of other strange events had occurred without my knowledge, without my participation. The great world moved on without me. I knew as little of it in my prison as a child knows of the sea, who bathes his little feet in the surf that breaks upon the beach at his father's door.

This great lapse of time, an entire manhood, so devoid of incident, so uninteresting to the general reader, was my real life. All that had happened previously was my childhood. It was in this fearful school of captivity and sorrow and labor and solitude and darkness, that I became a man and a Christian. Looking backward, I am filled with gratitude for the wisdom and goodness of God, which infused such health and blessing into the cup of bitterness which I was compelled to drink.

I passed through three great spiritual eras during my captivity. Life does not consist in external events, but in the revelation of spiritual states. This alone is the true biography.

The first era was one of intense resistance to my fate. My disagreeable surroundings annoyed and irritated me. The unaccustomed labor in the burning sun was almost too great for my strength. I loathed my companions and my keepers. I loathed my tasks. Still greater suffering was occasioned by my losses; the loss of friends and relatives; of books and study; of the delightful society of woman; of all the thousand little things which constitute the comfort and charm of civilized life.

Hope lingered long, and died a slow but painful death in my heart. I made many efforts to escape—all of which failed, and brought upon me terrible punishments. I was starved and scourged repeatedly, and finally branded for an attack made upon one of my keepers, in which I nearly succeeded in killing him. These things called out and developed all the evil qualities of my nature. Let the smoothest-faced, sweetest-tongued and gayest-hearted man in the world undergo what I have undergone, and he will discover how many unrecognized devils have been dormant in the serene and undisturbed depths of his being.

Wounded and bleeding in my self-love and self-respect, my sufferings, physical and mental, seemed to have a destructive effect upon my spiritual nature. Destruction of the old precedes a new order of things. Along with hope, faith also sickened and died. For a long time I consoled myself by recalling my wonderful experiences in the spiritual world. I prayed, and recited to myself the sweet promises of Scripture to those in affliction. But as months and years rolled away, despair overpowered me. I began to doubt the truth of religion, the reliability of my own memory, and even the very existence of God.

So little depth of earth had the good seed found in my heart! I, who thought I loved and believed in Christ; who had seen him in both worlds; who conceived myself ready and able to preach his true doctrine to mankind; thus tried in the fiery furnace of temptation, found myself all dross, thoroughly skeptical and wicked, worse than the ignorant convicts and keepers around me.

What mortal can comprehend the meaning of those mysterious words of the Divine Man on the cross: "My God! my God! why hast thou forsaken me?"

I felt also that God had forsaken me. When the little religious light I had, faded away in my soul, I was taken possession of by demons, male and female. I verily believe that I was, for a while, what the world calls insane. I became proud, and supercilious, and scoffing. I was ambitious as Simon, cruel as Magistus, sensual and abandoned as Helena. Escaped from those wretches in the body, my spirit became the sport and prey of infernal spirits similar to them. I envied the power, the glory, the magic of Simon. At night I dreamed only of bacchanalian orgies in a Grecian heaven, and awoke parched and feverish and excited and maddened, as if some syren-like Helena had kissed me in my sleep.

This wretched state lasted about ten years. It culminated in a great illness; for relief or death had become the alternative. The illness of a convict in prison! Cast upon my pallet of straw, without friends, without nurses, without proper diet or medicine, frequently without water; what days and nights of suffering and anguish did I experience!

It was a long, long sickness. The stage of excitement was accompanied with wild delirium, and my imagination was haunted by fiery figures of infernal spirits.

Then exhaustion came, and forgetfulness. Nature slowly rallied; after that, thought returned, strength and feeling came back. My sisters and Beltrezzor and Jesus loomed up away off, as pleasant pictures or beautiful dreams. Many sweet little scenes of my happy childhood revisited me in charming memories. I lay for hours in peaceful trances. I had consoling visions. The poor convict's cell was illumined with a glory not its own.

One night I saw the house that was building for me in the heavens. It was rising in stately grandeur. Oh it was beautiful! but still unfinished. Mary Magdalen was toiling away with earnest brow and face more angelic than ever. Many shining spirits were about her. I was lying some distance off, asleep in the shadow of a great rock. She said to her companions with a sweet smile:

"He will awake presently and help me build."

One day I heard the voice of my father saying to John the Baptist,

"The crisis is over; he will be saved; we must teach him the power of the Lord's Prayer."

I know not whether this was a dream or a genuine vision. But I repeated the Lord's Prayer feebly and with folded hands. The effect was wonderful. A great light shone around me. The air was full of little cherub forms. Heavenly music was heard in the distance. The deepest chords of my being were touched. The flood-gates of contrition were reopened. Faith returned. I wept. I was happy—oh, so happy!

This also may have been a dream, but it was a potent medicine; for after that, my recovery was amazingly rapid. I then entered into a second and very different phase of my spiritual life. The devil, after casting me repeatedly into the water and the fire, and rending me sorely, had departed. But I knew full well that he only departs for a season—that his return is as sure as the rising of the tides. I knew that the only way to keep him out, was to refurnish my house on the heavenly model.

Now my knowledge of spiritual things came to be of immense advantage. Not an abstract, theoretical knowledge of them, but a knowledge derived from sight and hearing. I had seen, felt and studied the angelic sphere of life. I knew what it was. I had discovered three great elements in that sphere, and determined to put them all into action in my own life, so as to bring my spirit into interior communion with angels and the Lord.

The first element was profound humility and reverence. God only enters the soul which is thoroughly emptied of self. A proud Christian is a devil in disguise. The angels are so thoroughly divested of the selfhood, that they live and labor only for others' good; and that is living and laboring for God.

Prayer is the means by which humility and reverence are cultivated. It does not change the Unchangeable; it only brings the soul into that state in which it is receptive of the divine love and wisdom. I determined, therefore, to pray—for I had long neglected prayer—and to pray regularly, systematically, earnestly, and especially in the form or after the manner that the Lord himself had appointed.

The second element of angelic life was cheerfulness. The cheerfulness of angels flows from the peace and joy in which they live. They cannot be present in a sphere of gloom and darkness. The silent, tearful, mourning, austere, ascetic Christian, cuts himself off from angelic consolations, and renders his regeneration doubly painful and difficult. Tears and fastings and scourgings and solitude and fantastic self-denials do not lead to heaven. They block up the way thither with needless difficulties.

I determined, therefore, to be cheerful; to accept my lot with graceful resignation; to have a genial word and pleasant smile for every one; to avoid reveries and broodings which kept the past continually in painful contrast with the present; to make a final surrender of all my grand ambitions and glorious expectations; and to take a heartfelt pleasure in the trifles of life, such as may be found even within the walls of a prison.

The third element of the angelic life was useful activity. An idle angel is an impossibility. They are all busy as bees; and like those little preachers to mankind, each labors intently, not for his own special benefit, but for the good of all the rest. Their cheerfulness and usefulness run in equal and parallel streams, and they are both proportioned to their reverence and humility.

I determined therefore to work willingly; to accept my hard tasks as those appointed of God; to be no longer an eye-servant but an earnest, faithful, intelligent co-operator in building, repairing and improving the magnificent temples, baths, aqueducts, walls, quays and fortifications of Antioch; to treat my fellow-laborers as brethren, not by descending to their gross level, but by striving to lift them as well as myself up to the height of a noble and unselfish manhood.

All this was facile and beautiful in theory, difficult and painful in practice. The struggle was intense; and many, many dark and miserable days alternated with my bright ones. It was the great warfare of my life, less imposing than my struggles with Magistus and Helena, but far more productive of results. It was a process by which good was substituted for evil; but as fast only as the evil was thoroughly repented of and put away. It was a process of growth by which the germ of the heavenly life, penetrating through the dead shell of the old nature, passed upward into a serener light and larger liberty. It was a death and a resurrection. How small an affair was my first resurrection in comparison with this!

Twenty years or more were spent in the great combat between my old natural man and the new spiritual man which was being conceived, born, nourished, instructed and vitalized within me. I am still engaged in the same conflict. But after twenty years, I felt that the good had attained a permanent ascendency—that duty had become pleasure—that self was so far subdued that I expected nothing, desired nothing for myself alone, and experienced a serene delight in promoting the happiness of others.

The reader need not think that a convict's prison afforded no opportunities for the great work of regeneration, and for the development of Christian character. The rainbow that shines in the cloud, and glitters in the dew-drop, is the same. The divine influx is identical in the greatest things and in the least. The patience, the meekness, the kindness to others, the obedience to law, the truthfulness, the industry, the honesty which can be exhibited in the lowliest sphere of human life, have no sweeter odor, no greater worth in the sight of heaven when they are displayed on the throne of the Cæsars.

I worked faithfully at all my tasks until my overseers respected me so much that they did not watch me at all. I was always ready to assist every one with word and deed, until my power over my fellow-prisoners was such that my voice of intercession could suspend a quarrel or even suppress a riot. I delighted to instruct these poor degraded fellows in the truths of religion; and when they turned a deaf ear to these, I could still please them with scraps of poetry or history or science. It was a special pleasure to nurse the sick; and in the course of twenty or thirty years, hundreds and even thousands felt the benefit and the blessing of my presence.

This steady growth of a good and useful character in spite of the sneers and rebuffs of the ill-disposed, and in the face of mighty difficulties, brought substantial comforts to myself also. I was released from strict confinement; I was made overseer of a considerable party; I was allowed liberties I had not known before; and I was fed with abundance from the officers' table. Thus, with advancing years, I became contented and happy, and my means of being useful to others were greatly increased.

I was permitted to plant flowers and vines in the interior courtyard of our prison. After long and patient labor I adorned and beautified the spot so greatly that it attracted the attention of every visitor.

The mission of flowers is like that of poetry, to enchant, to elevate, and to purify. Therefore the Spring comes annually to shower her myriads of fragrant little lyrics upon the world!

It seemed a shame to constrain these sweet and free children of the air and sunlight to illumine the interior of a dungeon and to live with criminals; but I remembered that the angels whom they represent, delight to visit the humblest spot and to assist the most forlorn and helpless creatures of God.

I had been in prison about fifteen years without seeing a book, when a singular old Greek character was confined with us for some nameless crime. He was taciturn and stately, and evidently a man of education. He had a copy of the Tragedies of Eschylus which the guard had not taken from him, although parchments so well executed as that, were of considerable value. He seemed to know Eschylus by heart, and he loaned the book to me. With what delight I devoured it!

It was to me a whole flower-garden of sweets and beauties. The sad fate of Orestes, haunted by the Furies, struck the tenderest chords in my heart; and I contemplated with the joy of kinship and sympathy the grandeur of Prometheus chained to the rock, for holding in his possession secret knowledge which no tortures could compel him to reveal.

I, too, was to learn the sanctity of silence!

One day the old Greek, when working on a pier, suddenly plunged twenty feet into the rapid Orontes. He struck out boldly down the river for the sea, and the boat sent after him did not overtake the desperate swimmer. He left Eschylus behind him.

I had been in prison about twenty-five years, when I came into possession of another and far greater book. A young Jew was condemned to hard labor for striking a Roman officer who had insulted his sister. He fell sick almost immediately, and was carried off by grief and a rapid consumption. I nursed him closely, and he seemed much attached to me until he discovered that I was a Christian. He became at once stern and cold and uncommunicative, and ended by requesting the keeper to provide him with another nurse or none at all.

He died not long after, and I was surprised at receiving a message from his deathbed. He thanked me for my kindness to him, and begged me to accept from him a beautiful little copy of the Psalms of David.

What a treasure I found it! It was a mirror of my own struggles; of my hopes and fears; of my deep humiliations and my ecstatic triumphs. It let me into the presence of angels. It was like the voice of God calling to little Samuel in the dead of night.

XXXI
FREE

One day I was summoned from my labors into a kind of reception-room to meet a visitor. A visitor! I had been imprisoned thirty years and no one had ever called to see me. I had forgotten the outer world and supposed it had forgotten me. It was with surprise and some trepidation that I advanced to present myself to the stranger.

He was of small size, ugly, stoop-shouldered and bald. His face was sallow, his nose aquiline, his brows heavy and joined between his eyes. His air was embarrassed and timid and his speech slow. With this unprepossessing appearance, his manner was cordial and engaging, his tones agreeable, and when warmed up in conversation, his features were radiant with thought and genius.

This remarkable man was Paul, the apostle to the Gentiles.

After satisfying himself that I had been thirty years in prison and that I was really Lazarus whom Christ raised from the dead, he became very animated and communicative.

"You will be interested," said he, "to know how I found you out. I was called, a few days before I left Rome on this tour to the Eastern churches, to see a dying man. He was one of the most miserable wrecks I have ever witnessed, bearing the mark of the beast and the seal of sin. He was a Greek and his name was Demetrius. He wished to be baptized into the Christian faith, and to confess his sins before he died. He told me that you had been sentenced for life under a false name to hard labor on the public works of Antioch. He begged, as a favor to a dying sinner, that I would visit you if possible, and beg your pardon for the crimes he had committed against you."

It seemed that all my friends supposed I had been burned as one of the Christian candles, on the eventful night of the death of Magistus. My sisters and the disciples had mourned for me as one of the first martyrs of the new faith. Mary and Martha had arrived safely in Gaul, and had founded a beautiful church with a convent and Christian schools at Marseilles. Their wealth had contributed immensely to the spread of Christianity. They were devoted and holy women, and Paul was eloquent in praise of their zeal and piety.

"And Mary Magdalen?" said I, with a slight tremor at pronouncing the name of a woman who had of late taken ardent possession of my thoughts.

"The humblest, sweetest, gentlest creature in the world! She always wears her black veil and devotes herself to the most menial offices. She is the grandest type I have yet seen of the purifying and sanctifying influence of the religion of Christ."

I felt a sweet glow of satisfaction at this announcement; and old man as I was, something like a blush mounted to my cheeks.

I learned from the great apostle the history of the Church from its infancy to the present time. He was modest and even depreciating in narrating his own share in the stupendous labors of the early disciples. I was not slow in detecting, from what he said, the immense changes in thought and spirit which had taken place in the Christian commonwealth since I had been withdrawn from its sphere.

Jesus Christ had left them a religion; Paul had made it a theology.

Paul drew from me a narration of my experiences in the spiritual world. I was very explicit and enthusiastic, for I deemed my revelations of the utmost importance to the Church and the world. He listened with interest, but with evident incredulity. We exchanged ideas at some length on all the leading questions of theology. I became more and more anxious to impress him with the truth of what I was saying.

"Remember," said I, "that the germs which you now plant in the Church, will expand in the form and direction you give them for hundreds and may be thousands of years. The slightest deviations now from the genuine truth, will grow into gigantic errors.

"If you teach the destructibility of this physical globe and the resurrection of our dead bodies from the dust, the Church will not have a true conception of the spiritual world, nor of the relation of that world to this.

"If you teach the separate and distinct personality of the Father, Son and Holy Ghost, the proper or supreme divinity of Jesus Christ will not be understood, and the germ of polytheism will take root in your creed.

"If you ignore the great judgment executed by Christ in the world of spirits, you will fail to comprehend the true object of his incarnation; and you will commit the sad mistake of supposing that the next and last judgment predicted, will take place in the world of nature.

"If you speak, as you did just now, of the blood of Christ cleansing from sin, your hearers may fall into the error of supposing that the material blood shed upon the cross is what cleanses and saves from sin; whereas the truth is, that the blood shed for the remission of sins, is the wine of the New Testament—the spiritual truth and spiritual life which flow forth from the Divine Man for the healing of the nations."

So I went on, reiterating all the grand points of doctrine which distinguished the teachings of the angels I had conversed with, from the teachings of Paul. He became more and more restive under my impetuous torrent of argument, and at last rose to depart. He excused himself on the plea of urgent business and short time. He said he would call again if possible, and would interest the Church in Antioch to labor for my release.

He left me with a pleasant smile. He passed into a gallery where he met the governor of the prison. They were conversing as they walked slowly along beneath a window at which I had stopped. I heard Paul say,

"He is evidently insane."

"I wish the world was full of such madmen," was the bluff answer of the governor.

And that was the result of my interview with the great thinker, the leading spirit of the Christian world!

Insane!

This visit of Paul was of immense service to me. It helped me to subdue one of the strongest points of my selfhood. I still cherished the dream that my spiritual knowledge had been entrusted to me for the special benefit of the Christian Church. My only reason for wishing to get out of prison, was that I might communicate the Doctrine of Christ, as it appears to the angels, to my fellow-men.

After mature reflection upon my conversation with Paul and its results, I came to the conclusion that I had labored under a great mistake and had cherished an impossible hope. There are certain successive steps in the grand evolution of the general human mind, which make one revelation of truth necessary and proper at one time and another at another. The world and the Church were not ready for the knowledges which had been given to me. The transition from Jewish darkness to angelic light was too great, too sudden. A long period of twilight must intervene—a period of literal interpretations, of janglings and wranglings and schisms. In the fullness of time, perhaps, and after another judgment in the world of spirits, another church may be instituted capable of receiving without adulteration the sublime verities of the spiritual world.

So I abandoned my mission. God knew better than I did, and I was satisfied.

It is strange what a new, sweet, beautiful life sprung up in my soul after I discovered that I had no mission in this world to fulfill, but to spread cement between stones, to plant flowers, to read the Psalms and to nurse my sick fellow-prisoners. I was a new creature.

I then entered upon what I have designated as the third state or era of my spiritual life. And this state was so marvelous, so exceptional to all the experiences of my fellow-men, that I shall not dwell long upon it. It may be a thousand or two thousand years before Providence repeats the phenomenon and produces another case like mine; and although in the far-off perfection of the world they will be common enough, the story of it will for centuries fall upon the ears of men as an idle dream.

The first intimation I had of a further change of state, was received while I was reading the Scriptures. The good Christians of Antioch, it seems, failed in procuring my release; but they contrived to send me a copy of the ancient Scriptures and the Gospel of Matthew. These were priceless jewels to an old man and a prisoner dead to all things except the life of religion.

One day when reading in the Psalms and applying the thoughts to my own individual experience, I became suddenly aware, by a kind of interior illumination, that the secret soul-life of the Lord Jesus Christ in his combats with the powers of hell, was embodied and concealed in the sacred pages. They contain more wonderful things than all the heights and depths of this external nature which we so much admire. They contain the mysteries of life and death.

Every day brought new revelations to my mind of the interior meaning of the sacred writings. I found that the spiritual history of the incarnation of Christ was concealed in the narrative of the lives of Abraham, Isaac and Jacob. The first chapters of Genesis, under the figure of the creation of the world, revealed the successive steps by which the human soul is built up from its original chaos into the image of God. The wanderings of the Israelites from Egypt to Canaan, was the spiritual history of every man's regeneration. And the prophets—oh, the prophets! with their dark sayings and grand imagery, concealed with a mystic veil the most beautiful and holy truths of the spiritual universe.

These things were not invented by my imagination. They were not discovered by my ingenuity. They pre-existed in the Scriptures, but are invisible to the mind which rests in the mere sense of the letter. Their existence was revealed to me by an interior light, the operation of which I did not comprehend. I learned also that this wonderful spiritual sense of the

Divine Word was clearly understood in heaven, and was the mental food of angels.

The Gospel of Matthew contains similar spiritual mysteries enfolded in the literal story of our Lord. The Epistles of Paul, however,—glowing, eloquent, devout, impressive as they are—contain no interior or spiritual signification. I saw at once that they had no organic connection with the heavens; in other words, that they were not divinely inspired. They were simply the earnest, saintly utterances of a great and good man to his brethren.

"And yet," said I to myself, "so potent has this zealous and eloquent apostle been in organizing the Church, and so dense is the darkness of the natural mind, that it would not surprise me, if in the far future the words of Paul are reckoned of equal value with the history of Jesus, or with the Law and the Prophets."

The peace and joy inspired by the spiritual perception of the Word, were ineffable. My mind was in a state of continual felicity. I began also to have the most exquisite and beautiful dreams. I was frequently awakened by strains of the most heavenly music, and the darkness of my little cell was illumined by flashes of light, auroral and rainbow colors darting and twinkling here and there in the most surprising manner. I felt that some organic change in my spiritual constitution was impending.

One Sabbath morning when I was reading in the Prophets, I became suddenly aware of a presence in my room; and lifting my eyes I beheld my father standing before me. He was as youthful and beautiful as ever. He was clad in shining garment, and said with a beaming smile:

"Do you understand what you read?"

"Better than I ever did before. But, O father! how is it that you have descended into the natural world?"

"Have you so soon forgotten your instructions in the world of spirits? I have not descended into the world of nature. I see nothing material which surrounds you. I am invisible to all eyes but yours. The change is in yourself. Your spiritual sight has been partially opened into the world of spirits where I am—enough to see my form, but not my surroundings. You seem to come to me, while I seem to come to you. You see me with your spiritual eyes and your material surroundings with your natural eyes."

It is needless to explain the philosophy, as it is impossible to describe the joy, of this happy reunion. Suffice it to say that my father came frequently to see me, or I went to see him, however the case may be interpreted. He assisted me in my studies of the Word, and we had many long discourses on the mysteries of regeneration. Many of these things are incommunicable in human language, for when my spiritual sight was open, I spoke unconsciously the language of spirits and not the language of men; and I find it impossible to embody in material expressions what was perfectly intelligible in my spiritual state.

"Your case," said my father, "so strange and exceptional at present, is a proof of the possibilities of the human spirit. As long as the powers of hell reign on earth, it will be fearfully dangerous for man to have communication with spirits; and the Lord in his mercy will, as far as may be possible, keep each world a secret from the other. When He comes again with an open Word and his angelic hosts in the far-off ages of terrestrial time, such cases as yours may occur not unfrequently, and will announce the approaching conjunction of heaven and earth."

This double life, this wheel within a wheel, is no part of my earthly autobiography. I must draw the veil over its mysteries. I am permitted, however, to tell my readers that my uncle Beltrezzor was revealed to my eyes. He appeared as a young man of unspeakable beauty, clad in a purple robe of dazzling splendor. He had become a member of a heavenly society situated nearest to the Sun of the spiritual world. The atmosphere in which they live is a tissue of golden light, and the emblem of their spiritual love is a flame of sacred fire.

Would you call that a convict's cell or the gate of paradise, which was brightened by the halo of such presences?

The old man who thus lived in both worlds, at once escaping the common limitations of time and space, was not withdrawn from the practical discharge of his homely and difficult duties. Never in his life was he more faithful, more zealous, more careful in the little every-day affairs which really make the happiness or the misery of life.

One day I was working on the walls of a new palace. The chief architect, a man of noble character and great influence, happened to approach very near me in one of his rounds of inspection. He said in a pleasant tone:

"You spread your cement with very great care."

"So it ought to be," said I, "for the cement is the brotherly love which binds the hearts of the brethren together."

He lifted his hand and made a certain signal.

I responded to it with another.

"I discover," he said, "that you are a member of that venerable and secret order instituted by king Solomon and Hiram Abiff, the widow's son."

"Yes—for more than forty years."

"And has it been of service to you?"

"Oh yes! I have discovered in it a mine of spiritual treasures. Its symbols and ceremonies embody a system of universal philosophy unknown even to its members. It is an epitome of the spiritual mysteries of the universe."

"How comes it," said he, "that a disciple of the square and compass, who has stood upon the tesselated pavement, is confined at hard labor as a criminal?"

"Ah sir! I was quite a youth when I came here. I was innocent, but I had none to defend me."

"Is it possible!" said he, and walked toward the governor of the prison, with whom he entered into conversation.

The next day I received a full discharge from my sentence, and a handsome present of money from the chief architect.

I was free!

XXXII
WHAT REMAINS?

I purchased some new clothes, and wandered all day about the streets of Antioch, astonished at my liberty. I dined at an eating-house where several languages were spoken by the different guests, and where every one stared at the long-bearded, long-haired old man, with the new robes and the rough, brown hands. Toward dark I began to feel very lonely and miserable, and at last returned to the prison like a dog to his kennel, and begged the favor of a night's lodging in my old cell.

Free! Free like a plant whose roots are dead, and which, with no attachment to the earth, trembles at the mercy of the wind!

I met next day with some of the Christians of Antioch. They seemed glad that I had been released and spoke kindly to me, but remembered the visit of Paul and his belief that I was insane. If my opinions had been orthodox, what a cordial reception they would have given to the man whom Christ raised from the dead! As I had learned the divine philosophy of silence, I said nothing to them on spiritual subjects.

I was sixty-five years old and everything was new and strange. The pages of history during my long incarceration had been written in blood and tears. Vespasian occupied the throne of the Roman empire, assisted by his son Titus, who had besieged and taken Jerusalem. The holy temple was reduced to ashes and the city of David was a pile of ruins. The judgment in the world of spirits had descended upon the earth.

I was shocked by the horrible details of the persecution which the Christian world had suffered from the detestable Nero; and of the crucifixion of Peter, the murder of Paul and the martyrdom of many prominent disciples. What Lelius had begun at the private instigation of a sorcerer on the little stage of Antioch, too insignificant for historical notice, had been repeated by the butcher of Rome on the theatre of the world.

During this terrible persecution my sisters had been driven from Marseilles. Flying for their lives, they reached the bleak and distant shores of Britain. There they planted the gospel banner and preached Christ to the pagan natives. There they were still living at the last accounts, lights in the darkness, warmth in the coldness around them.

Mary Magdalen had refused to fly from the Roman tyrants. Roused to a wild pitch of religious enthusiasm by the atrocities perpetrated upon her fellow-Christians, she rushed defiantly into the presence of the heathen officers and demanded the pleasure and the glory of dying for the name of Christ. Seeking martyrdom, she escaped it. Astounded at this eloquent and brave woman with disheveled hair and face flashing a wild spiritual light, the persecutors pronounced her mad, and refused to put her to death.

She retired to a mountain in Spain and occupied a cave overlooking the sea. There she lived in solitude and prayer, wearing out soul and body in contrition for the sins of her early youth. Her sanctity and power of healing were so great, that many pilgrims came from remote places to receive her benediction or be healed by her touch.

Helena, the beautiful syren from whom my soul had so narrowly escaped, deserted Simon for Lelius, and Lelius for some Roman general, and this last for a low favorite of Caligula. She was finally swallowed up in that hideous whirlpool of Roman life, which was kept in motion by the unbridled passions of male and female monsters, such as the world has rarely seen.

Simon Magus had been driven from Antioch at the instigation of Helena, who had unbounded control over the Roman legate. He retired into Samaria, where he acquired great power and fame by his magic and sorceries. Thousands of people in that rude country admitted his claim to divine power. It was there that he came into contact with the disciples of Christ.

Simon had discovered by his acute genius that a great change had taken place in the relations between the spiritual and natural worlds since the death and ascension of Jesus. The old demons who had governed the world of spirits had been cast into hell. No spells of incantation could recall Jabol-he-moth or any of the great spirits to his consultations. The magical formulas had lost their power. The pagan oracles were becoming silent. The influence formerly exercised by magicians over men and Nature was evidently waning. Simon became sad, suspicious, fearful. The ground was sinking under him.

He did not attribute these singular changes to the right cause. He believed that Jesus was only a magician more powerful than any or all others—one who, by some mysterious method had monopolized the subtle forces of spirit over matter. He therefore came to the disciples of Jesus, and was baptized into the Church. When he thought he had sufficiently ingratiated himself with the apostles, he offered them a large sum of money for the magical secret by which they healed the sick and raised the dead.

Peter answered him indignantly:

"Thy money perish with thee, because thou hast thought that the gift of God may be purchased with money!"

After that exposure he went to Rome, where his magical powers seemed to revive in the infernal atmosphere of that wicked city. His conduct became more and more eccentric, insolent and presumptuous. He was clearly obsessed by devils. He manifested great aversion to the name of Christ, and professed to repeat all of his miracles with the greatest ease. He announced in the height of his madness, that he would ascend to heaven with a chariot and horses on a certain day. The amphitheatre was crowded to suffocation. It was said that he rose about forty feet in the air, when his chariot and horses fell back into the arena and crushed him to death.

Thus perished a man whose character and actions will seem impossible to future generations, but who was one of the typical products of a corrupt and doomed civilization.

I had never known the earthly heaven of home and wife and child. I had no country; no resting place; for little Bethany also was laid in ashes. My old friends and my old enemies were dead. The little church to which I belonged in heart, was the feeblest of all religious powers; and even that would have repudiated and expelled me on a full declaration of my faith. The most advanced man in the world, I was the most desolate.

My face, my thoughts, my heart turned fondly to Britain. The last time I beheld my sisters was on that eventful night in Bethany, when they gave the supper to Jesus, and when Mary unwittingly anointed him for his burial. I must see them again! It was a long, dangerous, desolate journey for a poor old man to make alone. But my sisters called to me at evening from the golden shadows of the west, and beckoned to me in the night through the twinkling of the northern stars.

I sailed from Antioch to Rome. Not a Christian cared enough for the old man with heretical opinions, to pay a friendly visit or give a kindly farewell to him whom Christ had raised from the dead. As the ship passed close to one of the great piers, some old convicts who were working upon it recognized me and waved me a hearty good-bye. With tears in my eyes I kissed my hand to my only friends in the world.

On reaching Rome I was delighted to find the apostle John who had extricated Mary and Martha from the toils of Magistus, and who gave me a most cordial reception. This unexpected warmth of friendship and sympathy infused new life into me and almost made me happy again.

To my great surprise and pleasure, this disciple whom Jesus loved, and to whose care he committed his mother, agreed with almost everything I had to say. He broke the seal I had imposed upon my lips; for he had a sacred thirst for spiritual knowledge which I felt constrained to gratify. He received my doctrines of the resurrection of the spiritual instead of the natural body, of judgments in the spiritual and not in the natural world, and the grand central truth of all truths—the supreme divinity and absolute fatherhood of Jesus Christ.

John regretted deeply the dissensions which had already distressed the little Church, and foresaw the errors which would probably arise from certain dubious phrases and unwarranted doctrines which had crept into its theology. My whole story, he said, was so beautiful that it ought to be true; and if true, it certainly ought to be beautiful.

Thus John endorsed the very teachings for which Paul thought me insane!

Just as I was starting for Britain, news was brought from that cold region which rendered my journey unnecessary.

My sisters were dead!

Martha, when traversing one dark night a desolate moor to relieve a person in deep distress, was lost and perished in the snow. When the corpse was discovered and laid out in the little chapel of their convent, and Mary approached it, this new sorrow, added to the multiplied cares and labors of her life, was too much for the overburdened heart. The silver cord was gently broken, and she stretched her own body, like a funeral pall, upon that of her sister.

Conjoined in their lives! united in their death!

Beautiful spirits, clad always in virgin white! Brides of Christ! Twin-stars of heaven! Farewell!—until this old body also shall drop into the dust, and the strong bond of spiritual affinity shall draw us together again, and bind us, to each other for ever!

John, the beloved disciple, was only visiting Rome. He lived at Ephesus. He now entreated me to accompany him home and spend the remnant of my days in the peaceful shade of his humble cottage. I thanked him warmly, but declined his invitation. There was one more person upon earth whom I felt a strong desire to see. That person was Mary Magdalen, the last link which connected me with the past. The hunger of an old man's heart for home and friends, for sympathy and love, was reduced to this. It was all that was left me.

My feelings toward Mary Magdalen had become clearly defined in the last ten years of my captivity. The sad things of the past were buried and forgotten. I had outlived, outgrown the self-righteous conceit that I was better than she. Yea, I had discovered that she was far better than I. I was thoroughly ashamed of the neglect, almost amounting to scorn, with which I had treated her in my youth. Her grand devotion to the cause of Christ, her fiery zeal, her contrition, her penances, her humility, her self-sacrifice, her solitude, haunted my imagination. The martyrdom of her life was continually before me.

I resolved to make a pilgrimage to her shrine; for I now regarded her as the saint and myself as the repentant sinner. I would not mention love to a heart so sorely stricken with the wounds of conscience and the sorrows of life. I would tell her nothing. I would leave all that to the revealing light of the spiritual world, which was now so near us both.

I would merely see her and weep with her over the old, sweet memories of Jesus and Martha and Mary. I would live near her. I would work for her, without her knowledge. I would make her comfortable without her seeing whence it came. I would visit her in sickness. I would close her eyes in death. All the rest should be buried deep, deep in the recesses of a heart which had not grown old.

I reached Marseilles and surveyed with silent grief the ashes of the convent my sisters had built. I employed a snug little boat and coasted along, west and south-west, until we reached the shores of Spain, where the spurs of the Pyrenees jut out into the Great Sea.

Landing at a little village, I was directed to a considerable mountain near by. I made the ascent before the heat of the day. The path made a sudden turn from a crag which stood a thousand feet above the water; and I found myself at the dark mouth of a cave. Near the entrance, on the right, was a wooden cross planted in a little bed of violets, wildly overgrown. The sky was clear and beautiful. A perfect silence reigned around. My heart throbbed as I approached the last earthly home of the friend of my sisters.

I looked into the cave and started back. A fearful sense of awe came over my soul. My pilgrimage was in vain. I stood in the presence of the dead!

In that dim and damp and empty cavern, lay a human body, stretched upon a couch of stone. It was clad in rusty black, with a black veil thrown over the face. She had been long, long dead; for the feet which protruded from her robe were bones and not feet. A scourge of leather thongs had fallen from her hands. Engraven deeply in the moist rock of the wall, just above her prostrate figure, was the single word,

Magdalen.

I advanced no nearer. I knelt in prayer. I did not weep. He who has lived in both worlds, cannot be greatly stirred by the mutations of this. I turned away, thinking of our beautiful house in the heavens, and sighing to myself,

"It is well! It is well!"

My heart now turned to John. I sailed from Marseilles, bound for Alexandria, where I expected to take ship for Ephesus. We never reached Alexandria. After we passed the island of Sicily a series of terrible storms commenced, and our little vessel was driven about like a feather on the sea. Our hardships were great, and our labor in vain. After many days our vessel sprang a leak, and we were compelled to abandon her, or go to the bottom with her. Our boat stood bravely for the shore, where some lofty mountains loomed up through the night air. We were capsized, and I lost consciousness. When I recovered my senses it was daylight. The little boat was beached quite near me. My companions were all drowned. I was utterly alone.

I was wrecked at the foot of the western range of Mount Lebanon, on the coast of Phenicia. I found a large and dry cave half-way up the first great spur that overlooks the sea. I have made this my home. I turned fisherman for a living—for I had lost all with the ship—and the little boat was serviceable for that. I exchanged my fish with the people a little way from the coast, for other articles more needed.

Thus I have lived for several years. Here I have written this manuscript. I have chosen the Greek language for its composition, because I am familiar with it, and because I believe the words of Eschylus and Homer will be more durable than the marbles of Athens.

One more page and it will be finished. Its inspiration withdrawn from me, my life will be more desolate than ever. I shall seal it up carefully, and conceal it in some safe place for the eyes and ears of a future generation wiser and better than this. I shall then turn to Death and say, "I salute thee."

I shall not wait long. After I left my prison in Antioch and mingled with the turbulent tide of human life, my spiritual visions left me, my spiritual senses were closed. They are opening again. I have the old, beautiful dreams. I hear the same heavenly music. I see the same auroral and rainbow flashes of light. These now are prophecies of death—nay, rather of life, of heaven. The gates stand ajar.

My eyes, my hopes, my heart are steadily fixed on that Land of Beauty, where the Son of the Desert will be united to Martha; and John the Baptist to Mary; and Lazarus to Magdalen; and all—all to Christ!

without waiting for a reply, he incontinently arose and, putting away the bottle of rum and the glasses, went across the saloon—Barnaby watching him all the while like a man in a dream—and opened the door of a cabin like that which Barnaby had occupied a little while before. He was gone only for a moment, for almost immediately he came out again ushering a lady before him.

By now the daylight in the cabin was grown strong and clear, so that the light shining full upon her face, Barnaby True knew her the instant she appeared.

It was Miss Marjorie Malyoe, very white, but strangely composed, showing no terror, either in her countenance or in her expression.

It would not be possible for the writer to give any clear idea of the circumstances of the days that immediately followed, and which, within a week, brought Barnaby True and the enchanting object of his affections at once to the ending of their voyage, and of all these marvellous adventures. For when, in after times, our hero would endeavor to revive a memory of the several occurrences that then transpired, they all appeared as though in a dream or a bewitching phantasm.

All that he could recall were long days of delicious enjoyment followed by nights of dreaming. But how enchanting those days! How exquisite the distraction of those nights!

Upon occasions he and his charmer might sit together under the shade of the sail for an hour at a stretch, he holding her hand in his and neither saying a single word, though at times the transports of poor Barnaby's emotions would go far to suffocate him with their rapture. As for her face at such moments, it appeared sometimes to assume a transparency as though of a light shining from behind her countenance.

The vessel in which they found themselves was a brigantine of good size and build, but manned by a considerable crew, the most strange and outlandish in their appearance that Barnaby had ever beheld. For some were white, some were yellow, and some were black, and all were tricked out with gay colors, and gold ear-rings in their ears, and some with long mustachios, and others with handkerchiefs tied around their heads. And all these spoke together a jargon of which Barnaby True could not understand a single word, but which might have been Portuguese from one or two phrases he afterwards remembered. Nor did this outlandish crew, of God knows what sort of men, address any of their conversation either to Barnaby or to the young lady. They might now and then have looked at him and her out of the corners of their yellow eyes, but that was all; otherwise they were, indeed, like the creatures of a dream. Only he who was commander of this strange craft, when he would come down into the saloon to mix a glass of grog or to light a pipe of tobacco, would maybe favor Barnaby with a few words concerning the weather or something of the sort, and then to go on deck again about his business.

Indeed, it may be affirmed with pretty easy security that no such adventure as this ever happened before; for here were these two innocent young creatures upon board of a craft that no one, under such circumstances as those recounted above, could doubt was a pirate or buccaneer, the crew whereof had seen no one knows what wicked deeds; yet they two as remote from all that and as profoundly occupied with the transports of their passion and as innocent in their satisfaction thereof as were Corydon and Phyllis beside their purling streams and flowery meads, with nymphs and satyrs caracoling about them.

VIII

It is probable that the polite reader of this veracious narrative, instead of considering it as the effort of the author to set before him a sober and well-digested history, has been all this while amusing himself by regarding it only as a fanciful tale designed for his entertainment. If this be so, the writer may hardly hope to convince him that what is to follow is a serious narrative of that which, though never so ingenuous in its recapitulation, is an altogether inexplicable phenomenon. Accordingly, it is with extraordinary hesitation that the scribe now invites the confidence of his reader in the succinct truth of that which he has to relate. It is in brief as follows:

That upon the last night of this part of his voyage, Barnaby True was awakened from slumber by flashes of lightning shining into his cabin, and by the loud pealing of approaching thunder. At the same time observing the sound of footsteps moving back and forth as in great agitation overhead, and the loud shouting of orders, he became aware that a violent squall of wind must be approaching the vessel. Being convinced of this he arose from his berth, dressed quickly, and hurried upon deck, where he found a great confusion of men running hither and thither and scrambling up and down the rigging like monkeys, while the Captain, and one whom he had come to know as the Captain's mate, were shouting out orders in a strange foreign jargon.

A storm was indeed approaching with great rapidity, a prodigious circle of rain and clouds whirling overhead like smoke, while the lightning, every now and then, flashed with intense brightness, followed by loud peals of thunder.

By these flashes of lightning Barnaby observed that they had made land during the night, for in the sudden glare of bright light he beheld a mountainous headland and a long strip of sandy beach standing out against the blackness of the night beyond. So much he was able to distinguish, though what coast it might be he could not tell, for presently another flash falling from the sky, he saw that the shore was shut out by the approaching downfall of rain.

This rain came presently streaming down upon them with a great gust of wind and a deal of white foam across the water. This violent gale of wind suddenly striking the vessel, careened it to one side so that for a moment it was with much ado that he was able to keep his feet at all. Indeed, what with the noise of the tempest through the rigging and the flashes of lightning and the pealing of the thunder and the clapping of an unfurled sail in the darkness, and the shouting of orders in a strange language by the Captain of the craft, who was running up and down like a bedlamite, it was like pandemonium with all the devils of the pit broke loose into the night.

It was at this moment, and Barnaby True was holding to the back-stays, when a sudden, prolonged flash of lightning came after a continued space of darkness. So sharp and heavy was this shaft that for a moment the night was as bright as day, and in that instant occurred that which was so remarkable that it hath afforded the title of this story itself. For there, standing plain upon the deck and not far from the companionway, as though he had just come up from below, our hero beheld a figure the face of which he had seen so imperfectly once before by the flash of his own pistol in the darkness. Upon this occasion, however, the whole figure was stamped out with intense sharpness against the darkness, and Barnaby beheld, as clear as day, a great burly man, clad in a tawdry tinsel coat, with a cocked hat with gold braid upon his head. His legs, with petticoat breeches and cased in great leathern sea-boots pulled up to his knees, stood planted wide apart as though to brace against the slant of the deck. The face our hero beheld to be as white as dough, with fishy eyes and a bony forehead, on the side of which was a great smear as of blood.

All this, as was said, stood out as sharp and clear as daylight in that one flash of lightning, and then upon the instant was gone again, as though swallowed up into the darkness, while a terrible clap of thunder seemed to split the very heavens overhead and a strong smell as of brimstone filled the air around about.

At the same moment some voice cried out from the darkness, "William Brand, by God!"

Then, the rain clapping down in a deluge, Barnaby leaped into the saloon, pursued by he knew not what thoughts. For if that was indeed the image of old William Brand that he had seen once before and now again, then the grave must indeed have gaped and vomited out its dead into the storm of wind and lightning; for what he beheld that moment, he hath ever averred, he saw as clear as ever he saw his hand before his face.

This is the last account of which there is any record when the figure of Captain William Brand was beheld by the eyes of a living man. It must have occurred just off the Highlands below the Sandy Hook, for the next morning when Barnaby True came upon deck it was to find the sun shining brightly and the brigantine riding upon an even keel, at anchor off Staten Island, three or four cable-lengths distance from a small village on the shore, and the town of New York in plain sight across the water.

'Twas the last place in the world he had expected to see.

IX

And, indeed, it did seem vastly strange to lie there alongside Staten Island all that day, with New York town in plain sight across the water and yet so impossible to reach. For whether he desired to escape or no, Barnaby True could not but observe that both he and the young lady were so closely watched that they might as well have been prisoners, tied hand and foot and laid in the hold, so far as any hope of getting away was concerned.

Throughout that day there was a vast deal of mysterious coming and going aboard the brigantine, and in the afternoon a sail-boat went up to the town, carrying the Captain of the brigantine and a great load in the stern covered over with a tarpaulin. What was so taken up to the town Barnaby did not then guess, nor did he for a moment suspect of what vast importance it was to be for him.

About sundown the small boat returned, fetching the pirate Captain of the brigantine back again. Coming aboard and finding Barnaby on deck, the other requested him to come down into the saloon for he had a few serious words to say to him. In the saloon they found the young lady sitting, the broad light of the evening shining in through the skylight, and making it all pretty bright within.

The Captain commanded Barnaby to be seated, whereupon he chose a place alongside the young lady. So soon as he had composed himself the Captain began very seriously, with a preface somewhat thus: "Though you may think me the Captain of this brigantine, Master Barnaby True, I am not really so, but am under orders of a superior whom I have obeyed in all these things that I have done." Having said so much as this, he continued his address to say that there was one thing yet remaining for him to do, and that the greatest thing of all.

He said that this was something that both Barnaby and the young lady were to be called upon to perform, and he hoped that they would do their part willingly; but that whether they did it willingly or no, do it they must, for those also were the orders he had received.

You may guess how our hero was disturbed by this prologue. He had found the young lady's hand beneath the table and he now held it very closely in his own; but whatever might have been his expectations as to the final purport of the communications the other was about to favor him with, his most extreme expectations could not have equalled that which was demanded of him.

"My orders are these," said his interlocutor, continuing: "I am to take you and the young lady ashore, and to see that you are married before I quit you, and to that end a very good, decent, honest minister who lives ashore yonder in the village was chosen and hath been spoken to, and is now, no doubt, waiting for you to come. That is the last thing I am set to do; so now I will leave you and her young ladyship alone together for five minutes to talk it over, but be quick about it, for whether willing or not, this thing must be done."

Thereupon he incontinently went away, as he had promised, leaving those two alone together, our hero like one turned into stone, and the young lady, her face turned away, as red as fire, as Barnaby could easily distinguish by the fading light.

Nor can I tell what Barnaby said to her, nor what words or arguments he used, for so great was the distraction of his mind and the tumult of his emotions that he presently discovered that he was repeating to her over and over again that God knew he loved her, and that with all his heart and soul, and that there was nothing in all the world for him but her. After which, containing himself sufficiently to continue his address, he told her that if she would not have it as the man had said, and if she were not willing to marry him as she was bidden to do, he would rather die a thousand, aye, ten thousand, deaths than lend himself to forcing her to do such a thing as this. Nevertheless, he told her she must speak up and tell him yes or no, and that God knew he would give all the world if she would say "yes."

All this and much more he said in such a tumult that he was hardly aware of what he was speaking, and she sitting there, as though her breath stifled her. Nor did he know what she replied to him, only that she would marry him. Therewith he took her into his arms and for the first time set his lips to hers, in such a transport of ecstasy that everything seemed to his sight as though he were about to swoon.

So when the Captain returned to the saloon he found Barnaby sitting there holding her hand, she with her face turned away, and he so full of joy that the promise of heaven could not have made him happier.

The yawl-boat belonging to the brigantine was ready and waiting alongside when they came upon deck, and immediately they descended to it and took their seats. Reaching the shore, they landed, and walked up the village street in the twilight, she clinging to our hero's arm as though she would faint away. The Captain of the brigantine and two other men aboard accompanied them to the minister's house, where they found the good man waiting for them, smoking his pipe in the warm evening, and walking up and down in front of his own door. He immediately conducted them into the house, where, his wife having fetched a candle, and two others from the village being present, the good, pious man having asked several questions as to their names and their age and where they were from, and having added his blessing, the ceremony was performed, and the certificate duly signed by those present from the village—the men who had come ashore from the brigantine alone refusing to set their hands to any paper.

The same sail-boat that had taken the Captain up to the town was waiting for Barnaby and the young lady as they came down to the landing-place. There the Captain of the brigantine having wished them godspeed, and having shaken Barnaby very heartily by the hand, he helped to push off the boat, which with the slant of the wind presently sailed swiftly away, dropping the shore and those strange beings, and the brigantine in which they sailed, alike behind them into the night.

They could hear through the darkness the creaking of the sails being hoisted aboard of the pirate vessel; nor did Barnaby True ever set eyes upon it or the crew again, nor, so far as the writer is informed, did anybody else.

X

It was nigh midnight when they made Mr. Hartright's wharf at the foot of Beaver Street. There Barnaby and the boatmen assisted the young lady ashore, and our hero and she walked up through the now silent and deserted street to Mr. Hartright's house.

You may conceive of the wonder and amazement of our hero's dear step-father when aroused by Barnaby's continued knocking at the street door, and clad in a dressing-gown and carrying a lighted candle in his hand, he unlocked and unbarred the door, and so saw who it was had aroused him at such an hour of the night, and beheld the young and beautiful lady whom Barnaby had brought home with him.

The first thought of the good man was that the *Belle Helen* had come into port; nor did Barnaby undeceive him as he led the way into the house, but waited until they were all safe and sound together before he should unfold his strange and wonderful story.

"This was left for you by two foreign sailors this afternoon, Barnaby," the good man said, as he led the way through the hall, holding up the candle at the same time, so that Barnaby might see an object that stood against the wainscoting by the door of the dining-room.

It was with difficulty that our hero could believe his eyes when he beheld one of the treasure-chests that Sir John Malyoe had fetched with such particularity from Jamaica.

He bade his step-father hold the light nigher, and then, his mother having come down-stairs by this time, he flung back the lid and displayed to the dazzled sight of all the great treasure therein contained.

You are to suppose that there was no sleep for any of them that night, for what with Barnaby's narrative of his adventures, and what with the thousand questions asked of him, it was broad daylight before he had finished the half of all that he had to relate.

The next day but one brought the *Belle Helen* herself into port, with the terrible news not only of having been attacked at night by pirates, but also that Sir John Malyoe was dead. For whether it was the sudden fright that overset him, or whether it was the strain of passion that burst some blood-vessel upon his brain, it is certain that when the pirates quitted the *Belle Helen*, carrying with them the young lady and Barnaby and the travelling-trunks, they left Sir John Malyoe lying in a fit upon the floor, frothing at the mouth and black in the face, as though he had been choked. It was in this condition that he was raised and taken to his berth, where, the next morning about two o'clock, he died, without once having opened his eyes or spoken a single word.

As for the villain man-servant, no one ever saw him afterwards; though whether he jumped overboard, or whether the pirates who so attacked the ship had carried him away bodily, who shall say?

Mr. Hartright had been extremely perplexed as to the ownership of the chest of treasure that had been left by those men for Barnaby, but the news of the death of Sir John Malyoe made the matter very easy for him to decide. For surely if that treasure did not belong to Barnaby, there could be no doubt but that it belonged to his wife—she being Sir John Malyoe's legal heir. Thus it was that he satisfied himself, and thus that great fortune (in actual computation amounting to upward of sixty-three thousand pounds) fell to Barnaby True, the grandson of that famous pirate William Brand.

As for the other case of treasure, it was never heard of again, nor could Barnaby decide whether it was divided as booty among the pirates, or whether they had carried it away with them to some strange and foreign land, there to share it among themselves.

It is thus we reach the conclusion of our history, with only this to observe, that whether that strange appearance of Captain Brand was indeed a ghostly and spiritual visitation, or whether he was present on those two occasions in flesh and blood, he was, as has been said, never heard of again.

IV
A TRUE HISTORY OF THE DEVIL AT NEW HOPE

At the time of the beginning of the events about to be narrated—which the reader is to be informed occurred between the years 1740 and 1742— there stood upon the high and rugged crest of Pick-a-Neck-a-Sock Point (or Pig and Sow Point, as it had come to be called) the wooden ruins of a disused church, known throughout those parts as the Old Free Grace Meeting-house.

This humble edifice had been erected by a peculiar religious sect calling themselves the Free Grace Believers, the radical tenet of whose creed was a denial of the existence of such a place as Hell, and an affirmation of the universal mercy of God, to the intent that all souls should enjoy eternal happiness in the life to come.

For this dangerous heresy the Free Grace Believers were expelled from the Massachusetts Colony, and, after sundry peregrinations, settled at last in the Providence Plantations, upon Pick-a-Neck-a-Sock Point, coadjacent to the town of New Hope. There they built themselves a small cluster of huts, and a church wherein to worship; and there for a while they dwelt, earning a precarious livelihood from the ungenerous soil upon which they had established themselves.

As may be supposed, the presence of so strange a people was entertained with no great degree of complaisance by the vicinage, and at last an old deed granting Pick-a-Neck-a-Sock to Captain Isaiah Applebody was revived by the heirs of that renowned Indian-fighter, whereupon the Free Grace Believers were warned to leave their bleak and rocky refuge for some other abiding-place. Accordingly, driven forth into the world again, they embarked in the snow1 "Good Companion," of Bristol, for the Province of Pennsylvania, and were afterwards heard of no more in those parts. Their vacated houses crumbled away into ruins, and their church tottered to decay.

1 [A two-masted square-rigged vessel.]

So at the beginning of these events, upon the narrative of which the author now invites the reader to embark together with himself.

I
HOW THE DEVIL HAUNTED THE MEETING-HOUSE

At the period of this narrative the settlement of New Hope had grown into a very considerable seaport town, doing an extremely handsome trade with the West Indies in cornmeal and dried codfish for sugar, molasses, and rum.

Among the more important citizens of this now wealthy and elegant community, the most notable was Colonel William Belford—a magnate at once distinguished and honored in the civil and military affairs of the colony. This gentleman was an illegitimate son of the Earl of Clandennie by the daughter of a surgeon of the Sixty-seventh Regiment of Scots, and he had inherited a very considerable fortune upon the death of his father, from which he now enjoyed a comfortable competency.

Our Colonel made no little virtue of the circumstances of his exalted birth. He was wont to address his father's memory with a sobriety that lent to the fact of his illegitimacy a portentous air of seriousness, and he made no secret of the fact that he was the friend and the confidential correspondent of the present Earl of Clandennie. In his intercourse with the several Colonial governors he assumed an attitude of authority that only his lineage could have supported him in maintaining, and, possessing a large and commanding presence, he bore himself with a continent reserve that never failed to inspire with awe those whom he saw fit to favor with his conversation.

This noble and distinguished gentleman possessed in a brother an exact and perfect opposite to himself. Captain Obadiah Belford was a West Indian, an inhabitant of Kingston in the island of Jamaica. He was a cursing, swearing, hard-drinking renegado from virtue; an acknowledged dealer in negro slaves, and reputed to have been a buccaneer, if not an out-and-out pirate, such as then infested those tropical latitudes in prodigious numbers. He was not unknown in New Hope, which he had visited upon several occasions for a week or so at a time. During each period he lodged with his brother, whose household he scandalized by such freaks as smoking his pipe of tobacco in the parlor, offering questionable pleasantries to the female servants, and cursing and swearing in the hallways with a fecundity and an ingenuity that would have put the most godless sailor about the docks to the blush.

Accordingly, it may then be supposed into what a dismay it threw Colonel Belford when one fine day he received a letter from Captain Obadiah, in which our West Indian desperado informed his brother that he proposed quitting those torrid latitudes in which he had lived for so long a time, and that he intended thenceforth to make his home in New Hope.

Addressing Colonel Belford as "My dear Billy," he called upon that gentleman to rejoice at this determination, and informed him that he proposed in future to live "as decent a limb of grace as ever broke loose from hell," and added that he was going to fetch as a present for his niece Belinda a "dam pirty little black girl" to carry her prayer-book to church for her.

Accordingly, one fine morning, in pursuance of this promise, our West Indian suddenly appeared at New Hope with a prodigious quantity of chests and travelling-cases, and with so vociferous an acclamation that all the town knew of his arrival within a half-hour of that event.

When, however, he presented himself before Colonel Belford, it was to meet with a welcome so frigid and an address so reserved that a douche of cold water could not have quenched his verbosity more entirely. For our great man had no notion to submit to the continued infliction of the West Indian's presence. Accordingly, after the first words of greeting had passed, he addressed Captain Obadiah in a strain somewhat after this fashion:

"Indeed, I protest, my dear brother Obadiah, it is with the heartiest regrets in the world that I find myself obliged to confess that I cannot offer you a home with myself and my family. It is not alone that your manners displease me—though, as an elder to a younger, I may say to you that we of these more northern latitudes do not entertain the same tastes in such particulars as doubtless obtain in the West Indies—but the habits of my household are of such a nature that I could not hope to form them to your liking. I can, however, offer as my advice that you may find lodgings at the Blue Lion Tavern, which doubtless will be of a sort exactly to fit your inclinations. I have made inquiries, and I am sure you will find the very best apartments to be obtained at that excellent hostelry placed at your disposal."

To this astounding address our West Indian could, for a moment, make no other immediate reply than to open his eyes and to glare upon Colonel Belford, so that, what with his tall, lean person, his long neck, his stooping shoulders, and his yellow face stained upon one side an indigo blue by some premature explosion of gunpowder—what with all this and a prodigious hooked beak of a nose, he exactly resembled some hungry predatory bird of prey meditating a pounce upon an unsuspecting victim. At last, finding his voice, and rapping the ferrule of his ivory-headed cane upon the floor to emphasize his declamation, he cried out: "What! What! What! Is this the way to offer a welcome to a brother new returned to your house? Why, — — — —! who are you? Am not I your brother, who could buy you out twice over and have enough left to live in velvet? Why! Why!—Very well, then, have it your own way; but if I don't grind your face into the mud and roll you into the dirt my name is not Obadiah Belford!" Thereupon, striving to say more but finding no fit words for the occasion, he swung upon his heel and incontinently departed, banging the door behind him like a clap of thunder, and cursing and swearing so prodigiously as he strode away down the street that an infernal from the pit could scarcely have exceeded the fury of his maledictions.

However, he so far followed Colonel Belford's advice that he took up his lodgings at the Blue Lion Tavern, where, in a little while, he had gathered about him a court of all such as chose to take advantage of his extravagant bounty.

Indeed, he poured out his money with incredible profusion, declaring, with many ingenious and self-consuming oaths, that he could match fortunes with the best two men in New Hope, and then have enough left to buy up his brother from his hair to his boot-leathers. He made no secret of the rebuff he had sustained from Colonel Belford, for his grievance clung to him like hot pitch—itching the more he meddled with it. Sometimes his fury was such that he could scarcely contain himself. Upon such occasions, cursing and swearing like an infernal, he would call Heaven to witness that he would live in New Hope if for no other reason than to bring shame to his brother, and he would declare again and again, with incredible variety of expletives, that he would grind his brother's face into the dirt for him.

"HE WOULD SHOUT OPPROBRIOUS WORDS AFTER THE OTHER IN THE STREETS"

Accordingly he set himself assiduously at work to tease and torment the good man with every petty and malicious trick his malevolence could invent. He would shout opprobrious words after the other in the streets, to the entertainment of all who heard him; he would parade up and down before Colonel Belford's house singing obstreperous and unseemly songs at the top of his voice; he would even rattle the ferrule of his cane against the palings of the fence, or throw a stone at Madam Belford's cat in the wantonness of his malice.

Meantime he had purchased a considerable tract of land, embracing Pig and Sow Point, and including the Old Free Grace Meeting-House. Here, he declared, it was his intention to erect a house for himself that should put his brother's wooden shed to shame. Accordingly he presently began the erection of that edifice, so considerable in size and occupying so commanding a situation that it was the admiration of all those parts, and was known to fame as Belford's Palace. This magnificent residence was built entirely of brick, and Captain Obadiah made it a boast that the material therefor was brought all the way around from New York in flats. In the erection of this elegant structure all the carpenters and masons in the vicinage were employed, so that it grew up with an amazing rapidity. Meantime, upon the site of the building, rum and Hollands were kept upon draught for all comers, so that the place was made the common resort and the scene for the orgies of all such of the common people as possessed a taste for strong waters, many coming from so far away as Newport to enjoy our Captain's prodigality.

Meantime he himself strutted about the streets in his red coat trimmed with gilt braid, his hat cocked upon one side of his bony head, pleasing himself with the belief that he was the object of universal admiration, and swelling with a vast and consummate self-satisfaction as he boasted, with strident voice and extravagant enunciation, of the magnificence of the palace he was building.

At the same time, having, as he said, shingles to spare, he patched and repaired the Old Free Grace Meeting-House, so that its gray and hoary exterior, while rejuvenated as to the roof and walls, presented in a little while an appearance as of a sudden eruption of bright yellow shingles upon its aged hide. Nor would our Captain offer any other explanation for so odd a freak of fancy than to say that it pleased him to do as he chose with his own.

At last, the great house having been completed, and he himself having entered into it and furnished it to his satisfaction, our Captain presently began entertaining his friends therein with a profuseness of expenditure and an excess of extravagance that were the continued admiration of the whole colony. In more part the guests whom Captain Obadiah thus received with so lavish an indulgence were officers or government officials from the garrisons of Newport or of Boston, with whom, by some means or other, he had scraped an acquaintance. At times these gay gentlemen would fairly take possession of the town, parading up and down the street under conduct of their host, staring ladies out of countenance with the utmost coolness and effrontery, and offering loud and critical remarks concerning all that they beheld about them, expressing their opinions with the greatest freedom and jocularity.

Nor were the orgies at Belford's Palace limited to such extravagances as gaming and dicing and drinking, for sometimes the community would be scandalized by the presence of gayly dressed and high-colored ladies, who came, no one knew whence, to enjoy the convivialities at the great house on the hill, and concerning whom it pleased the respectable folk of New Hope to entertain the gravest suspicion.

At first these things raised such a smoke that nothing else was to be seen, but by-and-by other strange and singular circumstances began to be spoken of—at first among the common people, and then by others. It began to be whispered and then to be said that the Old Free Grace Meeting-House out on the Point was haunted by the Devil.

The first information concerning this dreadful obsession arose from a fisherman, who, coming into the harbor of a nightfall after a stormy day, had, as he affirmed, beheld the old meeting-house all of a blaze of light. Some time after, a tinker, making a short-cut from Stapleton by way of the old Indian road, had a view of a similar but a much more remarkable manifestation. This time, as the itinerant most solemnly declared, the meeting-house was not only seen all alight, but a bell was ringing as a signal somewhere off across the darkness of the water, where, as he protested, there suddenly appeared a red star, that, blazing like a meteor with a surpassing brightness for a few seconds, was presently swallowed up into inky darkness again. Upon another occasion a fiddler, returning home after midnight from Sprowle's Neck, seeing the church alight, had, with a temerity inflamed by rum, approached to a nearer distance, whence, lying in the grass, he had, he said, at the stroke of midnight, beheld a multitude of figures emerge from the building, crying most dolorously, and then had heard a voice, as of a lost spirit, calling aloud, "Six-and-twenty, all told!" whereat the light in the church was instantly extinguished into an impenetrable darkness.

It was said that when Captain Obadiah himself was first apprised of the suspicions entertained of the demoniacal possession of the old meeting-house, he had fixed upon his venturesome informant so threatening and ominous a gaze that the other could move neither hand nor foot under the malignant fury of his observation. Then, at last, clearing his countenance of its terrors, he had burst into a great, loud laugh, crying out: "Well, what then? Why not? You must know that the Devil and I have been very good friends in times past. I saw a deal of him in the West Indies, and I must tell you that I built up the old meeting-house again so that he and I could talk together now and then about old times without having a lot of — —, dried, codfish-eating, rum-drinking Yankee bacon-chewers to listen to every word we had to say to each other. If you must know, it was only last night that the ghost of Jezebel and I danced a fandango together in the graveyard up yonder, while the Devil himself sat cross-legged on old Daniel Root's tombstone and blew on a dry, dusty shank-bone by way of a flute. And now" (here he swore a terrific oath) "you know the worst that is to be known, with only this to say: if ever a man sets foot upon Pig and Sow Point again after nightfall to interfere with the Devil's sport and mine, hell suffer for it as sure as fire can burn or brimstone can scorch. So put that in your pipe and smoke it."

These terrible words, however extravagant, were, to be sure, in the nature of a direct confirmation of the very worst suspicion that could have been entertained concerning this dolorous affair. But if any further doubt lingered as to the significance of such malevolent rumors, Captain Obadiah himself soon put an end to the same.

The Reverend Josiah Pettibones was used of a Saturday to take supper at Colonel Belford's elegant residence. It was upon such an occasion and the reverend gentleman and his honored host were smoking a pipe of tobacco together in the library, when there fell a loud and importunate knocking at the house door, and presently the servant came ushering no less a personage than Captain Obadiah himself. After directing a most cunning, mischievous look at his brother, Captain Obadiah addressed himself directly to the Reverend Mr. Pettibones, folding his hands with a most indescribable air of mock humility. "Sir," says he—"Reverend sir, you see before you a humble and penitent sinner, who has fallen so desperately deep into iniquities that he knows not whether even so profound piety as yours can elevate him out of the pit in which he finds himself. Sir, it has got about the town that the Devil has taken possession of my old meeting-house, and, alas! I have to confess—*that it is the truth.*" Here our Captain hung his head down upon his breast as though overwhelmed with the terrible communication he had made.

"What is this that I hear?" cried the reverend gentleman. "Can I believe my ears?"

"Believe your ears!" exclaimed Colonel Belford. "To be sure you cannot believe your ears. Do you not see that this is a preposterous lie, and that he is telling it to you to tease and to mortify me?"

At this Captain Obadiah favored his brother with a look of exaggerated and sanctimonious humility. "Alas, brother," he cried out, "for accusing me so unjustly! Fie upon you! Would you check a penitent in his confession? But you must know that it is to this gentleman that I address myself, and not to you." Then directing his discourse once more to the Reverend Mr. Pettibones, he resumed his address thus: "Sir, you must know that while I was in the West Indies I embarked, among other things, in one of those ventures against the Spanish Main of which you may have heard."

"Do you mean piracy?" asked the Reverend Pettibones; and Captain Obadiah nodded his head.

"'Tis a lie!" cried Colonel Belford, smacking his hand upon the table. "He never possessed spirit enough for anything so dangerous as piracy or more mischievous than slave-trading."

"Sir," quoth Captain Obadiah to the reverend gentleman, "again I say 'tis to you I address my confession. Well, sir, one day we sighted a Spanish caravel very rich ladened with a prodigious quantity of plate, but were without so much as a capful of wind to fetch us up with her. 'I would,' says I, 'offer the Devil my soul for a bit of a breeze to bring us alongside.' 'Done,' says a voice beside me, and—alas that I must confess it!—there I saw a man with a very dark countenance, whom I had never before beheld aboard of our ship. 'Sign this,' says he, 'and the breeze is yours!' 'What is it upon the pen?' says I. "'Tis blood,' says he. Alas, sir! what was a poor wretch so tempted as I to do?"

"And did you sign?" asked Mr. Pettibones, all agog to hear the conclusion of so strange a narration.

"Woe is me, sir, that I should have done so!" quoth Captain Obadiah, rolling his eyes until little but the whites of them were to be seen.

"And did you catch the Spanish ship?"

"That we did, sir, and stripped her as clean as a whistle."

"'Tis all a prodigious lie!" cried Colonel Belford, in a fury. "Sir, can you sit so complacently and be made a fool of by so extravagant a fable?"

"Indeed it is unbelievable," said Mr. Pettibones.

At this faint reply, Captain Obadiah burst out laughing; then renewing his narrative—"Indeed, sir," he declared, "you may believe me or not, as you please. Nevertheless, I may tell you that, having so obtained my prize, and having time to think coolly over the bargain I had made, I says to myself, says I: 'Obediah Belford! Obadiah Belford, here is a pretty pickle you are in. 'Tis time you quit these parts and lived decent, or else you are damned to all eternity.' And so I came hither to New Hope, reverend sir, hoping to end my days in quiet. Alas, sir! would you believe it? scarce had I finished my fine new house up at the Point when hither comes that evil being to whom I had sold my sorrowful soul. 'Obadiah,' says he, 'Obadiah Belford, I have a mind to live in New Hope also,' 'Where?' says I. 'Well,' says he, 'you may patch up the old meetinghouse; 'twill serve my turn for a while.' 'Well,' thinks I to myself, 'there can be no harm in that,' And so I did as he bade me— and would not you do as much for one who had served you as well? Alas, your reverence! there he is now, and I cannot get rid of him, and 'tis over the whole town that he has the meeting-house in possession."

"Tis an incredible story!" cried the Reverend Pettibones.

"'Tis a lie from beginning to end!" cried the Colonel.

"And now how shall I get myself out of my pickle?" asked Captain Obadiah.

"Sir," said Mr. Pettibones, "if what you tell me is true, 'tis beyond my poor powers to aid you."

"Alas!" cried Captain Obadiah. "Alas! alas! Then, indeed, I'm damned!" And therewith flinging his arms into the air as though in the extremity of despair, he turned and incontinently departed, rushing forth out of the house as though stung by ten thousand furies.

It was the most prodigious piece of gossip that ever fell in the way of the Reverend Josiah, and for a fortnight he carried it with him wherever he went. "'Twas the most unbelievable tale I ever heard," he would cry. "And yet where there is so much smoke there must be some fire. As for the poor wretch, if ever I saw a lost soul I beheld him standing before me there in Colonel Belford's library." And then he would conclude: "Yes, yes, 'tis incredible and past all belief. But if it be true in ever so little a part, why, then there is justice in this—that the Devil should take possession of the sanctuary of that very heresy that would not only have denied him the power that every other Christian belief assigns to him, but would have destroyed that infernal habitation that hath been his dwelling-place for all eternity."

As for Captain Belford, if he desired privacy for himself upon Pig and Sow Point, he had taken the very best means to prevent the curious from spying upon him there after nightfall.

II
HOW THE DEVIL STOLE THE COLLECTOR'S SNUFFBOX

Lieutenant Thomas Goodhouse was the Collector of Customs in the town of New Hope. He was a character of no little notoriety in those parts, enjoying the reputation of being able to consume more pineapple rum with less effect upon his balance than any other man in the community. He possessed the voice of a stentor, a short, thick-set, broad-shouldered person, a face congested to a violent carnation, and red hair of such a color as to add infinitely to the consuming fire of his countenance.

The Custom Office was a little white frame building with green shutters, and overhanging the water as though to topple into the tide. Here at any time of the day betwixt the hours of ten in the morning and of five in the afternoon the Collector was to be found at his desk smoking his pipe of tobacco, the while a thin, phthisical clerk bent with unrelaxing assiduity over a multitude of account-books and papers accumulated before him.

For his post of Collectorship of the Royal Customs, Lieutenant Goodhouse was especially indebted to the patronage of Colonel Belford. The worthy Collector had, some years before, come to that gentleman with a written recommendation from the Earl of Clandennie of a very unusual sort. It was the Lieutenant's good-fortune to save the life of the Honorable Frederick Dunburne, second son of the Earl—a wild, rakish, undisciplined youth, much given to such mischievous enterprises as the twisting off of door-knockers, the beating of the watch, and the carrying away of tavern signs.

Having been a very famous swimmer at Eton, the Honorable Frederick undertook while at the Cowes to swim a certain considerable distance for a wager. In the midst of this enterprise he was suddenly seized with a cramp, and would inevitably have drowned had not the Lieutenant, who happened in a boat close at hand, leaped overboard and rescued the young gentleman from the watery grave in which he was about to be engulfed, thus restoring him once more to the arms of his grateful family.

For this fortunate act of rescue the Earl of Clandennie presented to his son's preserver a gold snuffbox filled with guineas, and inscribed with the following legend:

"To Lieutenant Thomas Goodhouse, who, under the Ruling of Beneficent Providence, was the Happy Preserver of a Beautiful and Precious Life of Virtuous Precocity, this Box is presented by the Father of Him whom He saved as a grateful acknowledgment of His Services.

Thomas Monkhouse Dunburne, Viscount of Dunburne and Earl of Clandennie.

August 17, 1752."

Having thus satisfied the immediate demands of his gratitude, it is very possible that the Earl of Clandennie did not choose to assume so great a responsibility as the future of his son's preserver entailed. Nevertheless, feeling that something should be done for him, he obtained for Lieutenant

Goodhouse a passage to the Americas, and wrote him a strong letter of recommendation to Colonel Belford. That gentleman, desiring to please the legitimate head of his family, used his influence so successfully that the Lieutenant was presently granted the position of Collector of Customs in the place of Captain Maull, who had lately deceased.

The Lieutenant, somewhat to the surprise of his patrons, filled his new official position as Collector not only with vigor, but with a not unbecoming dignity. He possessed an infinite appreciation of the responsibilities of his office, and he was more jealous to collect every farthing of the royal duties than he would have been had those moneys been gathered for his own emolument.

Under the old Collectorship of Captain Maull, it was no unusual thing for a barraco of superfine Hollands, a bolt of silk cloth, or a keg of brandy to find its way into the house of some influential merchant or Colonial dignitary. But in no such manner was Lieutenant Goodhouse derelict in his duties. He would have sacrificed his dearest friendship or his most precious attachment rather than fail in his duties to the Crown. In the intermission of his duties it might please him to relax into the softer humors of conviviality, but at ten o'clock in the morning, whatever his condition of sobriety, he assumed at once all the sterner panoply of a Collector of the Royal Customs.

Thus he set his virtues against his vices, and struck an even balance between them. When most unsteady upon his legs he most asserted his integrity, declaring that not a gill or a thread came into his port without paying its duty, and calling Heaven to witness that it had been his hand that had saved the life of a noble young gentleman. Thereupon, perhaps, drawing forth the gleaming token of his prowess—the gold snuffbox—from his breeches-pocket, and holding it tight in his brown and hairy fist, he would first offer his interlocutor a pinch of rappee, and would then call upon him to read the inscription engraved upon the lid of the case, demanding to know whether it mattered a fig if a man did drink a drop too much now and then, provided he collected every farthing of the royal revenues, and had been the means of saving the son of the Earl of Clandennie.

Never for an instant upon such an occasion would he permit his precious box to quit his possession. It was to him an emblem of those virtues that no one knew but himself, wherefore the more he misdoubted his own virtuousness the more valuable did the token of that rectitude become in his eyes. "Yes, you may look at it," he would say, "but damme if you shall handle it. I would not," he would cry, "let the Devil himself take it out of my hands."

The talk concerning the impious possession of the Old Free Grace Meeting-House was at its height when the official consciousness of the Collector, who was just then laboring under his constitutional infirmity, became suddenly seized with an irrepressible alarm. He declared that he smoked something worse than the Devil upon Pig and Sow Point, and protested that it was his opinion that Captain Obadiah was doing a bit of free-trade upon his own account, and that dutiable goods were being smuggled in at night under cover of these incredible stories. He registered a vow, sealing it with the most solemn protestations, and with a multiplicity of ingenious oaths that only a mind stimulated by the heat of intoxication could have invented, that he would make it his business, upon the first occasion that offered, to go down to Pig and Sow Point and to discover for himself whether it was the Devil or smugglers that had taken possession of the Old Free Grace Meeting-House. Thereupon, hauling out his precious snuffbox and rapping upon the lid, he offered a pinch around. Then calling attention to the inscription, he demanded to know whether a man who had behaved so well upon that occasion had need to be afraid of a whole churchful of devils. "I would," he cried, "offer the Devil a pinch, as I have offered it to you. Then I would bid him read this and tell me whether he dared to say that black was the white of my eye."

Nor were those words a vain boast upon the Collector's part, for, before a week had passed, it being reported that there had been a renewal of manifestations at the old church, the Collector, finding nobody with sufficient courage to accompany him, himself entered into a small boat and rowed down alone to Pig and Sow Point to investigate, for his own satisfaction, those appearances that so agitated the community.

It was dusk when the Collector departed upon that memorable and solitary expedition, and it was entirely dark before he had reached its conclusion. He had taken with him a bottle of Extra Reserve rum to drive, as he declared, the chill out of his bones. Accordingly it seemed to him to be a surprisingly brief interval before he found himself floating in his boat under the impenetrable shadow of the rocky promontory. The profound and infinite gloom of night overhung him with a portentous darkness, melting only into a liquid obscurity as it touched and dissolved into the stretch of waters across the bay. But above, on the high and rugged shoulder of the Point, the Collector, with dulled and swimming vision, beheld a row of dim and lurid lights, whereupon, collecting his faculties, he opined that the radiance he beheld was emitted from the windows of the Old Free Grace Meeting-House.

Having made fast his boat with a drunken gravity, the Collector walked directly, though with uncertain steps, up the steep and rugged path towards that mysterious illumination. Now and then he stumbled over the stones and cobbles that lay in his way, but he never quite lost his balance, neither did he for a moment remit his drunken gravity. So with a befuddled and obstinate perseverance he reached at last to the conclusion of his adventure and of his fate.

The old meeting-house was two stories in height, the lower story having been formerly used by the Free Grace Believers as a place wherein to celebrate certain obscure mysteries appertaining to their belief. The upper story, devoted to the more ordinary worship of their Sunday meetings, was reached by a tall, steep flight of steps that led from the ground to a covered porch which sheltered the doorway.

The Collector paused only long enough to observe that the shutters of the lower story were tight shut and barred, and that the dull and lurid light shone from the windows above. Then he directly mounted the steps with a courage and a perfect assurance that can only be entirely enjoyed by one in his peculiar condition of inebriety.

He paused to knock at the door, and it appeared to him that his knuckles had hardly fallen upon the panel before the valve was flung suddenly open. An indescribable and heavy odor fell upon him and for the moment overpowered his senses, and he found himself standing face to face with a figure prodigiously and portentously tall.

Even at this unexpected apparition the Collector lost possession of no part of his courage. Rather he stiffened himself to a more stubborn and obstinate resolution. Steadying himself for his address, "I know very well," quoth he, "who you are. You are the Divil, I dare say, but damme if you shall do business here without paying your duties to King George. I may drink a drop too much," he cried, "but I collect my duties—every farthing of 'em." Then drawing forth his snuffbox, he thrust it under the nose of the being to whom he spake. "Take a pinch and read that," he roared, "but don't handle it, for I wouldn't take all hell to let it out of my hand."

The being whom he addressed had stood for all this while as though bereft of speech and of movement, but at these last words he appeared to find his voice, for he gave forth a strident bellow of so dreadful and terrible a sort that the Collector, brave as he found himself, stepped back a pace or two before it. The next instant he was struck upon the wrist as though by a bolt of lightning, and the snuffbox, describing a yellow circle against the light of the door, disappeared into the darkness of the night beyond. Ere he could recover himself another blow smote him upon the breast, and he fell headlong from the platform, as through infinite space.

The next day the Collector did not present himself at the office at his accustomed hour, and the morning wore along without his appearing at his desk. By noon serious alarm began to take possession of the community, and about two o'clock, the tide being then set out pretty strong, Mr. Tompkins, the consumptive clerk, and two sailors from the *Sarah Goodrich*, then lying at Mr. Hoppins's wharf, went down in a yawl-boat to learn, if possible, what had befallen him. They coasted along the Point for above a half-hour before they discovered any vestige of the missing Collector. Then at last they saw him lying at a little distance upon a cobbled strip of beach, where, judging from his position and from the way he had composed himself to rest, he appeared to have been overcome by liquor.

At this place Mr. Tompkins put ashore, and making the best of his way over the slippery stones exposed at low water, came at last to where his chief was lying. The Collector was reposing with one arm over his eyes, as though to shelter them from the sun, but as soon as Mr. Tompkins had approached close enough to see his countenance, he uttered a great cry that was like a scream. For, by the blue and livid lips parted at the corners to show the yellow teeth, from the waxy whiteness of the fat and hairy hands—in short, from the appearance of the whole figure, he was aware in an instant that the Collector was dead.

His cry brought the two sailors running. They, with the utmost coolness imaginable, turned the Collector over, but discovered no marks of violence upon him, till of a sudden one of them called attention to the fact that his neck was broke. Upon this the other opined that he had fallen among the rocks and twisted his neck.

The two mariners then made an investigation of his pockets, the clerk standing by the while paralyzed with horror, his face the color of dough, his scalp creeping, and his hands and fingers twitching as though with the palsy. For there was something indescribably dreadful in the spectacle of those living hands searching into the dead's pockets, and he would freely have given a week's pay if he had never embarked upon the expedition for the recovery of his chief.

In the Collector's pockets they found a twist of tobacco, a red bandanna handkerchief of violent color, a purse meagrely filled with copper coins and silver pieces, a silver watch still ticking with a loud and insistent iteration, a piece of tarred string, and a clasp-knife.

The snuffbox which the Lieutenant had regarded with such prodigious pride as the one emblem of his otherwise dubious virtue was gone.

III
THE STRANGE ADVENTURES OF A
YOUNG GENTLEMAN OF QUALITY

The Honorable Frederick Dunburne, second son of the Earl of Clandennie, having won some six hundred pounds at écarté at a single sitting at Pintzennelli's, embarked with his two friends, Captain Blessington and Lord George Fitzhope, to conclude the night with a round of final dissipation in the more remote parts of London. Accordingly they embarked at York Stairs for the Three Cranes, ripe for any mischief. Upon the water the three young gentlemen amused themselves by shouting and singing, pausing only now and then to discharge a broadside of raillery at the occupants of some other and passing boat.

All went very well for a while, some of those in the passing boats laughing and railing in return, others shouting out angry replies. At last they fell in with a broad-beamed, flat-nosed, Dutch-appearing yawl-boat, pulling heavily up against the stream, and loaded with a crew of half-drunken sailors just come into port. In reply to the challenge of our young gentlemen, a man in the stern of the other boat, who appeared to be the captain of the crew—a fellow, as Dunburne could indefinitely perceive by the dim light of the lanthorn and the faint illumination of the misty half-moon, possessing a great, coarse red face and a bullet head surmounted by a mildewed and mangy fur cap— bawled out, in reply, that if they would only put their boat near enough for a minute or two he would give them a bellyful of something that would make them quiet for the rest of the night. He added that he would ask for nothing better than to have the opportunity of beating Dunburne's head to a pudding, and that he would give a crown to have the three of them within arm's-reach for a minute.

Upon this Captain Blessington swore that he should be immediately accommodated, and therewith delivered an order to that effect to the watermen. These obeyed so promptly that almost before Dunburne was aware of what had happened the two boats were side by side, with hardly a foot of space between the gunwales. Dunburne beheld one of the watermen of his own boat knock down one of the crew of the other with the blade of an oar, and then he himself was clutched by the collar in the grasp of the man with the fur cap. Him Dunburne struck twice in the face, and in the moonlight he saw that he had started the blood to running down from his assailant's nose. But his blows produced no other effect than to call forth a volley of the most horrible oaths that ever greeted his ears. Thereupon the boats drifted so far apart that our young gentleman was haled over the gunwale and soused in the cold water of the river. The next moment some one struck him upon the head with a belaying-pin or a billet of wood, a blow so crushing that the darkness seemed to split asunder with a prodigious flaming of lights and a myriad of circling stars, which presently disappeared into the profound and utter darkness of insensibility. How long this swoon continued our young gentleman could never tell, but when he regained so much of his consciousness as to be aware of the things about him, he beheld himself to be confined in a room, the walls whereof were yellow and greasy with dirt, he himself having been laid upon a bed so foul and so displeasing to his taste that he could not but regret the swoon from which he had emerged into consciousness. Looking down at his person, he beheld that his clothes had all been taken away from him, and that he was now clad in a shirt with only one sleeve, and a pair of breeches so tattered that they barely covered his nakedness. While he lay thus, dismally depressed by so sad a pickle as that into which he found himself plunged, he was strongly and painfully aware of an uproarious babble of loud and drunken voices and a continual clinking of glasses, which appeared to sound as from a tap-room beneath, these commingled now and then with oaths and scraps of discordant song bellowed out above the hubbub. His wounded head beat with tremendous and straining painfulness, as though it would burst asunder, and he was possessed by a burning thirst that seemed to consume his very vitals. He called aloud, and in reply a fat, one-eyed woman came, fetching him something to drink in a cup. This he swallowed with avidity, and thereupon (the liquor perhaps having been drugged) he dropped off into unconsciousness once more.

When at last he emerged for a second time into the light of reason, it was to find himself aboard a brig—the *Prophet Daniel*, he discovered her name to be—bound for Baltimore, in the Americas, and then pitching and plunging upon a westerly running stern-sea, and before a strong wind that drove the vessel with enormous velocity upon its course for those remote and unknown countries for which it was bound. The land was still in sight both astern and abeam, but before him lay the boundless and tremendously infinite stretch of the ocean. Dunburne found himself still to be clad in the one-armed shirt and tattered breeches that had adorned him in the house of the crimp in which he had first awakened. Now, however, an old tattered hat with only a part of the crown had been added to his costume. As though to complete the sad disorder of his appearance, he discovered, upon passing his hand over his countenance, that his beard and hair had started a bristling growth, and that the lump on his crown—which was even yet as big as a walnut— was still patched with pieces of dirty sticking-plaster. Indeed, had he but known it, he presented as miserable an appearance as the most miserable of those wretches who were daily ravished from the slums and streets of the great cities to be shipped to the Americas. Nor was he a long time in discovering that he was now one of the several such indentured servants who, upon the conclusion of their voyage, were to be sold for their passage in the plantations of Maryland.

Having learned so much of his miserable fate, and being now able to make shift to walk (though with weak and stumbling steps), our young gentleman lost no time in seeking the Captain, to whom he endeavored to explain the several accidents that had befallen him, acknowledging that he was the second son of the Earl of Clandennie, and declaring that if he, the Captain, would put the *Prophet Daniel* back into some English port again, his lordship would make it well worth his while to lose so much time for the sake of one so dear as a second son. To this address the Captain, supposing him either to be drunk or disordered in his mind, made no other reply than to knock him incontinently down upon the deck, bidding him return forward where he belonged.

Thereafter poor Dunburne found himself enjoying the reputation of a harmless madman. The name of the Earl of Rags was bestowed upon him, and the miserable companions of his wretched plight were never tired of tempting him to recount his adventures, for the sake of entertaining themselves by teasing that which they supposed to be his hapless mania.

Nor is it easy to conceive of all the torments that those miserable, obscene wretches were able to inflict upon him. Under the teasing sting of his companions' malevolent pleasantries, there were times when Dunburne might, as he confessed to himself, have committed a murder with the greatest satisfaction in the world. However, he was endowed with no small command of self-restraint, so that he was still able to curb his passions within the bounds of reason and of policy. He was, fortunately, a complete master of the French and Italian languages, so that when the fury of his irritation would become too excessive for him to control, he would ease his spirits by castigating his tormentors with a consuming verbosity in those foreign tongues, which, had his companions understood a single word of that which he uttered, would have earned for him a beating that would have landed him within an inch of his life. However, they attributed all that he said to the irrational gibbering of a maniac.

About midway of their voyage the *Prophet Daniel* encountered a tremendous storm, which drove her so far out of the Captain's reckoning that when land was sighted, in the afternoon of a tempestuous day in the latter part of August, the first mate, who had been for some years in the New England trade, opined that it was the coast of Rhode Island, and that if the Captain chose to do so he might run into New Hope Harbor and lie there until the southeaster had blown itself out. This advice the Captain immediately put into execution, so that by nightfall they had dropped anchor in the comparative quiet of that excellent harbor.

Dunburne was a most excellent and practised swimmer. That evening, when the dusk had pretty well fallen, he jumped overboard, dived under the brig, and came up on the other side. Thus leaving all hands aboard looking for him or for his dead body at the starboard side of the *Prophet Daniel*, he himself swam slowly away to the larboard. Now partly under water, now floating on his back, he directed his course towards a point of land about a mile away, whereon, as he had observed before the dark had settled down, there stood an old wooden building resembling a church, and a great brick house with tall, lean chimneys at a little farther distance inland.

The intemperate cold of the water of those parts of America was so much more excessive than Dunburne had been used to swim in that when he dragged himself out upon the rocky, bowlder-strewn beach he lay for a considerable time more dead than alive. His limbs appeared to possess hardly any vitality, so benumbed were they by the icy chill that had entered into the very marrow of his bones. Nor did he for a long while recover from this excessive rigor; his limbs still continued at intervals to twitch and shudder as with a convulsion, nor could he at such times at all control their trembling. At last, however, with a huge sigh, he aroused himself to some perception of his surroundings, which he acknowledged were of as dispiriting a sort as he could well have conceived of. His recovering senses were distracted by a ceaseless watery din, for the breaking waves, rushing with a prodigious swiftness from the harbor to the shore before the driving wind, fell with uproarious crashing into white foam among the rocks. Above this watery tumult spread the wet gloom of the night, full of the blackness and pelting chill of a fine slanting rain.

Through this shroud of mist and gloom Dunburne at last distinguished a faint light, blurred by the sheets of rain and darkness, and shining as though from a considerable distance. Cheered by this nearer presence of human life, our young gentleman presently gathered his benumbed powers together, arose, and after a while began slowly and feebly to climb a stony hill that lay between the rocky beach and that faint but encouraging illumination.

So, sorely buffeted by the tempest, he at last reached the black, square form of that structure from which the light shone. The building he perceived to be a little wooden church of two stories in height. The shutters of the lower story were tight fastened, as though bolted from within. Those above were open, and from them issued the light that had guided him in his approach from the beach. A tall flight of wooden steps, wet in the rain, reached to a small, enclosed porch or vestibule, whence a door, now tight shut, gave ingress into the second story of the church.

Thence, as Dunburne stood without, he could now distinguish the dull muttering of a man's voice, which he opined might be that of the preacher. Our young gentleman, as may be supposed, was in a wretched plight. He was ragged and unshaven; his only clothing was the miserable shirt and bepatched breeches that had served him as shelter throughout the long voyage. These abominable garments were now wet to the skin, and so displeasing was his appearance that he was forced to acknowledge to himself that he did not possess enough of humility to avow so great a misery to the light and to the eyes of strangers. Accordingly, finding some shelter afforded by the vestibule of the church, he crouched there in a corner, huddling his rags about him, and finding a certain poor warmth in thus hiding away from the buffeting of the chill and penetrating wind. As he so crouched he presently became aware of the sound of many voices, dull and groaning, coming from within the edifice, and then—now and again—the clanking as of a multitude of chains. Then of a sudden, and unexpectedly, the door near him was flung wide open, and a faint glow of reddish light fell across the passage. Instantly the figure of a man came forth, and following him came, not a congregation, as Dunburne might have supposed, but a most dolorous company of nearly, or quite, naked men and women, outlined blackly, as they emerged, against the dull illumination from behind. These wretched beings, sighing and groaning most piteously, with a monotonous wailing of many voices, were chained by the wrist, two and two together, and as they passed by close to Dunburne, his nostrils were overpowered by a heavy and fetid odor that came partly from within the building, partly from the wretched creatures that passed him by.

As the last of these miserable beings came forth from the bowels of that dreadful place, a loud voice, so near to Dunburne as to startle his ears with its sudden exclamation, cried out, "Six-and-twenty, all told," and thereat instantly the dull light from within was quenched into darkness.

In the gloom and the silence that followed, Dunburne could hear for a while nothing but the dash of the rain upon the roof and the ceaseless drip and trickle of the water running from the eaves into the puddles beneath the building.

Then, as he stood, still marvelling at what he had seen, there suddenly came a loud and startling crash, as of a trap-door let fall into its place. A faint circle of light shone within the darkness of the building, as though from a lantern carried in a man's hands. There was a sound of jingling, as of keys, of approaching footsteps, and of voices talking together, and presently there came out into the vestibule the dark figures of two men, one of them carrying a ship's lantern. One of these figures closed and locked the door behind him, and then both were about to turn away without having observed Dunburne, when, of a sudden, a circle from the roof of the lantern lit up his pale and melancholy face, and he instantly became aware that his presence had been discovered.

The next moment the lantern was flung up almost into his eyes, and in the light he saw the sharp, round rim of a pistol-barrel directed immediately against his forehead.

In that moment our young gentleman's life hung as a hair in the balance. In the intense instant of expectancy his brain appeared to expand as a bubble, and his ears tingled and hummed as though a cloud of flies were buzzing therein. Then suddenly a voice smote like a blow upon the silence—"Who are you, and what d'ye want?"

"Indeed," said Dunburne, "I do not know."

"What do you do here?"

"Nor do I know that, either."

He who held the lantern lifted it so that the illumination fell still more fully upon Dunburne's face and person. Then his interlocutor demanded, "How did you come here?"

Upon the moment Dunburne determined to answer so much of the truth as the question required. "'Twas by no fault of my own," he cried. "I was knocked on the head and kidnapped in England, with the design of being sold in Baltimore. The vessel that fetched me put into the harbor over yonder to wait for good weather, and I jumped overboard and swam ashore, to stumble into the cursed pickle in which I now find myself."

"Have you, then, an education? To be sure, you talk so."

"Indeed I have," said Dunburne—"a decent enough education to fit me for a gentleman, if the opportunity offered. But what of that?" he exclaimed, desperately. "I might as well have no more learning than a beggar under the bush, for all the good it does me." The other once more flashed the light of his lantern over our young gentleman's miserable and barefoot figure. "I had a mind," says he, "to blow your brains out against the wall. I have a notion now, however, to turn you to some use instead, so I'll just spare your life for a little while, till I see how you behave."

He spoke with so much more of jocularity than he had heretofore used that Dunburne recovered in great part his dawning assurance. "I am infinitely obliged to you," he cried, "for sparing my brains; but I protest I doubt if you will ever find so good an opportunity again to murder me as you have just enjoyed."

This speech seemed to tickle the other prodigiously, for he burst into a loud and boisterous laugh, under cover of which he thrust his pistol back into his coat-pocket again. "Come with me, and I'll fit you with victuals and decent clothes, of both of which you appear to stand in no little need," he said. Thereupon, and without another word, he turned and quitted the place, accompanied by his companion, who for all this time had uttered not a single sound. A little way from the church these two parted company, with only a brief word spoken between them.

Dunburne's interlocutor, with our young gentleman following close behind him, led the way in silence for a considerable distance through the long, wet grass and the tempestuous darkness, until at last, still in unbroken silence, they reached the confines of an enclosure, and presently stood before a large and imposing house built of brick.

Dunburne's mysterious guide, still carrying the lantern, conducted him directly up a broad flight of steps, and opening the door, ushered him into a hallway of no inconsiderable pretensions. Thence he led the way to a dining-room beyond, where our young gentleman observed a long mahogany table, and a sideboard of carved mahogany illuminated by three or four candles. In answer to the call of his conductor, a negro servant appeared, whom the master of the house ordered to fetch some bread and cheese and a bottle of rum for his wretched guest. While the servant was gone to execute the commission the master seated himself at his ease and favored Dunburne with a long and most minute regard. Then he suddenly asked our young gentleman what was his name.

Upon the instant Dunburne did not offer a reply to this interrogation. He had been so miserably abused when he had told the truth upon the voyage that he knew not now whether to confess or deny his identity. He possessed no great aptitude at lying, so that it was with no little hesitation that he determined to maintain his incognito. Having reached this conclusion, he answered his host that his name was Tom Robinson. The other, however, appeared to notice neither his hesitation nor the name which he had seen fit to assume. Instead, he appeared to be lost in a reverie, which he broke only to bid our young gentleman to sit down and tell the story of the several adventures that had befallen him. He advised him to leave nothing untold, however shameful it might be. "Be assured," said he, "that no matter what crimes you may have committed, the more intolerable your wickedness, the better you will please me for the purpose I have in view."

Being thus encouraged, and having already embarked in disingenuosity, our young gentleman, desiring to please his host, began at random a tale composed in great part of what he recollected of the story of *Colonel Jack*, seasoned occasionally with extracts from Mr. Smollett's ingenious novel of *Ferdinand, Count Fathom*. There was hardly a petty crime or a mean action mentioned in either of these entertaining fictions that he was not willing to attribute to himself. Meanwhile he discovered, to his surprise, that lying was not really so difficult an art as he had supposed it to be. His host listened for a considerable while in silence, but at last he was obliged to call upon his penitent to stop. "To tell you the truth, Mr. What's-a-name," he cried, "I do not believe a single word you are telling me. However, I am satisfied that in you I have discovered, as I have every reason to hope, one of the most preposterous liars I have for a long time fell in with. Indeed, I protest that any one who can with so steady a countenance lie so tremendously as you have just done may be capable, if not of a great crime, at least of no inconsiderable deceit, and perhaps of treachery. If this be so, you will suit my purposes very well, though I would rather have had you an escaped criminal or a murderer or a thief."

"Sir," said Dunburne, very seriously, "I am sorry that I am not more to your mind. As you say, I can, I find, lie very easily, and if you will give me sufficient time, I dare say I can become sufficiently expert in other and more criminal matters to please even your fancy. I cannot, I fear, commit a murder, nor would I choose to embark upon an attempt at arson; but I could easily learn to cheat at cards; or I could, if it would please you better, make shift to forge your own name to a bill for a hundred pounds. I confess, however, I am entirely in the dark as to why you choose to have me enjoy so evil a reputation."

At these words the other burst into a great and vociferous laugh. "I protest," he cried, "you are the coolest rascal ever I fell in with. But come," he added, sobering suddenly, "what did you say was your name?"

"I declare, sir," said Dunburne, with the most ingenuous frankness, "I have clean forgot. Was it Tom or John Robinson?"

Again the other burst out laughing. "Well," he said, "what does it matter? Thomas or John—'tis all one. I see that you are a ragged, lousy beggar, and I believe you to be a runaway servant. Even if that is the worst to be said of you, you will suit me very well. As for a name, I myself will fit you with one, and it shall be of the best. I will give you a home here in the house, and will for three months clothe you like a lord. You shall live upon the best, and shall meet plenty of the genteelest company the Colonies can afford. All that I demand of you is that you shall do exactly as I tell you for the three months that I so entertain you. Come. Is it a bargain?"

Dunburne sat for a while thinking very seriously. "First of all," said he, "I must know what is the name you have a mind to bestow upon me."

The other looked distrustfully at him for a time, and then, as though suddenly fetching up resolution, he cried out: "Well, what then? What of it? Why should I be afraid? I'll tell you. Your name shall be Frederick Dunburne, and you shall be the second son of the Earl of Clandennie."

Had a thunder-bolt fallen from heaven at Dunburne's feet he could not have been struck more entirely dumb than he was at those astounding words. He knew not for the moment where to look or what to think. At that instant the negro man came into the room, fetching the bottle of rum and the bread and cheese he had been sent for. As the sound of his entrance struck upon our young gentleman's senses he came to himself with the shock, and suddenly exploded into a burst of laughter so shrill and discordant that Captain Obadiah sat staring at him as though he believed his ragged beneficiary had gone clean out of his senses.

IV
A ROMANTIC EPISODE IN THE LIFE OF A YOUNG LADY

Miss Belinda Belford, the daughter and only child of Colonel William Belford, was a young lady possessed of no small pretensions to personal charms of the most exalted order. Indeed, many excellent judges in such matters regarded her, without doubt, as the reigning belle of the Northern Colonies. Of a medium height, of a slight but generously rounded figure, she bore herself with an indescribable grace and dignity of carriage. Her hair, which was occasionally permitted to curl in ringlets upon her snowy neck, was of a brown so dark and so soft as at times to deceive the admiring observer into a belief that it was black. Her eyes, likewise of a dark-brown color, were of a most melting and liquid lustre; her nose, though slight, was sufficiently high, and modelled with so exquisite a delicacy as to lend an exceeding charm to her whole countenance. She was easily the belle of every assembly which she graced with her presence, and her name was the toast of every garrison town of the Northern provinces.

Madam Belford and her lovely daughter were engaged one pleasant morning in entertaining a number of friends, in the genteel English manner, with a dish of tea and a bit of gossip. Upon this charming company Colonel Belford suddenly intruded, his countenance displaying an excessive though not displeasing agitation.

"My dear! my dear!" he cried, "what a piece of news have I for you! It is incredible and past all belief! Who, ladies, do you suppose is here in New Hope? Nay, you cannot guess; I shall have to enlighten you. 'Tis none other than Frederick Dunburne, my lordship's second son. Yes, you may well look amazed. I saw and spoke with him this very morning, and that not above a half-hour ago. He is travelling incognito, but my brother Obadiah discovered his identity, and is now entertaining him at his new house upon the Point. A large party of young officers from the garrison are there, all very gay with cards and dice, I am told. My noble young gentleman knew me so soon as he clapped eyes upon me. 'This,' says he, 'if I am not mistook, must be Colonel Belford, my father's honored friend.' He is," exclaimed the speaker, "a most interesting and ingenuous youth, with extremely lively and elegant manners, and a person exactly resembling that of his dear and honored father."

It may be supposed into what a flutter this piece of news cast those who heard it. "My dear," cried Madam Belford, as soon as the first extravagance of the general surprise had passed by to an easier acceptance of Colonel Belford's tidings—"my dear, why did you not bring him with you to present him to us all? What an opportunity have you lost!"

"Indeed, my dear," said Colonel Belford, "I did not forget to invite him hither. He protested that nothing could afford him greater pleasure, did he not have an engagement with some young gentlemen from the garrison. But, believe me, I would not let him go without a promise. He is to dine with us to-morrow at two; and, Belinda, my dear" —here Colonel Belford pinched his daughter's blushing cheek—"you must assume your best appearance for so serious an occasion. I am informed that my noble gentleman is extremely particular in his tastes in the matter of female excellence."

"Indeed, papa," cried the young lady, with great vivacity, "I shall attempt no extraordinary graces upon my young gentleman's account, and that I promise you. I protest," she exclaimed, with spirit, "I have no great opinion of him who would come thus to New Hope without a single word to you, who are his father's confidential correspondent. Nor do I admire the taste of one who would choose to cast himself upon the hospitality of my uncle Obadiah rather than upon yours."

"My dear," said Colonel Belford, very soberly, "you express your opinion with a most unwarranted levity, considering the exalted position how they were leaning over the rail of the vessel looking out towards the westward, she fallen mightily quiet as though occupied with very serious thoughts.

Of a sudden she began, without any preface whatever, to speak to Barnaby about herself and her affairs, in a most confidential manner, such as she had never used to him before. She told him that she and her grandfather were going to New York that they might take passage thence to Boston, in Massachusetts, where they were to meet her cousin Captain Malyoe, who was stationed in garrison at that place. Continuing, she said that Captain Malyoe was the next heir to the Devonshire estate, and that she and he were to be married in the fall.

You may conceive into what a confusion of distress such a confession as this, delivered so suddenly, must have cast poor Barnaby. He could answer her not a single word, but stood staring in another direction than hers, endeavoring to compose himself into some equanimity of spirit. For indeed it was a sudden, terrible blow, and his breath came as hot and dry as ashes in his throat. Meanwhile the young lady went on to say, though in a mightily constrained voice, that she had liked him from the very first moment she had seen him, and had been very happy for these days she had passed in his society, and that she would always think of him as a dear friend who had been very kind to her, who had so little pleasure in her life.

At last Barnaby made shift to say, though in a hoarse and croaking voice, that Captain Malyoe must be a very happy man, and that if he were in Captain Malyoe's place he would be the happiest man in the world. Thereupon, having so found his voice, he went on to tell her, though in a prodigious confusion and perturbation of spirit, that he too loved her, and that what she had told him struck him to the heart, and made him the most miserable, unhappy wretch in the whole world.

She exhibited no anger at what he said, nor did she turn to look at him, but only replied, in a low voice, that he should not talk so, for that it could only be a pain to them both to speak of such things, and that whether she would or no, she must do everything her grandfather bade her, he being indeed a terrible man.

To this poor Barnaby could only repeat that he loved her with all his heart, that he had hoped for nothing in his love, but that he was now the most miserable man in the world.

It was at this moment, so momentous to our hero, that some one who had been hiding unseen nigh them for all the while suddenly moved away, and Barnaby, in spite of the gathering darkness, could perceive that it was that villain man-servant of Sir John Malyoe's. Nor could he but know that the wretch must have overheard all that had been said.

As he looked he beheld this fellow go straight to the great cabin, where he disappeared with a cunning leer upon his face, so that our hero could not but be aware that the purpose of the eavesdropper must be to communicate all that he had overheard to his master. At this thought the last drop of bitterness was added to his trouble, for what could be more distressing to any man of honor than to possess the consciousness that such a wretch should have overheard so sacred a conversation as that which he had enjoyed with the young lady. She, upon her part, could not have been aware that the man had listened to what she had been saying, for she still continued leaning over the rail, and Barnaby remained standing by her side, without moving, but so distracted by a tumult of many passions that he knew not how or where to look.

After a pretty long time of this silence, the young lady looked up to see why her companion had not spoken for so great a while, and at that very moment Sir John Malyoe comes flinging out of the cabin without his hat, but carrying his gold-headed cane. He ran straight across the deck towards where Barnaby and the young lady stood, swinging his cane this way and that with a most furious and threatening countenance, while the informer, grinning like an ape, followed close at his heels. As Sir John approached them, he cried out in so loud a voice that all on deck might have heard him, "You hussy!" (And all the time, you are to remember, he was swinging his cane as though he would have struck the young lady, who, upon her part, shrank back from him almost upon the deck as though to escape such a blow.) "You hussy! What do you do here, talking with a misbred Yankee supercargo not fit for a gentlewoman to wipe her feet upon, and you stand there and listen to his fool talk! Go to your room, you hussy"—only 'twas something worse he called her this time—"before I lay this cane across you!"

You may suppose into what fury such words as these, spoken in Barnaby's hearing, not to mention that vile slur set upon himself, must have cast our hero. To be sure he scarcely knew what he did, but he put his hand against Sir John Malyoe's breast and thrust him back most violently, crying out upon him at the same time for daring so to threaten a young lady, and that for a farthing he would wrench the stick out of his hand and throw it overboard.

A little farther and Sir John would have fallen flat upon the deck with the push Barnaby gave him. But he contrived, by catching hold of the rail, to save his balance. Whereupon, having recovered himself, he came running at our hero like a wild beast, whirling his cane about, and I do believe would have struck him (and God knows then what might have happened) had not his man-servant caught him and held him back.

"Keep back!" cried out our hero, still mighty hoarse. "Keep back! If you strike me with that stick I'll fling you overboard!"

By this time, what with the sound of loud voices and the stamping of feet, some of the crew and others aboard were hurrying up to the scene of action. At the same time Captain Manly and the first mate, Mr. Freesden, came running out of the cabin. As for our hero, having got set agoing, he was not to be stopped so easily.

"And who are you, anyhow," he cries, his voice mightily hoarse even in his own ears, "to threaten to strike me! You may be a bloody pirate, and you may shoot a man from behind, as you shot poor Captain Brand on the Cobra River, but you won't dare strike me face to face. I know who you are and what you are!"

As for Sir John Malyoe, had he been struck of a sudden by palsy, he could not have stopped more dead short in his attack upon our hero. There he stood, his great, bulging eyes staring like those of a fish, his face as purple as a cherry. As for Master Informer, Barnaby had the satisfaction of seeing that he had stopped his grinning by now and was holding his master's arm as though to restrain him from any further act of violence.

By this time Captain Manly had come bustling up and demanded to know what all the disturbance meant. Whereupon our hero cried out, still in the extremity of passion:

"The villain insulted me and insulted the young lady; he threatened to strike me with his cane. But he sha'n't strike me. I know who he is and what he is. I know what he's got in his cabin in those two trunks, and I know where he found it, and whom it belongs to."

At this Captain Manly clapped his hand upon our hero's shoulder and fell to shaking him so that he could hardly stand, crying out to him the while to be silent. Says he: "How do you dare, an officer of this ship, to quarrel with a passenger of mine! Go straight to your cabin, and stay there till I give you leave to come out again."

At this Master Barnaby came somewhat back to himself. "But he threatened to strike me with his cane," he says, "and that I won't stand from any man!"

"No matter for that," says Captain Manly, very sternly. "Go to your cabin, as I bid you, and stay there till I tell you to come out again, and when we get to New York I'll take pains to inform your step-father of how you have behaved. I'll have no such rioting as this aboard my ship."

By this time, as you may suppose, the young lady was gone. As for Sir John Malyoe, he stood in the light of a lantern, his face that had been so red now gone as white as ashes, and if a look could kill, to be sure he would have destroyed Barnaby True where he stood.

It was thus that the events of that memorable day came to a conclusion. How little did any of the actors of the scene suspect that a portentous Fate was overhanging them, and was so soon to transform all their present circumstances into others that were to be perfectly different!

And how little did our hero suspect what was in store for him upon the morrow, as with hanging head he went to his cabin, and shutting the door upon himself, and flinging himself down upon his berth, there yielded himself over to the profoundest depths of humiliation and despair.

V

From his melancholy meditations Barnaby, by-and-by and in spite of himself, began dropping off into a loose slumber, disturbed by extravagant dreams of all sorts, in which Sir John Malyoe played some important and malignant part.

From one of these dreams he was aroused to meet a new and startling fate, by hearing the sudden and violent explosion of a pistol-shot ring out as though in his ears. This was followed immediately by the sound of several other shots exchanged in rapid succession as coming from the deck above. At the same instant a blow of such excessive violence shook the *Belle Helen* that the vessel heeled over before it, and Barnaby was at once aware that another craft—whether by accident or with intention he did not know—must have run afoul of them.

Upon this point, and as to whether or not the collision was designed, he was, however, not left a moment in doubt, for even as the *Belle Helen* righted to her true keel, there was the sound of many footsteps running across the deck and down into the great cabin. Then proceeded a prodigious uproar of voices, together with the struggling of men's bodies being tossed about, striking violently against the partitions and bulkheads. At the same instant arose a screaming of women's voices, and one voice, that of Sir John Malyoe, crying out as in the greatest extremity: "You villains! You damned villains!" and with that the sudden detonation of a pistol fired into the close space of the great cabin.

Long before this time Barnaby was out in the middle of his own cabin. Taking only sufficient time to snatch down one of the pistols that hung at the head of his berth, he flung out into the great cabin, to find it as black as night, the lantern slung there having been either blown out or dashed out into darkness. All was as black as coal, and the gloom was filled with a hubbub of uproar and confusion, above which sounded continually the shrieking of women's voices. Nor had our hero taken above a couple of steps before he pitched headlong over two or three men struggling together upon the deck, falling with a great clatter and the loss of his pistol, which, however, he regained almost immediately.

What all the uproar portended he could only guess, but presently hearing Captain Manly's voice calling out, "You bloody pirate, would you choke me to death?" he became immediately aware of what had befallen the *Belle Helen*, and that they had been attacked by some of those buccaneers who at that time infested the waters of America in prodigious numbers.

It was with this thought in his mind that, looking towards the companionway, he beheld, outlined against the darkness of the night without, the form of a man's figure, standing still and motionless as a statue in the midst of all this tumult, and thereupon, as by some instinct, knew that that must be the master-maker of all this devil's brew. Therewith, still kneeling upon the deck, he covered the bosom of that figure point-blank, as he supposed, with his pistol, and instantly pulled the trigger.

In the light of the pistol fire, Barnaby had only sufficient opportunity to distinguish a flat face wearing a large pair of mustachios, a cocked hat trimmed with gold lace, a red scarf, and brass buttons. Then the darkness, very thick and black, again swallowed everything.

But if our hero failed to clearly perceive the countenance towards which he had discharged his weapon, there was one who appeared to have recognized some likeness in it, for Sir John Malyoe's voice, almost at Barnaby's elbow, cried out thrice in loud and violent tones, "William Brand! William Brand! William Brand!" and thereat came the sound of some heavy body falling down upon the deck.

This was the last that our hero may remember of that notable attack, for the next moment whether by accident or design he never knew, he felt himself struck so terrible a blow upon the side of the head, that he instantly swooned dead away and knew no more.

VI

When Barnaby True came back to his senses again, it was to become aware that he was being cared for with great skill and nicety, that his head had been bathed with cold water, and that a bandage was being bound about it as carefully as though a chirurgeon was attending to him.

He had been half conscious of people about him, but could not immediately recall what had happened to him, nor until he had opened his eyes to find himself in a perfectly strange cabin of narrow dimensions but extremely well fitted and painted with white and gold. By the light of a lantern shining in his eyes, together with the gray of the early day through the deadlight, he could perceive that two men were bending over him — one, a negro in a striped shirt, with a yellow handkerchief around his head and silver ear-rings in his ears; the other, a white man, clad in a strange, outlandish dress of a foreign make, with great mustachios hanging down below his chin, and with gold ear-rings in his ears.

It was this last who was attending to Barnaby's hurt with such extreme care and gentleness.

All this Barnaby saw with his first clear consciousness after his swoon. Then remembering what had befallen him, and his head beating as though it would split asunder, he shut his eyes again, contriving with great effort to keep himself from groaning aloud, and wondering as to what sort of pirates these could be, who would first knock a man in the head so terrible a blow as that which he had suffered, and then take such care to fetch him back to life again, and to make him easy and comfortable.

Nor did he open his eyes again, but lay there marvelling thus until the bandage was properly tied about his head and sewed together. Then once more he opened his eyes and looked up to ask where he was.

Upon hearing him speak, his attendants showed excessive signs of joy, nodding their heads and smiling at him as though to reassure him. But either because they did not choose to reply, or else because they could not speak English, they made no answer, excepting by those signs and gestures. The white man, however, made several motions that our hero was to arise, and, still grinning and nodding his head, pointed as though towards a saloon beyond. At the same time the negro held up our hero's coat and beckoned for him to put it on. Accordingly Barnaby, seeing that it was required of him to quit the place in which he then lay, arose, though with a good deal of effort, and permitted the negro to help him on with his coat, though feeling mightily dizzy and much put about to keep upon his legs — his head beating fit to split asunder and the vessel rolling and pitching at a great rate, as though upon a heavy cross-sea.

So, still sick and dizzy, he went out into what he found was, indeed, a fine saloon beyond, painted in white and gilt like the cabin he had just quitted. This saloon was fitted in the most excellent taste imaginable. A table extended the length of the room, and a quantity of bottles, and glasses clear as crystal, were arranged in rows in a hanging rack above.

But what most attracted our hero's attention was a man sitting with his back to him, his figure clad in a rough pea-jacket, and with a red handkerchief tied around his throat. His feet were stretched under the table out before him, and he was smoking a pipe of tobacco with all the ease and comfort imaginable. As Barnaby came in he turned round, and, to the profound astonishment of our hero, presented to him in the light of the lantern, the dawn shining pretty strong through the skylight, the face of that very man who had conducted the mysterious expedition that night across Kingston Harbor to the Cobra River.

VII

This man looked steadily at Barnaby True for above half a minute and then burst out a-laughing. And, indeed, Barnaby, standing there with the bandage about his head, must have looked a very droll picture of that astonishment he felt so profoundly at finding who was this pirate into whose hands he had fallen. "Well," says the other, "and so you be up at last, and no great harm done, I'll be bound. And how does your head feel by now, my young master?"

To this Barnaby made no reply, but, what with wonder and the dizziness of his head, seated himself at the table over against his interlocutor, who pushed a bottle of rum towards him, together with a glass from the hanging rack. He watched Barnaby fill his glass, and so soon as he had done so began immediately by saying: "I do suppose you think you were treated mightily ill to be so handled last night. Well, so you were treated ill enough, though who hit you that crack upon the head I know no more than a child unborn. Well, I am sorry for the way you were handled, but there is this much to say, and of that you may feel well assured, that nothing was meant to you but kindness, and before you are through with us all you will believe that without my having to tell you so."

Here he helped himself to a taste of grog, and sucking in his lips went on again with what he had to say. "Do you remember," says he, "that expedition of ours in Kingston Harbor, and how we were all of us balked that night?" then, without waiting for Barnaby's reply: "And do you remember what I said to that villain Jack Malyoe that night as his boat went by us? I says to him, 'Jack Malyoe,' says I, 'you've got the better of us once again, but next time it will be our turn, even if William Brand himself has to come back from the grave to settle with you.'"

"I remember something of the sort," said Barnaby, "but I profess I am all in the dark as to what you are driving at."

At this the other burst out in a great fit of laughing. "Very well, then," said he, "this night's work is only the ending of what was so ill begun there. Look yonder"—pointing to a corner of the cabin—"and then maybe you will be in the dark no longer." Barnaby turned his head and there beheld in the corner of the saloon those very two travelling-cases that Sir John Malyoe had been so particular to keep in his cabin and under his own eyes through all the voyage from Jamaica.

"I'll show you what is in 'em," says the other, and thereupon arose, and Barnaby with him, and so went over to where the two travelling-cases stood.

Our hero had a strong enough suspicion as to what the cases contained. But, Lord! what were suspicions to what his two eyes beheld when that man lifted the lid of one of them—the locks thereof having already been forced—and, flinging it back, displayed to Barnaby's astonished and bedazzled sight a great treasure of gold and silver, some of it tied up in leathern bags, to be sure, but so many of the coins, big and little, yellow and white, lying loose in the cases as to make our hero think that a great part of the treasures of the Indies lay there before him.

"Well, and what do you think of that?" said the other. "Is it not enough for a man to turn pirate for?" and thereupon burst out a-laughing and clapped down the lid again. Then suddenly turning serious: "Come Master Barnaby," says he. "I am to have some very sober talk with you, so fill up your glass again and then we will heave at it."

Nor even in after years, nor in the light of that which afterwards occurred, could Barnaby repeat all that was said to him upon that occasion, for what with the pounding and beating of his aching head, and what with the wonder of what he had seen, he was altogether in the dark as to the greater part of what the other told him. That other began by saying that Barnaby, instead of being sorry that he was William Brand's grandson, might thank God for it; that he (Barnaby) had been watched and cared for for twenty years in more ways than he would ever know; that Sir John Malyoe had been watched also for all that while, and that it was a vastly strange thing that Sir John Malyoe's debts in England and Barnaby's coming of age should have brought them so together in Jamaica—though, after all, it was all for the best, as Barnaby himself should presently see, and thank God for that also. For now all the debts against that villain Jack Malyoe were settled in full, principal and interest, to the last penny, and Barnaby was to enjoy it the most of all. Here the fellow took a very comfortable sip of his grog, and then went on to say with a very cunning and knowing wink of the eye that Barnaby was not the only passenger aboard, but that there was another in whose company he would be glad enough, no doubt, to finish the balance of the voyage he was now upon. So now, if Barnaby was sufficiently composed, he should be introduced to that other passenger. Thereupon,

your subject occupies. I may, however, explain to you that he came to America quite unexpectedly and by an accident. Nor would he have declared his incognito, had not my brother Obadiah discovered it almost immediately upon his arrival. He would not, he declared, have visited New Hope at all, had not Captain Obadiah Belford urged his hospitality in such a manner as to preclude all denial."

But to this reproof Miss Belinda who, was, indeed, greatly indulged by her parents, made no other reply than to toss her head with a pretty sauciness, and to pout her cherry lips in an infinitely becoming manner.

But though our young lady protested so emphatically against assuming any unusual charms for the entertainment of their expected visitor, she none the less devoted no small consideration to that very thing that she had so exclaimed against. Accordingly, when she was presented to her father's noble guest, what with her heightened color and her eyes sparkling with the emotions evoked by the occasion, she so impressed our young gentleman that he could do little but stand regarding her with an astonishment that for the moment caused him to forget those graces of deportment that the demands of elegance called upon him to assume.

However, he recovered himself immediately, and proceeded to take such advantage of his introduction that by the time they were seated at the dinner-table he found himself conversing with his fair partner with all the ease and vivacity imaginable. Nor in this exchange of polite raillery did he discover her wit to be in any degree less than her personal charms.

"Indeed, madam," he exclaimed, "I am now more than ready to thank that happy accident that has transported me, however much against my will, from England to America. The scenery, how beautiful! Nature, how fertile! Woman, how exquisite! Your country," he exclaimed, with enthusiasm, "is like heaven!"

"Indeed, sir," cried the young lady, vivaciously, "I do not take your praise for a compliment. I protest I am acquainted with no young gentleman who would not defer his enjoyment of heaven to the very last extremity."

"To be sure," quoth our hero, "an ambition for the abode of saints is of too extreme a nature to recommend itself to a modest young fellow of parts. But when one finds himself thrown into the society of an houri—"

"And do you indeed have houris in England?" exclaimed the young lady. "In America you must be content with society of a much more earthly constitution!"

"Upon my word, miss," cried our young gentleman, "you compel me to confess that I find myself in the society of one vastly more to my inclination than that of any houri of my acquaintance."

With such lively badinage, occasionally lapsing into more serious discourse, the dinner passed off with a great deal of pleasantness to our young gentleman, who had prepared himself for something prodigiously dull and heavy. After the repast, a pipe of tobacco in the summer-house and a walk in the garden so far completed his cheerful impressions that when he rode away towards Pig and Sow Point he found himself accompanied by the most lively, agreeable thoughts imaginable. Her wit, how subtle! Her person, how beautiful! He surprised himself smiling with a fatuous indulgence of his enjoyable fancies.

Nor did the young lady's thoughts, though doubtless of a more moderate sort, assume a less pleasing perspective. Our young gentleman was favored with a tall, erect figure, a high nose, and a fine, thin face expressive of excellent breeding. It seemed to her that his manners possessed an elegance and a grace that she had never before discovered beyond the leaves of Mr. Richardson's ingenious novels. Nor was she unaware of the admiration of herself that his countenance had expressed. Upon so slender a foundation she amused herself for above an hour, erecting such castles in the air that, had any one discovered her thought, she would have perished of mortification.

But though our young lady so yielded herself to the enjoyment of such silly dreams as might occur to any miss of a lively imagination and vivacious temperament, the reader is to understand that she has yet so much dignity and spirit as to cover these foolish and romantic fancies with a cloak of so delicate and so subtle a reserve that when the young gentleman called to pay his respects the next afternoon he quitted her presence ten times more infatuated with her charms than he had been the day before.

Nor can it be denied that our young lady knew perfectly well how to make the greatest use of such opportunities. She already possessed a great deal of experience in teasing the other sex with those delicious though innocent torments that cause the eyes of the victim to remain awake at night and the fancy to dream throughout the day.

Such presently became the condition of our young gentleman that at the end of the month he knew not whether his present life had continued for weeks or for years; in the charming infatuation that overpowered him he considered nothing of time, every other consideration being engulfed in his desire for the society of his charmer. Cards and dice lost for him their accustomed pleasure, and when a gay society would be at Belford's Palace it was with the utmost difficulty that he assumed so much patience as to take his part in those dissipations that there obtained. Relieved from them, he flew with redoubled ardor back to the gratification of his passion again.

In the mean time Captain Obadiah had become so accustomed to the presence of his guest that he made no pretence of any concealment of that iniquitous, dreadful avocation that lent to Pig and Sow Point so great a terror in those parts. Rather did the West Indian appear to court the open observation of his dependant.

One exquisite day in the last of October our young gentleman had spent the greater part of the afternoon in the society of the beautiful object of his regard. The leaves, though fallen from the trees in great abundance, appeared thereby only to have admitted of the passage of a riper radiance of golden sunlight through the thinning branches. This and the ardor of his passion had so transported our hero that when he had departed from her presence he seemed to walk as light as a feather, and knew not whether it was the warmth of the sunlight or the heat of his own impetuous transports that filled the universe with so extreme a brightness.

Overpowered with these absorbing and transcendent introspections, he approached his now odious home upon Pig and Sow Point by way of the old meeting-house. There of a sudden he came upon his patron, Captain Obadiah, superintending the burial of the last of three victims of his odious commerce, who had died that afternoon. Two had already been interred, and the third new-made grave was in the process of being filled. Two men, one a negro and the other a white, had nearly completed their labor, tramping down the crumbling earth as they shovelled it into the shallow excavation. Meanwhile Captain Obadiah stood near by, his red coat flaming in the slanting light, himself smoking a pipe of tobacco with all the ease and coolness imaginable. His hands, clasped behind his back, held his ivory-headed cane, and as our hero approached he turned an evil countenance upon him, and greeted him with a grin at once droll, mischievous, and malevolent in the extreme. "And how is our pretty charmer this afternoon?" quoth Captain Obadiah.

Conceive, if you please, of a man floating in the most ecstatic delight of heaven pulled suddenly thence down into the most filthy extremity of hell, and then you shall understand the motions of disgust and repugnance and loathing that overpowered our hero, who, awakening thus suddenly out of his dream of love, found himself in the presence of that grim and obscene spectacle of death—who, arousing from such absorbing and exquisite meditations, heard his ears greeted with so rude and vulgar an address.

Acknowledging to himself that he did not dare offer an immediate reply to his host, he turned upon his heel and walked away, without expressing a single word.

He was not, however, permitted to escape thus easily. He had not taken above twenty steps, when, hearing footsteps behind him, he turned his head to discover Captain Obadiah skipping rapidly after him in a prodigious hurry, swinging his cane and chuckling preposterously to himself, as though in the enjoyment of some most exquisite piece of drollery. "What!" he cried, as soon as he could catch his breath from his hurry. "What! What! Can't you answer, you villain? Why, blind my eyes! a body would think you were a lord's son indeed, instead of being, as I know you, a beggarly runaway servant whom I took in like a mangy cat out of the rain. But come, come—no offence, my boy! I'll be no hard master to you. I've heard how the wind blows, and I've kept my ears open to all your doings. I know who is your sweetheart. Harkee, you rascal! You have a fancy for my niece, have you? Well, your apple is ripe if you choose to pick it. Marry your charmer and be damned; and if you'll serve me by taking her thus in hand, I'll pay you twenty pounds upon your wedding-day. Now what do you say to that, you lousy beggar in borrowed clothes?"

Our young gentleman stopped short and looked his tormentor full in the face. The thought of his father's anger alone had saved him from entangling himself in the web of his passions; this he forgot upon the instant. "Captain Obadiah Belford," quoth he, "you're the most consummate villain ever I beheld in all of my life; but if I have the good-fortune to please the young lady, I wish I may die if I don't serve you in this!"

At these words Captain Obadiah, who appeared to take no offence at his guest's opinion of his honesty, burst out into a great boisterous laugh, flinging back his head and dropping his lower jaw so preposterously that the setting sun shone straight down his wide and cavernous gullet.

V
HOW THE DEVIL WAS CAST OUT
OF THE MEETING-HOUSE

The news that the Honorable Frederick Dunburne, second son of the Earl of Clandennie, was to marry Miss Belinda Belford, the daughter and only child of Colonel William Belford, of New Hope, was of a sort to arouse the keenest and most lively interest in all those parts of the Northern Colonies of America.

The day had been fixed, and all the circumstances arranged with such particularity that an invitation was regarded as the highest honor that could befall the fortunate recipient. There were to be present on this interesting occasion two Colonial governors and their ladies, an English general, the captain of the flag-ship *Achilles*, and above a score of Colonial magnates and ladies of distinction.

Captain Obadiah had not been bidden to either the ceremony or the breakfast. This rebuff he had accepted with prodigious amusement, which, not limiting itself to the immediate occasion, broke forth at intervals for above two weeks. Now it might express itself in chuckles of the most delicious entertainment, vented as our Captain walked up and down the hall of his great house, smoking his pipe and cracking the knuckles of his fingers; at other times he would burst forth into incontrollable fits of laughter at the extravagant deceit which he believed himself to be imposing upon his brother, Colonel Belford.

At length came the wedding-day, with such circumstances of pomp and display as the exceeding wealth and Colonial dignity of Colonel Belford could surround it. For the wedding-breakfast the great folding-doors between the drawing-room and the dining-room of Colonel Belford's house were flung wide open, and a table extending the whole length of the two apartments was set with the most sumptuous and exquisite display of plate and china. Around the board were collected the distinguished company, and the occasion was remarkable not less for the richness of its display than for the exquisite nature of the repast intended to celebrate so auspicious an occasion.

At the head of the board sat the young couple, radiant with an engrossing happiness that took no thought of what the future might have in store for it, but was contented with the triumphant ecstasy of the moment.

These elegant festivities were at their height, when there suddenly arose a considerable disputation in the hallway beyond, and before any one could inquire as to what was occurring, Captain Obadiah Belford came stumping into the room, swinging his ivory-headed cane, and with an expression of the most malicious triumph impressed upon his countenance. Directing his address to the bridegroom, and paying no attention to any other one of the company, he cried out: "Though not bidden to this entertainment, I have come to pay you a debt I owe. Here is twenty pounds I promised to pay you for marrying my niece."

Therewith he drew a silk purse full of gold pieces from his pocket, which he hung over the ferrule of his cane and reached across the table to the bridegroom. That gentleman, upon his part (having expected some such episode as this), arose, and with a most polite and elaborate bow accepted the same and thrust it into his pocket.

"And now, my young gentleman," cried Captain Obadiah, folding his arms and tucking his cane under his armpit, looking the while from under his brows upon the company with a most malevolent and extravagant grin— "and now, my young gentleman, perhaps you will favor the ladies and gentlemen here present with an account of what services they are I thus pay for."

"To be sure I will," cried out our hero, "and that with the utmost willingness in the world."

During all this while the elegant company had sat as with suspended animation, overwhelmed with wonder at the singular address of the intruder. Even the servants stood still with the dishes in their hands the better to hear the outcome of the affair. The bride, overwhelmed by a sudden and inexplicable anxiety, felt the color quit her face, and reaching out, seized her lover's hand, who took hers very readily, holding it tight within his grasp. As for Colonel and Madam Belford, not knowing what this remarkable address portended, they sat as though turned to stone, the one gone as white as ashes, and the other as red in the face as a cherry. Our young gentleman, however, maintained the utmost coolness and composure of demeanor. Pointing his finger towards the intruder, he exclaimed: "In Captain Obadiah Belford, ladies and gentlemen, you behold the most unmitigated villain that ever I met in all of my life. With an incredible spite and vindictiveness he not only pursued my honored father-in-law, Colonel Belford, but has sought to wreak an unwarranted revenge upon the innocent and virtuous young lady whom I have now the honor to call my wife. But how has he overreached himself in his machinations! How has he entangled his feet in the net which he himself has spread! I will tell you my history, as he bids me to do, and you may then judge for yourselves!"

At this unexpected address Captain Obadiah's face fell from its expression of malicious triumph, growing longer and longer, until at last it was overclouded with so much doubt and anxiety that, had he been threatened by the loss of a thousand pounds, he could not have assumed a greater appearance of mortification and dejection. Meantime, regarding him with a mischievous smile, our young gentleman began the history of all those adventures that had befallen him from the time he embarked upon the memorable expedition with his two companions in dissipation from York Stairs. As his account proceeded Captain Obadiah's face altered by degrees from its natural brown to a sickly yellow, and then to so leaden a hue that it could not have assumed a more ghastly appearance were he about to swoon dead away. Great beads of sweat gathered upon his forehead and trickled down his cheeks. At last he could endure no more, but with a great and strident voice, such as might burst forth from a devil tormented, he cried out: "'Tis a lie! 'Tis all a monstrous lie! He is a beggarly runaway servant whom I took in out of the rain and fed and housed—to have him turn thus against me and strike the hand that has benefited him!"

"Sir," replied our young gentleman, with a moderate and easy voice, "what I tell you is no lie, but the truth. If any here misdoubts my veracity, see, here is a letter received by the last packet from my honored father. You, Colonel Belford, know his handwriting perfectly well. Look at this and tell me if I am deceiving you."

At these words Colonel Belford took the letter with a hand that trembled as though with palsy. He cast his eyes over it, but it is to be doubted whether he read a single word therein contained. Nevertheless, he saw enough to satisfy his doubts, and he could have wept, so great was the relief from the miserable and overwhelming anxiety that had taken possession of him since the beginning of his brother's discourse.

Meantime our young gentleman, turning to Captain Obadiah, cried out, "Sir, I am indeed an instrument of Providence sent hither to call your wickedness to account," and this he spoke with so virtuous an air as to command the admiration of all who heard him. "I have," he continued, "lived with you now for nearly three odious months, and I know every particular of your habits and such circumstances of your life as you are aware of. I now proclaim how you have wickedly and sacrilegiously turned the Old Free Grace Meeting-House into a slave-pen, whence for above a year you have conducted a nefarious and most inhuman commerce with the West Indies."

At these words Captain Obadiah, being thrown so suddenly upon his defence, forced himself to give forth a huge and boisterous laugh. "What then?" he cried. "What wickedness is there in that? What if I have provided a few sugar plantations with negro slaves? Are there not those here present who would do no better if the opportunity offered? The place is mine, and I break no law by a bit of quiet slave-trading."

"I marvel," cried our young gentleman, still in the same virtuous strain—"I marvel that you can pass over so wicked a thing thus easily. I myself have counted above fifty graves of your victims on Pig and Sow Point. Repent, sir, while there is yet time."

But to this adjuration Captain Obadiah returned no other reply than to burst into a most wicked, impudent laugh.

"Is it so?" cried our young gentleman. "Do you dare me to further exposures? Then I have here another evidence to confront you that may move you to a more serious consideration." With these words he drew forth from his pocket a packet wrapped in soft white paper. This he unfolded, holding up to the gaze of all a bright and shining object. "This," he exclaimed, "I found in Captain Obadiah's writing-desk while I was hunting for some wax with which to seal a letter." It was the gold snuffbox of the late Collector Goodhouse. "What," he cried, "have you, sir, to offer in explanation of the manner in which this came into your possession? See, here engraved upon the lid is the owner's name and the circumstance of his having saved my own poor life. It was that first called my attention to it, for I well recollect how my father compelled me to present it to my savior. How came it into your possession, and why have you hidden it away so carefully for all this while? Sir, in the death of Lieutenant Goodhouse I suspect you of a more sinister fault than that of converting yonder poor sanctuary into a slave-pen. So soon as Captain Morris of your slave-ship returns from Jamaica I shall have him arrested, and shall compel him to explain what he knows of the circumstances of the Lieutenant's unfortunate murder."

At the sight of so unexpected an object in the young gentleman's hand Captain Obadiah's jaw fell, and his cavernous mouth gaped as though he had suddenly been stricken with a palsy. He lifted a trembling hand and slowly and mechanically passed it along that cheek which was so discolored with gunpowder stain. Then, suddenly gathering himself together and regaining those powers that appeared for a moment to have fled from him, he cried out, aloud: "I swear to God 'twas all an accident! I pushed him down the steps, and he fell and broke his neck!"

Our young gentleman regarded him with a cold and collected smile. "That, sir," said he, "you shall have the opportunity to explain to the proper authorities—unless," he added, "you choose to take yourself away from these parts, and to escape the just resentment of those laws to which you may be responsible for your misdemeanors."

"I shall," roared Captain Obadiah, "stand my trial in spite of you all! I shall live to see you in torments yet! I shall—" He gaped and stuttered, but could find no further words with which to convey his infinite rage and disappointed spite. Then turning, and with a furious gesture, he rushed forth and out of the house, thrusting those aside who stood in his way, and leaving behind him a string of curses fit to set the whole world into a blaze.

He had destroyed all the gaiety of the wedding-breakfast, but the relief from the prodigious doubts and anxieties that had at first overwhelmed those whom he had intended to ruin was of so great a nature that they thought nothing of so inconsiderable a circumstance.

As for our young gentleman, he had come forth from the adventure with such dignity of deportment and with so exalted an air of generous rectitude that those present could not sufficiently admire at the continent discretion of one so young. The young lady whom he had married, if she had before regarded him as a Paris and an Achilles incorporated into one person, now added the wisdom of a Nestor to the category of his accomplishments.

Captain Obadiah, in spite of the defiance he had fulminated against his enemies, and in spite of the determination he had expressed to remain and to stand his trial, was within a few days known to have suddenly and mysteriously departed from New Hope. Whether or not he misdoubted his own rectitude too greatly to put it to the test of a trial, or whether the mortification incident upon the failure of his plot was too great for him to support, it was clearly his purpose never to return again. For within a month the more valuable of his belongings were removed from his great house upon Pig and Sow Point and were loaded upon a bark that came into the harbor for that purpose. Thence they were transported no one knew whither, for Captain Obadiah was never afterwards observed in those parts.

Nor was the old meeting-house ever again disturbed by such manifestations as had terrified the community for so long a time. Nevertheless, though the Devil was thus exorcised from his abiding-place, the old church never lost its evil reputation, until it was finally destroyed by fire about ten years after the incidents herein narrated.

In conclusion it is only necessary to say that when the Honorable Frederick Dunburne presented his wife to his noble family at home, he was easily forgiven his *mésalliance* in view of her extreme beauty and vivacity. Within a year or two Lord Carrickford, his elder brother, died of excessive dissipation in Florence, where he was then attached to the English Embassy, so that our young gentleman thus became the heir-apparent to his father's title, and so both branches of the family were united into one.